Praise for

KRAKEN

"With his tale of a giant-squid corpse, Miéville, never predictable, lobs a grenade into the urban-fantasy genre, remaking it into wild comedy. . . . Anyone who reads this is never going to think about natural-history museums — or aquariums — in the same way again. A–"
—*Entertainment Weekly*

"*Kraken* fairly throbs with the fantastical. . . . With its playful, densely pyrotechnic prose and its blizzard of references to other works, *Kraken* defies easy characterization."
—*The New York Times*

"If the fact that his plot is powered by a case of squid-napping does not give away Miéville's less than serious intent, the abundance of other puns, injokes and pop-cultural references surely do. . . . And Miéville sets about his dark comedy with almost unseemly relish. Squid, however gigantic, are merely an appetiser for the feast of weirdness he lays out . . . for Miéville's dedicated and growing readership, *Kraken* succeeds in reforming the urban fantasy around a tougher, funnier and more intellectually demanding core."
—*The Guardian* (UK)

"*Kraken* is a thriller that combines weirdness with humor and excitement. Miéville's London is filled with interesting, eccentric and dangerous people in a world that is always larger than it seems."
—*The Denver Post*

"Highly recommended...Miéville's sprawling saga calls to mind the works of H. P. Lovecraft and H. G. Wells with a distinctive 21st century spin."

—*Library Journal*

"Miéville's fantasy is a rich literary work, full of wordplay and imagery that will appeal to literary-fiction fans as much to fantasy readers."

—*Booklist*

"Simultaneously reverent and brimming with punky attitude, *Kraken* proves Miéville is ever forging new ground, even when walking the same grey pavements as his readers."

—*The Independent* (UK)

While Miéville is often cited as having massive crossover appeal between speculative fiction and literary fiction, he doesn't concede a single thing to the mainstream here. Instead, *Kraken* is full-strength, grade-A geekitude. And as such, it's brilliant.

—The Onion A.V. Club

"Enormously fun to read."

—io9

"*Kraken* is a solid and epic contribution to the genre...one hell of a summer read."

—Baltimore *City Paper*

"Miéville is a master world-builder. . . . [he] has done what all great science-fiction has done—and great so-called literary fiction, when it gets around to it—provided a nuanced, highly imagined critique of zeitgeist, dressed up in a crackerjack story."

—*Time Out Chicago*

"Miéville more than delivers."

—*San Francisco Chronicle*

BY CHINA MIÉVILLE

King Rat

Perdido Street Station

The Scar

Iron Council

Looking for Jake: Stories

Un Lun Dun

The City & The City

Kraken

Embassytown

Railsea

Three Moments of an Explosion

This Census-Taker

The Last Days of New Paris

KRAKEN

KRAKEN

AN ANATOMY

China Miéville

BALLANTINE BOOKS

NEW YORK

2011 Del Rey Trade Paperback Edition

Copyright © 2010 by China Miéville

All rights reserved.

Published in the United States by Del Rey, an imprint of The Random House Publishing Group, a division of Random House, Inc., New York.

DEL REY is a registered trademark and the Del Rey colophon is a trademark of Random House, Inc.

Originally published in the United States by Del Rey, an imprint of The Random House Publishing Group, a division of Random House, Inc., in 2010.

Grateful acknowledgment is made to Hiromi Kozuka for permission to reprint "The Kraken Wakes" by Hugh Cook. Reprinted by permission of Hiromi Kozuka.

Library of /Congress Cataloging-to-Publication Date

Miéville, China.
Kraken : an anatomy / China Miéville.
p. cm.
ISBN 978-0-345-49750-5
eBook 978-0-345-52185-9
1. Museum curators—England—Fiction. 2. Giant squids—Fiction.
3. Magic—Fiction. 4. Cults—Fiction. I. Title.
PR6063.I265K73 2010
823'.914—dc22   2010013893

Printed in the United States of America

www.delreybooks.com

Book design by Karin Batten

To Mark Bould
Comrade-in-tentacles

ACKNOWLEDGMENTS

For all their help with this book I'm extremely grateful to Mark Bould, Mic Cheetham, Julie Crisp, Melisande Echanique, Penelope Haynes, Chloe Healy, Kaitlin Heller, Deanna Hoak, Simon Kavanagh, Peter Lavery, Jemima Miéville, David Moensch, Sandy Rankin, Max Schaefer, Jesse Soodalter, and to my editors Chris Schluep and Jeremy Trevathan. My sincere thanks to all at Del Rey and Macmillan.

The Natural History Museum and Darwin Centre are, of course, real places—the latter containing a real *Architeuthis*—but the questionable versions depicted here are entirely my responsibility. For their extraordinary hospitality and behind-the-scenes access, I am enormously grateful to those who work in the real institutions, particularly Patrick Campbell, Oliver Crimmen, Mandy Holloway, Karen James, and John Lambshead.

The poem in chapter 19, "The Kraken Wakes," is copyright Hugh Cook, and I am very grateful to his family for permission to reproduce it. Among the countless writers, musicians, artists, and researchers to whom I'm indebted, those I'm particularly aware of and grateful to with regard to this book include Hugh Cook, Burial, Hugh Harman and Rudy Ising, William Hope Hodgson, Pop Will Eat Itself, Tsunemi Kubodera and Kyoichi Mori, Jules Verne, H. G. Wells, and Japetus Steenstrup.

"The green waves break from my sides
As I roll up, forced by my season"

—HUGH COOK, "The Kraken Wakes"

The sea is full of saints. You know that? You know that: you're a big boy.

The sea's full of saints and it's been full of saints for years. Since longer than anything. Saints were there before there were even gods. They were waiting for them, and they're still there now.

Saints eat fish and shellfish. Some of them catch jellyfish and some of them eat rubbish. Some saints eat anything they can find. They hide under rocks; they turn themselves inside out; they spit up spirals. There's nothing saints don't do.

Make this shape with your hands. Like that. Move your fingers. There, you made a saint. Look out, here comes another one! Now they're fighting! Yours won.

There aren't any big corkscrew saints anymore, but there are still ones like sacks and ones like coils, and ones like robes with flapping sleeves. What's your favourite saint? I'll tell you mine. But wait a minute, first, do you know what it is makes them all saints? They're all a holy family, they're all cousins. Of each other, and of . . . you know what else they're cousins of?

That's right. Of gods.

Alright now. Who was it made you? You know what to say.

Who made you?

PART ONE

SPECIMENS

Chapter One

AN EVERYDAY DOOMSAYER IN SANDWICH-BOARD ABRUPTLY walked away from what over the last several days had been his pitch, by the gates of a museum. The sign on his front was an old-school prophecy of the end: the one bobbing on his back read FORGET IT.

INSIDE, A MAN WALKED THROUGH THE BIG HALL, PAST A DOUBLE stair and a giant skeleton, his steps loud on the marble. Stone animals watched him. "Right then," he kept saying.

His name was Billy Harrow. He glanced at the great fabricated bones and nodded. It looked as if he was saying hello. It was a little after eleven on a morning in October. The room was filling up. A group waited for him by the entrance desk, eyeing each other with polite shyness.

There were two men in their twenties with geek-chic haircuts. A woman and man barely out of teens teased each other. She was obviously indulging him with this visit. There was an older couple, and a father in his thirties holding his young son. "Look, that's a monkey," he said. He pointed at animals carved in vines on the museum pillars. "And you see that lizard?"

The boy peeped. He looked at the bone apatosaurus that Billy had seemed to greet. Or maybe, Billy thought, he was looking at the glyptodon beyond it. All the children had a favourite inhabitant of the Natural History Museum's first hall, and the glyptodon, that half-globe armadillo giant, had been Billy's.

Billy smiled at the woman who dispensed tickets, and the guard behind her. "This them?" he said. "Right then, everyone. Shall we do this thing?"

HE CLEANED HIS GLASSES AND BLINKED WHILE HE WAS DOING IT, replicating a look and motion an ex had once told him was adorable. He was a little shy of thirty and looked younger: he had freckles, and not enough stubble to justify "Bill." As he got older, Billy suspected, he would, DiCaprio-like, simply become like an increasingly wizened child.

Billy's black hair was tousled in halfheartedly fashionable style. He wore a not-too-hopeless top, cheap jeans. When he had first started at the centre, he had liked to think that he was unexpectedly cool-looking for such a job. Now he knew that he surprised no one, that no one expected scientists to look like scientists anymore.

"So you're all here for the tour of the Darwin Centre," he said. He was acting as if he thought they were present to investigate a whole research site, to look at the laboratories and offices, the filing, the cabinets of paperwork. Rather than to see one and only the one thing within the building.

"I'm Billy," he said. "I'm a curator. What that means is I do a lot of the cataloguing and preserving, stuff like that. I've been here awhile. When I first came here I wanted to specialise in marine molluscs— know what a mollusc is?" he asked the boy, who nodded and hid. "Snails, that's right." Mollusca had been the subject of his master's thesis.

"Alright, folks." He put his glasses on. "Follow me. This is a work-ing environment, so please keep the noise down, and I beg you not to touch anything. We've got caustics, toxins, all manner of horrible stuff all over the place."

One of the young men started to say, "When do we see—?" Billy raised his hand.

"Can I just . . . ?" he said. "Let me explain about what'll happen when we're in there." Billy had evolved his own pointless idio-superstitions, according to one of which it was bad luck for anyone to speak the name of what they were all there for, before they reached it.

"I'm going to show you a bunch of the places we work," he said lamely. "Any questions, you can ask me at the end: we're a little bit time constrained. Let's get the tour done first."

No curator or researcher was obliged to perform this guide-work. But many did. Billy no longer grumbled when it was his turn.

They went out and through the garden, approaching the Darwin with a building site on one side and the brick filigrees of the Natural History Museum on the other.

"No photos please," Billy said. He did not care if they obeyed: his obligation was to repeat the rule. "This building here opened in 2002," he said. "And you can see we're expanding. We'll have a new building in 2008. We've got seven floors of wet specimens in the Darwin Centre. That means stuff in Formalin."

Everyday hallways led to a stench. "Jesus," someone muttered.

"Indeed," said Billy. "This is called the dermestarium." Through interior windows there were steel containers like little coffins. "This is where we clean up skeletons. Get rid of all the gunk on them. *Dermestes maculatus.*"

A computer screen by the boxes was showing some disgusting salty-looking fish being eaten by insect swarms. "Eeurgh," someone said.

"There's a camera in the box," said Billy. "Hide beetles is their English name. They go through everything, just leave bones behind."

The boy grinned and tugged his father's hand. The rest of the group smiled, embarrassed. Flesh-eating bugs: sometimes life really was a B-movie.

Billy noticed one of the young men. He wore a past-it suit, a shabby-genteel outfit odd for someone young. He wore a pin on his lapel, a design like a long-armed asterisk, two of the spokes ending in curls. The man was taking notes. He was filling the pad he carried at a great rate.

A taxonomiser by inclination as well as profession, Billy had decided there were not so many kinds of people who took this tour.

There were children: mostly young boys, shy and beside themselves with excitement, and vastly knowledgeable about what they saw. There were their parents. There were sheepish people in their twenties, as geeky-eager as the kids. There were their girlfriends and boyfriends, performing patience. A few tourists on an unusual byway.

And there were the obsessives.

They were the only people who knew more than the young children. Sometimes they did not speak: sometimes they would interrupt Billy's explanations with too-loud questions, or correct him on scientific detail with exhausting fussy anxiety. He had noticed more of such visitors than usual in the last several weeks.

"It's like late summer brings out the weirdos," Billy had said to his friend Leon, a few nights back, as they drank at a Thames pub. "Someone came in all Starfleet badges today. Not on my shift, sadly."

"Fascist," Leon had said. "Why are you so prejudiced against nerds?"

"Please," Billy said. "That would be a bit self-hating, wouldn't it?"

"Yeah, but you pass. You're like, you're in deep cover," Leon said. "You can sneak out of the nerd ghetto and hide the badge and bring back food and clothes and word of the outside world."

"Mmm, tasteful."

"Alright," Billy said as colleagues passed him. "Kath," he said to an ichthyologist; "Brendan," to another curator, who answered him, "Alright Tubular?"

"Onward please," said Billy. "And don't worry, we're getting to the good stuff."

Tubular? Billy could see one or two of his escortees wondering if they had misheard.

The nickname resulted from a drinking session in Liverpool with colleagues, back in his first year at the centre. It was the annual conference of the professional curatorial society. After a day of talks on methodologies and histories of preservation, on museum schemes and the politics of display, the evening's wind-down had started with polite how-did-you-get-into-this?, turned into everyone at the bar one by one talking about their childhoods, these meanderings, in boozy turn, becoming a session of what someone had christened Biography Bluff. Everyone had to cite some supposedly extravagant fact about themselves—they once ate a slug, they'd been part of a foursome, they tried to burn their school down, and so on—the truth of which the others would then brayingly debate.

Billy had straight-faced claimed that he had been the result of the world's first-ever successful *in vitro* fertilisation, but that he had been disavowed by the laboratory because of internal politics and a question mark over issues of consent, which was why the official laurel had gone to someone else a few months after his birth. Interrogated about details, he had with drunken effortlessness named doctors, the location, a minor complication of the procedure. But before bets were made and his reveal made, the conversation had taken a sudden turn and the game had been abandoned. It was two days later, back in London, before a lab-mate asked him if it was true.

"Absolutely," Billy had said, in an expressionless teasing way that meant either "of course," or "of course not." He had stuck by that response since. Though he doubted anyone believed him, the nickname "Test-tube" and variants were still used.

They passed another guard: a big, truculent man, all shaved head and muscular fatness. He was some years older than Billy, named Dane Something, from what Billy had overheard. Billy nodded and tried to meet his eye, as he always did. Dane Whatever, as he always did, ignored the little greeting, to Billy's disproportionate resentment.

As the door swung shut, though, Billy saw Dane acknowledge someone else. The guard nodded momentarily at the intense young man with the lapel pin, the obsessive whose eyes flickered in the briefest response. Billy saw that, in surprise—and just before the door closed between them—Dane looking at him.

Dane's acquaintance did not meet his eyes. "You feel it get cool?" Billy said, shaking his head. He sped them through time-release doors. "To stop evaporation. We have to be careful about fire. Because, you know, there's a fair old bit of alcohol in here, so . . ." With his hands he made a soft explosion.

The visitors stopped still. They were in a specimen maze. Ranked intricacies. Kilometres of shelves and jars. In each was a motionless floating animal. Even sound sounded bottled suddenly, as if something had put a lid on it all.

The specimens mindlessly concentrated, some posing with their own colourless guts. Flatfish in browning tanks. Jars of huddled mice gone sepia, grotesque mouthfuls like pickled onions. There were sports with excess limbs, foetuses in arcane shapes. They were as carefully shelved as books. "See?" Billy said.

One more door and they would be with what they were there to see. Billy knew from repeated experience how this would go.

When they entered the tank room, the chamber at the heart of the Darwin Centre, he would give the visitors a moment without prattle. The big room was walled with more shelves. There were hundreds more bottles, from those chest-high down to those the size of a glass of water. All of them contained lugubrious animal faces. It was a Linnaean décor; species clined into each other. There were steel bins, pulleys that hung like vines. No one would notice. Everyone would be staring at the great tank in the centre of the room.

This was what they came for, that pinkly enormous thing. For all its immobility; the wounds of its slow-motion decay, the scabbing that clouded its solution; despite its eyes being shrivelled and lost; its sick colour; despite the twist in its skein of limbs, as if it were being wrung out. For all that, it was what they were there for.

It would hang, an absurdly massive tentacled sepia event. *Architeuthis dux*. The giant squid.

"It's eight point sixty two metres long," Billy would say at last. "Not the largest we've ever seen, but no tiddler either." The visitors would circle the glass. "They found it in 2004, off the Falkland Islands.

"It's in a saline-Formalin mix. That tank was made by the same people that do the ones for Damien Hirst. You know, the one he put the shark in?" Any children would be leaning in to the squid, as close as they could get.

"Its eyes would have been twenty-three or twenty-four centimetres across," Billy would say. People would measure with their fingers, and children opened their own eyes mimicry-wide. "Yeah, like plates. Like dinner plates." He said it every time, every time thinking of Hans Christian Andersen's dog. "But it's very hard to keep eyes fresh, so they're gone. We injected it with the same stuff that's in the tank to stop it rotting from the inside.

"It was alive when it was caught."

That would mean gasps all over again. Visions of an army of coils, twenty thousand leagues, an axe-fight against a blasphemy from the deep below. A predatory meat cylinder, rope limbs unrolling, finding a ship's rail with ghastly prehensility.

It had been nothing like that. A giant squid at the surface was a weak, disoriented, moribund thing. Horrified by air, crushed by its own self, it had probably just wheezed through its siphon and palsied, a gel mass of dying. That did not matter. Its breach was hardly reducible to however it had actually been.

The squid would stare with its handspan empty sockets and Billy would answer familiar questions—"It's name is Archie." "Because of *Architeuthis*. Get it?" "Yes, even though we think it's a girl."

When it had come, wrapped in ice and preservative cloth, Billy had helped unswaddle it. It was he who had massaged its dead flesh, kneading the tissue to feel where preservatives had spread. He had been so busy on it it was as if he had not noticed it, quite, somehow. It was only when they were done and finished, and it was tanked, that it had hit him, had really got him. He had watched refraction make it shift as he approached or moved away, a magic motionless motion.

It wasn't a type-specimen, one of those bottled Platonic essences that define everything like them. Still, the squid was complete, and it would never be cut.

Other specimens in the room would eventually snare a bit of visitor attention. A ribbon-folded oarfish, an echidna, bottles of monkeys. And there at the end of the room was a glass-fronted cabinet containing thirteen small jars.

"Anyone know what these are?" Billy would say. "Let me show you."

They were distinguished by the browning ink and antique

angularity of the hand that had labelled them. "These were collected by someone quite special," Billy would say to any children. "Can you read that word? Anyone know what that means? 'The *Beagle*'?"

Some people got it. If they did they would gape at the subcollection that sat there unbelievably on an everyday shelf. Little animals collected, euthanized, preserved and catalogued on a journey to the South American seas, two centuries before, by the young naturalist Charles Darwin.

"That's his writing," Billy would say. "He was young, he hadn't sorted out his really big notions when he found these. These are part of what gave him the whole idea. They're not finches, but these are what got the whole thing started. It's the anniversary of his trip soon."

Very rarely, someone would try to argue with him over Darwin's insight. Billy would not have that debate.

Even those thirteen glass eggs of evolutionary theory, and all the centuries'-worth of tea-coloured crocodiles and deep-sea absurdities, evinced only a little interest next to the squid. Billy knew the importance of that Darwin stuff, whether visitors did or not. No matter. Enter that room and you breached a Schwarzschild radius of something not canny, and that cephalopod corpse was the singularity.

That, Billy knew, was how it would go. But this time when he opened the door he stopped, and stared for several seconds. The visitors came in behind him, stumbling past his immobility. They waited, unsure of what they were being shown.

The centre of the room was empty. All the jars looked over the scene of a crime. The nine-metre tank, the thousands of gallons of brine-Formalin, the dead giant squid itself were gone.

Chapter Two

A<small>S SOON AS</small> B<small>ILLY</small> <small>STARTED CLAMOURING HE WAS SURROUNDED</small> by colleagues, all gaping and demanding to know what was going on and what the hell, where was, where was the goddamn squid?

They hurried the visitors out of the building. Afterward, all Billy recalled of that rushed dismissal was the little boy sobbing, desolate that he had not been shown what he had come to see. Biologists, guards, curators came and stared with stupid faces at the enormous lack in the tank room. "What . . . ?" they said, just like Billy had, and "Where did . . . ?"

Word spread. People ran from place to place as if they were looking for something, as if they had misplaced something, and might find it under a cupboard.

"It can't have, it can't have," a biophysicist called Josie said, and yes, no, it couldn't have, not disappeared, so many metres of abyss meat could not have gone. There were no suspicious cranes. There were no giant tank- nor squid-shaped holes cartoon-style in the wall. It could not have gone, but there it was, not.

There was no protocol for this. What to do in the event of a chemical spill—that was planned. If a specimen jar broke, if results did not tally, even if a tour member became violent, you run a particular algorithm. *This though*, Billy thought. *What the hell?*

• • •

The police arrived at last, coming in a stampy gang. The staff stood waiting, huddled exactly as if cold, as if drenched in benthic water. Officers tried to take statements.

"I don't understand, I'm afraid . . ." one might say.

"It's *gone*."

The crime scene was off-limits, but since Billy was the discoverer he was allowed to stay. He gave his statement, standing by the lack. When he was done and his questioner distracted, he stepped aside. He watched the police work. Officers looked at the antique once-animals that eyed them back, at the no giant tank, at the nowhere anything so big and missing as *Architeuthis* could be.

They measured the room as if maybe the dimensions were hiding things. Billy had no better ideas. The room looked huge. All the other tanks looked forlorn and far away, the specimens apologetic.

Billy stared at the stands on which the *Architeuthis* tank should be. He was still adrenalized. He listened to the officers.

"Search me for a fucking clue, mate . . ."

"Shit, you know what this means, don't you?"

"Don't even get me started. Hand me that tape measure."

"Seriously, I'm telling you, this is a handover, no question . . ."

"What are you waiting for, mate? Mate?" That was to Billy, at last. An officer was telling him just-courteously to fuck off. He joined the rest of the staff outside. They milled and muttered, congregating roughly by jobs. Billy saw a debate among directors.

"What's that about?" he said.

"Whether or not to close the museum," Josie said. She was biting her nails.

"What?" Billy said. He took off his glasses and blinked at them aggressively. "What's the sodding debate? How big does something have to be before its nickage closes us down?"

"Ladies and Gents." A senior policeman clapped his hands for attention. His officers surrounded him. They were muttering to and listening to their shoulders. "I'm Chief Inspector Mulholland. Thanks for your patience. I'm sorry to've kept you all waiting." The staff huffed, shifted, bit their nails.

"I'm going to ask you to please *not talk* about this, ladies and gents," Mulholland said. A young female officer slipped into the room. Her uniform was unkempt. She was speaking on some phone hands-free, muttering at nothing visible. Billy watched her. "Please don't talk about this," Mulholland said again. The whispering in the room mostly ceased.

"Now," Mulholland said, after a pause. "Who was it found it gone?" Billy put up his hand. "You, then, would be Mr. Harrow," Mulholland said. "Can I ask the rest of you to wait, even if you've already told us what you know? My officers'll speak to you all."

"Mr. Harrow." Mulholland approached him as the staff obeyed. "I've read your statement. I'd be grateful if you'd show me around. Could you take me on exactly the route you did with your tour?" Billy saw that the young female officer had gone.

"What is it you're looking for?" he said. "You think you're going to find it . . . ?"

Mulholland looked at him kindly, as if Billy were slow. "Evidence."

Evidence. Billy ran his hand through his hair. He imagined marks on the floor where some huge perfidious pulley system might have been. Drying puddles of preserver in a trail as telltale as crumbs. Right.

Mulholland summoned colleagues, and had Billy walk them through the centre. Billy pointed out what they passed in a terse parody of his usual performance. The officers poked at bits and pieces and asked what they were. "An enzyme solution," Billy said, or, "That's a time sheet."

Mulholland said: "Are you alright, Mr. Harrow?"

"It's kind of a big thing, you know?"

That wasn't the only reason Billy glanced repeatedly behind him. He thought he heard a noise. A very faint clattering, a clanking like a dropped and rolling beaker. It was not the first time he had heard that. He had been catching little snips of such misplaced sound at random moments since a year after he had started at the centre. More than once he had, trying to find the cause, opened a door onto an empty room, or heard a faint grind of glass in a hallway no one could have entered.

He had concluded a long time ago that it was his mind inventing these just-heard noises. They correlated with moments of anxiety. He had mentioned the phenomenon to people, and though some had reacted with alarm, many told some anecdote about horripilation or twitches when they were under pressure, and Billy remained fairly sanguine.

In the tank room the forensic team was still dusting, photographing, measuring tabletops. Billy folded his arms and shook his head.

"It's those Californian sods." When he returned to where most of the staff were waiting he joked quietly about rival institutes to a workmate outside the tank room. About disputes over preservation methodology that had taken a dramatic turn. "It's the Kiwis," Billy said. "O'Shea finally gave in to temptation."

He did not go straight back to his flat. He had a long-standing arrangement to meet a friend.

Billy had known Leon since they had been undergraduates at the same institute, though in different departments. Leon was enrolled in a PhD course in a literature department in London, though he never talked about it. He had since forever been working on a book called *Uncanny Blossom*. When Leon had told him, Billy had said, "I had no idea you were entering the Shit Title Olympics."

"If you didn't swim in your sump of ignorance you'd know that title's designed to fuck with the French. Neither word's translatable into their ridiculous language."

Leon lived in a just-plausible rim of Hoxton. He camped up his role as Virgil to Billy's Dante, taking Billy to art happenings or telling him about those he could not attend, exaggerating and lying about what they entailed. Their game was that Billy was in permanent anecdote overdraft, always owed Leon stories. Leon, skinny and shaven-headed and in a foolish jacket, sat in the cold outside the pizzeria with his long legs stretched out.

"Where've you been all my life, Richmal?" he shouted. He had long ago decided that blue-eyed Billy was named for another naughty boy, the William of *Just William*, and had illogically rechristened him for the book's author.

"Chipping Norton," said Billy, patting Leon's head. "Theydon Bois. How's the life of the mind?"

Marge, Leon's partner, inclined her face for a kiss. The crucifix she always wore glinted.

He had only met her a few times. "She a god-botherer?" Billy had asked Leon after he first met her.

"Hardly. Convent girl. Hence tiny Jesus-shaped guilt trip between her tits."

She was, as Leon's girlfriends were more often than not, attractive and a little heavy, somewhat older than Leon, too old for the dilute emo-goth look she maintained. "Say Rubenesque or zaftig at your peril," Leon had said.

"What's zaftig?" Billy said.

"And fuck you 'too old,' Pauley Perrette's way older."

"Who's that?"

Marge worked part-time at Southwark Housing Department and made video art. She had met Leon at a gig, some drone band playing in a gallery. Leon had deflected Billy's Simpsons joke and told him that she was one of those people who had renamed herself, that Marge was short for Marginalia.

"Oh *what?* What's her real name?"

"Billy," Leon had said. "Don't be such a wet blanket."

"We've been watching a weird bunch of pigeons outside a bank is what we've been up to," Leon said as Billy sat.

"We've been arguing about books," said Marge.

"Best sort of argument," said Billy. "What was the substance?"

"Don't sidetrack him," said Leon, but Marge was already answering: "Virginia Woolf versus Edward Lear."

"Christ Alive," said Billy. "Are those my only choices?"

"I went for Lear," said Leon. "Partly out of fidelity to the letter L. Partly because given the choice between nonsense and boojy wittering you blatantly have to choose nonsense."

"You obviously haven't read the glossary to *Three Guineas*," said Marge. "You want nonsense? She calls 'soldiers' 'gutsgruzzlers,' 'heroism' equals 'botulism,' 'hero' equals 'bottle.'"

"Lear?" Billy said. "Really? In the Land of the Fiddly-Faddly, the BinkerlyBonkerly roams." He took off his glasses and pinched the top of his nose. "Alright, let me tell you something. Here's the thing," he said at last and then whatever, it stalled. Leon and Marge stared at him.

Billy tried again. He shook his head. He clucked as if something were stuck in his mouth. He had at last almost to shove the information past his own teeth. "One of . . . Our giant squid is missing." Saying it felt like puncturing a lid.

"What?" Leon said.

"I don't . . ." Marge said.

"No, it doesn't make any more sense to me." He told them, step by impossible step.

"Gone? What do you mean 'gone'? Why haven't I heard anything about it?" Leon said at last.

"I don't know. I'd have thought it would have . . . I mean, the police asked us to keep it secret—oops, look what I did—but I didn't expect that to actually work. I'd thought it would be all over the *Standard* by now."

"Maybe it's a what-d'you-call-it, a D-Notice?" Leon said. "You know, one of those things where they stop journalists talking about stuff?"

Billy shrugged. "They're not going to be able to . . . Half that tour group have probably blogged the shit out of it by now."

"Someone's probably registered bigsquidgone dot com," Marge said.

Billy shrugged. "Maybe. You know, when I was on my way, I was thinking about maybe I shouldn't . . . I almost didn't tell you myself. Obviously put the fear of God in me. But the big issue for me's not that the cops didn't want us to tell: it's the whole 'totally impossible' thing."

THERE WAS A STORM THAT NIGHT AS HE HEADED HOME, A HORRIBLE one that filled the air with bad electricity. Clouds turned the sky dark brown. The roofs streamed like urinals.

As he entered his Haringay flat, precisely at the second he crossed the threshold, Billy's phone rang. He stared through the window at the sodden trees and roofs. Across the street, a twirl of rubbishy wind was gusting around some klaggy-looking squirrel on a rooftop. The squirrel shook its head and watched him.

"Hello?" he said. "Yeah, this is Billy Harrow."

"... somethingsomething, 'bout damn time you got back. So you're coming in, yeah?" a woman on the line said.

"Wait, what?" The squirrel was still staring at him. Billy gave it the finger and mouthed *Sod off.* He turned from the window and tried to pay attention. "Who is this, sorry?" he said.

"Will you bloody listen? Better at shooting your mouth than listening, ain't you? Police, mate. Tomorrow. Got it?"

"Police?" he said. "You want me back to the museum? You want—"

"*No.* The station. Fuck's sake clean your ears." Silence. "You there?"

"... Look, I don't appreciate the way you're—"

"Yeah, I don't appreciate you gabbing away when you was told not to." She gave him an address. He frowned as he scribbled it on some takeout menu.

"Where? That's *Cricklewood.* That's nowhere near the museum. What's ... ? Why did they send someone from up there down to the museum ... ?"

"We're done, mate. Just get there. Tomorrow." She rang off and left him staring at the mouthpiece in his chilly room. The windows made sounds in the wind, as if they were bowing. Billy stared at the phone. He was annoyed that he felt obliged to acquiesce to that last order.

Chapter Three

Billy had bad dreams. He was not the only one. There was no way yet he could know that night sweats were citywide. Hundreds of people who did not know each other, who did not compare their symptoms, slept harried. It was not the weather.

It meant a trek, that meeting to which he had been ordered, that he pretended to himself to consider ignoring. He considered, or, again, pretended to consider, calling his father. Of course he did not. He started to dial Leon's number but again did not. There was nothing to add to what he had said. He wanted to tell someone else about the disappearance, that strange theft. He auditioned recipients of that phone call in his mind, but his energy to do so, to say anything, kept spilling out, left him repeatedly.

That squirrel was still there. He was sure it was the same animal that watched him from behind the gutter, like a dug-in soldier. Billy did not go in to work. Was not even sure if anyone was in that day and did not call to check. He called no one.

At last—late, as the sky became grey and flat, later than his rude interlocutor had desired, in some feeble faux disobedience—he set out from his block by a commercial yard near Manor House for a 253 bus. He walked through scuffing food wrappers, through news-papers, through flyers urging repentance being peeled one by one by the wind from a discarded pile. In the bus he looked down on the low flat roofs of bus shelters, plinths for leaves.

In Camden he took a Tube, came up again a few steps on for another bus. He checked his mobile repeatedly, but all he received was one text from Leon—LOST NE MORE TREASURES?? On that last leg Billy looked into areas of London he did not know but that felt tuggingly familiar, with their middling businesses and cheap eateries, the lampposts where unlit Christmas street ornaments put up early in readiness or left unplucked a whole year dangled like strange washing. He wore headphones, listened to a soundclash between MIA and an up-and-coming rapper. Billy wondered why he had not thought to insist the police just pick him up, if they were going to have their HQ in this ridiculously out-of-the-way patch.

Walking, even through his headphones Billy was startled by noises. For the first time ever outside the corridors of the Darwin Centre, he heard or imagined that glass noise. The light in that early evening was wrong. *Everything's screwed up,* he thought. As if the fat spindle of the *Architeuthis*'s body had been slotted in and holding something in place. Billy felt like a lid unsecured and banging in the wind.

The station was just off the high street, much larger than he expected. It was one of those very ugly London buildings in mustard bricks that, instead of weathering grandly like their red Victorian ancestors, never age, but just get dirtier and dirtier.

He waited a long time in the waiting area. Twice he got up and asked to see Mulholland. "We'll be with you shortly, sir," said the first officer he asked. "And who the fuck's he?" said the second. Billy grew more and more irritated, turning the pages of old magazines.

"Mr. Harrow? Billy Harrow?"

The man coming toward him was not Mulholland. He was small and skinny and trimly kempt. In his fifties, in plain clothes, a dated brown suit. He had his hands behind his back. As he waited, he leaned forward and up on his toes more than once, a dancey little tic.

"Mr. Harrow?" he said in a voice thin like his moustache. He shook Billy's hand. "I'm Chief Inspector Baron. You met my colleague, Mulholland?"

"Yeah, where is he?"

"Yes, no. He's not here. I'm taking over this investigation, Mr. Harrow. Sort of." He tilted his head. "Apologies for keeping you waiting, and thank you very much for coming in."

"What do you mean you're taking over?" Billy said. "Whoever it was spoke to me last night didn't . . . She was bloody rude, to be honest."

"Though I suppose with us lot taking over your labs," Baron said, "where else were you going to go, eh? I suppose there'll be no pickling for you till we're done, I'm afraid. Maybe you can think of it as a holiday."

"Seriously, what's the score?" Baron led Billy down striplit corridors. In the white light Billy realised how dirty his glasses were. "Why've you taken over? And you're way out here . . . I mean, no offense . . ."

"Anyway," said Baron. "I promise we won't keep you any longer than we have to."

"I'm not sure what it is I can do for you," Billy said. "I already told you lot everything I know. I mean, that was Mulholland. Did he mess up then? Are you a cleaner-upper?"

Baron stopped and faced Billy. "It's like a film, this, isn't it?" he said. He smiled. "You say, 'But I've told your officers everything,' and I say, 'Well now you can tell me,' and you don't trust me and we dance a little bit and then eventually after a few more questions you get to look horrified and say, 'What, you think *I* had something to do with this?' And we go round and round."

Billy was speechless. Baron did not stop smiling.

"Rest assured, Mr. Harrow," he said. "That is not what's going on here. My absolute honour." He held his hand up in a scout pledge.

"I never thought . . ." Billy managed to say.

"So having made that clear," Baron said, "do you reckon we can dispense with the rest of the script and you can give me a hand? That's a blinder, Mr. Harrow." His little voice fluted. "That's peachy. Now let's get this done."

It was Billy's first time in an interview room. It was just like on telly. Small, beige, windowless. On the far side of a table were a woman and another man. The man was in his forties, tall and powerful. He wore a nondescript dark suit. His hair was receding, his haircut severe. He clasped his heavy hands and regarded Billy levelly.

The first thing Billy noticed about the woman was her youth. She was out of her teens maybe, but not by much. She was, he realized, the policewoman who'd done a brief cameo at the museum. She had on a blue Metropolitan Police uniform, but it was worn more informally than he would have expected her to get away with. It was not buttoned up, was a bit thrown-on. Clean, but rucked, hitched, and tweaked. She had on more makeup than he would have thought permissible, too, and her blonde hair was messily fancily styled. She looked like a pupil obeying the letter but straining against the spirit of school uniform rules. She did not even glance at him, and he could not see her face more clearly.

"Right then," said Baron. The other man nodded. The young PC leaned against the wall and fiddled with a mobile phone.

"Tea?" said Baron, gesturing Billy to a chair. "Coffee? Absinthe? I'm joking of course. I would say 'Cigarette?' but these days, you know."

"No, I'm fine." Billy said. "I'd like to just—"

"Of course, of course. Alright then." Baron sat and pulled bits of paper from his pockets and searched through them. The scattiness was not convincing. "Tell me about yourself, Mr. Harrow. You're a curator, I think?"

"Yeah."

"Which means what?"

"Preserving, cataloguing, that sort of stuff." Billy fiddled with his glasses so he did not have to meet anyone's eye. He tried to see which way the woman was looking. "Consulting on displays, keeping stuff in good nick."

"Always done it?"

"Pretty much."

"And . . ." Baron squinted at a note. "It was you who prepared the squid, I'm told."

"No. It was all of us. I was . . . it was a group effort." The other man sat by Baron, saying nothing and looking at his own hands. The young woman sighed and prodded her phone. She appeared to be playing a game on it. She clicked her tongue.

"You were at the museum, weren't you?" Billy said to her. She glanced at him. "Was it you who called me? Last night?" Her Winehousey hair was distinctive. She said nothing.

"You . . ." Baron was pointing at Billy with a pen, still sorting through the papers, "are too modest. You are the squid man."

"I don't know what you mean." Billy shifted. "Something like that comes in, you know . . . We were all working on it. All hands on deck. I mean . . ." He indicated hugeness with his hands.

"Come come," said Baron. "You've got a way with them, haven't you?" Baron met his eye. "Everyone says so."

"I don't know." Billy shrugged. "I like molluscs."

"You are an endearingly modest young man," Baron said. "And you are fooling no one."

Curators worked across taxonomies. But it was a standing claim in the centre that Billy's molluscs in particular were special. The stress could be on either word—it was *Billy's* molluscs, and Billy's *molluscs*, that kept pristine for ages in their solutions, that fell into particularly dramatic enjarred poses and held them well. It made no sense: one could hardly be any better at preserving a cuttlefish than a gecko or a house mouse. But the joke did not die, because there was a tiny something to it. Though in truth Billy had been pretty cack-handed when he had started. He had shattered his way through a fair few beakers, tubes, and flasks; had splayed more than one dead animal sodden on the lab floor before rather abruptly coming into his skills.

"What's this got to do with anything?" Billy said.

"It has the following to do with what for," Baron said. "See we've got you down here, or up here, depending which way you hold your map, for two reasons, Mr. Harrow. One, you're the person who found the giant squid missing. And two, something a bit more specific. Something you mentioned.

"You know, I have to tell you," Baron said. "I've never seen anything like this. I mean I've heard of stealing horses before. Plenty of dogs, of course. A cat or two. But . . ." He chuckled and shook his head. "Your guards've got a lot to answer for, haven't they? I gather there's a fair old degree of mea culpa-ing going on right now, as it goes."

"Dane and that lot?" Billy said. "I guess so, I don't know."

"I didn't mean Dane, actually. Interesting you bring him up. I was referring as they say to the *other* guards. But certainly Dane Parnell and his colleagues, too, must be feeling a bit daft. And of them more later. Recognise this?"

Baron slipped the page of a notepad across the table. On it was a vaguely asterisk design. Maybe it was a burst of radial sunbeams from a sun. Two of the several arms coiled at their ends, longer than the others.

"Yeah," said Billy. "I drew that. It was what that bloke on the tour was wearing. I drew it for the guy interviewing me yesterday."

"Do you know what this is, Mr. Harrow?" said Baron. "Can I call you Billy? Do you know?"

"How should I know? But the bloke who had this on, he was with me all the time. He never had any time to go off and do anything, you know, dodgy. I would've seen . . ."

"Have you seen this before?" The other man spoke, for the first time. He gripped his hands as if holding them back from something. His accent was classless and without any regional pitch—neutral enough that it had to have been cultivated. "Does it *jog your memory?*"

Billy hesitated. "I'm sorry," he said. "Can I just . . . Who are you?"

Baron shook his head. The large man's face did not change but for a slow blink. The woman glanced up from her phone, at last, and made some little tooth-kissing noise.

"This is Patrick Vardy, Mr. Harrow," Baron said. Vardy clenched his fingers. "Vardy's helping with our investigation."

No rank, Billy thought. All the police he had met had been *Constable So-and-so, DC This, Inspector That*. But not Vardy. Vardy stood and walked to the edge of the room, out of the immediate light, made himself an illegitimate topic.

"So *have* you seen this before?" said Baron, tapping the paper. "Little squiggle ring any bells?"

"I don't know," said Billy. "Don't think so. What is it? Do I get to know?"

"You told our colleagues back Kensington-side that the man wearing this seemed quote *het up* unquote, or something?" Baron said. "What about that?"

"Yeah, I told Mulholland," Billy said. "I don't know whether the bloke was weird or what," Billy said to Baron. He shrugged. "Some people who come see the squid are a bit . . ."

"Seen more like that recently?" Baron said. "The, ah, oddballs?"

Vardy leaned forward and muttered something in his ear. The police-man nodded. "Any people getting unusually excited?"

"Squid geeks?" Billy said. "I don't know. Maybe. There's been a couple in costumes or weird clothes." The woman made a note of something. He watched her do so.

"Alright, now tell me this," Baron said. "Has anything strange been going on outside the museum recently? Any interesting leaflets being handed out, any pickets? Any *protests*? Have you clocked any other interesting bits of jewellery on any other visitors? I know, I'm asking as if you're a magpie, all googly-eyed at shinies. But you know."

"I don't," Billy said. "I don't know. It has happened that we get nut-ters outside. As for this bloke, ask Dane Parnell." He shrugged. "Like I said yesterday, I think he recognised the guy."

"We would of course indeed like to have words with Dane Parnell. What with him and Mystery Pin Man seeming like they know each other and so forth. But we can't." Vardy whispered something else to him and Baron continued. "Because a bit like the specimen he was paid to look after, and indeed like Pin Man, Dane Parnell's disappeared."

"Disappeared?"

Baron nodded. "Whereabouts unknown," he said. "No one on the phone. Give the dog a bone. Not at home. Why might he disappear, you might ask. We are *very keen* to have him help us with the old enquiries."

"You spoken to him?" said the PC abruptly. Billy jumped in his chair and stared at her. She put her weight on one hip. She spoke quickly, with a London accent. "You talk a lot, don't you? All sorts of chatting you shouldn't be supposed to."

"What . . . ?" Billy said. "We haven't said more than ten words to each other since he started working there."

"What did he do before that?" Baron said.

"I've got *no clue* . . ."

"Listen to him squeak!" The woman sounded delighted.

Billy blinked. He tried to take it in good humour, smiled, tried to get her to smile back, failed. "To be honest," he said, "I don't even like the bloke. He's chippy. Couldn't be bothered to say hello, let alone anything else."

Baron, Vardy and the woman looked at each other in speechless conclave. They communicated something with waggled eyebrows and pouted lips, repeated quick nods.

Baron said, slowly, "Well if you should think of anything, Mr. Harrow, do please let us know."

"Yeah." Billy shook his head. "Yeah, I will." He put up surrender hands.

"Good man." Baron stood. He gave Billy a card, shook his hand as if the gratitude were genuine, pointed him to the door. "Don't go anywhere, will you? We might want to have another chat."

"Yeah, I think we will," the woman said.

"What did you mean 'Pin Man's disappeared'?" said Billy.

Baron shrugged. "Everything and everyone's vanishing, isn't it? Not that he 'disappeared' really; that would imply he was ever there. Your visitors have to book and leave a number. We've called everyone you were escorting yesterday. And the gentleman with the sparkle on his lapel . . ." Baron tap-tapped the design. "Ed, he told your desk his name was. Right, *Ed*. The number he gave's unregistered, and no one's answering."

"Hie thee to your books, Billy," Vardy said as Billy opened the door. "I'm disappointed in you." He tapped the paper. "See what Kooby Derry and Morry can show you." The words were weird but weirdly familiar.

"Wait, what?" said Billy from the doorway. "What was that?" Vardy waved him away.

Billy TRIED AND FAILED TO PARSE THE ENCOUNTER ON HIS BEWILdered way south. He had not been under arrest: he could have left at any time. He had his phone out, ready to do a tirade for Leon, but again for reasons he could not put into words, he did not make the call.

Nor did he go home. Instead, full of an unending sense of being under observation, Billy went to the centre of London. From café to bookshop café, mooching through paperbacks on his way through too much tea.

He did not have a phone with Internet connection, nor did he have his laptop with him, so could not test his intuition that his own reveal the previous night notwithstanding, there would be no information about the squid's disappearance in the news. The London papers certainly did not cover it. He did not eat, though he stayed out late enough, hours, that it was past time, until it was evening, then early night. He did not really do anything but moodily consider and grow frustrated, did not call the centre, only tried to consider possibilities.

What came back and back to him, what grew to gnaw him most throughout those hours, were the names that Vardy had said. Billy was absolutely certain he had heard them, that they meant something to him. He regretted that he hadn't insisted on more from Vardy: he did not even know how to spell them. He scribbled possibilities on a scrap of paper, *kubi derry, morry, moray, kobadara,* and more.

Got some bloody poking around to do, he thought.

On his way home at last his attention was drawn, he was not sure why, to a man on the backseat of his bus. He tried to work out what he had noticed. He could not get a clear view.

The guy was big and broad, in a hoodie, looking down. Whenever Billy turned, he was hunched over or with his face to the glass. Everything they passed tried to grab Billy's attention.

It was as if he were watched by the city's night animals and buildings, and by every passenger. *I shouldn't feel like this,* Billy thought. Neither should things. He watched a woman and man who had just got on. He imagined the couple shifting straight through the metal chair behind him, out of his sight.

A gust of pigeons shadowed the bus. They should be sleeping. They flew when the bus moved, stopped when it stopped. He wished he had a mirror, so he could watch without turning his head, see that man in back's evasive face.

They were on the top deck, above the most garish of central London's neon, by low treetops and first-floor windows, the tops of street signs. The light zones were reversed from their oceanic order, rising, not pitching, into dark. The street on which lamps shone and that was glared by shopwindow fluorescence was the shallowest and lightest place: the sky was the abyss, pointed by stars like bioluminescence. In the bus's upper deck they were at the edges of deep, the fringe of the dysphotic zone, where empty offices murked up out of sight. Billy looked up as if down into a deep-sea trench. The man behind him was looking up, too.

At the next stop, which was not his, Billy waited until the doors had closed before bolting from his seat and down the stairs, shouting, "Wait, wait, sorry!"

The bus left him and headed into the dark like a submersible. Through the dirty window at the rear of the top, he saw the man look straight at him.

"Shit," Billy said. "Shit."

He jerked his hand defensively out. The glass flexed and the man jerked backward as the bus receded. Billy's own glasses shivered on his face. He saw no one moving behind the window, past a crack in the glass that had suddenly bisected it. The man he had seen was Dane Parnell.

Chapter Four

Billy sat up late that weird deep night. He closed the curtains of his living room, imagining the unsavoury squirrel watching him as he poked around on his laptop. Why would Dane have followed him? How? He tried to think like a detective. He was bad at it.

He could call the police. He'd seen Dane commit no crime, but still. He should. He could call Baron, as he had requested. But despite his discomfort—call it fear—Billy did not want to do that.

There had been such a strange gaming edge to all his interactions with Baron, Vardy and the woman. It had been so clear that he was being played, that information was being held from him, that they had no consideration for him at all except insofar as he pushed forward whatever their opaque agenda was. He did not want to be involved. Or, and or, he wanted to understand this himself.

He slept a very little at last. In the morning, he discovered that it was not as hard to regain entry to the Darwin Centre as he had imagined. The two police at the entrance were not terribly interested, and examined his pass peremptorily. They interrupted his carefully constructed story of why he had to go back in to sort out some stuff on his desk that wouldn't wait but that he'd be careful and quick and blah blah. They just waved him past.

"Can't go to the tank room," one of them said. *Alright,* Billy thought. *Whatever.*

He was looking for something, but he had no idea what. He hesitated by retorts and sinks, by plastic containers of diaphonized fish, their flesh made invisible by enzymes, their bones made blue. A common room was full of stacks of posters for the Beagle Project, a retracing of those crucial early days of Darwin's journeys, a rerun in a floating laboratory kitschly made to look like the *Beagle.*

"Hey, Billy," said Sara, another curator who'd been granted entry, for whatever reason. "Did you hear?" She looked around and lowered her voice, passed on some rumour so evanescent and vapid it left his head as soon as she said it. Folklore was self-generating. Billy nodded as if he agreed, shook his head as if it were a shocking possibility, whatever it was she was talking about.

"Did you hear?" she said as well. "Dane Parnell's disappeared."

Well *that* he heard. It gave Billy another cold sensation, as he had had the previous night when he had seen Dane all those yards away, through the bus's glass, and as if Billy had touched him back.

"I was talking to one of the police," Sara said, "doing stuff in the tank room, and he was saying that they've heard things since, you know, it went. Something clattering."

"Whooo," said Billy, like a ghost. She smiled. But *Those are* my *hallucinations,* he thought. It was like theft. Those were his imaginings that the police were hearing.

He logged in at a workstation and searched, trying endless different spellings of the names Vardy had said, referring to his scribbled paper and crossing them off, one by one. Eventually he entered the renditions "Kubodera" and "Mori." "Oh man," he whispered. Stared at the screen and sat back. "Of course."

No wonder those names had tantalised. He was ashamed of himself. Kubodera and Mori were the researchers who, a few months previously, had been the first researchers to catch the giant squid on camera in the wild.

He downloaded their essay. He looked again at the pictures. "First-ever observations of a live giant squid in the wild" the paper was called, as if ten-year-olds had taken control of the *Proceedings of the Royal Society B*. First *ever*.

More than one of his colleagues had printouts of those pictures above their desks. When the images were released, Billy himself had turned up at the office with two bottles of Cava, and had proposed that the anniversary should henceforth be an annual holiday, Squid-day. Because these pictures, as he had said to Leon at the time, were momentous shit.

The first was the most famous, the one they had used on the news. Ajut into view in dark water almost a kilometre down, an eight-metre squid. Its arms blossomed, curved left and right around the bait at the end of the perspectived line. But it was the second picture at which Billy stared.

Again the line descended; again there in ominous water was the animal. But this time it was coming mouth-on. It was caught in a near-perfect radial limb-burst: at the apex, the bite. The two hunting arms, longer limbs with paddle-shaped hands, were recoiled in the dark.

A tentacular explosion. That picture banished all slanderous theories of *Architeuthis* as sluggish predator-by-accident, tentacles adangle in deepwater lethargy for prey to bumble into, no more a hunter than some idiot jellyfish.

That image had been cherished by fan-partisans of *Mesonychoteuthis*, the "colossal squid," *Architeuthis*'s huge, squat-bodied rival. Which, *Mesonychoteuthis*, yes, had also been emerging into the camera and video gaze with highly and historically unusual enthusiasm recently. And it was, yes, a terrifying animal. True, it had greater mass; its mantle was longer; granted, its tentacles grabbed not with suckers but with cruel cat-curved claws. But whatever its shape, however its stats and the *Architeuthis*'s compared, it would never be the *giant squid*. It was a parvenu monster. Hence the trash-talk of those who researched it, eager to demote the long-term kraken for their new favourite: "without parallel," ". . . even larger," "an order of magnitude meaner."

But observe the Kubodera/Mori images. Hardly the weak opportunist the haters had dreamed up. *Architeuthis* did not wait and dangle. *Architeuthis* loomed, jetted from the abyss, hunting.

Billy stared at the screen. Ten arms, five lines crisscrossing; two longer than the others. The silver design on the pin he'd seen was of this predator incoming. As seen by prey.

He walked the corridors carrying papers so he looked as if he was going from somewhere to somewhere else. He entered rooms he was allowed to enter, nodded in greeting to the police guarding those he was not. His revelation notwithstanding, he still had no idea what it was he was hoping to find.

He left the Darwin Centre for the main museum. He saw no police there. He walked the route he used to take as a boy, past the staring ichthyosaur, stone ammonites, past where was now the café. There at last, in the middle of everything and everyone, he thought perhaps he heard a sound. The noise of a jar rolling. Very faint.

It came—or sounded as if it did to him, he corrected himself—from a door off-limits to visitors, that led downstairs to storage areas and undercorridors. He listened at it, crowds to his back. He heard nothing. He entered the keycode and descended.

Billy walked windowless halls underground. He told himself that he did not think he was listening for anything real. That whatever hint it was he was looking for came from inside him. *So alright*, he said to himself. *Help me out. What am I looking for? What are you— what am I—on about?*

Guards and curators raised their hands as he passed in brief greetings. The rooms and hallways were lined with industrial shelving, on which were cardboard boxes labelled in thick pen; glass cases empty, or full of surplus specimens; papers; unneeded furniture. There below the heating pipes, by high brick walls and pillars, Billy heard the noise again. From around a corner. He followed it like bread crumbs.

The corridor opened out, not a room but a sudden large hallway. It was stacked quite full of taxidermy, charnel Victoriana. Mammal heads watched from walls, like a hundred Faladas; bisons stiff as aging soldiers by a plaster iguanodon and a tatty emu. There was a thicket of the preserved necks-up of giraffes, their heads a canopy above.

A clink, a clack. Under the striplights the stuffed bodies shed hard shadows. Billy heard another tiny noise. It came from the dark by the wall, deep in the specimen undergrowth.

Billy stepped off the path. He pressed through unyielding antique bodies, shouldering deeper into the little forest of animal remains. He glanced up as if at birds and pressed toward the whitewashed walls. He did not hear another of the sounds, only his own efforts and the brush of his clothes on dry skins. He rounded a stack of hippo parts, and came abruptly up against something of which he could for moments not make sense.

Glass, an old glass container as large as any he had seen. A chest-high lidded cylinder with scalloped base, full of pee-coloured pre-server, and a specimen at which he stared. Something rather too big for the container, shoved crudely inside. Part-peeled, with eyes and paws up against the glass and ragged skin suspended like open wings, but even as he thought that he shook his head *no.*

Billy saw that what he had thought pelt was a ruined shirt, what he had thought peeled was hairlessness and bloat, that *oh my Jesus fuck-ing Christ* what stared deadly at him in broken pose pressed up and misshaped against the bottle's inside was a man.

BILLY STAYED OUT OF THE POLICE'S WAY. IT WAS NOT EVEN HIM WHO called them. In those initial terrified moments, when he had torn upstairs unable to breathe, he had not thought to make the call. He had instead run to the two officers guarding the Darwin Centre and screamed, "Quick! Quick!"

Their colleagues came quickly in numbers, cordoning off more of the museum, declaring the basement out of bounds. They took Billy's prints. Gave him hot chocolate for shock.

No one questioned him. They put him in a conference room and told him not to leave, but no one asked how he had found what he had found. Billy waited by an overhead projector, a TV on a rolling base. He listened to the museum being cleared, the consternation of the crowds.

He wanted solitude more than he wanted fresh air. He wanted his body to stop the last of its panicked shaking, so he sat and waited, as he had been told to, his glasses steaming when he sipped, until the door opened and Baron peered in.

"Mr. Harrow," Baron said, and shook his head. "*Mister Hah-row* . . .

"Mr. Harrow, Billy, Billy Harrow. What *have* you been up to?"

Chapter Five

Baron sat next to Billy and shrugged at him sympathetically.

"Bit of a shock," he said.

"What the *hell?*" Billy said. "What the hell, how did they get that . . . ? What even happened?"

"Gives a whole new meaning to 'Someone getting bottled,' doesn't it? I apologise, I apologise," Baron said. "Morgue humour. Defence mechanism. You've had a horrible shock, I do know. Believe me."

"What's going on?" Billy said. Baron said nothing. "I saw Dane," Billy said.

"Is that right?" Baron said slowly. "Really now?"

"I was coming home. Last night. On a bus. He was on there. He must've been following me. Unless he could've just . . . no. He must've been there deliberately. It wouldn't be hard for him to find out where I live . . ."

"Alright. Alright, now, listen . . ."

"I feel like I'm going mad," Billy said. "Even before that . . . Before what's in the basement. I've been feeling like I'm being followed. I didn't say anything because, it's stupid, you know . . ." The wind shook the windows abruptly. "I tell you I'm losing it . . . What happened downstairs? Did Dane do *that?*"

"Let me think for a second, Mr. Harrow," Baron said.

"When I was in with you, why was there a psychology professor there? Vardy. That's what he does. I looked him up. Come on, Baron, don't look like that—all it took was a bit of an online poke about. I could tell he wasn't a cop."

"Is that so? You can ask him yourself in a bit."

"Was he there because . . . Is it that you think I'm mad, Baron?" There was another silence. "Is that what you think's going on with me? Because, Jesus . . ." Billy breathed out shakily. "Right at the moment, I think you have a point."

"No," said Baron. "None of us think you're losing it. Rather the opposite." He glanced at his watch. This time, when he arrived, Vardy shook Billy's hand. He had one of those unpleasant too-hard grips. He was carrying a briefcase.

"Did you have a look?" Baron said.

"It's pretty much as you'd expect," Vardy said.

"*What?*" Billy shouted. "What you'd *expect?* What about it did you expect, exactly?"

"We'll discuss that," Vardy said. "We'll discuss that, Billy. Now wait. I gather you saw Dane Parnell."

Billy ran his fingers through his hair. Vardy seemed too large for the chair he was in: he squeezed his shoulders together, as if to avoid spilling himself. He and Baron looked at each other, sharing another unspoken moment.

"Right then," said Baron. "Let's have another go. Patrick Vardy, Billy Harrow, curator. Billy Harrow, Patrick Vardy. Professor of psychology at Central London University. As I gather you know."

"Yeah, like I say," Billy muttered. "My Google-fu is strong."

"I owe you an apology, Mr. Harrow," Baron said. "I sort of assumed you'd be as half-arsed as most people. Wouldn't even occur to them to look up our names."

"So how much do you know about us?" Vardy said. "About me?"

"You're a psych." Billy shrugged. "You work with the cops. So I figure . . . You're a profiler, aren't you? Like Cracker? Like *Silence of the Lambs?*" Vardy smiled, a bit. "That poor sod shoved into the bottle, downstairs," Billy said. "He's not the first. Is that it? That's it, isn't it. You're looking for someone . . . You're looking for Dane. Dane's some kind of serial killer. You're here to work out what his thing is. And, oh Christ, he wants me, doesn't he? He's following *me*. And it's something to do with . . ."

But he stopped. How did any of this make sense of the squid? Baron pursed his lips.

"Not exactly," said Baron. "It's not quite right." He chopped his hands through the air onto the tabletop, organising invisible thoughts.

"Look, Mr. Harrow," Baron said. "Here's the thing. Go back a step. Who'd want to steal a giant squid? Never mind *how* just yet. That's not important. Right now, focus on why. It seems like you might be able to help us, and we might be able to help you. I'm not saying you're in danger, but I'm saying that—"

"Oh Christ . . ."

"Billy Harrow, *listen* to me. You need to know what's going on. We've talked it over. We're going to tell you the full story. And this is in *confidence*. Which this time please keep, thank you. Now, all this is not the sort of thing we normally lay out for people. We think it might help you to know, and to be perfectly frank we think it might help us too."

"Why does Dane want me?" Billy said.

"I wasn't on this case originally, as you know. There are certain flags that go up, you might say, under certain circumstances. Certain sorts of crime. The disappearance of your squid. Plus there are aspects of what's downstairs that are . . . relevant. Like for example the fact that the diameter of that jar's opening isn't big enough to have got that gentleman inside."

"What?"

"But what really clinched our interest," Baron said, "what really rang my bell—and I mean that literally, there's a bell on my desk—is when you drew us that picture."

From his briefcase Vardy pulled a photocopy of the druggily exaggerated asterisk.

"I know what that is," said Billy. "Kubodera and Mori—"

"So," Baron said, "I head up a specialist unit."

"What unit?"

Vardy pushed another piece of paper across the table. It was the sign again, the ten-armed spread with two longer limbs. But not the one Billy had drawn. The angles, the lengths of the arms, were slightly different.

"That was drawn a little over a month ago," Baron said. "A bookshop got busted into one night and a bunch of stuff was taken. Bloke wearing this sign had come in a couple of days running beforehand, not buying anything, looking around. Nervous."

"If this were a question of a couple of kids both wearing *Obey Giant* T-shirts, we'd not be bothered," Vardy said, quickly, in his deep voice. "This is not a bloody meme. Though it may be going that way and thank you very much that'll complicate things very nicely." Billy blinked. "Are you a graffiti aficionado? It's started to crop up. Early days. It'll be on stickers on lampposts and student rucksacks soon. Turns out that this"—he flicked the paper—"is appropriate for the times."

"It just fits," said Baron.

"But not quite yet," Vardy said. "So when it turns up twice, we sniff a pattern."

"The guy who was burgled," Baron said. "It's Charing Cross Road. He stocks a lot of junk and a little bit of proper antiquarian stuff. Six books nicked that night. Five had just come in. Maybe two, three hundred quids' worth. They were all on the desk up front, waiting to be sorted. At first he thought that was all that was gone.

"But where there are locked cabinets, the glass's broken and something's missing from a top shelf." He held up a finger. "One book. From a bunch of old academic journals. He worked out what it was was gone."

Baron looked down and read laboriously. "*For-hand-linger . . . ved de Skandinav*—something," he said. "The 1857 volume."

"How's your Danish, Billy?" said Vardy. "Ring any bells?"

"Some villain wants to make it look like he's rushed in and snagged at random," Baron said. "So he grabs a load of books off the counter. But he then runs twenty feet down a corridor, to one *specific* locked bookshelf, breaks one specific pane of glass, takes one specific old book." Baron shook his head. "It was that one journal. *That*'s what this was all about."

"So we asked the Danish Royal Academy for the contents," Vardy said. "Too old to be on databases."

"To be honest, we didn't think much of it at the time," Baron said. "It wasn't a priority. It only got passed to us because we'd seen that symbol knocking around a bit. When the list came in from Copenhagen nothing stood out. But. When we heard the symbol'd turned up here, and just what'd happened, one of those articles nicked weeks ago came back sharpish."

"Pages one eighty-two to one eighty-five," Vardy said.

"I won't try the Scandiwegian," Baron said, reading. "It's an article about *blaeksprutter,* so they say. Translation: Japetus Steenstrup. 'Several Particulars about the Giant Cuttlefish of the Atlantic.'"

"To recap," Baron said. "Weeks before your squid was snaffled, someone pinched an original copy of that article."

"You'll have heard of the author," Vardy said. Billy's mouth was open. He had. The giant squid was *Architeuthis dux,* but its genus was named for the man who had taxonomised it: *Architeuthis Steenstrup.*

"Now," Vardy said. "Two crimes united by a questionable necklace do not a conspiracy make. However. Two crimes—three, now, with the chap downstairs—united by such jewellery *and* by giant squid, and our radar does indeed tend to ping."

"That is the sort of thing that gets us interested," Baron said.

"'Us'?" Billy said at last. "Who *is* 'us'?"

"We," said Baron, "are the FSRC."

"The what?"

Baron folded his hands. "Do you remember that lot calling themselves New Rosicrucians?" he said. "Who kidnapped that girl in Walthamstow?" Baron thumbed in Vardy's direction. "Found them. And he was I suppose you'd call it *consulting* during seven/seven, too. That sort of thing. It's an area of concern."

"*What* area?"

"Alright, alright," Baron said. "You sound like you're about to cry." Vardy handed Billy a piece of paper. It was, oddly, his CV. His PhD was in psychology, but his master's was in theology. His first degree divinity. Billy pushed his glasses on and scanned the publications list, the Positions Currently Held.

"You're an editor of *The Journal of Fundamentalism Studies?*" Billy said. This was a test.

Baron said, "The FSRC is the Fundamentalist and Sect-Related Crime Unit."

Billy stared at him, at Vardy, at the CV again. "You *are* a profiler," he said. "You're a cult profiler."

Vardy even smiled.

"THERE'S . . ." BARON COUNTED ON HIS FINGERS. "AUM SHINRIKYO . . . The Returner Sect . . . Church of Christ Hunter . . . Kratosians, close to home some of them . . . Do you have any idea the increase in cult-related violence in the last ten years? Of course you don't, because unless it's, boo, Al Qaeda and the Al-Qaedalinos, it doesn't come close to the news. But they're the least of our worries. And part of the reason you haven't heard about this is because *we* are good at our job. We've been keeping the streets safe.

"That's why you were encouraged to keep shtum. But you told someone something. Which A, you should not have done, and B, is not unimpressive. Collingswood's going to have to ask you again, a bit harder.

"It's not as if we're exactly secret," he said. "It's not so much 'plausible denial'—that's not the best strategy these days. It's more 'plausibly uninteresting.' Everyone'll be like, 'FSRC? Why on earth you asking about them? Silly nonsense, bit of an embarrassment . . .'" He smiled. "You get the idea."

Billy could hear officers in the corridors outside. Phones were ringing.

"So," said Billy at last. "So you're cult people. So what's this got to do with that poor sod in the basement? And what's it got to do with *me?*"

Vardy brought up a video file on his laptop and placed it where all three men could watch. An office, a tidy desk, books on the walls, a printer and PC. There was Vardy, sitting three-quarters toward the camera, another man with his back to the lens. All that could be seen of him was slicked-back thinning hair and a grey jacket. The colours were not very good.

". . . *so.*" Billy heard the hidden-faced man say. "*I done a stint with that bunch in Epping, bog-standard manickies they are I think, balance balance balance not very interesting, I wouldn't waste your time.*"

"*What about this?*" said video-Vardy, and held out what Billy could see was the symbol he himself had drawn.

The obscured man leaned in. "*Oh right,*" he said. He spoke in a breathless conspiratorial drone. "*The tooths, the toothies,*" he said. "*Yeah no I don't know,*" he said. "*The toothies they're new I think I hen't seen them much except they been drawing that leaving it about. A sign a sign. You been to Camden? Saw it and I thought I'll have some of that but they're odd ones, they sort of wave hello but then you can't find much of them. So. Are they secret?*"

"*Are they?*" said video-Vardy.

"*Well you tell me you tell me. I can't get to them and you know me so it's, you know it's tantalising is what it is.*"

"*Tenets?*"

"*Got me. What I hear,*" the man made gossip-talk movements with his fingers, "*all I can tell you is they talk about the dark, the rise, the you know the reaching out. They love that the outreaching, hafay . . .*"

"*What?*"

"*Hafay hafay, where's your Greek professor? Alpha phi eta, hafe, hapsis if you like, touchy touchy, that's what they say—it's a haptic story, this one.*"

Vardy froze the picture. "He's sort of a freelance research assistant. A *fan.* He's a collector."

"Of what?" Billy said.

"Religions. Cults."

"How the hell do you collect a cult?"

"By joining it."

OUTSIDE THE WINDOW WERE THE WIND-BOISTEROUS LIMBS OF trees. The room felt very close. Billy looked away from the light outside.

The man on-screen was not the only one, Vardy said. A small obsessive tribe. Heresy geeks, going sect to sect, accumulating creeds as greedy as any Renfields. Soldiers of the Saviour Worm one week,

Opus Dei or the Bobo Dreds the next, with genius for devotion and sudden brief bursts of sincerity sufficient to be welcomed as neophytes. Some were always cynically in it for the notch on the bedpost, others Damascene certain for two or three days that *this one was different,* until they remembered their own natures and excommunicated themselves with indulgent chuckles.

They gathered to compare gnoses, in Edgware Road cafés over sheesha or pubs in Primrose Hill or somewhere called Almagan Yard, mostly their favoured hangouts in the "trap streets," Vardy said. They traded dissident mysteries in vague competition, as if faiths were Top Trumps cards.

"What about your apocalypse, then?" "Well, the universe is a leaf on the time-tree, and come autumn it's going to shrivel and fall off into hell." Murmurs of admiration. "Ooh, nice one. My new lot say ants are going to eat the sun."

"He wants to join these 'toothies,' you see," Vardy said. "He's a completist. But he can't find them."

"What's a trap street?" Billy was ignored.

"*Toothies,*" Baron said. "Get it? Harrow, sit down." Billy had stood up and was walking toward the door. "*Toothies,*" Baron said. "Get it? Tyuh-tyuh-tyuh-*Tyoothies.*"

"I've had enough," Billy said.

"Sit down," Vardy said.

"We're the bloody cult squad, Harrow," Baron said. "Why d'you think we're called in? Who do you think's responsible for what's going on?"

"Teuthies." Vardy smiled. "Worshippers of the giant squid."

Chapter Six

"THE ARTICLE THAT GOT NICKED," SAID BARON. BILLY STOOD still, his hand on the doorknob. "It's where old Japetus names *Architeuthis* for the first time. 'Course you can get hold of a reprint, but originals are a bit special, aren't they?"

"He was refuting folklore," said Vardy. "The whole piece is him pooh-poohing some fairy story, and saying, 'No no, there's a rational explanation, gentlemen.' You could say it's where the sea monster meets . . ." He gestured around him. "This. The *modern world*." The stress was mockery. "Out of fable into science. The end of an old order. Right?" He wagged his finger *no*. Baron watched him indulgently.

"Death of legend?" Vardy said. "Because he gives it a name? He said it was *Ar-chi-teu-this*. Not 'great' squid, Billy. Not 'big,' not even 'giant.' '*Ruling*.'" He blinked. "It *rules*? That's him being faithful to the Enlightenment? He shoves it into taxonomy, yeah, but as what? As a bloody demiurge.

"He was a prophet. At the end of the lecture, you know what he did? Oh, he had props. He was a performer like Billy Graham. Brings out a jar, and what's in it? A beak." Vardy snap-snapped his fingers. "Of a giant squid."

The light was going: some cloud cover arriving, as if summoned by drama. Billy stared at Vardy. He had his glasses in his hand, so

Vardy was a touch hazy. Billy had actually heard this story, or its outlines, he remembered: an anecdote in a lecture hall. Where they
could, his lecturers, with vicarious panache, would spice the stories of
their forebears' theories. They told anecdotes of a polymath Faraday;
read Feynman's achingly sad letter to his dead wife; described Edison's
swagger; eulogised Curie and Bogdanov martyred to their utopian
researches. Steenstrup had been part of that dashing company.

The way Vardy spoke was almost as if he could no-shit *see* Steenstrup's performance. As if he were looking at the black weapon thing
Steenstrup had lifted from the jar. That leviathan part, more like a
tool of alien design than any mouth. Preserved, precious, manifest
like the finger bone of a saint. Whatever he had claimed, Steenstrup's
bottle had been a reliquary.

"That article," Vardy said. "It's a fulcrum. With a certain way of
looking at things, it would easily be worth breaking the law for.
Because it's sacred text. It's *gospel.*"

Billy shook his head. He felt as if his ears were ringing.

"And that," Baron said, audibly amused, "is what the professor gets
paid for."

"What our thieves have been doing is building a library," said
Vardy. "I bet you good money that over the last few months stuff by
Verrill and Ritchie and Murray and other, you know, classic *teuthic*
literature has also been nicked."

"Jesus," said Billy. "How do you know so much about this?" Vardy
swatted the question away—literally, with his hand—as if it were an
insect.

"It's what the man do," Baron said. "Zero to guru in forty-eight
hours."

"Let's move on," said Vardy.

"So," Billy said. "You think this cult nicked the book, took the
squid, and killed that guy? And now they want me?"

"Did I say that?" Vardy said. "I can't be sure these squiddists did
anything. Something doesn't add up, to be honest."

Billy started up unhappy performed laughter at that. "*D'you
think?*" he said.

But Vardy ignored him and went on. "But it's something to do with them."

"Come on," said Billy. "This is *batshit*." He pleaded. "A religion about squid?"

The little room felt like a trap. Baron and Vardy watched him. "Come on now," Vardy said. "You can have faith in anything," Vardy said. "Everything's fit to be worshipped."

"You going to say this is all a coincidence?" Baron said.

"Your squid just disappeared, right?" Vardy said.

"And no one's watching you," Baron said. "And no one did anything to that poor sod downstairs. It was suicide by bottle."

"And you," said Vardy, staring at Billy, "you don't feel anything's wrong with the world, right now. Ah, you do, though, don't you? I can see. You want to hear this."

A silence. "How did they do it?" said Billy.

"Sometimes you can't get bogged down in the *how*," Baron said. "Sometimes things happen that shouldn't, and you can't let that detain you. But the *why?* we can make headway with."

Vardy walked to the window. He was against its light, a dark shape. Billy could not tell if Vardy was facing him or facing out.

"It's always bells and smells," Vardy said, from his obscurity. "Always high-church. They might . . . *abjure the world*"—he rolled the pomp of the phrase around—"but for sects like this it's all rites and icons. That's the point. Not many cults have had their reformation." He walked out of the window's glare. "Or if they have, hello you poor buggers in Freezone, along comes a Council of Trent and the old order bites back. They really have to have their sacraments." He shook his head.

Billy paced between posters, cheap artworks and pinboard message exchanges between colleagues he did not know. "If you worship that animal . . . I'll put it simply," Vardy said. "You, your *Darwin Centre* . . ." Billy did not understand the scorn there. "You and your colleagues, Billy—you put God on display. Now, who would a devotee be not to liberate it?

"It's lying there pickled. Their touchy hunter god. You can imagine how that plays out in psalms. How God's described."

"Right," Billy said. "Right, you know what? I really need to get out of here."

Vardy seemed to quote: "'It moves through darkness, emptying into that ink ink of its own.' Something like that. Shall we say *a black cloud in water already black?* There's a koan for you, Billy. It's a tactile god with as many tentacles as we have fingers, and *is that coincidence?* Because *that*," he added, in a more everyday voice, "is how this works, you see?"

Baron beckoned Billy to the door. "They'll have verses about its mouth," Vardy said behind them. "The *hard maw of a sky-bird* in the deep trenches of water." He shrugged. "Something like that. You're sceptical? Au contraire: it's a *perfect* god, Billy. It's the bloody choicest perfect simon-pure exact god for today, for right now. Because it's bugger-all like us. Alien. That old beardy bully was never plausible, was he?"

"Plausible enough for you, you bloody hypocrite," Baron said jovially. Billy followed him into the corridor.

"They venerate the thing," Vardy said, following. "They have to save it from the insult of what I strongly suspect is your cheerful affection. I bet you have a nickname for it, don't you?" He tilted his head. "I bet that nickname is 'Archie.' I see I'm right. Now, you tell me. What person of faith could possibly allow that?"

THEY TRACED THROUGH THE MUSEUM'S CORRIDORS, AND BILLY HAD no idea where they were going. He felt absolutely untethered. As if he were not there. The hallways were all deserted. The darks and woods of the museum closed up behind him.

"How do you . . . ? What is it you're doing?" he said to Vardy as the man took a breath, mid-insight. *What do you call that?* Billy thought. That reconstitutive intelligence, berserker meme-splicing, seeing in nothings first patterns, then correspondence, then causality and dissident sense.

Vardy even smiled. "Paranoia," he said. "Theology."

They reached an exit Billy had never used, and he gasped in the cool air of the outside. The day blustered: the trees wriggled in wind and clouds raced as if on missions. Billy sat on the stone steps.

"So the guy in the basement . . ." he said.

"Don't know yet," Vardy said. "He got in the way. Dissident, guard, sacrifice, something. At the moment I'm talking about the shape of something."

"None of this should be your business," Baron said. With his hands in his pockets he addressed his remarks to one of the building's stonework animals. The air shoved Billy's hair and clothes around. "You shouldn't have to fuss with any of this. But here's the thing. What with Parnell on the bus, what with that sort of attention, it just seems like for whatever reasons . . . they've noticed you, Mr. Harrow."

He caught Billy's eye. Billy twitched in the attention. He glanced around the grounds, beyond the gate to the street, into the shifting plant life. Bits of rubbish shifted in gusts, crawled on the pavement like bottom-feeders.

"You're part of some conspiracy that trapped their god," Vardy said. "But more than that. You're the go-to squid guy, Mr. Harrow. You seem to have got someone interested. As far as they're concerned, you're a person of interest."

He stood between Billy and the wind. "*You* found the squid gone," he said. "You put it there in the first place. It's always been you who's had magic mollusc fingers." He twiddled his own. "Now *you* found this dead bloke. Is it any wonder they're interested?"

"You've been feeling . . . like stuff's going on," Baron said. "Would that be fair to say?"

"What's happening to me?" Billy managed to speak calmly.

"Don't worry, Billy Harrow. That's perspicacity, not paranoia, that, what you're feeling." Baron turned, taking in the London panorama, and wherever he looked, whenever he paused facing some particular patch of blackness, Billy looked too. "There *is* something wrong. And it's noticed you. That's not always the best place to be." Billy sat in the middle of that world's notice, like a tiny prey.

"What is it you want to do?" Billy said. "I mean, find out who killed that guy. Right? But what about me? Are you going to get the squid back?"

"That would be our intent, yes," Baron said. "Cult robbery, after all, is part of our remit. And now there's murder, too. Yes. And your safety is of, shall we say, no little concern to us."

"What do they want? What's Dane in all this?" Billy said. "And you're some secret cult squad, right? So why are you telling me this?"

"I know, I know, you're feeling a little exposed," Baron said. "A bit out in the glare of it all. There are ways we might help. And you could help us back."

"Like it or not, you're already part of this," Vardy said.

"We have a proposal," Baron said. "Come on in out of the cold. Shoot on over with us back to the Darwin Centre. There's a proposition on the table, and there's someone you should meet."

Chapter Seven

THE ROOMS SETTLED AROUND THEM, AS IF FINICKETY *GENII LOCI* were adjusting. Billy felt like an outsider. Was that glass he heard, clank-sliding out of sight? A clatter that might be bones?

The two uniforms guarding the tank room did not react to Baron with any visible respect. "Clocked that, did you?" Baron muttered to Billy. "Right now they're coming up with hilarious jokes about what FSRC stands for. The first half is always 'Fucking Stupid.'"

Inside was the disdainful young woman again, glancing at Billy perhaps a shade more friendly than before, her uniform as casual as ever. She had a laptop open on the table where the squid no longer was. "Alright?" she said. She mock-saluted Vardy and Baron, raised an eyebrow at Billy. She typed one-handed.

"I'm Billy."

She looked *oh-really?* "There's trace, man," she said to Baron.

"Billy Harrow, PC Kath Collingswood," Baron said. She clucked her tongue or chewing gum and turned her computer round, but not enough that Billy could see.

"Quite a spike," Vardy murmured.

"With the strike and all that, you wouldn't expect to see shit like this," she said. Vardy looked lengthily around the room, as if the dead animals might be responsible.

"Do you want to know what any of these things are?" said Billy.

"No no," said Vardy thoughtfully. He approached the oarfish caught decades before. He looked at an antique alligator baby. "Ha," he said.

He circumnavigated. "Ha!" he said again abruptly. He had reached the cabinet of *Beagle* specimens. He wore an unrecognisable expression.

"This is them," he said after awhile.

"Yeah," said Billy.

"My good God," Vardy said softly. "Good God." He leaned very close and read their labels a long time. When finally he rejoined Collingswood, as she ran information through the computer, he glanced back at the *Beagle* cabinet more than once. Collingswood followed his glance.

"Oh yeah," she said to the jars. "That's what I'm talking about."

"Are you who I'm supposed to meet?" Billy said.

"Yeah," she said. "I'm him. Come down the pub."

"Uh . . ." Billy said. "I don't think that's in my plans . . ."

"Best thing for you, a drink," Baron said. "Best thing. Coming?" he said to Vardy.

Vardy shook his head. "I'm not the persuasive one." He waved them out.

"Nah," said Collingswood to Billy. "Not so much. It ain't that he's not *interested* in, like, persuasiveness, get me? He's *interested* in it. Like something in a jar."

"Come on, Billy," Baron said. "Come and have a drink on the Metropolitan Police."

The world was swaying when they left. Too many people speaking in too many street-corner hushes, too much foreclosure, the sky closing some deal. Collingswood frowned at the clouds, like she did not like what they wrote. The pub was a dark drinkerie decorated with old London road signs and copies of antique maps. They sat in an out-of-the-way corner. Even so, the other punters, a mix of seedy geezers and office workers, were clearly unsettled by Kath Collingswood's uniformed—if unorthodoxly—presence.

"So . . ." Billy said. He had no idea what to say. Collingswood seemed unbothered. She just watched him while Baron went to the bar. Collingswood offered a cigarette.

"I think it's no smoking," Billy said. She looked at him and lit. The smoke surrounded her in dramatic shapes. He waited.

"Here's the thing," Baron said, delivering the drinks. "You heard Vardy. Parnell and the toothies have eyes on you. So you aren't necessarily in the safest of all situations."

"But I'm nothing," Billy said. "You know that."

"Hardly the point," Baron said. It surprised him how hard it jarred him to see Collingswood drink and smoke in uniform. "Let's take stock," Baron said. "Now, Vardy . . . You saw him in action. You know the sort of thing he does. For all our expertise, in this case, vis-à-vis—that is to say, what's going on at the moment—we could do with some input. From a specialist. Like yourself. We're dealing with fanatics. And fanatics are always experts. So we need experts of our own. And that is where you come in."

Billy stared at him. He even laughed a bit. "I wondered if you were going to say something like this, but then I was like, don't be mad."

"None of us knows shit about giant squid," Collingswood said. The animal's name sounded absurd in her sarky London voice. "'Cause we don't give a shit about it, granted, but, you know."

"Fine, then, so leave me alone," Billy said. "Not as if I'm an expert anyway."

"Oh come on, don't be like that."

"Don't just mean book-smarts, Harrow." Baron said. "I have a healthy respect for cultists. And *they* think you're something special, which says a lot, no matter what *you* think. Remember when you saw Dane Parnell? Remember about the bus window?"

"What?" said Billy. "That it was broken?"

"What you said to us was you saw it *break*. How do you suppose that happened?" Baron let the question sit. "The way we, the FSRC I mean, do things . . . we need a subtler approach than the rest of the force. It's handy to have members *out*side of the actual service."

"You actually are actually trying to get me to join," Billy said, incredulous.

"There's certain privileges," Baron said. "A few responsibilities. Official Secrets, whatnot. Bit of dosh. Not enough to really make a big difference, to be honest, but, you know, it's a couple of pizzas . . ."

"And tell me, does anyone in the FSRC," Billy said, "ever make a blind bit of sense?" He looked at his drinking partners blearily. "I was not expecting to be recruited today."

"Yeah, and by the filth, too," Collingswood said. She blew gusts, gave him a little smirk. Still no one was telling her to stop smoking.

"We want you onside, Billy," Baron said. "You could help Vardy. You know the books. You'll understand the squid stuff. Any investigation, we always start with beliefs, but the biology's going to be part of all that.

"You know, I have to tell you . . ." Baron shifted as if broaching a painful subject. "You might have heard, it's an old standard that if you're looking for whodunit, you start with whoever finds the body. And you did have access to the tank, too."

Billy's eyes widened. He began to rise. Baron pulled him back down, laughing. "Sit down, you pillock," he said. "I'm just saying that if we wanted to, we could approach this a whole other way. Where were you on the night of, et cetera and so on. But you and us can scratch each other's backs. We want insight and you want protection. Win-win, mate."

"So why are you threatening me?" Billy said. "And I told you, I don't have any insight . . ."

"You going to tell me," Baron interrupted, tilting his chin in a *come now* look, "you've got no sense of the bloody awesomeness of that thing?"

". . . The squid?"

"The *Archi*-bloody-*teuthis*, Billy Harrow, yes. The giant squid. That thing in the jar. That. That got took. And is been and gone. Are you really surprised someone might worship it? Don't you want a better idea why? What the stakes are? You know stuff's going on, now. Don't you want to know more?"

"There's new life and new civilisations," Collingswood said. She did her face in a hand mirror.

Billy shook his head and said, "Bloody hell."

"Nah," Collingswood said. "That's a different unit."

Billy closed his eyes, opened them at the sound of the glasses vibrating on the table. Collingswood and Baron looked at each other.

"Did he just . . . ?" Collingswood said. She looked at Billy again, with interest.

"We know you've been unsettled," Baron said carefully. "Makes you a great candidate . . ."

"*Unsettled?*" Billy thought of the jarred man. "That's one way to put it. And now you want me to, to go looking stuff up for you? That's it?"

"For a starter."

"I do not think so," Billy said. "I'd rather go home and forget all about whatever's going on."

"*Right,*" said Collingswood. She took a drag. The low light glimmered on her gold trimmings. "Like you can forget about it. Like you can forget about all *this.*" She swayed in her chair. "Good luck with that, bruv."

"No one doubts you'd rather," Baron said. "But choice, alas, is not given to all of us. Even if you're not interested in it, it's interested in you. Let me just let that stand for a tick.

"Thing is, Billy, we should be outdated. FSRC got set up a little bit before 2000. Cobbled together from a couple of older outfits. Supposed to be temporary. It was the millennium: we were waiting for some devout nutters to set fire to the Houses of Parliament. Sacrifice Cherie Blair to their goat overlords, something."

"No luck there," Collingswood said. She did the French breathing thing with her smoke. Disgusting as it was, Billy couldn't take his eyes off it.

"Sweet FA," said Baron. "A little bit of silly buggery, but the big Y2K explosion of . . . well, *millennialism,* that we'd been expecting . . . didn't happen."

"Not *then,*" said Collingswood.

"Do you even remember the millennium?" Billy said. "Weren't you watching *Teletubbies*?" She smirked.

"She's right," Baron said. "Stuff was delayed. It came after. Eventually we ended up busier than ever. Look, I don't care what these groups want to do, so long as they keep to themselves. Paint yourself blue and boff cactuses, just do it indoors and don't involve civilians. Live and let live. But that's not what causes the trouble." He tapped the table with each word that followed. "All these groups are all about revelations, apocrypha . . ."

"Always boils down to the same thing," Collingswood said.

"It does a bit," said Baron. "Any holy book, it's the last chapter that gets us interested."

"John the fucking Divine," Collingswood said. "Bish bash fucking bosh."

"What my colleague is getting at," Baron said, "is we're facing a wave of St. Johns. A bit of an epidemic of eschatologies. We live," he said, too flatly for any humour to be audible, "in the epoch of competing ends."

Collingswood said, "Ragnarok versus Ghost Dance versus Kali Yuga versus Qiyamah yadda yadda."

"That's what gets converts these days," Baron said. "It's a buyers' market in apocalypse. What's hot in heresy's Armageddon."

"It was all chat, for ages," Collingswood said. "But since suddenly, something's actually going on."

"And they're all still insisting it's *their* apocalypse that's going to happen," Baron said. "And that means trouble. Because they're fighting about it."

"What do you mean *something's going on?*" Billy said, but what with his head all over the place and the blatantly actual fact of impossibilities, the scorn he tried to put in it didn't really take. Collingswood prodded the air, rubbed her fingers together to indicate that she felt something, as if the world had left residue on her.

"You got to be worried when they're agreeing about anything," she said. "Prophets. That's the last bloody thing you want prophets to do. Even if, especially if, they still don't agree on details. Heard about them hoodies and asbos rucking in East London?" She shook her head. "Brothers of Vulpus went at it with a bunch of druids. Nasty. Them sickles are sharp. And all over how the world's going to end."

"We're overstretched, Harrow," said Baron. "'Course we do other stuff; sacrificed kiddies, animal cruelty, whatnot. But it's ends-of-the-world where the action is. It's harder and harder to deal with the apocalypse rumbles. We can't cope," he said. "I'm being frank with you. Let alone now something this big has happened. Don't get me wrong—I got no more time for fortune cookies than you have. Still though. Little while ago, half the prophets in London began to know—know—that the world's on its way out." He did not sound as if he was mocking the knowledge. "And I am utterly buggered if I know what that's about, but then it suddenly got a lot more definite. Round about when you-know-what happened."

"Your squid went *poof*," Collingswood said.

"It is not my squid."

"Oh it is, though," she said. "Come on, it is, though." It felt like his, when she said that. "It happened again," she said to Baron. "It got closer again."

"They brought the public into it," Baron said. "And that is not on. We go out of our way to keep civies out. But if someone like you, someone with knowledge I mean, does get his face rubbed in it, well, we take advantage."

"Some people make better recruits'n others," Collingswood said. She watched Billy closely. She leaned closer. "Open your gob a minute," she said. He did not consider saying no. She peered past his teeth. "You shouldn't have told your mates about the squid," she said. "You shouldn't have *could*."

"Vardy doesn't need me," Billy said. "He can research all this himself. And I don't need you."

"The professor can be a touch off-putting, I know," Baron said. He took one of Collingswood's cigarettes.

"The way he was talking," Billy said. "About the squid people. It was like he was one of them."

"You've put your finger on it," Baron said. "It is *just* like he's one of them. He has a little revelation."

"Takes one to know one," said Collingswood. "Oh yeah."

"What?" said Billy. "He was one of . . . ?"

"Man of faith," Baron said. "Grew up one of your ultra-born-agains. Creationist, literalist. His dad was an elder. He was in it for years. Lost his faith but not his interest, lucky for us, and not his nous, neither. Every group we look at, he gets it like a convert"— Baron thumped his chest—"because for a moment or two he *is*."

"It's more than that," Collingswood said. "He don't just get it," she said. She grinned smoke at Billy. She put her hand to her lips, as if she were whispering, though she was not. "He *misses* it. He's miserable. He didn't used to have to put up with none of this random reality cack. He's pissed off with the world for being all godless and pointless, get me? He'd go back to his old faith tomorrow if he could. But he's too smart now."

"That's his cross to bear," said Baron. "Boom-boom! I thank you."

"He knows religion is bollocks," Collingswood said. "He just wishes he didn't. That's why he understands the nutters. That's why he hunts them. He misses pure faith. He's jealous."

Chapter Eight

In late drab rain, Baron drove Billy back to his flat. "Kath's going to take a look at your security," he said.

"Haven't got any."

"Well quite."

"I don't want to let nothing happen to you now," she said. "Not now you're precious." He looked at her sideways. "And don't let anyone in you don't know for a few days, either."

"Are you joking?"

"Look, they're not stupid," Baron said. "They're going to know we're watching. But they've got some questions about you, for obvious, and curiosity can be a bit of a millstone. So safety first, eh?" He turned to look at Billy in the backseat. "I don't like it any more than you. Alright, perhaps you like it even less than me." He laughed.

"Shouldn't you be protecting me?" Billy said.

"Wanna be in my gang, my gang, my gang," Collingswood sang.

"Gary Glitter?" Billy said. "Really?"

"I wouldn't say *danger*," said Baron. "I'd say at the very worst it's *dangish*. We're not saying don't have anyone over—"

"I bloody am," said Collingswood, but Baron continued, "if it's someone you trust, that's all peachy. Just being cautious. You're small fry. They've got what they want."

"The squid," said Billy.

"Collingswood's going to install a good solid security set. You'll be fine. And you know, if you take us up on our offer, we might upgrade it."

Billy stared at them. "This isn't a job offer. It's a protection racket. Literally, protection."

Collingswood tutted. "Little drama queen, ain't you?" she said. She patted his cheek. "It's benefits, innit? All jobs have them."

Baron steered Billy toward the kitchen while Collingswood milled by the front door. She looked thoughtfully around the hallway, the cabinet on which Billy left his keys and post. She made a sight, trendily unkempt, up on tiptoe, cigarette loose between her lips as if in a French film, prodding at the upper corner of his doorway with confidence and precision Billy did not associate with someone so young.

"Understand what we're talking about," Baron said. He poked around without asking, looking for coffee. "You'd keep your job. Just a day off a week, something, to put in time with us. For training. Extreme theology, self-defence. And there'd be that bit of dosh." He sipped. "I suppose this must all be a bit much."

"Are you taking the piss?" Billy said. "A bit much? I just found a man *pickled*. I'm being recruited by cops who tell me the Cthulhu cult might be after me . . ."

"Alright," Baron said. He did not, Billy noticed, need any explanation as to what Cthulhu was. "Calm down. Let me tell you what I think. Someone's watching you. As in, look-but-don't-touch. Maybe they're going to go for a conversion. You know how creationists are chuffed to the bollocks when they have members who are scientists or whatever? Think what it would be to this lot to have a genuine squidologist in the congregation."

"Oh good," said Billy. "That's very reassuring. Unless it's that they want to cut out my heart."

"Vardy can get into these headspaces," Baron said. "If he doesn't think these cultists are out for you, they're not."

There was a banging, a rasp, from the other room. "What's she doing?" said Billy.

"Focus, Harrow. In my professional opinion, and Vardy's, the squiddoes are trying to work out what you represent."

"I represent bugger-all!"

"Yeah, but they don't know that. And in this world where you now are, *everything* represents something. Get it? It's really important you get that. Everything represents something."

"It ain't going to win any prizes," Collingswood said, entering, hands in her pockets. She shrugged. "It'll do the necessary. Invite only. It'll hold till Doc Octopus here makes up his mind. Don't touch." She wagged her finger at Billy. "Hands off."

"You said Vardy thought I had nothing to be worried about," Billy said. "I thought he was never wrong."

"Never is," she said, and shrugged. "Never know, though, know what I mean?"

"This is just basic precautions," Baron said. "You should see my house. Stick around here a couple of days, while you chew stuff over. We'll keep you in the loop. We've got feelers out, we know what we're looking for. The offer's on the table. Get back to us soon, eh?"

Billy shook his head hopelessly. "Jesus, give me a chance . . ."

"Think all you want," Baron said, "but think to yourself, alright? Kath?" Collingswood lightly touched his Adam's apple. He recoiled.

"What was . . . ?" he said.

"Try chatting now," she said. "For your own sake. Trust me."

"I do not trust you."

"Wise man."

"Pay attention. This is my number." Baron gave him a card.

"You don't get mine yet," Collingswood said. "You got to earn that sort of shit."

"Anything worrying, anything strange," Baron said, "or, on the other hand, when you decide you're on board . . ."

"If," Billy said.

"When you decide you're on board, call."

Anything strange. Billy remembered the bottled corpse. That greyed skin, those drowned eyes.

"Seriously." He spoke quietly. "What did they do to that guy? How did they get the squid out of there?"

"Now, Mr. Harrow," Baron said. He shook his head, friendly. "I told you. All those *why*s is not a helpful way of looking at things. And blimey, there's plenty of stuff you've not even seen yet. How could you possibly understand what's going on? If you even wanted to. Which, as I say, dot dot dot.

"So. Rather than trying to get to grips with things you can't possibly, I'd just say wait. Wait and see. Because you will see. There's more to come. Good-bye now."

Chapter Nine

AT THE ENTRANCE TO THE FLAT, WHERE COLLINGSWOOD HAD fiddled, there were marks. Tiny scratches. A little balsa lid, flush with the wood. He flicked it with his fingernail.

Billy was hesitant to trust whatever protection it was he'd been afforded. He double-locked his door. He stared out through glass at the rooftop where that dirty bloody squirrel lay unseen. He wished it drowned in rainwater.

He hunted online but failed to find a single detail of the FSRC. Thousands of organisations of those initials, but Baron's unit was nowhere. On his university page Billy read Vardy's publications list. "Oedipus, Charisma and Jim Jones"; "Sayyid Qutb and the Problem of Psychological Organisation"; "The Dialectics of Waco."

Billy drank wine in front of the television on mute, a bottled shadow-show. How often, he thought, are such offers made? A knight emerging from a wardrobe with the offer of another place *but you have to come now*. Was the squid out there, or destroyed? He did not trust his potential colleagues. He did not appreciate their recruitment methods.

In the television light he watched the curtains hang limply, remembering the obscene discovery in the museum basement. He did not think he was particularly exhausted. He imagined the window beyond the fabric. He woke abruptly in a panic on his sofa.

When the hell had he fallen asleep? He remembered no transition. The book he did not even remember starting to read slid from him like an inadequate blanket. It was dark. Billy realised he had heard tapping at his door.

A patter like the feet of a gecko on the other side of the wood. A nail scratching and, yes, a whisper. Billy was silent. He told himself it was some remnant dream, but it was not. It sounded again.

Billy crept to the kitchen and picked up a knife. The faint faint noise continued. He pressed his ear to the door. He unlocked it, watching his own bravery and ninja stealth, bewildered. As he pushed, Billy realised that he should be calling Baron, of course, instead of indulging this incompetent vigilantism. But momentum had him, the door was opening.

The hallway was empty.

He peered at his neighbours' entrances. There were no evidential drafts, no slips of air to insinuate doors quickly closed. No dust dancing. Billy looked at nothing. He stood there for moments, then minutes. He leaned out like a figurehead, to see as far down those corridors as he could, keeping his feet inside his flat. Still there was nothing.

He did not sleep in his bed that night. He took his duvet to the sofa, closer to the front door, so he could hear. There were no more sounds, but he slept hardly at all.

IN THE MORNING HE ATE TOAST IN A TOO-SILENT FLAT, WITH MORE silence from outside weighing on the windows. He pulled the curtains apart enough to look at a grubby grey day, at knots of wood and leaves and blown plastic bags, at the unlikely haunt of the squirrel voyeur.

He was never one with a plethora of friends, but Billy did not often feel lonely, not like this. CN U COME OVER, he texted Leon. STUFF 2 TELL U. PLEASE. He felt he was yanking out of a trap in which Collingswood and Baron had placed him. Brave, rebellious animal. He hoped this escape was not a gnawing off of his own limb.

When Leon arrived Billy hung out from the doorframe again. "What kind of arsing around is this?" said Leon. "It's a bloody weird night, I just had about three fights on the way here, and me such a peaceable soul. I brought your mail up. Also wine." He held out a plastic bag. "Early though it is. What the hell's going on? To what do I owe . . . ? Jesus, Billy."

"Come in." Billy took the bag and envelopes.

"As I was saying, to what do I owe two visits in such quick succession?"

"Have a drink. You aren't going to believe this."

Billy sat opposite Leon and opened his mouth to tell him everything. But could not work out whether to start with the body in the jar, or the police and their strange offer. His tongue flopped over, momentarily meatlike. He swallowed. As if recovering from some dental treatment.

"You don't understand," he told Leon. "I never had a big bust-up with my dad, we just sort of dropped out of touch." He was continuing a conversation from months before, he realised. "My bro I never liked. That was deliberate, dropping him. My dad, though . . ."

He had found his father boring, was all. He had always had the sense that the faintly aggressive man, who lived alone after Billy's mother's death, had found Billy the same. It had been several years since he had let contact wither.

"Do you remember Saturday morning television?" he said. He had meant to tell Leon about the man in the jar. "I remember this one time." Showing his father some cartoon that had enthralled him, Billy had seen the bewilderment on the man's face. The inability to empathise with his boy's passion, or pretend to. Years later he reflected that that was the moment—and he no older than ten—Billy started to suspect that the two of them did not have much of a shot of it.

"I've still got that cartoon, you know," he said. "I found it recently, streamed on some website. You want to see it?" A 1936 Harman-Ising production, he had watched it many times. The glass-jar inhabitants of an apothecary's shelves on an adventure. It was extraordinary, and frightening.

"You know what happens," Billy said. "Sometimes when I'm preserving something or doing something in the wet labs or whatever, I clock that I'm singing one of the songs from it. "Spirits of amo-o-o-onia . . .'"

"Billy." Leon held out a hand. "What's going on?"

Billy stopped and tried again to say what had happened. He swallowed and worked against his own mouth, as if expelling some glutinous intruder. And with a breath finally he began to speak what he had intended. What he had found in the basement. He told him what the police had offered.

Leon did not smile. "Should you be telling me this?" he said at last. Billy laughed.

"No, but, you know."

"I mean, it's literally impossible, what happened," Leon said.

"I know. I know it is."

They stared at each other a long time. Leon said, "There are . . . maybe there are more things in heaven and earth . . ."

"If you quote Shakespeare at me I will kill you dead. Jesus, Leon, I found a dead man in a *jar*."

"This is heavy shit. And they've asked you to join? You going to be a cop?"

"A consultant."

When Leon had visited the squid, months before, he had said *wow*. *Wow* like you might *wow* a dinosaur skeleton, the Crown Jewels, a Turner watercolour. *Wow* said like the parents and partners who came to the Darwin Centre for someone else. Billy had been disappointed.

"What are you going to do?" Leon said.

"I don't know." Billy looked at the mail that Leon had brought from downstairs. Two bills and a card and a heavy package in brown paper, tied up old-style with hairy string. He put on his glasses and cut the string.

"Are you seeing Marginalia later?" he said.

"Yeah, and don't take that tone when you say her name or I'll get her to explain it to you," Leon said. He fiddled with his phone. "She has a whole riff."

"Please," said Billy. "Let me guess. 'The key to the text is not the actual text itself, but . . . '" He frowned. He did not understand what he was unwrapping. Inside the package was a rectangle of black cotton.

"I'm texting her, she'll love this," Leon said.

"Oh Leon, *don't* tell her what I've been saying," Billy said. "I've already said more than I should . . ." He prodded the cloth.

The package moved.

"*Fuck* . . ."

"What? What? What?"

They were both standing. Billy stared at the package, unmoving on the table where he had dropped it. There was silence. Billy took a pen from his pocket and poked the cotton gently.

The cloth gave. The package opened.

It bloomed. With a gasp of air it concertinaed, expanding, out-flicking and filling out, and what reached from its end was a hand. A man's arm, in a dark jacket sleeve. The flash of white shirt at its end. The emergent hand grabbed Billy by the neck.

"*Jesus*—" Leon pulled Billy away, and the package, still gripping, pulled *back*, braced against nothing.

Billy was held, and the package continued to unfold. Tongues of cotton flap-flapped open, black and blue and *shoes* now at the end of limbs bulking into presence, as if the matter of them was uncramp-ing. More arms unrolled clumsy as fire hoses and shoved Leon hard away.

Like plants in sped-up motion, emitting grunts of release, a stale sweat-and-fart smell, and a man and a boy stood suddenly on Billy's table. The boy stared at Leon staggering to rise. The man still gripped Billy's throat.

"Blow *ME*," the man said. He jumped off the table, without releasing Billy. The man was wiry, wore old jeans and a dirty jacket. He shook long greying hair. "Shiver me, that was horrible." He looked at Leon. "Eh?" he shouted, as if wanting sympathy.

The boy stepped slowly onto a chair and then to the floor. He wore a clean, oversized suit: Sunday best. "Come here, lad." The man licked the fingers of his free hand and pressed down the boy's mussed hair.

Billy couldn't breathe. Darkness closed on him. The man threw him against the wall.

"Right then." The man pointed at Leon, who froze, as if pinned by the gesture. "Watch him, Subby. Watch him like a little night-badger."

He pointed two fingers at his own eyes, then at Leon. "He makes a move, give him what-for. Now then." The boy stared at Leon with too-wide eyes.

"Yeah," the man said. He sniffed at the doorframe. "She ain't bad. Good notion, this, if I say so my own self, out of my boy's head. As because what we do *not* have here is anything nixing *egress*. Now we're in there's nothing to stop us getting out." He leaned toward Billy. "I say, there's nothing to stop us getting *out*. Didn't think of that, did you? You ferocious little whatnot."

Billy made a scratchy sound in his throat. The man put a finger to his lips, glancing expectantly at the boy, who slowly did as he did, and gestured *shhhh* at Billy, too.

"Goss and Subby do it again," the man said. He unrolled his tongue and tasted the air. He clamped his hand over Billy's mouth and Billy sputtered into the cool palm. The man went room to room, tugging Billy, licking floor, walls, light switches. He drew his tongue across the face of the television, leaving a spit-path in the dust.

"What what what specimens *have* you got here, lepidopterist?" he said to the bookshelves. He pulled out books and dropped them. "Nah," he said. "I can't taste not but shit of it."

Leon was suddenly up and running at him. The man *whoops-a-daisy*-ed and sent Leon sprawling. "And who might you be?" he said. "One of the young master's friends, hm? I'm afraid the doctors all agree that the lad needs complete isolation, and while your hijinks I'm sure are a tonic, they're not what young Mr. Billiam needs. I may have to eat you, you unfortunate young macaroon."

Leon moved and the boy stepped toward him, all predator-fish eyes. The man wheezed out smoke, though he had no cigarette, had sucked no smoke in.

"No . . ." Leon said. The man opened his mouth, the mouth kept going, and Leon was gone. The man dabbed the corners of his mouth like a cartoon cat.

"Alright you," he said to Billy, who gasped and fought the relentless fingers. "Got your jim-jams? Toothbrush packed? Left a message for the milkman? Good then, let's off. You know what airports are like and little Thomas doesn't travel well and I don't want to get stuck in a queue behind a group-booking to Ayia Napa, can you *imagine?* You promised and promised me a quiet weekend away and it's time, Billy, it's really time." He clasped his hands and raised an eyebrow. "You can hush your noise and all," he said to the boy. "I don't know, I really don't, you two! Onward."

Tugging him by the neck, the man took Billy out.

PART TWO

UNIVERSAL
SLEEPER

Chapter Ten

For THE BULK OF HER TWEENS AND TEENS, MOST OF KATH Collingswood's teachers had either been indifferent or mildly antipathetic to her. One man, her biology teacher, had more actively disliked her. She had known it pretty early in their relationship, and had even been able to express and evaluate his reasons to herself with some clarity.

His opinion of her as sulky she conceded, but considered no more his business than his disapproval of her friends. He thought her a bully, which was, she would say, 65 percent fair. Certainly she found it easy to intimidate more than half her class, and did so. But they were minor cruelties perpetrated without glee, vaguely, almost dutifully, to keep people off her back.

Collingswood had not much reflected on how easy such misery-mongering was for her, how often nothing but a glance or word, if even that, had palpable effects. The first time she thought about it was when she stopped that teacher's mouth.

She was thirteen. Some altercation had left a classmate crestfallen, and Mr. Bearing had shaken his whiteboard marker at Collingswood like a baton and said, "You're a nasty piece of work, aren't you? A nasty piece of work."

He had turned, shaking his head, to write on the board, but Collingswood had been abruptly enraged. She was completely unwilling to submit to the description. She had not even looked at the back of Mr. Bearing's head, had stared furiously at her nails and clucked her tongue, and something like a bubble of cold had swelled in her chest, and burst.

Collingswood did look up then. Mr. Bearing had stopped writing. He stood still, hand to the board. Two or three other children were looking around in confusion.

With a sense of great interest, with a sense of pleased curiosity, Kath Collingswood had known that Mr. Bearing would never call her a nasty piece of work again.

That was that. He picked up his writing. He did not turn to look at her. She put off till later the questions of what had happened, and how she had known that it had. She had leaned back, instead, on the rear legs of her chair.

After that moment, Collingswood took more mind of her unspoken interventions: the times she knew what her friends or enemies were about to say; when she silenced someone across a room; found a lost thing that was frankly unlikely to be wherever she uncovered it. She started to think things through.

Not that she was a poor student, but Collingswood's teachers might have been impressed to see the rigour with which she had pursued this research project. She started with a little tentative poking around online, put together a list of books and documents. Most she was able to download from absurd websites, copyright not being particularly apropos for such texts. The titles of those she could not track down she laboriously copied and requested from surprised, even concerned, librarians and booksellers. Once or twice she even found them.

She picked her way, more than once, through a weed-littered old carpark and bust windows into a small long-deserted hospital near her house. In the quiet of what had once been a maternity ward she dutifully acted out the idiotic actions the texts described. Certainly she felt stupid, but she performed as required, recited all the phrases.

She kept a record in her notebook of what she had tried, where she had read it, what if anything had occurred. BOOK OF THOTH = BOOK OF BOLLOCKS MORE LIKE, she wrote. LIBER NULL = NULL POINTS.

Mostly there were no effects at all, or just enough to keep her at it (a scuttling noise here, an unwarranted shadow there). But it was when she got exasperated and restless and thought *fuck it* to her studies, when she was resultingly imprecise, that she made the best progress.

"That's it for today. You can go early." Packing up her books with the rest of the class, Collingswood watched Miss Ambly's shock at her own words. The woman touched her mouth in bewilderment. Collingswood flicked her fingers. A pen spun off Miss Ambly's desk.

And later: "What's it doing, sir?" some girl asked of a bemused teacher, pointing at the class goldfish, which was swimming with highly unnatural motions. Collingswood, unnoticed, continued what she had started on an exasperated whim, scratching her hands on the desk as if DJing to a classmate's ringtone, which rhythms quite unexpectedly dictated the fish's back-and-forth motion.

That had been years ago. There had been a lot of work since then, of course, much tinkering, plenty of experiments, but Collingswood's baseline impatience continued to truncate her researches. She came to understand that this would ultimately limit her. That she was without question a bit of a talent if she said it herself, and yes she could make it her career no problem, but she would never be one of the very best. Since those days, she had met one or two of them, those very best at this. She had known them the moment they had walked into the room.

But her limits had unexpected effects, and not all negative. The lack of the sternest rigour to perform these competencies at the highest level blurred them, mixed their elements, gave them little swills of backwash. Mostly ignorable effects or demerits, but only mostly.

In the case of the alarm system she had installed in Billy's doorway, for example, she had primed it specifically for ingress. That it might trip, even faintly, in the case of *egress*, was a product not of design but of Collingswood's powerful but slapdash methods.

That would have bothered a perfectionist. But then that perfectionist would not have been alerted when intruders removed Billy from the flat that they had never broken into, as Collingswood, lurching awake and for several moments confused, her heart gonging and an aching in her ears, was.

Chapter Eleven

They were in a beat-up car. The man Goss drove. In the back, the boy, Subby, held Billy's arm.

Subby had no weapon and did not grip hard, but Billy did not move. He was frozen by the man and boy having unfolded in his room—the intrusion, the drugged dragging of the world. Billy's thoughts stuttered in loops. He felt dragged across time. A smear of pigeons was behind the car, pigeons that seemed to have been following him for days. *What the hell what the hell,* he thought, and *Leon.*

The car smelt of food and dust and sometimes of smoke. Goss had a face wrong for the time. He looked stolen from some fifties. There was a postwar cruelty to him.

Twice Billy's hand twitched and he imagined a quick bundle and rush, throwing open the door and rolling into the street, away from these arcane kidnappers. Begging help from the shoppers in that Turkish grocer and the Wimpy hamburger place, running through, where were they, Balham? Each time the thought came Goss made a *tch-tch* noise and Subby's hand would squeeze, and Billy would sit still.

He had no cigarette, but every few breaths Goss would exhale sweet woody smoke that would fill the car and go again. "What a ruddy night for it, eh?" he said. "Eh, Subby? What's that pootling about? Someone's out for a walk what oughtn't was, don't you coco? Someone's woke up, Subby." He wound down the window, an old hand-crank handle, looked up at the sky, wound it up again.

They hauled through streets of which Billy had lost all sense. They must be out in zone three or four where shops were keycutters and independent stationers. They passed no major chains. No west-coast coffee, not a Tescos. How could these be streets? Garages, timber-yards, judo gyms, cold pavements where rubbish moved quietly. The sky closed its last crack and it was night. Billy and his abductors were following rails, shadowing a lit-up train. It ushered them somewhere. They stopped by a dark arch.

"Chop chop," said Goss. He looked up suspiciously and sniffed. He pulled Billy from the car. Billy thought he might puke. He reeled. Goss exhaled one of his smoky exhalations. He unlocked a door in corrugated iron and pushed Billy through into the black. Subby tugged from somewhere.

Goss spoke, as if Billy and he were in dialogue: "Is he then?" "Don't know, might be, you got everything?" "Alright now, get the door, ready?"

Something opened. There was a change in the air on Billy's face. Goss whispered, "*Hush now.*"

The room they were in smelt of damp and sweat. Something shifted. There was sound, a sputtering and crack. Lights came up.

There were no windows. The floor was dirty cement. The bricks sloped overhead were mapped with mildew. The chamber was huge. Goss stood by the wall holding a lever he had thrown. The room was full of lights, dangling on wires and jutting mushrooms from wall cracks.

Goss swore mildly as if at curious pigs. Billy heard a radio. A circle of people waited. Figures in leather jackets, dark jeans, boots, gloves. Some in band T-shirts, all in motorbike helmets. They held pistols, knives, cartoonishly vile nail-studded clubs. A radio played staticky classical music, fuzzed. There was a naked man on all fours. His lips fluttered. He had dials pushed into him, above each nipple. Unbleed-ing but extruding clearly from his body. It was from his open mouth that the radio sounds came. His lips moved to make the music, inter-ference, the ghosts of other stations.

On a brick dais was a man. An older scrawny punk with spiked-up hair. A bandanna hid his mouth. His eyes were so wide he looked unhinged. He breathed hard, the cloth of his mask gusting in and out, and he was sweating in the cold. He was topless. He sat on a stool, his hands in his lap.

Billy was dizzy and sick from everything that night. Billy tried not to believe what he was seeing. Tried to imagine he might wake.

"Billy bloody Harrow," the man said. "Check what that little bitch is doing."

One of the figures in helmets twisted a dial on the radio-man's chest, and radio-man's mouth changed to sudden new shapes as the song ended. He whispered in little bursts and spoke barely audible interactions, men's voices and women's.

"*Roger that ic-two, Sarge,*" he said, and, "*Have a word with Vardy, will you?,*" and, "*ETA fifteen minutes, over.*"

"Not there yet," the bandanna man said. "They're visiting your old house." His voice was loud and low, London-accented. Goss shoved Billy closer. "Send that lot, then," he said. "Are you going to make me go through various motions, Billy Harrow? Can you just tell me who it is you're with and what it is you're doing? Can you tell me *puh-lease* what is going on tonight, what it is you set walking. Because something's out there. And more to the bloody point, what, pray bloody tell, is your interest?"

"What is this?" Billy whispered at last. "What did you do to Leon?"

"Leon?"

"You know how it is," Goss said. "You're both vying for the best vol-au-vent, and the next thing it's all been eaten."

Goss held Billy as if he were a puppet. Little Subby's hands clutched Billy's own.

"What's going on?" Billy said. He stared everywhere, at the radio-man; he struggled. "What is this?"

The sitting man sighed. "Bugger," he said. "You're going to do this." His staring eyes did not change at all. "Let me put it to you this way, Billy. What the fuck are you?"

He twisted on his stool. He raised his hands a little. He was blink-ing violently. "Who are you working with?" he said. "What are you?" Billy realised that the kerchief was not cowboy-style but was haphaz-ardly balled in his mouth. The man was gagged. He shook his hands and Billy saw he wore handcuffs.

"*Turn your fucking head!*" the voice continued, from this man who could not be speaking. "*Turn around.*" One of the helmeted guards slapped him hard across his face, and he screamed muffled into his gag. "Stand this bugger up." Two guards hauled him up by his armpits. His head lolled. "Let's see," the voice said. The guards turned the man to face the back wall.

Colours appeared. The whole of the topless man's back was a tat-too. At its edges it was wisps of coloured swirl, crossbred Celtic-knot fractals. In the centre was a big, dark-outlined, stylised face. Bold and expertly done. A man's face, in unnatural colours. A sharp old face with red eyes, something between a professor and a devil. Billy stared.

The Tattoo moved. Its heavy-lidded eyes met his. Billy stared at it and the Tattoo stared back.

Chapter Twelve

Billy shouted in shock and tried to scrabble backward. Goss held him.

The guards held the punk-haired man still. The Tattoo's inked eyes went side to side, like an animation, as if it were a cartoon projected onto him. The thick black edges travelled, the shaded blue, blue-green, copper sections of skin shifting as the Tattoo pursed its lips, watched Billy, raised its eyebrows at him. It opened its mouth, and a hole of dark ink opened, a drawn throat. It spoke in that deep London voice.

"Where's the kraken, Harrow? What's your angle? What does Baron's gang want with you?" The radio-man whispered static.

"What are you . . . ?"

"Let me explain our problem," the tattoo said. The man whose back it was on struggled in the guards' grip. "My problem is no one knows you, Billy Harrow. You come out of nowhere. No one knows your percentage. And normally I couldn't give a monkey's what you're up to, but that kraken, man. That kraken's *choice*, mate. And it's gone. And that's trouble. Something like that, angel watching over it. If not very well, eh? Here's the thing—I can't make sense of what you've done, or how. So how about you fill me in?"

Billy tried to think for anything, anything to say to make these impossible abductors let him go. He would tell them anything. But not a solitary word of the Tattoo's questions made any sense at all.

The shadows shifted. "You're running with Baron's mob," the Tattoo said. "Shit taste, but I can save you from yourself. Now you and me work together, we can't have secrets. So bring me up to speed." The Tattoo stared. "What's the story?"

Men unfold and people are generators and ink rides a man.

"Look at him," the Tattoo said. "This little prick's a Christ, is he? You said there's nothing in his house?"

"Buggery I could taste," said Goss. He hawked and swallowed what he raised.

"Who took the kraken, Billy?" the Tattoo said. Billy tried. There was a long silence.

"Look," Goss said. "He's got knowledges."

"No," the Tattoo said, slowly. "No. You're wrong. He don't. I think we're going to want to workshop this." The man shook and moaned, and a guard hit him again. The Tattoo rocked with the body that bore it. "You know what we need," the Tattoo said. "Take him to the workshop." The man who was a radio whispered an ill-tuned-in weather report.

GOSS DRAGGED BILLY, MAKING HIS LEGS MOVE WITH A NEW LOCO-motion like a cartoon caper. Little Subby followed.

"Get *off* me," Billy gasped abruptly. Goss smiled like a grandfather.

"Attention one and all," said Goss. "I love it when you're very very quiet. Beyond this door," Goss said, "just over the road, we can open up the old bonnet, take a look inside, see what's making the old girl seize up like that." He tapped Billy's belly. "We're all recyclers; we all have to do our bit, don't we, for the global warming and the polar bears and that. We'll find new life for her as a fridge."

"Wait," whispered Billy. Whispering was all he could do. "Listen, I can . . ."

"You can what, poppet?" said Goss. "I couldn't live with myself if I let you get in the way of progress. There's white-hot innovation around the corner, and we all have to be ready. We've never had it so good."

Goss opened the door into the cold and a girder of streetlamp light. Subby went out. Goss sent Billy after him, onto his hands and knees. Goss came after him. Billy put up his hands. He felt a rush. He heard splintering glass.

Billy crawled away. Goss did not follow. Subby did not move. The air was still. Billy did not understand. Nothing moved but him, for one, two seconds, and he could hear nothing but his own heart. Then air rushed past his ears again, and only then, too late, glass from whatever window had broken hit the ground, and Goss moved, his head shaking in a moment's confusion as he looked at space where Billy no longer quite was.

Something met Subby. "Huff," Subby said, and hurtled metres away. A man-shape in darkness gripped a pipework club. Goss shrieked. The attacker slammed the metal into him. It rang as if he were metal too. Goss did not even stagger. He ran to where Subby lay supine, blinking.

The man with the pipe grabbed Billy. He was big, bulky but fast-moving, his hair cut close, his clothes black and scruffy. There was a faint edge of streetlight on him.

"Dane?" Billy gasped. "*Dane.*"

THEY RAN ALONG THE DIRTY LITTLE NON-STREET, BY THE RAISED tracks, away from the terrible archway. A train passed, rumbling lights in the sky. Somewhere behind them Goss knelt by Subby.

"Come on," Dane said. Something ran along the bricks beside them, something Billy did not make out. "We've got two minutes before they're up. We've got one minute before their boss realises what's happened. You're bleeding. Goss can taste it."

Another train passed. From streets away came the noise of traffic. Dane bundled Billy on. "No way I can take them," Dane said. "I only got him 'cause they weren't expecting anything. Plus there was . . ."

Dane ran them an intricate route until they emerged from the brick maze. They were by a park, the only figures in the street. By the silhouettes of massed trees Dane unlocked a car and shoved Billy in.

Billy wore a beard of blood, he realised. His shirt was stained with it. At some point, the night's rough handling had split his lip. He dripped.

"Shit," he mumbled. "Shit, sorry, I . . ."

"One of his knuckleheads." Dane said. "Put your seat belt on." Something filthy scudded from the wall across the deserted road, out of a gutter into the car. The squirrel, coiling under a seat. Billy stared.

"Shtum," Dane said. He pulled out and drove, fast. "If it weren't for little sodding nutkin I wouldn't have found you. It got onto Goss's car."

They turned into lights, reached a street where there were shoppers and drinkers by late cafés and amusement arcades. Billy felt as if he would cry, to see people. It felt like the breaching of some meniscus, like he had entered a real night at last. Dane passed him a tissue.

"Wipe your mouth."

"Leon . . ."

"Wipe the blood. We don't want to be stopped."

"We have to stop, we have to go to the police . . ." *Really?* Billy thought even as he said that. *You're not there anymore.*

"No," Dane said, as if he were listening to that monologue. "We do not." *You know that, right?* "We're just going to drive. Wipe your mouth. I'm going to get you out of here."

Billy watched a quadrant of London he recognised no more than if it were Tripoli go by.

Chapter Thirteen

"**W**ELL THIS IS BLOODY FABULOUS, ISN'T IT? THIS IS BLOODY perfect." Baron stomped around Billy's flat. He shook his head at the walls, folded and refolded his arms. "This is just how it was supposed to go. This is peachy."

He stamped past the team powdering for fingerprints. She had her back to them, but from where she stood examining Billy's doorway, Collingswood got gusts of their resentment.

She could not hear thoughts. So far as she knew, no one could: they spilt from each individual head in too many overlapping and counterflowing streams, and the words that part-constituted some of those streams were contradictory and misleading. But irritation that strong communicated, and knowing it to be mistranslation, she—like most of those with any knack at all for that kind of thing—automatically translated into text.

whos this twat think he is
wankers shd fuck off let real coppers work
y r we leting that litl bitch smoke

She turned and spoke to the thinker of that last fragment. "Because you been told to let us do whatever we want, innit?" she said, and watched the blood leave his face. She stepped over dropped books and followed Baron. She picked up the post on the table.

"Well?" Baron said. "Any ideas?"

Collingswood unlistened, focused on the traces of Billyness. Touched with a fingertip the doorframe, where stains of Billy's attention read to her like messages squint-seen through a broken screen.

whats this she did that girl

cant get in

shes fit i wouldn't mind

"What are you bloody smirking at?" Baron said. "Got something?"

"Nothing, boss," she said. "You know what? No. You got me. This thing was still primed when I got here, you know? That's why I had to let you in. No entry without invite, and you saw Billy boy—he was way too chickenshit to let anyone he didn't know in after what we told him."

"So what's happened? He's hardly just gone for a bloody walk, has he?"

"Nah." She shrugged at the signs of scuffles. "Someone's took him."

"Someone who couldn't get in."

She nodded. "Someone who didn't get in," she said.

Vardy emerged from the bedroom, where he had been examining Billy's bits and pieces. He joined them in the kitchen.

"That ain't all," Collingswood said. She made shapes with her hands, chopped the air up. "Something big happened tonight. Big like when the kraken got took. I don't know what it is, but something's wandering around out there."

Baron nodded slowly. "Prof," Baron said. "Any thoughts from your good self? Wish to *revise* your opinion about the unlikelihood of any attacks by your teuthists?"

"No," said Vardy shortly. He folded his arms. "I do not. Care to revise your tone? Can't tell you what's gone on here or who's done what to whom, but seeing as you ask, *no*. This does *not* read teuthism to me." He closed his eyes. His colleagues watched him channelling whatever it was he channelled when he did what he did. "No," he said, "this does not feel like them."

"Well," Baron said. He sighed. "We're on the back foot here, ladies and gents. Our star witness and intended colleague is gone AWOL. We know the guard system was up and running. Doing what it was supposed to. But we also know it had both been tripped and not been tripped. Do I have that right?"

"Sort of," Collingswood said. "It went off in reverse. Woke me up. I couldn't work out what it was at first."

"It would cover windows, too?" Vardy said. She stared at him. "Fine," he said. "I have to ask."

"No you don't," she said. "I told you. No one could get in."

"No one?"

"What's your point? I ain't saying there's no one stronger'n me out there—you know there is. If anyone got in, it would go off and I'd know. No one broke in . . ." She stopped. She looked one by one at the post. She looked at the cardboard book box. "No one broke *in*," she said. "Someone sent him something. Look. There's no stamp, this was hand-delivered." She hefted it. She sniffed it.

Vardy unfolded his arms. Collingswood moved her fingers over the paper, whispered, ran little routines and subroutines.

"What is it?" Baron said.

"Alright," she said finally. In the other room the grumbles of the other police were audible and ignored. "Everything remembers how it used to be, right? So like, this . . ." She shook the container. "This remembers when it was heavier. It was a full parcel and now it's empty, right? It remembers being heavier but that ain't the thing, the weird thing."

She moved her fingers again, coaxed the cardboard. Of all the skills necessary for her work, what she was perhaps worst at was being polite to inanimate things. "It's that it remembers being not heavier enough.

"Guv," she said to Baron. "What do you know about how to . . ." She opened and clenched her hands. "How to make big shit go into something little?"

Chapter Fourteen

"WHAT HAPPENED TO LEON?" BILLY SAID.

Dane glanced at him and shook his head.

"I wasn't there, was I? I don't know. Was it Goss?"

"That man Goss, and that boy. It looked like he—"

"I wasn't there. But you got to face facts." Dane glanced again. "You saw what you saw. I'm sorry."

What did I see? Billy thought.

"Tell me what he said," Dane said.

"What?"

"The Tattoo. Tell me what he said."

"What *was* that?" Billy said. "*No.* You can tell *me* some stuff. Where did you even come from?" They turned through streets he did not know.

"Not now," Dane said. "We ain't got time."

"*Get the police* . . ." Beneath Billy's seat the squirrel made a throat noise.

"*Shit,*" Dane said. "We don't have time for this. You're smart, you know what's going on." He clicked his fingers. Where his fingers percussed, there was a faint burst of light. "We do *not* have time."

He braked, swore. Red lights disappeared in front of them. "So can we please cut the crap? You can't go home. You know that. That's where they got you. You can't call Baron's crew. You think that's going to help? Old Bill sort you out?"

"Wait . . ."

"That flat ain't your home anymore." He spoke in little stabs. "Those ain't your clothes, they ain't your books, that ain't your computer, you get it? You saw what you saw. You know you saw what you saw." Dane snapped his finger under Billy's nose and the light glowed again. He steered hard. "We clear?"

Yes, no, yes they were clear. "Why did you come?" Billy said. "Baron and Vardy said . . . I thought you were hunting me."

"I'm sorry about your mate. I've been there. Do you know what you are?"

"I'm not anything."

"You know what you did? I felt it. If you hadn't done that I wouldn't've got there in time, and they would've took you to the workshop. Something's *out*." Billy remembered a clenching inside, glass breaking, a moment of drag. "Goss'll be licking for us now. It's the man on the back you need to worry about."

"The Tattoo was *talking*."

"Do not start that. Miracles are getting more common, mate. We knew this was coming." He cried with gruff emotion, touched his chest near his heart. "It's the ends of the world."

"End of the world?"

"Ends."

It was like buildings self-aggregated out of angles and shade in front of the car, dissipated behind. Something very certain was out that night.

"It's war," Dane said. "This is where gods live, Billy. And they've gone to war."

"What? I'm not on anyone's side . . ."

"Oh, you are," Dane said. "You *are* a side."

Billy shivered. "That tattoo's a god?"

"*Fuck* no. It's a criminal. A fucking villain is what he is. Thinks you're up against him. Thinks you stole the kraken. Maybe you used to run with Grisamentum." Now that was a singsong name, a snip from scripture. "They never got on."

"Where's the squid?"

"That's the question, isn't it?" Dane turned the wheel hard. "You telling me you ain't felt what's going on? You ain't noticed signs? *They* are coming out of the darkness. This is gods' time. They been rising."

"What . . . ?"

"In liquid, through Perspex or glass. This is in your *blood*, Billy. Coming up out of heaven. Forced by their season. Australia, here, New Zealand." All places *Architeuthis* and *Mesonychoteuthis* had breached.

They were at a community hall, a sign reading SOUTH LONDON CHURCH. The street stank of fox. Dane held open the door. The squirrel leaped from the car and in two, three sine-curves was gone.

"You better start making sense, Dane," Billy said, "or I'm just . . . going to . . ."

"Billy please. Didn't I just save you? Let me help you."

BILLY SHIVERED. DANE LED INDOORS, THROUGH UNTIDY ROWS OF plastic chairs facing a lectern, to a room at the back. The windows were covered with collages of torn coloured tissue paper, faux stained glass. There were leaflets advertising mother-and-child meetings, house-clearance sales. A storeroom full of engine bits and mouldering papers, a bent bicycle, the detritus of years. "The congregation'll hide us," Dane said. "You don't want to mess with them. We scratch their back." He pulled open a trapdoor. Light reached up.

"Down there?" said Billy.

Concrete stairs led to a striplit hallway, a sliding gate like the door of an industrial elevator. Behind a grille an older man and a shaven-headed boy in boiler suits held up shotguns. The ambient night sound of London disappeared.

"Is that . . . ?" one of the guards said. "Who is that?"

"You know who *I* am?" Dane said. "Yeah you fucking do. Go tell his holiness I'm here and let us in." Brusque, but with a gentleness Billy could feel, Dane pushed Billy inside.

Beyond the gate the walls were not featureless. Billy's mouth opened. Still concrete and windowless, the walls were intricately moulded. Stained by London dirt no scrubbing could remove, a nautilus entwined with an octopus, with a cuttlefish, its flattened frilled mantle like a skirt edge. It encoiled limbs with an argonaut bobbing below its extruded eggcase-house. And squid everywhere. Shaped when the walls were wet.

What a corridor, this council-office walkway. A tentacular border of Disney-malevolent vampire squid; ornery Humboldt; whiplash squid in tuning-fork posture. Their bodies were rendered similar sizes, specificities effaced by shared squidness, teuthic quiddity. Their—the word came to Billy and would not lie down—squiddity. *Architeuthis* in the shabby matter of the building.

The buried room where Dane took Billy was tiny as a ship's cabin. There was a little bed, a steel toilet. On a table was a plate of curry, a cup of something hot. Billy almost wept at the smell.

"You're in shock," Dane said, "and you're starving and knackered. You don't understand what's going on. Get that down you and we'll talk."

Dane took a forkful—to show it was safe, Billy thought. He ate. The drink was too-sweet chocolate.

"Where are we?"

"The Teuthex'll explain."

What's a Teuthex? Billy felt like he was swimming. His exhaustion increased. He saw against a dark background. His thoughts faded in and out like a radio station. This was more, he realised, than tiredness.

"Oh," he said. A welling of alarm.

"Now don't worry," said Dane.

"You, what's, you . . ." Billy jiggled the cup and stared at it. Put the spiked thing heavily down before he dropped it, as if that mattered. Black came in at him like an ink cloud. "What did you do?"

"Don't worry," Dane said.

"You need this," Dane said.

Dane said another thing but his voice was too far away now. *Bastards,* Billy tried to say. Part of him told another part of him that Dane would not rescue him just to kill him now, but most of him was too tired to be afraid. Billy was in the dark quiet, and just before it closed behind him and over him he swung his own legs onto the bed and lay down, proud that no one did it for him.

INTO SLEEP'S BENTHOS AND DEEPER. A SLANDER THAT THE DEEPEST parts are lightless. There are moments of phosphor with animal movement. Somatic glimmers, and in this trench of sleep those lights were tiny dreams.

A long time sleep, and blinks of vision. Awe, not fear.

Billy might surface and for a moment open his flesh eyelids not his dream ones, and two or three times saw people looking down at him. He heard always only the close-up swirl of water, except in deep dream once through muffling miles of sea a woman said, "When'll he wake?"

He was night-krill was what he was, a single minuscule eye, looking at absence specked with presence. Plankton-Billy saw an instant's symmetry. A flower of limbflesh outreaching. Slivers of fin on a mantle. Red rubber meat. That much he knew already.

He saw something small or in the distance. Then black after black, then it came back closer. Straight-edged, hard-lined. An anomaly of angles in that curved vorago.

It was the specimen. It was his kraken, his giant squid quite still—still in suspension in its tank, the tank and its motionless dead-thing contents adrift in deep. Sinking toward where there is no below. The once-squid going home.

One last thing, that might have announced itself as such, the finality was so unequivocal. Something beneath the descending tank, at which from way above though already deep in pitch tiny Billy-ness stared.

Under the tank was something utter and dark and moving, something so slowly rising, and endless.

Chapter Fifteen

COLLINGSWOOD, WHOSE BRIEF THIS SORT OF THING WAS, HAD spent a couple of hours talking to a woman who referred to herself as an "asset" about some of the esoterica of material science. The woman had emailed a list of names, of researchers and grifters. "This sort of stuff changes all the time," she had warned. "Can't vouch for any of them in particular."

"I called the first couple, guv," Collingswood said, "but it was a bit tricky on the phone, you get me? Some of them gave me more names. I don't think any of them knew what I was on about. I need to see them face-to-face. You sure you want to come? Ain't you got shit to do?" She could rarely parse Baron's brain, which was to be expected: it was only the inexperienced and unskilled who sent their thinkings all over the place, profligate and foolish.

"Indeed," Baron said. "But that's what mobile phones are for, aren't they? This is the best lead we have."

They traced a zigzag route through London, Baron in his plain clothes, Collingswood in her costume-like uniform, hoping to surprise their informers into helpful candour. There were not many names on the list—infolding and weightomancy were arcana among the arcane, a geeky byway. Baron and Collingswood went to offices, community colleges, the back rooms of high-street shops. "Is there somewhere private we can talk?" Baron would say, or Collingswood would open with, "What d'you know about making big shit little?"

One name on the list was a science teacher. "Come on, boss, let's give the class a treat, eh?" Collingswood said, and marched in past pupils gaping from behind Bunsen burners. "George Carr?" Collingswood said. "What do you know about making big shit little?"

"ENJOY THAT?" CARR SAID. THEY WERE WALKING IN THE PLAY-ground. "What was it, some science teacher tell you you'd never amount to anything?"

"Nah," she said. "They all knew I'd amount to fucking loads."

"What the hell does a cult squad want with me?"

"We're just chasing a few leads, sir," Baron said.

"Ever flog your skills?" Collingswood said. "Shrinkage for hire?"

"No. I'm not good enough and not interested enough. I get what I need out of it."

"Which is what?"

"Come on holiday with me one day," he said. "Three weeks of clothes in one carry-on bag."

"Could I bring my dog?" Baron said.

"What? No way. Condensing something that complicated's out of my league. I might just get it in, maybe, but Fido's not going to be fetching sticks on the beach at the other end."

"But it's possible."

"Sure. There's a few people could do it." He stroked his stubble. "Has anyone given you Anders's name?"

Baron and Collingswood glanced at each other. "Anders?" Baron said.

"Anders Hooper. Runs a shop in Chelsea. Funny little specialist place. He's very good."

"So why haven't we heard of him?" Baron said, waving his list.

"Because he's only just started. Been doing it about a year, professionally. Now *he's* good enough and keen enough to do it for lucre."

"So how come *you've* heard of him?" Collingswood said.

Carr smiled. "I taught him how to do it. Tell him his Mr. Miyagi says hi."

• • •

Hooper's shop shared space on a terrace with a delicatessen, a travel bookshop, a florist. It was called Nippon This! Characters stared from the window with manga enthusiasm beside robot kits and nunchuck tat. Inside, a third of the small shelf space was taken up with books on the philosophy, mathematics, and design of origami. There were stacks of books of fold patterns. Incredible examples—dinosaurs, fish, klein bottles, geometric intricacies, all made from single uncut sheets.

"Alright," said Collingswood. She smiled in appreciation. "Alright, that's quite cool."

A young man came out from the back. "Morning," he said. Anders Hooper was tall, mixed-race, wearing a Gundam T-shirt. "Can I . . ." He hesitated at sight of Collingswood's uniform. "Help you?"

"Might be," she said. "Sell enough to make your rent on this place?"

"Who are you?"

"Answer the question, Mr. Hooper," said Baron.

". . . Sure. There's a lot of interest in anime and stuff. We're one of the best suppliers . . ."

"You can get all this shit off the Internet," Collingswood said. "People come here?"

"Sure. There's . . ."

"What about your orifuckinggami?" she said. He blinked.

"What about it? That's more specialist, of course . . ." He kept his mind pretty cloudy, but *what they know*? Collingswood got from him, as abruptly as if announced by a beep.

"And you're the man, right? Shit, we're in effing Chelsea. How d'you pay? We spoke to Mr. Carr. Says hello by the way. He told us you do custom folding. Special jobs. Sound right, Anders?"

He leaned on the counter. Looked from Baron to Collingswood. He glanced to either side as if someone might be listening.

"What is it you want to know?" he said. "I haven't done anything illegal."

"No one said you did," Collingswood said. "Someone fucking did though. Why did you get into all this?"

"For minimisation," Anders said. "It's not just about pressure, or forcing things. It's about topography, that sort of thing. Someone like Carr—and I'm not being disrespectful, it was him who got me started—but basically, you know, you're sort of . . ." He made kneading motions. "You're shoving stuff in. You're stuffing a suitcase."

"More or less what he said," Baron said.

"If that's what you want to do, then, you know, fine. But . . ." His hands tried to describe something. "What you're trying to do with planurgy is get things into other spaces, you know? Real things, with edges and surfaces, and all that. With origami you're still dealing with all that surface area. There's no cutting, you know? The point is you can unfold it, too. You get it?"

"And you don't have any problems with the fact that this is all, you know, *solid*," said Collingswood.

"Not as much as you might think. There's been a revolution in origami over the last few years . . . What?"

Collingswood was pissing herself laughing. Baron joined in. After a couple of seconds Anders had the grace to snigger.

"Well, I'm sorry," he said, "but there has been. Computers've helped. We're in the era of—alright, you'll like this one, too—*extreme* origami. It's all about maths." He looked at Collingswood. "What's your tradition?"

"Traditions are for ponces," she said.

He laughed. "If you say so. When you start bringing in a bit of abmaths, factoring in visionary numbers, that sort of thing—does this mean anything to you?"

"Get on with it."

"Sorry. My point is, there are ways of . . ." He leaned over the cash register and held the little digital display between fingertip and thumb. He folded it over.

Collingswood watched it go. Anders flipped it over and over, tucked it behind the keys. He gently concertinaed. The bulky thing collapsed on itself in fold-lines, different aspects of unbroken planes slipping behind each other as if seen from several directions at once. Anders folded, and within a minute and a half what lay on the desk, still connected to a power cord (which now slipped behind an impossible crease into the things' innards), was a hand-sized Japanese crane. The showing face of one of the bird's wings was a corner of the cash display, the other was the front of the money drawer. Its neck was a flattened wedge of its buttons. "If you pull there you can make its wings flap," Anders said.

"Cool," said Collingswood. "And it ain't broke?"

"That's the point." He manipulated its edges, unfolded the thing back into its original shape. Pressed its keys and it pinged and opened with a little cash chink.

"Nice," said Baron. "So you make a bit of dosh folding cash registers into birds."

"Oh yeah," Anders deadpanned. "Very lucrative."

"But wouldn't that still weigh the same?"

"There's ways of folding into sort of forgettable space, I suppose you could say, so the world won't notice the weight until you open it."

"How much would you charge to," Baron said, "for example, fold up a person? Into a package? That you could post?"

"Ah. Well. There's a lot of surfaces in a person, and you've got to keep track of them all. That's a lot of folds. Is that what this is about? That bloke who wanted to surprise his friend?"

Collingswood and Baron stared at him. "Which bloke," Baron said, "would that be?"

"Shit, did something happen? The guy was playing a trick on his mate. Had me make him and his son up like a book. Paid me extra to hand-deliver him. Said he didn't trust the post. I say *said*—took me ages to have a clue what he was on about, the way he talked. Pain in my arse getting there, but he made it worth my—"

"Getting where?" Baron said.

He recited Billy's address. "What happened?" Anders said.

"Tell us *everything you can* about this man," Baron said. He held up his notebook. Collingswood spread her hands, tried to feel residues in the room. "And what," said Baron, "do you mean 'his son'?"

"The bloke," Anders said. "Who had me fold him up. It was his kid, too. His boy." He blinked in Baron's and Collingswood's stares.

Baron whispered, "Describe them."

"The guy was in his fifties. Long hair. Smelt, to be honest. Smoke. I was a bit surprised he could pay—it wasn't cheap. His son was . . . a bit not all there." He tapped his head. "Never said a word . . . What? *What?* Jesus, what is it?"

Baron stepped back and dropped his arms to his sides, his notebook dangling. Collingswood stood, her mouth opening, her eyes widening. Their faces went white in time.

"Oh fuck," whispered Collingswood.

"My good God, this didn't, this didn't sound any alarm bells at all?" Baron said. "You didn't for a bloody second wonder who you might be dealing with?"

"I don't know what the hell you're talking about!"

"He doesn't fucking know," Collingswood said. Her voice grated. "This fucking newbie cunt has no idea. That's why they came here. 'Cause he's new. That's why he got the job, 'cause he's green. They knew he had no clue who the fucking shit he was dealing with."

"Who *was* I dealing with?" said Anders, shrilly. "What did I do?"

"It is," said Collingswood. "It is, isn't it, guv?"

"Oh my good Christ. It sounds like it. My God, it does sound like it." They shivered in a room suddenly made cold.

Collingswood whispered, "It's Goss and Subby."

Chapter Sixteen

Billy woke. The fog, the dark water in his head, was all gone.

He sat up. He was bruised but not tired. He wore the same clothes he had gone to sleep in, but they had been removed and cleaned. He closed his eyes and saw the oceanic things from his doped sleep.

By the door was a man in a tracksuit. Billy scrabbled back on the bed to see him, into some half-cringe, half-pugnacious uncoiling. "They're waiting for you," the man said. He opened the door. Billy slowly lowered his hands. He felt, he realised, better than he had for a long time.

"You drugged me," he said.

"I don't know anything about that," the man said anxiously. "But they're waiting for you."

Billy followed him past the industrial-rendered decapods and octopuses, illuminated by fluorescent lights. The presence of Billy's dream was persistent, like water in his ears. He hung back until the man turned a corner, then ducked away and ran as quietly as he could, accelerating through the echoes of his footfalls. He held his breath. At a junction he stopped, pressed his back against a wall and looked around.

Different subspecies in cement. Perhaps he could track his way by remembering cephalopods. He had no idea where to go. He heard the footfall of his escort seconds before the man reappeared. The man gestured at him, an uncomfortable beckoning.

"They're waiting for you," he said. Billy followed the man through the hollowed-out churchland into a hall big enough and unexpected enough that Billy gasped. All without windows, all scooped out from under London.

"Teuthex'll be here in a minute," the man said, and left.

There were pews, each with a slot behind its backrest, a space for hymnals. They faced a plain Shaker-style altar. Above it was a huge, beautifully wrought version of that many-armed symbol, all elongate S-curves in silver and wood. The walls were covered in pictures like ersatz windows. Every one was of giant squid.

There were grainy deep-sea photos. They looked much older than should have been possible. There were engravings from antique bestiaries. There were paintings. Pen-and-ink renditions, pastels, suggestive op-art geometries with fractal suckers. He recognised not a single one. Billy had grown up on pictures of kraken and books of antique monstrosities. He sought an image he knew. Where was de Montfort's impossible octopus hauling down a ship? Where the familiar old renderings of Verne's *poulpes*?

One eighteenth-century giant-squid pastoral—a large, camp rendition of a young *Architeuthis* gambolling in spume, near a shore from where fishermen watched it. A semiabstract rendition, an interweaving of pipelike brown jags, a nest of wedges.

"That's Braque," someone said behind him. "What did you dream?"

Billy turned. Dane was there, his arms folded. In front of him was the man who had spoken. He was a priest. The man was in his sixties, with white hair, neatly trimmed beard and moustache. He was *exactly* a priest. He wore a long black robe, white dog collar. Just a little battered-looking. His hands were clasped behind him. He wore a chain, from which dangled the squid symbol. They three stood in the sheer silence of that submerged chamber, staring at each other.

"You poisoned me," Billy said.

"Come come," said the priest. Billy held a pew and watched him.

"You poisoned me," Billy said.

"You're here, aren't you?"

"Why?" said Billy. "Why am I? What's going on? You owe me . . . an explanation."

"Indeed," said the priest. "And you owe us your life." His smile disarmed. "So we're both indebted. Look, I know you want to know what's happened. And we want to explain. Believe me, you *need* to understand." He spoke in a carefully neutral accent, but there was a little Essex to it.

"Are you going to tell me what all this is?" Billy glanced around for exits. "All I got from Dane yesterday was—"

"It was a bad day," the man said. "I hope you feel better. How did you dream?" He rubbed his hands.

"What did you give me?"

"Ink. Of course."

"Bullshit. Squid ink doesn't give you *visions*. That was acid or something . . ."

"It was ink," the man said. "What did you see? If you saw things, it was down to you. I'm sorry that it was all a bit of a rude submersion. We really had no choice. Time is not on our side."

"But why?"

"Because you *need* to *know*." The man stared. "You need to see. You need to know what's going on. We didn't give you any visions, Billy. What you saw came from you. You can see things clearer than anyone."

The man stepped closer to the picture. "I was saying, Braque," he said, "in 1908. Bertrand Hubert, the only French Teuthex we've ever had, took him out to sea. They were in the Bay of Biscay for four days. Hubert performed a particular ritual, of which sadly we no longer have much record, and brought up a little god.

"He must have been pretty powerful. He's the only one since Steenstrup who's been able to tickle up more than images. The actual . . . fry. So the godling waited while Braque, falling over himself and nearly overboard, apparently, sketched it. It went under waving a hunting arm as Braque said '*exactement comme un garçon qui dit <au revoir> aux amis.*'" He smiled. "Silly beggar. Not the slightest idea. It was "*comme*" nothing of the sort. Sounds odd, but he said it was the *coiliness* of what he saw that made him think in angles. He said no curves could do justice to the coils he'd seen."

Cubism as failure. Billy walked to another picture. More tradition-ally representational—a fat, flattened giant squid mouldering on a slab, surrounded by legs in waders. Quick, wisping brushstrokes. "Why did you drug me?"

"That's Renoir. That over there, Constable. Pre-Steenstrup, so it's what we call the atramentous epoch. Before we emerged from the ink-cloud." The works around Billy looked suddenly like Manets. Like Piranesis, Bacons, Breughels, Kahlos.

"Moore's my name," the priest said. "I am very sorry about your friend. I sincerely wish we could have stopped that."

"I don't even know what happened," Billy said. "I couldn't tell what that man . . ." He swallowed into silence. Moore cleared his throat. Behind heavily framed glass was a flattish surface, a slatey plane. It was brown-grey rock perhaps two feet square. In organic lines, in charcoal ink and stained a dried-blood red, overlooked by outlined human figures, was a torpedo shape; a conclave of spiral whips; a round black eye.

"That's from the Chauvet Cave," Moore said. "Thirty-five thou-sand years old." The carbon eye of the squid looked across epochs at them. Billy felt vertigo at the preantique rendition. Was it meant to be seen in the licking of a fire light? Women and men with sticks and deft fingertip smuts rendering what had visited at the edge of the sea. What had raised many arms in deepwater greeting while they waved from rockpools.

"We've always commissioned," Moore said. "We show them god." He smiled. "Or god's young. That's what we used to do.

"Since the end of the atrament we can generally only offer dreams. As we did you. How Hubert called up a young god we don't know. Even the sea won't tell us. And we've asked it. You've seen the young, Billy. Baby Jesu." He smiled at his little blasphemy. "That's what you preserved. *Architeuthis* is kraken-spawn. Gods are oviparous. Not just our gods, all gods. God-spawn's everywhere if you know where to look."

"What was that tattoo?" Billy said.

"Those kraken that make it to the last stage?" Moore jerked his thumb at the cave painting. "They sleepeth, is what they do," he quoted. "'Battening upon huge seaworms,' as they say. They'll rise only at the final end. Only in the *end*, when 'latter fire heats the deeps'"—he did quote fingers—"only then to be seen *once*, roaring they shall rise and on the surface die."

Billy looked past him. He wondered how the search of his almost-colleagues was going, whether Baron, Vardy, and Collingswood were making headway as they looked for him, as they must be doing. With a moment's startling clarity he imagined Collingswood with her so un-uniform uniform and swagger knocking heads together to find him.

"We were there at the beginning," Moore said. "And we're here now. At the end. Baby gods have started manifesting all over. Kubodera and Mori. That was just the first. Pictures, video, making themselves known. *Architeuthis, Mesonychoteuthis*, unknowns. After all those years of silence. They're *rising*.

"On the twenty-eighth of February, 2006, the kraken appeared in London." He smiled. "In Melbourne they keep theirs in a block of *ice*. Can you imagine? I can't help thinking of it as a godsicle. You know they're planning one for Paris which is going to be, what do they call it, *plastinated*? Like that strange German man does to people. *That's* how they're going to show god." Dane shook his head. Moore shook his head. "But, not you. You treated it . . . right, Billy. You laid it out with a *kindness*." Odd stilted formulation. "With respect. You kept it behind glass."

His squid had been a relic in a reliquary. "This is kraken year zero," Moore said. "This is *Anno Teuthis*. We're in the end times. What d'you think's been going on? You think it's just bloody chance that when you bring god up and treat it as you do, the world suddenly starts ending? Why do you think we kept coming to see? Why do you think we had someone on the inside?" Dane bent his head. "We had to know. We had to watch. We had to protect it too, find out what was going on. We knew something was going to happen.

"You realise the reason you *had* a kraken to work on is because in roaring it rose and on the surface died?"

Chapter Seventeen

IF YOU GOT INVOLVED WITH LEON, MARGE HAD ALWAYS UNDER-
stood, you took certain behaviours for granted. It wasn't a bad
thing—it gave leeway for your own behaviour, the indulgences of
which might have caused all manner of resentments and bad bloods
with previous lovers.

For example, Marge felt no compunction about cancelling a night
out if she was working on a piece and it was going well. "Sorry sweet,"
she'd said, many times, leaning over the battered video equipment
that she rescued from skips and eBay. "I've got something going. Can
we raincheck?"

When Leon did the same, even if it annoyed her, it also often came
with satisfaction, the knowledge that these were credits she could
cash in later. For similar reasons, knowing she had no intent to
become monogamous when they got together, she found his own
occasional non-her-focused sexual liaisons (mostly obviously
telegraphed) rather a relief.

In and of itself, she would not have thought much or anything of
not hearing from Leon for two, three, five days, a week at a time. That
was nothing, any more than was a last-minute cancellation. What,
however, gave her some anxiety, some pause, was that they had had a
specific arrangement—they had been going to see a James Bond
marathon, because "it'll be hilarious"—and that he had not called to

change plans. He had simply texted her some nonsense—that itself not news—and not turned up. And now was ignoring her messages.

She texted him, she emailed him. *Where are you?* she wrote. *Tell me or i'm going to get worried. Call rsvp text carrier pigeon whatever you prefer xx.*

Marge had deleted the last message Leon had sent, thinking it some drunk foolishness. Of course she regretted it deeply now. It had said something like: *billy says theres a squid cult.*

"Fathers and mothers and uncaring aunts and uncles in freezing darkness we implore you."

"We implore you." The congregation mumbled in time, in response to Moore the Teuthex's phrases.

"We are your cells and synapses, your prey and your parasites."

"Parasites."

"And if you care for us at all we know it not."

"Not."

Billy sat at the back of the church. He did not stand and sit with the small congregation, nor did he murmur meaningless phonemes in polite lag of their words. He watched. There were fewer than twenty people in the room. Mostly white, but not all, mostly dressed inexpensively, mostly middle-aged or older, but, a strange demographic blip, with four or five tough-looking young men, grim and devout and obedient, in one row.

Dane stood like a hulking altar boy. His eyes were closed, his mouth moving. The lights were low, there were shadows all over the place.

The Teuthex recited the service, his words drifting in and out of English, into Latin or Pig Latin, into what sounded like Greek, into strange slippery syllables that were perhaps dreams of sunken languages or the invented muttering of squidherds, Atlantean, Hyperborean, the pretend tongue of R'lyeh. Billy had expected ecstasy, the febrile devotions of the desperate speaking in tongues or tentacles, but this fervour—and fervour it was, he could see the tears and gripping hands of the devout—was controlled. The flavour of the sect was vicarly, noncharismatic, an Anglo-Catholicism of mollusc-worship.

Such a tiny group. Where were others? The room itself, the seats themselves, could have contained three times as many people as were there. Had the space always been aspirational, or was this a religion in decline?

"Reach out to enfold us," Moore said, and the congregation said, "Fold us," and made motions with their fingers.

"We know," the Teuthex said. A sermon. "We know this is a strange time. There are those who think it's the end." He made another motion of some dismissal. "I'm asking you all to have faith. Don't be afraid. 'How could it have gone?' people have asked me. 'Why aren't the gods doing anything?' Remember two things. The gods don't owe us anything. That's not why we worship. We worship because they're gods. This is their universe, not ours. What they choose they choose and it's not ours to know why."

Christ, thought Billy, *what a grim theology.* It was a wonder they could keep anyone in the room, without the emotional quid pro quo of hope. That's what Billy thought, but he saw that it was not nihilism in that room. That it was full of hope, whatever the Teuthex said; and he the Teuthex, Billy thought, quietly hopeful too. Doctrine was not quite doctrine.

"And second," said Moore. "Remember the movement that looks like not moving." A small frisson at that.

There was no communion, no passing out of, what, sacred calamari? Only some discordant and clunky wordless hymn, a silent prayer, and the worshippers left. Each as they filed out glanced at Billy with a strange and needy look. The young men looked positively hungry, and nervous to meet his eye.

Dane and Moore came to meet him. "So," said the Teuthex. "That was your first service."

"What was that squirrel?" Billy said.

"Freelancer," Dane said.

"What? Freelance what?"

"Familiar." *Familiar.* "Don't look like that. Familiar. Don't act like you've never heard of one."

Billy thought of black cats. "Where is it now?"

"I don't know, I don't want to know. It did what I paid it for." Dane did not look at him. "Job done. So it's gone."

"What did you pay it?"

"I paid it nuts, Billy. What would you think I'd pay a squirrel?" Dane's face was so deadpan flat Billy could not tell if what he was facing was the truth or contempt. Welcome to this world of work. Magic animals got paid in something, nuts or something. Billy examined the pictures and books in Moore's own dark grey chambers.

"Baron . . ." Billy said.

"Oh, we know Baron," said Dane. "And his little friends."

"He told me some books got stolen."

"They're in the library," said the Teuthex. He poured tea. "Can't use a photocopy to persuade the world."

Billy nodded as if that made sense. He faced Moore. "What's happening?" he said. "What did that . . . man . . . want? And why are you keeping me prisoner?"

Moore looked quizzical. "Prisoner? Where is it you want to go?"

There was a silence. "I'm getting out of here," Billy said. And then very quickly he said, "What did . . . Goss . . . do to Leon?"

"Would you be very offended if I said I don't believe you?" Moore said. "That you want to get out? I'm not sure you do." He met Billy's stare. "What did you see?" Billy almost recoiled at the eagerness in his voice. "Last night. What did you dream? You don't even know why you're not safe, Billy. And if you go to Baron and Vardy you'll be considerably less so.

"I know what they said about us." He almost twinkled, a vicar being a good sport. "But that little faith-gang called 'police' can't help, you know. You're in the Tattoo's sights, now."

"Think about the Tattoo," Dane said. "That face. That man's face on another man's back. How was you going to deal with that, Billy?" After a silence Dane said, "How you going to get the police to deal with that?"

"It isn't just that, either," Moore said. "As if that weren't enough. I know it's all a bit . . . Well. But it isn't just the Tattoo, even. Suddenly, ever since something or other, everyone agrees the end's in sight. Nothing unusual in that, you might say, and you'd be right except that I do mean *everyone*. That has . . . ramifications for you. You need to be with a power. Let me tell you. We are the Congregation of God Kraken. And this is our time."

They explained.

London was full of dissident gods.

Why? Well they have to live somewhere. A city living in its own afterlife. Why not?

Of course, they're all over, gods are. Theurgic vermin, those once worshipped or still worshipped in secret, those half worshipped, those feared and resented, petty divinities: they infect everybloody-where. The ecosystems of godhead are fecund, because there's nothing and nowhere that can't generate the awe on which they graze. But just because there are cockroaches everywhere doesn't mean there aren't cockroaches in particular in a New York kitchen. And just because angels keep their ancient places and every stone, cigarette packet, tor and town has its deities, doesn't mean there's nothing special about London.

The streets of London are stone synapses hardwired for worship. Walk the right or wrong way down Tooting Bec you're invoking something or other. You may not be interested in the gods of London, but they're interested in you.

And where gods live there are knacks, and money, and rackets. Halfway-house devotional murderers, gunfarmers and self-styled reavers. A city of scholars, hustlers, witches, popes and villains. Crim-inarchs like the Tattoo, those illicit kings. The Tattoo had run with the Krays, before he was Tattoo, but really you couldn't leave your front door unlocked. Nobody remembered what his name had been: that was part of what had happened to him. Whatever nasty miracle it was had en-dermed him had thrown away his name as well as his body. Everyone knew they used to know what he was called, including him, but no one recalled it now.

"The one who got him like that was smart," Dane said. "It was bet-ter when he was around, old Griz. I used to know some of his guys."

There was a many-dimensional grid of geography, economy, obli-gation and punishment. Crime overlapped with faith—"Neasden's run by the Dharma Bastards," Dane said—though many guerrilla entrepreneurs were secular, agnostic, atheist or philistine ecumenical. But faith contoured the landscape.

"Who's Goss and Subby?" Billy said. He sat guarded between them, looking from one to the other. Dane looked down at his own big fists. Moore sighed.

"Goss and Subby," Moore said.

"What's their . . . ?" Billy said.

"Everything you can think of is what."

"Badness," Dane said. "Goss sells his badness."

"Why did he kill that guy? In the cellar?" Billy said.

"The preserved man," the Teuthex said. "If that was his handiwork."

Billy said, "That Tattoo thought I stole the squid."

"That's why he was hunting you," Dane said. "See? That's why I had that familiar watching you."

"You preserved it, Billy. You opened the door and found it gone," Moore said. Pointed at him. "No wonder Baron wanted you. No wonder the Tattoo wanted you, and no wonder we were watching."

"But he could tell I didn't," Billy pleaded. "He said I had nothing to do with anything."

"Yeah," said Dane. "But then I rescued you."

"We got you out, so we're allies," Moore said. "So you *are* his enemy now."

"You're under our protection," said Dane. "And because of that you need it."

"How did you take the *Architeuthis*?" Billy said at last.

"It wasn't us," said Moore quietly.

"What?" But it was a relic. They would fight for it, surely, like a devout of Rome might fight for a shroud, a fervent Buddhist might liberate a stolen Sura. "So who?"

"Well," said Moore. "Quite.

"Look," he said. "You have to persuade the universe that things make sense a certain way. That's what knacking is." Billy blinked at this abrupt conversational twist, that word unfamiliarly verbed. "You use whatever you can."

"Snap," said Dane. He clicked his fingers, and with the sound came a tiny fluorescent glow in the air just where the percussion had been. Billy stared and knew it was not a parlour trick. "That's just skin and hand."

"You use what you can," Moore said, "and some what-you-cans are better than others."

Billy realised that Dane and his priest were not, in fact, changing the subject.

"A giant squid is . . ." Billy petered out but he was thinking, *Is powerful medicine, a big thing, a massive deal. It's magic, is what it is. For knacking.* "That's why it's been taken. That's why that tattoo wants it. But this is *craziness*," he added. He couldn't stop himself. "This is craziness."

"I know, I know," Moore said. "Mad beliefs like that, eh? Must be some *metaphor*, right? Must mean something else?" Shook his head. "What an awfully arrogant thing. What if faiths are exactly what they are? And mean exactly what they say?"

"Stop trying to make sense of it and just listen," Dane said.

"And what," Moore said, "if a large part of the reason they're so tenacious is that they're perfectly accurate?" He waited, and Billy said nothing. "This is all perfectly real. The Tattoo wants that body, Billy, to do something *himself*, or stop someone *else* doing something," Moore said.

"All these things have their powers, Billy," he said intensely. "'There are plenty of currents on the way down deep' is what we'd say. But some go deeper, quicker, than others. Some are *right*." He smiled not like someone joking.

"What would someone do with it?" Billy said.

"Whatever it is," Dane said, "I'm against it."

"What wouldn't they?" Moore said. "What couldn't they? With something that holy."

"That's why we need to get out there," Dane said. "To find it."

"Dane," said Moore.

"It's a duty of care," Dane said.

"Dane. We need understanding, certainly," Moore said. "But we have to have faith."

"What could show more faith than getting out there?" Dane asked.

"You understand what's going on?" Dane said to Billy. "How dangerous it all is? The Tattoo wants you, and *someone has a kraken*. That's a god, Billy. And we don't know who, or why."

A GOD, BILLY THOUGHT. THE THIEF HAD A BLEACHY FORMALIN-preserved mass of rubbery stink. But he knew truths were not true.

"God can take care of itself," Moore said to Dane. "You know things are happening, Billy. You've known for days."

"I *seen* you feel it," Dane said. "I seen you watching the sky."

"This is an end," Moore said. "And it's our god's doing it, and it isn't in our control. And that's not right." He splayed his fingers in a ludicrous prayer-motion. "That's why you're here, Billy. You know things you don't even know," he said. The fervour in it gave Billy a chill. "You've *worked on its holy flesh*."

Chapter Eighteen

"YOU COULD JUST STAMP YOUR LITTLE FEET, COULDN'T YOU, Subby? You could unbuckle your shoe and throw it in the lake."

Goss stamped. Subby walked a few paces behind him, his hands behind his back in crude mimicry of the man's pose. Goss was bent forward and beetling with energy. He uncoupled his hands repeatedly and wiped them on his mucky top. Subby watched him and did the same.

"Where are we now?" Goss said. "Well you may ask. Well you may ask. Where indeed are we now? Not often his nibs is wrong, but that Mr. Harrow clearly not so butter-wouldn't-melt as he'd give you to think, if he's got bouncers like that ready to spirit him away. Still not sure who that was who banged your bonce, you poor lad. You doing better?" He ruffled Subby's hair to the boy's openmouthed gaze.

"What *is* he like? He's all snotted up in this like slurry in alveoli. Still our best lead, of which his skin-inked eminence now admits, and, what do you say, once is never enough. We've caught up with him before, we'll do it again.

"Where? That's the question mark indeed, my young apprentice.

"Ears to the ground, Subby, tongues aflap." He did as he said and tasted where they were, and if pedestrians or shoppers in that pre-suburban shopping precinct noticed his slurping snake lick they pretended not to. "Mostly we're after Fluffy, so any flavours of the you-know-what, a distinct and meaty-bleachy-gamey bouquet I'm told, then veer we go, but otherwise, seems Mr. Harrow knows a little smidgeon, and of him I still recall the savour."

THERE WERE ALL KINDS OF DRAMAS OCCURRING IN THE CITY IN those days: machinations, betrayals, insinuations and misunderstandings between groups with distinct and overlapping interests. In the offices, workshops, laboratories and libraries of angry scholars and self-employed theorist-manipulators were screamed arguments between them and those nonhuman companions still around. "How can you do this to me?" was the sentence most regularly spoken, followed by, "Oh go fuck yourself."

In the headquarters of the Confederation of British Industry was a hallway between a much-frequented toilet and a small meeting room, that, if most members of the organisation noticed, they did so to briefly wonder why they had never done so before; and they tended not to again after that first time. It was not as brightly lit as it should be. The watercolours on its walls looked a bit vague: they were there, certainly, but rather difficult to pay attention to.

At the end of the corridor a plastic plaque read STOREROOM or OUT OF ORDER or something—some phrase tricky to recall with exactitude but the gist of which was *not this door, go somewhere else.* Two figures ignored that gist. In front was a large man wearing an expensive suit and a black motorcycle helmet. Just behind him, her hand in his, a woman in her sixties stumbled and tripped like an anxious animal. She was slack-faced, dressed in a threadbare trench coat.

The man knocked and opened without waiting for an answer. Inside was a small office. A man stood to greet them, indicated the two seats in front of his desk. The suited man did not sit. He pushed the woman into one of the chairs. He kept his hands on her shoulders. Her coat swung open and she wore nothing beneath it. Her skin was cold- and sick-looking.

For several seconds nothing happened. Then the woman moved her mouth extraordinarily. She made a ringing noise.

"Hello?" said the man behind the desk.

"Hello," said the woman, clicking and hollow-sounding, in a man's voice, a London voice. Her eyes were blank as a mannequin's. "Am I speaking to Mr. Dewey of the CBI?"

"You are. Thank you for contacting me so quickly."

"Not a problem," the woman said. She drooled slightly. "I understand you have a proposal for me. With regard to the, ah, current dispute."

"I do, Mr. . . . I do. We were wondering whether you might be able to help us."

It was in Cricklewood that, after a consultation based on highly specific geographopathic criteria, the Metropolitan Police had located its abquotidian operatives: the FSRC and their highly specialist support staff—secretaries unfazed by the information they were required to type, pathologists who would autopsy whatever bodies were put in front of them, no matter how unorthodox their arrangements or causes of death. Vardy, Baron and Collingswood met in the cold lab of one such, Dr. Harris, a tall woman vastly unfazed by absurd and knacked evidence. They had her show them the remains from the basement of the museum one more time.

"You told me to leave it in one piece," she had said.

"Now I'm telling you to open the ruddy thing," Baron had said, and half an hour later, after a crack and careful prising, the jar rocked in two pieces on the steel. Between them, the man who had been inside almost retained his cylindrically constrained form. The edges of his flesh, the pose of his hands, still looked as if he were pressed up against the glass.

"There," Harris said. She laser-pointed. The man stared at her with the intensity of the drowned. "Like I told you," she said. She indicated the bottle's neck. "There's no way he could have got in there." The FSRC operatives looked at each other.

"Thought perhaps you might have had a change of heart about that," Baron said.

"Couldn't have happened. He couldn't have been in there unless he was put in when he was born and left to grow up in it. Which given that he has several tattoos, plus for all the other obvious impossibility-related reasons, is not what happened."

"Alright," Baron said. "That's not what we're concerned with here. Right, ladies and gentlemen? What do we know of the methods of our suspects? Do we see any signature moves here? Our question *here* is about Goss and Subby."

GOSS AND SUBBY. GOSS AND SUBBY!

Collingswood was sure she was right. Anders Hooper was a good origamist, but the main reason he had got the job was because he was new, young, and did not recognise his employer.

He was no younger than she, of course, but as Vardy had said, with stern approval, "Collingswood doesn't count." Her research might have been unorthodox, her learning partial, but she took seriously knowledge of the world in which she operated. She read its histories in chaotic order, but she read them. How could she fail to know of Goss and Subby?

The notorious "Soho Goats" pub crawl with Crowley, that had ended in quadruple murder, memory of the photographs of which still made Collingswood close her eyes. The Dismembering of the Singers, while London struggled to recover from the Great Fire. In 1812, Walkers on the Face-Road had been Goss and Subby. Had to have been. Goss, King of the Murderspivs—that designation given him by a Roma intellectual who had, doubtless extremely carefully, resisted identification. Subby, whom the smart money said was the subject of Margaret Cavendish's poem about the "babe of meat and malevolence."

Goss and fucking Subby. Sliding shifty through Albion's history, disappearing for ten, thirty, a hundred blessed years at a time, to return, *evening all*, wink wink, with a twinkle of a sociopathic eye, to unleash some charnel-degradation-for-hire.

There was no specificity to Goss and Subby. Try to get what information you can about precisely what their knacks were, what Collingswood still thought of as their superpowers, and all you'd get was that Goss was a *murderous shit like no other*. Supershit; Wondershit; Captain Total Bastard. Nothing funny about it. Call it banal if it makes you feel better but evil's evil. Goss might stretch his mouth to do one person, stories said, might punch a hole in another, might find himself spitting flames to burn up a third. Whatever.

The first time Collingswood had read of them, it had been in a facsimile of a document from the seventeenth century, a description of the "long-fingered bad giver and his dead alive son," and for some weeks afterward, unfamiliar with old fonts, she had thought them Goff and Fubby. She and Baron had had a good laugh at that.

"Fo," she said. "Iff it? Iff it the work of Goff and Fubby?" Baron did, in fact, briefly, laugh. "Iff it their MO?"

And there was the problem. Goss and Subby had no such thing as an MO. Baron, Vardy and Collingswood peered at the preserved man. They referred to their notes, made more, circumnavigated the corpse, muttered to themselves and each other.

"All we can say for sure," said Baron at last, peering, leaning in, "is that so far as we know, there's no record of them having done anyone in like this before. I pulled the files. Vardy?"

Vardy shrugged. "We're flying blind," he said. "We all know that. But you want my opinion? Ultimately I think . . . my opinion's no. What I know of their methods, it's always been up-close, hands, bones. This is . . . something else. I don't know what this is, but this isn't that, I don't think."

"Alright," said Baron. "So we're after Goss and bloody Subby, and we're also looking for someone *else*, who pickles their enemies." He shook his head. "Lord, for a bloody Grievous Bodily Harm. Alright, ladies and gents, let's get moving on this fellow. We need an ID on the poor sod ASAP. Among many other bloody things."

Chapter Nineteen

Into new London? The city's vast unsympathetic attention's on you, the Teuthex said. *You're hunted.* Billy imagined himself emerging big-eyed as a fish, and London—where the Tattoo, Goss, Subby, the workshop waited—noticing. *Oh* there *you are.*

He walked almost as if free under the city. More than once Krakenists passed him and stared and he stared back at them, but they did not interrupt him. In places the grey bas-reliefs of cephalopods were crumbled and beneath were antique bricks. He found a door into a bright-lit room.

It made him gasp. It had the side-to-side proportions of a small sitting room, but its floor was way below. Absurdly deep. Steps angled down. It was a shaft of roomness, shelved with books. Ladders dangled from the stacks. As the church's holdings grew, Billy thought, horizontal constraints required generations of kraken worshippers to dig for their library.

Billy read titles on his way down. *A Tibetan Book of the Dead* by the Bhagavad Gita, by two or three Qur'ans, testaments old and new, arcana and Aztec theonomicons. Krakenlore. Cephalopod folklore; biology; humour; art and oceanography; cheap paperbacks and antiquarian rarities. *Moby-Dick,* shapes etched onto its cover. Verne's *20,000 Leagues.* A Pulitzer medal escutcheon stapled to a single page of one book, on which the line "Great squid propelling themselves over the floor of the sea in the cold darkness" was the only part left visible below paint. *The Highest Tide*, Jim Lynch, nailed upside down like something unholy.

Tennyson and a book of poems by Hugh Cook faced each other, open to competing pages. Billy read the counter to Alfred Lord.

THE KRAKEN WAKES

The little silver fish
Scatter like shrapnel
As I plunge upward
From the black underworld.
The green waves break from my sides
As I roll up, forced by my season,
And before the tenth second
I can feel my own heat—
The wind can never cool as oceans do.

By mid-morning,
My skin has sweated into agony.
The turmoil of my intestines
Bloats out against my skin.
I'm too sick to struggle—I hang
In the thermals of pain,
Screaming against the slow, slow, slow
Rise toward descent.

And the madness of my pain
Seems to have infected everything—
Cities hack each other into blood;
Ships sink in firestorm; armies
Flail with sticks and crutches;
Obesity staggers toward coronary
Down the streets of starvation.

"Jesus," Billy whispered.

Samizdat, sumptuous hardbacks, handwritten texts, dubious-looking output from small presses. *Apocrypha Tentacula; On Worship of Kraken; The Gospel According to Saint Steenstrup.*

We cannot see the universe, Billy read in a text taken at random. It was cobbled in incompetent typeface.

> We cannot see the universe. We are in the darkness of a trench, a deep cut, dark water heavier than earth, presences lit by our own blood, little biolumes, heroic and pathetic Promethei too afraid or weak to steal fire but able still to glow. Gods are among us and they care nothing and are nothing like us.
>
> This is how we are brave: we worship them anyway.

Old volumes bulged with addenda, were embossed *Catechismata*. Scrapbooks with glued-in snips. Annotated and those notes annotated, and on in unstinting interpretation, a merciless teuthic hermeneutic.

He read the names Dickins and Jelliss, *Alice Chess.* A spread about mutant versions of the game with arcane rules, bishops and pawns given strange powers, transmogrified pieces called saurians, torals and anti-kings, and one called a kraken. The "universal leaper" was usually thought the most powerful piece, he read, as it could go from where it was to any other square on the board. But it was not. Kraken was. *Kraken = universal leaper + zero,* he read, *= universal sleeper.* It could move to any square *including the one it was already on.* Anywhere including nowhere.

> On the board & in life for Kraken in the void nothing is not nothing. Kraken stillness is not lack. Its zero is ubiquity. This is the movement that looks like not moving, & it is the most powerful move of all.

Price rises were a function of neutral buoyancy, Billy read. Art Nouveau was coil-envy. Wars were meagre reflections of speculated kraken politics.

After uncounted hours Billy looked up and saw, by the room's raised entrance, a young woman. He remembered her from one of the moments during his visions. She stood in her nondescript London uniform of hoodie and jeans. She bit her lip.

"Hi," she said, shy. "It's an honour. They said that, like, everyone out there's looking for you. The angel of memory and everything, Dane said." Billy blinked. "Teuthex said do you want to come, and they'd be glad if you was . . . if you want follow me because they're waiting."

He followed her to a smaller room, containing one big table and many people. Dane and Moore were there. A few of the other men and women were in robes like the Teuthex's; most were in civvies. Everyone looked angry. On the table was a digital recorder. The noise of rowdy debate stopped with his entry. Dane stood.

"Billy," said Moore after a moment. "Please join us."

"I protest," someone said. There were murmurs.

"Billy, please join us," Moore said.

"What is this?" Billy said.

"There's never been a time like this," Moore said. "Are you interested in the future?" Billy said nothing. "Do you ever read your horoscope?"

"No."

"Sensible. You can't see *the* future, there's no such thing. It's all bets. You'll never get the same answer from two seers. But that doesn't mean either of them's wrong."

"Might be," Dane said.

"They might," Moore said. "But it's all degrees of might. You *want* your prognosticators to argue. You never told us what you dreamed, Billy. Something coming up? Everyone can feel something coming up. Since the kraken disappeared. And *no one disagrees.*" He brought together his hands in a reverse explosion. "And that's wrong.

"This is a recording we made of a consultation with the Londonmancers," he said.

"What's . . . ?" Billy said.

"Well you may ask," said Dane.

"Voices of the city," Moore said.

"They wish."

"Dane, please. Oldest oracles in the M25."

"Sorry," Dane said. "But Fitch has been off for years. Just tells you what you want to hear. People just go for tradition . . ."

"Some of the others are sharper," said someone else.

"You're forgetting," the Teuthex said. "It was the Londonmancers called it first. Fitch may be past it, true. People go out of tradition, true."

"Sentiment," Dane said.

"Maybe," Moore said. "But this time it was him called it. He's been begging people to pay attention." He pressed Play.

"—*best if you ask,*" said a curt digital voice.

"That's Saira," Moore said.

"—*what you're here for.*"

"*Something's coming up, underneath everything.*" It was the Teuthex. "*We're looking for a path between possible—*"

"*Not this time.*" An old man's voice. He muttered in and out of sense. He sounded urgent, in a confused way. "*Have faith, but you have to do something, understand? You're right, it's coming, and you have to . . . It's all ending.*"

"*Have faith in what?*" the Teuthex said. "*In London?*"

The old man Fitch maundered about back streets and hidden histories, described pentacles in the banalities of town planning. "*Time was I'd have said that,*" he abruptly said.

"*I don't understand . . .*"

"*No one does. I know what you think. What did they tell you? Did anyone tell you what's coming? Did they? No. They all know something is. None of them saw any way past it, did they? Something,*" Fitch said, and his voice sounded like the voice of dust, "*is coming. London's been telling you. Something happened and there's no running the numbers. No argument this time. No getting away from it.*"

"*What is it?*"

"*The world's closing in. Something rises. And an end. If any augur augurs you otherwise, sack 'em.*" Billy heard despair. "*Because they're lying, or they're wrong.*"

"We need to be looking," Dane said. "We need to be out there finding God. The Tattoo runs things. He won't let anyone else have something that powerful."

"What about the man you said was his enemy?" Billy said. "Might it be him who took it?"

"Grisamentum," Dane said. "No. He weren't a villain and he weren't a man of gods. And he died."

"Don't people think *you* took it?" said Billy. Everyone stared at him.

"Everyone knows we wouldn't," the Teuthex said. "It's not *ours*. It's no one's." They were, Billy understood, the last people who would take it, that asymptote of their faith.

"What is it you want to do?" Dane said. "You say we need to understand the situation, but we have to *hunt*. We can deliver it from evil."

"*Enough,*" the Teuthex said, silencing everyone else. "Does it not occur to you that this is a test? You really think *God* . . . needs *rescuing?*" He held himself like the head of a church, for the first time. "Do you know your catechism? What's the most powerful piece on the board?"

At last Dane muttered, "Kraken's the most powerful piece on the board."

"Why?"

". . . The movement that looks like not moving."

"Act like you understand what that means."

Moore stood and walked out. Billy waited. Dane walked out. The congregation left, one by one.

Chapter Twenty

FSRC HEADQUARTERS, ONE MIDDLE-SIZED ROOM CONTAINING cheap armchairs and Ikea office furniture. Collingswood rarely used a desk and had never claimed one of the various of them for herself, working instead with a laptop in a deep chair.

"What's up with grumpy twat?" Collingswood said.

"By which we mean whom, today?" Baron said.

"Vardy. He's been even quieter and grumpier than usual since this squid business."

"You think? Seems pretty standard surly to me."

"Nah." Collingswood leaned in toward her screen. "What's he even doing, anyway?"

"Getting to grips with the squid cult."

"Right. Having a kip, then."

Collingswood had seen Vardy's methods. He crossed London, interrogating informants. He did a great deal of online trawling. Sometimes he would pursue a frenetic and focused following of a trail from book to book, reading a paragraph in one, dropping it and grabbing another from the sliding scree of them on his desk, or jumping up and finding one on the shelves that faced him, reading it as he returned so that by the time he sat down again he was already done with it. It was as if he had found a single compelling story smuggled in bits into countless books. There was also his channelling. He would sit, his fingers arching in front of his mouth, his eyes closed. He might rock. He would slip into that reverie and stay in it for minutes, maybe an hour.

"What do you think's behind all the pangolin bones?" Baron might ask him, of some emerged oddball sect, or, "Any clue what that priestess meant by 'stick-blood'?" or, "Where do we think they might sacrifice that boy?"

"Not sure," Vardy would say. "Couple of ideas. I'll have a think." And his colleagues would be quieter, and Collingswood, if she were in the room, would make *what a twat* motions, or pretend to intend to spill her drink on him or something.

He would stay like that a long time, at last snap open his eyes and say something like, "It's not to do with the armour. Pangolins are *bipedal.* That's what this is about. That's why they kidnapped that dancer . . ." Or: "Greenford. Of *course.* The changing rooms of some disused swimming pool. Quick, we haven't got long."

"He can't move for squid stuff," Baron said. "Last time I looked he had the notes on Archie's preservation and a bunch of articles on squid metabolism. And some leaflets for that *Beagle* trip."

Collingswood raised her eyebrows. "I can't get any sniff about that business in Putney," she said. "Too much going on. The fucking squid's got everyone on edge. The number of cranks calling in you would not believe."

"How are you doing with it all?"

She made a rude noise. "Fuck off, guv," she said. She did not tell him about her new recurring nightmare, of being thrown from a car, hurtling toward a brick wall.

"It's definitely for us though, this Putney thing?"

"If I had to put dosh down," said Collingswood. "Bruises like that." A body had been listlessly humping the stony shoreline with the slap-slap of the water. He was a journalist with a special interest in labour, who appeared to have been crushed. The murder had been passed to FSRC when a pathologist had pointed out that the four huge bludgeoning wounds on the man's chest looked a bit like a single punch from an impossibly large fist.

Baron glanced at his screen. "Email from Harris."

"Am I right then?" Collingswood said. She had mooted the possibility that the body they had found in the basement—"Leave aside the doesn't-fit-in-the-fucking-jar thing for a minute, boss"—was nothing to do with the squid case. Was, in fact, some many-years-old arcane gangland hit that Billy had stumbled onto at that moment of heightened sensitivities. "He's got something," she had said. "A bit of nous. Maybe all stressed he sniffed something."

"Hah," said Baron, and sat back. "Alright then. You're going to like this, Kath. You're right."

"What?" She sat up fast enough to spill her coffee. "Bollocks. Really, guv?"

"Harris says the body was put in the bottle, she reckons, a good hundred years ago. That's how long it's been in that muck."

"Holy shit. Bit of a turn-up, isn't it?"

"Just you wait. That's not all. There's an 'and.' Or maybe I should say a 'but.' Isn't there some word that means both?"

"Get on with it, guv."

"So that body's been preserved like that for a century. But-stroke-and. Have you heard of GG Allin?"

"Who the eff's that?"

"Search me. Luckily Dr. Harris is a dab hand with Google. He was a singer, says here. Though it also says that stretches the definition. Delightful. 'Scum rocker,' it says here. More of a Queen man myself. 'Don't stand in the front row,' Harris says. Anyway, he died about a decade ago."

"So what?"

"So we should probably not ignore the fact that one of our deceased chap's tattoos reads 'GG Allin and the Murder Junkies.'"

"Oh, shit."

"Indeed. He was apparently pickled several decades before he got his tattoo." They looked at each other.

"You want me to find out who he was, don't you?"

"No need," he said. "We got a hit. He's on the database."

"*What?*"

"Fingerprints, DNA, the whole lot. That would be the DNA that is both a century old, and also gives his DOB as 1969. Name of Al Adler. AKA various stupid things. They do love their nicknames."

"What did he get done for?"

"Burglary. But that was because of a bargain, he got to do a bit of regular bird. The original charge was on the other list." Codes against illicit magery. Adler had been breaking and entering by esoteric means.

"Associates?"

"Freelance when he was starting out. Did a stint as some sort of stringer for a coven in Deptford. Spent the last four years of his working life full-time with *Grisamentum,* it looks like. Disappeared when Griz died. Grisabloodymentum, eh?"

"Before my time," Collingswood said. "I never met the bloke."

"Don't remind me," Baron said. "It should be illegal to be so much younger than me. He was alright, Grisamentum. I mean, you never know who you can trust, but he helped out a few times."

"So I bloody gather. Geezer does crop up. What exactly did he do?"

"He was a bit of a one," Baron said. "Finger in a lot of pies. Sort of a player. It's all gone a bit tits-up since he died. He was a good counterweight."

"Didn't you tell me he didn't die with . . ."

"Yeah, no. It wasn't anything battley and dramatic. He got sick. Everyone knew about it. Worst-kept secret. I tell you what though: his funeral was pretty bloody amazing."

"You were there?"

"Certainly I was."

The Metropolitan Police could not not mark so important a passing. So advertised a good-bye. The details of where and how Grisamentum would valedictory the city had been leaked so ostentatiously they were clearly summonses.

"How'd you finesse it?" Collingswood said. Baron smiled.

"A not-very-competent surveillance, ooh, look at us, you all saw us, tish, we're so silly." He waggled his head.

Collingswood was long-enough inducted, subtle enough in her policeness now, stalwart of the FSRC and London protocols to understand. The police could not officially attend the passing of so questionably licit a figure, but nor could they ignore that public event, show disrespect or ingratitude. Hence a mummery, an act designed to be seen through, the putative incompetence of their spying on the event leaving them seen, and understood to have attended.

Collingswood said, "So what did Adler do? To get bottled?"

"Who knows? What he did to piss somebody off, your guess is as good as mine."

"My guess is *way* better than yours, guv," she said. "Get the necessary, I'll fetch my shit."

She went to her locker for an old glyph-fucked board, a candle, a pot of unpleasant tallow. Baron sent Harris an email, requesting a rag of Adler's skin, a bone, a hank of his hair.

HE COULD NOT LEAVE, BUT HE WAS NOT OTHERWISE RESTRAINED. Billy spent hours in the sunken library. He saturated himself in deepwater theology and poetics. He looked for specifics about the teuthic apocalypse.

A swallowing up and a shitting out, taken from darkness, in darkness. A terrible biting. The elect like, what, skin-bugs, little parasites on or in the great holy squid body, carried through the vortex. Or not, depending on specifics. But it wasn't like this. When at last one time he sighed and took off his glasses and reshelved verses on the tentacular, blinked and rubbed his eyes, he was startled to see several men and women who had been in the meeting with the Teuthex. He stood. They were various in age and clothes, though not in their respectful expressions. He had not heard them enter or descend.

"How long've you been here?" he said.

"We had a question," said a woman in a gown, gold tentacle-sigil winking. "You worked on it. Was there anything about this kraken that was . . . special?"

Billy ran his hands through his hair. "You mean was it specially special? Unusual *for a giant squid?*" He shook his head hopelessly. "How would I know?" He shrugged. "You tell me. I'm not one of your prophets."

Whoa. Something rushed around the room at that. Everyone looked sheepish. *What . . . ?* thought Billy. *What was—?* Oh.

Of *course* he was one of their prophets.

"Oh shit," he said. He slumped against the bookshelf. He closed his eyes. That was why they had given him dreams. They weren't just *anyone's* dreams: they were there to be read.

Billy looked at the books, textbooks next to the visions. He tried, like Vardy, to channel vicarious Damascene scenes. He could imagine these faithful seeing cephalopod biologists as unknowing saints, their vision unknown even to themselves and the purer for that, stripped of ego. And him? Billy had touched the body of God. Kept it safe, preserved it against time, ushered in *Anno Teuthis*. And because of Goss and the Tattoo, he had suffered for God, too. That was why this congregation protected him. He was not just another saint. Billy was the preserver. Giant-squid John the Baptist. The shyness he saw in the Krakenists was devotion. It was awe.

"Oh for God's sake," he said.

The men and women stared. He could see them attempting exegesis on his outburst.

ANY MOMENT CALLED *NOW* IS ALWAYS FULL OF POSSIBLES. AT TIMES of excess might-bes, London sensitives occasionally had to lie down in the dark. Some were prone to nausea brought on by a surfeit of apocalypse. Endsick, they called it, and at moments of planetary conjuncture, calendrical bad luck or mooncalf births, its sufferers would moan and puke, struck down by the side effects of revelations in which they had no faith.

Right then it was swings and roundabouts. On the one hand, such attacks were getting rarer. After years of being martyrs to somebody else's martyrs, the endsick had never been so free of the trouble. On the other hand, this was because the very proliferation, the drunkenness of an unclosed universe that had always played merry hell with their inner ear, was collapsing. And something was replacing it. Instead of all those maybes, underlying them all, approaching dimly and with gathering speed, was something simple and absolutely final.

What was this queasiness that had come in in place of the other queasiness, the sensitives wondered? What was this new discomfort, this new cold illness? Oh, right, they began to realise. That's what it is. It's fear.

Animals were afraid, too. Rats went to ground. Seagulls went back to the sea. London foxes rutted in a terrified hormonal swill, and their adrenalin made them good quarries for the secret urban hunts.

For most Londoners, all this was so far visible only in an epidemic of birdlime, the guano of terror, as pigeons began to shit themselves. Shops were covered. In Chelsea, Anders Hooper stared at the window of Nippon This! and shook his head in disgust. With a little *ding* his door opened. Goss and Subby walked in.

"Bertrand!" Goss said, and gave him a friendly wave. Subby stared. "You got me so excited, I had another question for you!"

Anders backed away. He felt for his mobile phone. "You call us if you hear anything else from them, right?" Baron had said, and given him a card, the location of which he was trying to remember. Anders bumped into the wall. Goss leaned on the counter.

"So anyway," Goss said. "There we are, Subby and me and, oh, you know, *all* of us. You know. 'Course you know, you of all bleeding mathematicians, eh? So the question is, what's the skinny?" He smiled. He breathed out cigarette smoke he had never breathed in.

"I don't understand," Anders said. In his pocket, he thumbed for the 9 button.

"No, of course," Goss said. Subby walked under the flap in the counter and stood next to Anders. Touched his arm. Tugged his sleeve. Anders failed to dial. Tried again.

"I couldn't agree more," Goss said. He pronounced it *mo-wah.* "I could *not* agree *more.* It's all a bit much at the jockey club, which is why we had to put that doping little saddler bang to rights. Imagine my surprise when I heard my name. Eh? All for the best." He tapped the side of his nose, and winked. "Those rozzers, eh! My name! My name, can you Adam and Eve it?"

Anders felt as if cold water filled his belly. "Wait."

"Did you was be chatting up my gob handle? Would I be right in that? Now all manner of whatnots are asking after me!" Goss laughed. "It's all a bit of a pony. Say my name, say my name! You said my name."

"I *didn't.* I didn't even *know* your name . . ."

Anders brought his thumb down, but there was a rush of air, a fast and cut-off bang. Anders saw no motion. All he knew was that Goss was on one side of the counter, Anders pressed the button on his phone, there was noise, the hatch was still sailing slowly through the air in a trail of splinters, and Goss was on the other side of the counter, in front of him, up close to him, holding his wrist and squeezing it so that Anders let go of his phone and gasped.

The hatch hit the floor. Goss made a chat-chat motion with his free hand. "You talky little fellow," he said. "You and Subby, never a bloody word in!"

Anders could smell Goss's hair. Could see the veins below the skin of his face. Goss pulled his face up close. His breath smelt of nothing at all. It was like air wafted by a paper fan. Until another breath and smoke came. Anders began to whimper.

"I read them books," Goss said. Inclined his head toward the origami shelves. "I read them to Subby. He was *enthralled*. En. Fucking. Thralled. Never you *Very Hungry Caterpillar* me, with this one it was all 'Oh, now tell me how to make a carp! Now how do I make a horsey?' I'm ever so good at that one now. Let me show you."

"I never told anyone," Anders said. "I don't know who you are . . ."

"Shall we make an apple tree?" Goss said. "Shall we make a tortoise? Fold and fold and fold." He began to fold. Anders began to scream. "I'm not as good at it as you!" Goss laughed.

Goss folded, with wet-flesh sounds, and cracks. Eventually Anders stopped screaming, but Goss continued to fold.

"I don't know, Subby," he said, at last. He wiped his hands on Anders's coat. He squinted at his handiwork. "I need more practice, Subby," he said. "It isn't quite as much like a lotus as I'd have liked."

Chapter Twenty-One

Billy woke as if rising out of water. He gasped. He put his head in his trembling hands. In that deep dream, what he had seen was this.

He had been a point of awareness, a soul-spot, a sentient submerged node, and had drifted over an ocean floor that he had seen in monochrome, lightless as it would have been, and that had pitched suddenly into a crevasse, a Mariana Trench of water like clotted shadow. His little selfless self had drifted. And after an inconceivably long time of that drifting, again he had seen a thing below him, rising. A flattening of the dark, coming up out of dark. Beggaring perspective. Dream-Billy knew what it would be, and was afraid of its arms, its many limbs and endless body. But when it came into water faintly lit enough that he could see its contours, it was a landscape he recognised, because it was him. A Billy Harrow face, Atlantean, eyes open and staring into the sky all the way above. The huge him was long lifeless. Pickled. Skin scabbed, church-sized eyes cataracted by preservation, vast clammy lips peeled back from teeth too big to imagine. A conserved Billy-corpse thrown up by some submerged cataclysm.

Billy shivered on his bed. He had no idea if it was the start of a day outside, or if whatever schedule he was given came according to the church's clockless grooves. He wanted suddenly and very much to tell

Marge that Leon was dead. He had not thought of her, until then, and he was ashamed. He shut his eyes tight and held his breath at the thought of Leon. Billy tried to flex whatever inner thing it was that he had touched when Goss had come for him, when the glass had broken and hesitated.

On his tray was a glass of murky drink. The inky posset. No one would spike him secretly anymore—the choice was his. The offer was there, the hope, though he was dreaming without the ink's help. Billy was a hostage-prophet, augur-inmate. He was being played as a piece in a variant game of apocalypse.

You were supposed to run the numbers. Fortune-telling was quantum betting, a competitive scrying of variably likely outcomes. That variation, the disagreements, indispensable to the calculation. Triangulating possibilities. No one knew what to do now prognosticators all agreed. Billy gripped the frame of the bed. He stared at the ink-intoxicant.

There was a knock and Dane entered. He leaned against the wall. He wore a coat and carried a bag. For a long time, neither man spoke. They just looked at each other.

"I'm not your prophet, Dane," Billy said. "Thanks for saving my life. I never said that yet. I'm sorry about that. But this is . . . You have to let me go." Still sought, yes, but. "You can help me."

Dane closed his eyes. "I was born in the church," he said. "My mum and dad met through it. It was my granddad, my dad's dad, who was the one really into it. It was him taught me. He used to do catechism with me. But I mean, that's bollocks, ain't it? It's not about reciting like a parrot. It's about understanding. He used to talk me through it."

He opened his eyes and took equipment out of his bag, checked it, put it back. A spearhead emerged from the muzzle of what looked like a pistol. "Most of my friends . . . Well you know what it's like with church and kids. They don't stick with it, do they? Me, though . . . I had a calling. You know what the Teuthex said." Dane examined his kit. "We can protect you. You're being hunted by Goss and fucking Subby. Everyone wants what's in your head, Billy. I know, I know, don't tell me, there's nothing in your head. Whatever."

"What are you doing?" Billy said.

"My job. I done such things for the church. You can't ask me all the things I done for the church, 'cause I won't tell you. All the faiths got their . . ." There was a pause during which even the empty hallways seemed to wait.

"Crusaders," Billy said.

Dane shrugged. "I was going to say oddjobsmen. Go-to guys." The hashish-eaters; the Hospitallers; Francis X. Killy. Sanctioned wet-workers of the devout. "Everyone's got apocalypse brigades, Billy, for when it all goes down. Waiting like kings under hills. They couldn't exactly go undercover." He laughed. "They couldn't exactly get a job at the Darwin Centre."

Dane lifted his shirt. His skin was studded with keloid marks. He pointed and one by one named them like little pets. "Clockworkers," he said. "Saviour Sect. Mary Martyrs. This one . . ." A long and snaky path. "That's not from a godfight, that one, just a straight-on face-off with a crook. He was stealing from us."

Footsteps approached but passed on. Dane looked at the ceiling. "You know what the question is?" he said. "What is it you're loyal to. God? The church? The pope? What if they don't agree?" He kept his gaze up. "What you want and what I want ain't the same thing. You want to be safe, and . . . not to be a prisoner. Which do you want more? Because it's safer here. You want a bit of revenge, too? What I want's my god. Maybe that's in the same direction for a bit.

"If we do this, Billy, you and me, I got to know you're not going to run. I ain't threatening you—I'm telling you you'll die if you try to deal with shit on your own. If we do this I'll help you, but you have to help me. That means you got to trust me.

"It ain't going to be safe even a tiny bit, understand? If we go. You got *everyone* after you." He lifted the bag.

"You'll be safer if you stay here. But they won't let you go. They want to know what you see." He tapped his head.

"Why are you doing this?" Billy's heart was speeding again.

"Because it ain't our place just to *watch*. There's a god to save."

"They think it's the right thing," Billy said. "I read about the movement without movement. Moore thinks he's doing the holy thing, moving like a kraken on a board. By not moving."

"Well ain't it convenient that this interpretation lets him sit on his arse? They won't let you go. I want your help, but I ain't going to force you. Time ain't with us. So?"

"I'm not what you think," Billy said. "I'm not a saint, Dane, just because I cut up a squid."

"Are you more worried about being a prisoner or a saint?" Dane said. "I ain't asking you to be anything."

"What are you going to do?"

"You fallen in the middle of a war. I'm not going to bullshit you, I'm not going to tell you you can get your revenge for your mate. You can't take Goss and neither can I. That ain't what I'm offering. We don't know who has the kraken, but we know the Tattoo's after it. If he gets hold of something like that . . ."

"It's him who got your friend killed. The best way to ruin his day's to get the god back. Best I can do."

Billy could stay among obsequious jailers. Offering him hallucinogen, taking devout and monkish notes on whatever drivel he subsequently raved.

"Will they come after you?" Billy said. "If you go rogue?"

What this renegacy would mean! Dane would be without the church that made him, an apostate hero taking faith into the heart of darkness, a paladin in hell. A lifetime of obedience, followed by what?

"Oh yeah," Dane said.

Billy nodded. He pocketed the ink. He said, "Let's go."

THE TWO MEN ON DUTY AT THE GATE LOOKED SHOCKED AS DANE approached. They nodded. They piously averted their eyes from Billy. It made him want to pretend to speak in tongues.

"I'm out," Dane said. "On a job."

"Sure," said the younger doorman. He transferred his shotgun from arm to arm. "Let us just . . ." He fumbled with the door. "Only," he said, and pointed at Billy. "Teuthex said we need his permission . . ."

Dane rolled his eyes. "Don't bugger me around," he said. "I'm on a mission. And I need him for a moment to taste some stuff out. Need what's in there." Tapped Billy's head. "You know who he is? What he knows? Don't waste my time, I'm bringing him straight back." The two men looked at each other. Dane said, in a low voice, "Do *not* waste my *time*."

What, were they going to disobey *Dane Parnell?* They opened the gate.

"Don't lock it," Dane said. "He'll be back in a second." He led Billy up the stairs, Billy behind him risking a tiny backward glance. Dane pushed open the trapdoor and pulled him out past bulwarks of rubbish, into the rear room of the South London Church of Christ.

LIGHT BURST THROUGH WINDOWS. LONDON DUST SETTLED AROUND them. Billy blinked.

"Welcome to exile," Dane said quietly, lowering the door. He was a traitor now, in his fidelity to his duty. "Come on." They went past the kitchen, the toilet, the bric-a-brac. In the main room, chairs were circled. Billy and Dane came out into a meeting of mostly elderly women, who broke off chatting.

"Alright love?" one said, and another, "Is everything okay, sweetheart?" Dane ignored them.

"Do they . . ." Billy whispered. "Do they worship the, the kraken . . . ?"

"No, they're Baptists. Mutual protection. Any second the Teuthex's going to find out we're gone. So we've got to get far away, fast. Follow me close and do exactly what I say, when I say. You try to go off on your own, Billy, and you will be found and you will die. Neither of us wants that. You understand? Walk quickly but don't run.

"Are you ready?"

Chapter Twenty-Two

THERE WAS NO PLEASURE, NO I-TOLD-YOU-SO AMONG THE hedge-seers who had for so long predicted that the end was on its way. Now that everyone who cared to think about it agreed with them—though they might abjure the insight—those who found themselves suddenly and unexpectedly the advance guard of mainstream opinion were at a bit of a loss. What was the point of dedicating your life to giving warnings if everyone who might have listened—because the majority were still unbothered and would possibly remain so till the sun went out—merely nodded and agreed?

A plague of ennui afflicted London's manic prophets. Warning signs were discarded, pamphlets pulped, megaphones thrown into cupboards. Those who could count questionable presences insisted that ever since the *Architeuthis* had disappeared, something new had been walking. Something driven and intense and intent on itself. And since shortly after that, it had unfolded again and become something a little *more* itself, emerged from a pupa of unspecificity into sentience, an obsessive moment of now that trod heavy in time.

No, they didn't really know what that meant, either, but that was their very strong impression. And it was freaking them out.

BILLY STUMBLED AT THE DAY, THE COLD SUNLIGHT, THE PASSERSBY. At people in everyday clothes carrying papers and bags and on their way to south London shops. None of them looked twice at him. The trees leaflessly scratched the sky. It was all washed out by the winter.

A clutch of pigeons rose, wheeled and disappeared over the aerials. Dane stared at their retreating forms with frank suspicion. He beckoned Billy.

"Move," Dane said. "I don't like the look of those birds."

Billy listened to the flatness of his footsteps on tarmac, not echoing at all. His pulse was fast. There was a stretch of low skyline and neglected brickwork. The church behind them was little more than a big shed. "I really do not like the look of those birds," Dane said.

They went past newsagents, past bins spilling from their rims, dogshit by trees, a row of shops. Dane walked them to a car. It was not the same one as before. He opened the door. There was a whisper.

"What?" Dane said. He looked up. "Was that . . . ?" There was no other noise. He was looking at a crude clay dragon, a little Victorian flourish in the matter of a roof, ajut from its vertex. He hustled Billy into the car.

"What was that?" Billy said. Dane let out a shaking breath as he drove.

"Nothing," Dane said. "It's a thought, though. God knows we need some help. We need to put some mileage behind us." Billy did not recognise any streets. "Any second now London's going to be teeming with my pissed-off crew. Ex-crew."

"So where are we going?"

"We get underground. Then we start hunting."

"And . . . what *about* the cops?" Billy said.

"We *ain't* going to the *police*." Dane smacked the wheel. "They can't do shit. And if they could, it wouldn't be what we want them to. Why do you think *they're* looking? They want it for themselves."

"So what are you going to do with it if you find it, Dane?"

Dane looked at him. "I'm going to make sure no one else gets it."

DANE HAD HIS HIDES. IN EMPTY-LOOKING SHELLS, IN SHABBY squats, in neat-seeming places that appeared to have permanent tenants holding down jobs respectable and unrespectable.

"We move, we stay a day or two at a time," Dane said. "We get hunting."

"Surely the church'll find us," Billy said. "These are safe houses, right?"

"Not even the Teuthex knows these. When you do the work I do, you have to have leeway. The less they know the better. Keep their hands clean. It ain't ours to kill, *we* ain't the predators, get me? But needs must." To defend heaven you unleash hell, that sort of sophistry.

"Are you the only one?" Billy said.

"No," Dane said. "I'm the best, though."

Billy put his head back on the seat and watched London go. "Goss just opened his mouth," he said. "And Leon was . . ." He shook his head. "Is that his . . . knack?"

"His knack is that he's an unspeakable bastard," Dane said. "A jobsworth." He unfolded a piece of paper with one hand. "This is a list of movers," he said. "We've got a god to find. This is who might've done the job."

Billy watched Dane for a while, watched anger come and go across his face, and moments of aghast uncertainty. They dossed down finally near the river, in a one-bedroom flat decorated like student digs. There were books on biology and chemistry on cheap shelves, a System Of A Down poster on the wall, the paraphernalia of dope.

"Whose is all this?" he said.

"In case it gets broken into," Dane said. "Or remote-viewed. Scried or whatever. Got to be convincing." A toothbrush crusted with paste-spit was in the bathroom, a half-used soap and shampoo. There were clothes in the drawers, all suited to the invented inhabitant: all the same size and unpleasant style. Billy picked up the phone but it was not connected.

Dane checked tiny bones tied in bundles on the windowsill. Ugly little clots of magicky stuff. From a cabinet below the bed he took a machine made of rusty old equipment and nonsense: a motherboard, an old oscilloscope, crocodile-clipped to knickknacks. When he plugged it in there was a thud, waves fluxed on the screen and the air felt dryer.

"Alright," Dane said. "Bit of security."

Alarm systems and signal-jammers fucking with the flows of sentience and sensation—magic. *Call it "knocking,"* Billy told himself. The occult machines left not nothing, not a void that would attract attention like a missing tooth, but projected a shred of presence for remote-sensors, a construct soul. The residue of a pretend person.

When Dane went to the bathroom, Billy did not try to leave. He did not even stand by the door and wonder.

"Why don't you want this?" Billy said when Dane returned. He raised his hands to indicate everything. "The end, I mean. You say it's ending. I mean, it's your kraken doing it . . ."

"No, it ain't," Dane said. "Or not like it's supposed to."

It would have made sense to Billy, had Dane hedged and hemmed and hawed, dissembled and evaded. It could not be so uncommon a phenomenon, the last-minute cold feet of the devout. Absolutely I was all signed up for the apocalypse but right *now?* Like *this?* It would have made sense, but that was not what this was. Billy knew then and quite certainly that had Dane trusted that this *was* the horizon of which he had read and catechised since his feisty fervent youth, he would have gone along with it. But this was not quite the right kraken apocalypse. That was the problem. It was according to some other plan. Some other schema. Something had hijacked the squid finality. This was and was not the intended end.

"I need to get a message to someone," Billy said. Dane sighed. "Hey." Billy was surprised by the speed of his own anger, as he squared up. The big man looked surprised too. "I'm not your pet. You can't order me around. My best friend *died,* and his girlfriend needs to know."

"That's well and good," Dane said. He swallowed. His effort to stay calm was alarming. "But there's one *mistake* there. You say I can't order you around. Oh I can. I *have* to. You do what I tell you or Goss or Subby or the Tattoo or any one of all the others out there looking for you will *find* you, and then if you're *very* lucky you'll just die. *You understand?*" He prodded Billy's chest one, two, three times. "I just exiled myself, Billy. I am not having a good day."

They stared at each other. "Tomorrow the real shit begins," Dane said. "Right now, there's nowhere as much knacking floating around as you'd think. There's what you could call a power shortage. That gives us opportunities. I don't just know church people, you know." He opened his bag. "We might not have to do this totally alone."

"Let's make sure," Billy said carefully. "Just answer me this. I mean . . . I know you don't want to get the police in, but . . . What about just Collingswood? She's not like the leader of that lot—she's a constable—but she's obviously got something. We could call her . . ." The flat anger of Dane's face hushed him.

"We *ain't dealing* with that lot," he said. "You think they'll keep us safe? They won't mess with us? You think she ain't going to hand us right over?"

"But . . ."

"'But' fuckity shite, Billy. We stick to who *I* know." Dane brought out maps of London felt-tipped with additions, sigils on parkland and routes traced through streets. A speargun, Billy saw to his surprise, like a scuba diver might carry.

"You've never shot, right?" Dane said. "Maybe we need to get you something. I didn't . . . I didn't have time to plan this a whole lot, you know? I'm thinking who might help. Who I've run with." He counted off on his fingers, and scribbled names. "My man Jason. Wati. Oh, man, Wati. He's going to be angry. If we want to get a talisman or anything we need to go to Butler."

"Are these kraken people?"

"Hell no, the church is out," Dane said. "That's closed. We can't go there. These are people I've run with. Wati's a red, good guy. Butler, it's all about what he saw: he can get you defences. Jason, Jason Smyle, he's a good bet."

"Hey, I know that name," Billy said. "Did he work at . . . the museum?" Dane smiled and shook his head. *No*, thought Billy, the familiarity abruptly gone.

They ate from the bag of junk food Dane had bought. There were two beds, but like campers they dossed down on the living room floor. This was a landscape through which they were passing, a forest glade. They lay without speaking some time.

"How did it feel?" Dane said. "To work on the kraken."

". . . Like smelly rubber," Billy said at last. Dane looked as if he would thunder disapproval, but then he laughed.

"Oh man," said Dane. "You're bad." He shook his head. His grin was guilty. "Seriously. You telling me there was *nothing*? You've got something." He clicked his fingers, made that spot of biophosphor, like a deep-sea squid. "You didn't feel nothing?"

Billy lay back. "No," he said. "Not then. It was earlier. I was rubbish at what I did, the first few months I was there. I didn't even know if I'd stick it. But then all of a sudden I got much better. *That* was when it felt something special. Like I could preserve anything, any way I wanted."

"What about in the alley?" Dane said. Billy looked at him across the dark room. Dane spoke carefully. "When Goss was coming for you. You did something, then. Did that feel like something?"

"I didn't do anything."

"If you say so, Billy," Dane said. "My granddad was a holy man. He used to ask me who my favourite saint was. He said you could tell a lot about someone if you knew that. So I'd say Kraken, because I wanted to be a good boy, and that was the right answer to most . . . religious questions. And he'd say, *No, that's cheating. Which* saint? I couldn't decide for ages, but suddenly one day I did. I told him.

"*Saint Argonaut,* I said. *Really?* he says. He wasn't angry or nothing, he was just, like, surprised. But I think he liked that. *Really?* he goes. *Not Saint Blue-Ring? Not Saint Humboldt? They're your fighting saints.* He said that because I was big like him and everyone knew I was going to be a soldier. *Why Saint Argonaut?* he goes. *Because of that pretty spiral it makes,* I says."

Dane smiled beautifully, and Billy smiled back. He pictured the intricately fanned fractal eggcase Dane was describing, which gave the argonaut its other name. "Paper nautilus," he said.

"He was a tough man, but he loved that," Dane said.

When Dane went to the bathroom again, Billy opened the little bottle and dripped several bitter drops of the squid ink onto his tongue. He lay back and waited in the dark. But even with all the adrenalin of that day, and the inadequate snack supper, he went quickly to blank sleep, and outraced any visions or dreams.

Chapter Twenty-Three

WHAT MARGINALIA WAS THINKING WAS, *WHAT THE HELL IS going on?*

When Leon still did not answer any messages, she tried Billy, who did not answer either. She managed to persuade a locksmith of her bona fides, and at last got into Leon's flat. Nothing was out of place. There was no hint to his location. She did not know Billy's friends or family to call them.

Marge had walked into the police station closest to her when Leon had gone and not come back, when neither he nor Billy would answer their phones. She had reported two missing persons. The officers treated her with brusque sympathy, but they told her the number of people who disappeared every year, every week, and they told her how many soon returned from drunken trips or absentminded weekends. They told her it was best if she didn't worry too much, and they warned her not to expect too much.

To her own great surprise, Marge began to cry in the station. The police were embarrassed and cack-handedly sweet, offering her tea and tissues. When she calmed down she went home, expecting nothing and not knowing what to do. But within an hour and a half of getting back (certain keywords coming up in the report of her visit, correlating with other words, the names she had mentioned attracting attention, Leon's imperfectly recollected but telling last text, red-flagged on computer systems not nearly so hopeless as ostentatiously cynical commentators would claim) there was a knock at her door. A middle-aged man in a suit and a very young blonde woman offhandedly in police uniform. The woman carried a leash, but was not followed by any dog.

"Hello," the man said. He had a thin voice. "It's Miss Tilley, isn't it? My name's Baron. DCI Baron. This is my colleague PC Collingswood. We need a word. I wonder if we might come in?"

Inside, Collingswood turned slowly, a full circle, taking in the dark walls, the posters for video events and basement electronica parties. Baron and Collingswood did not sit, though Marge gestured them at the sofa. She got a breath of some earthy, porky smell, and blinked.

"I gather you've mislaid some friends, Miss Tilley," Baron said. Marge considered correcting him, *Ms.* did not bother.

"I wasn't expecting to see you," she said. "At your office they told me you couldn't really do anything."

"Ah, well, they don't know what we know. What relation are you to Billy Harrow?"

"Billy? None at all. It's Leon I'm with."

"With?"

"I told you."

"You haven't told me anything, Miss Tilley."

"I told them at the station. He's my lover."

Collingswood rolled her eyes and wobbled her head, *La di fucking da.* She click-clicked, as if at an animal, gestured with her chin toward the other rooms.

"And you haven't heard anything from Leon since he went to meet Billy?" Baron said.

"I didn't even know for sure that's where he'd gone. How come you came so fast? I mean they said not to expect . . ." She opened her mouth in a sudden zero of terror. "Oh God, have you *found* him . . . ?"

"No no," said Baron. "Nothing like that. What it is is this is one of those dovetailing situations. Collingswood and I, we're not generally Missing Persons, you see. We're from a different squad. But we got a heads-up about your problem, because it may have bearing on our case."

Marge stared at him. ". . . The squid thing? Is that what you're investigating?"

"Fu-u-u-ck!" said Collingswood. "I *knew* it. That little bastard."

"Ah." Baron raised his eyebrows mildly. "Yes. We sort of wondered if Billy'd been able to resist a natter."

"Got to give it to him, boss, for someone who don't know what he's doing, he's got some clout. Come on, you." She said the last to no one, so far as Marge could tell.

"We'd much rather you kept whatever he mentioned to yourself, if you don't mind, Miss Tilley."

"You think this has something to do with Leon going missing?" Marge said, incredulous. "And Billy? Where do you think they are?"

"Well, that's what we're looking into," Baron said. "And you can rest assured we'll let you know as soon as we know anything. Was Billy talking a lot about the squid? Had Leon been to see it? Was he a regular at the museum?"

"What? No, not at all. I mean, he'd seen it once, I think. But he wasn't that interested."

"Did he talk to you about it?"

"Leon?" she said. "You mean did he tell me about it disappearing? He thought it was hilarious. I mean he knew it was a big deal for Billy. But it was so weird, you know? He had to take the piss. I wasn't even a hundred percent sure if Billy was bullshitting, you know?"

"Yeah, no," Collingswood said.

"Why on earth would you think he'd make something like that up?" Baron said.

"Well. It hasn't been in the news or anything, has it?"

"No," said Baron. "Ah, but therein, therein is a tale. Of gag orders the like of which you've no idea." He smiled.

"Anyway, it's not like Leon *approved* of it. He just . . . the whole idea of it made him laugh. He texted me some joke about it before he . . ."

"Oh yeah," said Collingswood. "It is quite the riot."

"Come on," said Marge. "Someone nicked a giant squid. Come on."

"What can you tell us about Billy?" Baron said. "What do you think of him?"

"Billy? I don't know. He's alright. I don't really know him. He's Leon's friend. Why are you asking?"

Baron glanced at Collingswood. She shook her head and tugged the lead. "Not a sausage," she said. "Ooh, sorry Perky."

"What's going on?" Marge said.

"We're just doing some detecting, Miss Tilley," Baron said.

"Should I . . . ? How worried should I be?"

"Oh, not very," he said. "Would you, Kath?"

"Nah." Collingswood was texting someone.

"You know the more I think about it, I don't think this is related to what we're up to. So if I were you I wouldn't worry."

"Yeah," said Collingswood, still thumbing her message. "Nah."

"Now," said Baron, "obviously we'll let you know if we realise otherwise. But I must say I'm doubtful. Many thanks." He nodded. He touched his forefinger to the brow of his nonexistent cap; *Cheerio then.*

"Hey, what?" Marge said. "Is that it?" Collingswood was already by the door, popping her collars like a dandy. She winked at Marge. "What just happened?" Marge said. "Are you going? What happens now?"

Collingswood said to her, "Rest assured we're going to leave no stone unturned in our search for wossname and thingy."

Marge gasped. Baron said, "Now, Kath." He shook his head, rolled his eyes at Marge like a tired father. "Miss Tilley, as soon as we have any ideas of what's going on, we'll be straight back in touch."

"Did you *hear* what she *said*?"

"Kath," Baron said, "off you go, get in the car. I did, I did, Miss Tilley. And I apologise."

"I want to make a complaint." Marge shook. She clenched and unclenched her fists.

"Of course. It's absolutely your right to do so. You have to understand it's just a question of Collingswood's gallows humour. She's an excellent officer, and that's her way of dealing with the trauma we have to see every day. Not that it's any excuse, I grant you. So you go ahead, it might shape her up." He paused on his way out, his hand on the doorway. "I'll let her know I'm very disappointed in her."

"Wait, you can't just leave now. How do I get in touch with you if I need . . . ?"

"Your local station gave you a contact officer, right?" Baron said. "Go through her. She'll pass on any information to me and my squad."

"What the *hell*? You can't just suddenly . . ." But the door was closing, and though she shouted demands to know what was going on, Marge did not follow the officers. She leaned against the door until a strong feeling that she would cry passed. She said to herself out loud, "What the fuck was that?"

What was it? It was a judgement call, and a bad one. It had been a hunch of the kind one infrequently hears about: a hunch that was wrong.

"Not a fucking thing," Collingswood said. She lit a cigarette. The little winter wind snatched its smoke. "She doesn't know shit," Collingswood said.

"Agreed," said Baron.

"And none of this has shit to do with her. We're not going to get anything with that one."

"Agreed," said Baron.

"No one's hexed bollock all anywhere near that flat," Collingswood said. "Not like bloody Billy's." Someone or someones with soul or souls starched with witchery of one or other sort had certainly been *there*. At Billy's place her poor aetherial animal companion had swivelled and whined and squealed so loud even Baron could hear him.

"You know there ain't much stuff going on at the moment," Collingswood said. "With everyone scared shitless of the UMA. So whatever trails get left would stick out more. You saw the piggy." She shook the lead. "Well, I mean, you didn't, but you know what I mean. Bloody nothing. So what's the story? This Leon geezer part of something?"

"Doubtful," Baron said. "From everything we can get he's absolutely nothing. Just some typical everyday tosser." He made a *brrrr* sound with his lips. "If he's got anything to do with the kraken he's been in deep cover for God knows how long. I think he's just got snagged." Collingswood listened for text-thoughts. She felt for her brief familiar sniffing the faint para-scent trails of what magery was in that street.

"Well, poor little sod," she said.

"Quite. I doubt we'll see him again. Or Billy."

"Unless Billy's our villain." They pondered. "Did you hear what Vardy was going on about this morning?"

"Where *is* that man?" Baron said. "What's he up to?"

Collingswood shrugged. "I dunno. He said something about chasing up Adler's religious life."

"Did he have one?"

"I dunno, guv. I'm not the one chasing. But did you hear what he said this morning? About the Krakenists?"

There were rumours already, of course, about all aspects of the theft, the murder, the mysteries. Nothing could stop rumours moving faster than horses. It was part of Baron's and Collingswood's job to overhear them. Vardy's theological snitches had told him, and he had told his colleagues, that there were whispers of the shunning of high-profile worshippers in the teuthic church.

There was also, still, that growing apocalypse mutter.

It was a seller's market for relics right then. Who could doubt that religion and organised crime were linked? As the bishops of one secret Catholic order asked whenever questions of business ethics arose, was Saint Calvi martyred to teach us *nothing*?

"So do we still think it's definitely godders did this?" Collingswood said. She sniffed. "Krakenists or whatnot? Or is it maybe just fucking crooks?"

"Your guess," Baron said, "is as good as mine. Fact it's probably considerably better."

"I'm still getting bollock all from snitches," Collingswood said. She sniffed again.

"Whoa," Baron said. "You're . . . here." He handed her a tissue. Her nose was bleeding.

"Oh you little fucking wankface," Collingswood said. She pinched the top of her nose. "You cuntbandit."

"Jesus, Kath, you alright? What's all that?"

"It's just tension, boss."

"Tense? On a beautiful day like this?" She glared at him. "What's got your goat?"

"Nothing. It's not like that. It's just . . ." She raised her hands. "It's all this. It's the fucking Panda."

Through a meandering chain of half-arsed jokes, that was the name Collingswood and Baron had given the end on the edge of things. The end for which even the most tentatively apocalyptic faith was preparing. The magic reek of it had Collingswood, as a knack-smith, on edge: toothached, crampy, unsettled. She had been referring to that fearful approaching whatever-it-was repeatedly, until Baron had suggested giving it a shorthand. It had started as Big Bad Wolf, from where it had quickly become Sausage Dog, and ultimately Panda. The nickname did not help Collingswood feel any better about it.

"Whatever it is has to do with the fucking squid," she said. "If we knew who'd taken the bugger . . ."

"We know who the top suspects are. Certainly if anyone in the office asks." The devout might pay a lot for the corpse of a god. The FSRC listened and *fished*, ho ho, for word of the secretive Church of God Kraken. But the disappearance might be a more profane, though knacked and abnatural, crime. And that would be a complication.

Bureaucracies turf-war. The FSRC were the only officers in the Met who were anything other than blitheringly inadequate to deal with the eldritch nonsense of knackery. They were the state's witches and hammers of witches. But their remit was a historical quirk. There were no Wizardry Squads in the UK Police. No SO21 to police Crimes of Magic. The Flying Squad did not. There was only the FSRC, and technically they were not concerned with the powers of ley lines, charmed words, invoked entities, et cetera—they were a *cult* squad, specifically.

In practice of course it was staffed by and kept watch on all those with questionable talents. FSRC computers were loaded with occult hexware and abgrades (Geas 2.0, iScry). But the unit was obliged to maintain appearances by describing all its work in terms of the policing of religion. They had to take care, if they concluded that it *was* purely secular abcriminality behind the *Architeuthis* disappearance, to stress what links they could with London's heresiarchs. Otherwise they would lose jurisdiction. Without cult-games at the heart of the squidnapping, it would be handed over to some brusque unsubtle unit—Serious Crime, Organised Crime. Antiquities.

"God preserve us," Collingswood said.

"Just hypothetically," Baron said. "Between you and me. If this *is* crims, not godsquadders, you know who our top suspect is."

"Tat-fucking-too," said Collingswood.

Baron's phone went. "Yeah," he said into it. He listened and stopped walking. He looked sick, and sicker, and old.

"What?" Collingswood said. "What, boss?"

"Alright," he said. "We'll be there." He shut the phone. "Goss and Subby," he said. "I think they found out that Anders gave them to us. Someone . . . Oh, bugger me. You'll see."

Chapter Twenty-Four

WHEN BILLY WOKE HE REALISED THAT HIS DREAMS HAD BEEN nothing but the usual cobbled-together fag-ends of meaning.

Why wouldn't the gods of the world be giant squid? What better beast? It wouldn't take much to imagine those tentacles closing around the world, now would it?

He knew he was at war now. Billy stepped out into it. It wasn't his city anymore, it was a combat zone. He looked up at sudden noises. He was a guerrilla, behind Dane. Dane wanted his god; Billy wanted freedom and revenge. Whatever Dane said, Billy wanted revenge for Leon and for the loss of any sense of his own life, and being at war with the Tattoo gave him at least a tiny chance for that. Right?

They were simply disguised. Hair flattened out for Billy, teased up for Dane. Dane wore a tracksuit; Billy was absurd in clothes stolen from the imaginary student. He blinked like the escapee he was, watched Londoners hurrying. Dane took a couple of seconds to open a new car.

"You got some magic key?" Billy said.

"Don't be a twat," Dane said. He was just using some criminal finger technique. Billy looked around the vehicle's interior—there was a paperback, empty water bottles, scattered paper. He hoped with a hopeless sense of fret that this theft would not hurt someone he would *like*, someone *nice*. It was a pitiful equivocation.

"So . . ." Billy said. Here he was, in the trenches. "What's the plan? We're taking it to them, right?"

"Hunting," Dane said. "We have leads to follow. But this is dangerous? I'm . . . Now I'm rogue you and me need some help. It ain't true we got no allies. I know a few people. We're going to the BL."

"What?"

"The British Library."

"*What?* I thought you wanted us to keep a low profile."

"Yeah. I know. It ain't a good place for us."

"So why . . ."

"Because we have a god to find," Dane snapped. "Alright? And because we need help. It's a risk, yeah, but it's mostly beginners' territory. People who know what they want go other places."

There was magery there, he said, but strictly newbie. For serious stuff you looked elsewhere. A deserted swimming pool in Peckham; the tower of Kilburn's Gaumont State, no longer a cinema nor a bingo hall. In the meat locker of an Angus Steak House off Shaftsbury Avenue were the texts powerful enough to shift position when the librarians were not looking, which were said to whisper lies they wanted the reader to hear.

"Keep your mouth shut, keep your eyes open, watch and learn, show respect," Dane said. "And don't forget we're hunted, so you see *anything*, tell me. Keep your head down. Be ready to run."

It rained, briefly. When it rains, Dane quoted his grandfather, it's a kraken shaking the water off its tentacles. When the wind blows, it's the breath from its siphon. The sun, Dane said, is a glint of biophosphor in a kraken's skin.

"I keep thinking about Leon," Billy said. "I need to . . . I should tell his family. Or Marge. She should know . . ." It was nearly too heavy to articulate his feelings like that, and he had to stop speaking.

"You ain't telling no one," Dane said. "You ain't talking to no one. You stay underground."

The city felt like it was hesitating. Like a bowling ball on a hilltop, fat with potential energy. Billy recalled the snake unhinging of Goss's jaw, bones jostling and a mouth with precipitous reconfiguration a doorway. Dane drove past a small gallery and a dry cleaners, a market collection of junk, tchotchkes in multiplicity, urban twee.

• • •

IN FRONT OF THE BRITISH LIBRARY, IN THE GREAT FORECOURT, A little crowd was gathered. Students and other researchers, laptops clutched, in trendy severe spectacles and woolly scarves. They were gaping and laughing.

What they stared at was a little group of cats, walking in a complicated quadrille, languidly purposeful. Four were black, one tortoiseshell. They circled and circled. They were not scattering nor squabbling. They described their routes in dignified fashion.

Far enough away to be safe but still startlingly close were three pigeons. They strutted in their own circle. The paths of the two groups of animals almost overlapped.

"Can you believe it?" said one girl. She smiled at Billy in his foolish clothes. "You ever seen such a well-behaved bunch? I love cats."

Most of the students, after a minute or two of amused watching, went past the cats into the library. There were a very few among the crowd, though, who looked not in humour but consternation. None of these men or women entered. They did not cross the stalked lines. Though it was early and they had only just arrived, on seeing the little gathering they would leave.

"What's going on?" said Billy. Dane headed to the centre of the forecourt, where a giant figure waited. He was uneasy being out. He looked constantly to all sides, led Billy with a kind of cringing pugnacity toward the twenty-foot statue of Newton. The imagined scientist hunched, examining the earth, his compass measuring distance. A tremendous misunderstanding, it seemed, Blake's glowering ecstatic grumble at myopia mistranslated by Paolozzi as splendid and autarch.

A broad man stood by the figure, in a puffy jacket and woolly hat and glasses. He carried a plastic bag. He looked to be muttering to himself. "Dane," someone said. Billy turned, but there was no one in earshot. The hatted man waved at Dane, warily. His bag was full of copies of a left-wing newspaper.

"Martin," said Dane. "Wati." He nodded to the man, and the statue. "Wati, I need your help—"

"Shut your mouth," a voice said. Dane stepped backward in obvious shock. "I will talk to you in a sodding minute."

It spoke in a whisper, with a unique accent. It was between London and something bizarre and unplaced. It was a metal whisper. Billy knew it was the statue that spoke.

"Uh, okay," the man with the newspapers said. "You've got stuff to do, I'm going to split. I'll see you Wednesday."

"Alright," the statue said. Its lips did not move. It did not move at all—it was a statue—but the voice was whispered from its barrel-sized mouth. "Tell herself I said hi."

"Alright," the man said. "Later. Good luck. Solidarity to that lot." He glanced at the cats. A nod good-bye to Dane, and one to Billy too. The man left a paper between Isaac Newton's feet.

Dane and Billy stood together. The statue stayed heavily sat. "You come to me?" it said. "To *me*? You have got some nerve, Dane."

Dane shook his head. He said quietly, "Oh, man. You heard . . ."

"I thought there'd been a mistake," the voice said. "I got told, and I was like, no, that's not possible, Dane wouldn't do that. He'd never do that. I put a couple of watchers on your place *to get you off the hook*. Understand? How long I known you, Dane? I can't believe you."

"Wati," said Dane. He was plaintive. Billy had never heard him like this before. Even arguing with the Teuthex, his pope, he had been surly. Now he wheedled. "Please, Wati, you have to believe me. I had no choice. Please hear me out."

"What do you think you can say to me?" the Newton said.

"Wati, please. I ain't saying what I done was right, but you owe me to at least listen. Don't you? Just that?"

Billy looked between the hunching metal man and the kraken-cultist. "You know Davey's café?" the statue said. "I'll see you there in a minute. And as far as I'm concerned it's to say good-bye, Dane. I just can't believe you, Dane. I can't believe you were scabbing."

Noiselessly, something went. Billy blinked.

"What was that?" he said. "Who've we been talking to?"

"An old friend of mine," Dane said heavily. "Who's rightly pissed off. Rightly. That fucking squirrel. Idiot I am. I didn't have time, I didn't think I could risk it. I was racing." He looked at Billy. "It's your bloody fault. Nah, mate, I'm not really blaming you. You didn't know." He sighed. "This is . . ." He gestured at the statue, now empty.

Billy did not know how he knew that. "That was, I mean, the head of the committee. The shop steward."

Readers approached the library, saw the little groups of animals, laughed and continued or, those who looked as if they understood something, hesitated and left. The presence of the circling creatures barred them.

"You see what's going on," Dane said. Miserably he ran his hands over his head. "*That* is a picket line, and *I* am in trouble."

"A picket? The cats and birds?"

Dane nodded. "The familiars are on strike."

Chapter Twenty-Five

FROM THE ELEVENTH DYNASTY, THE DAWN OF THE MIDDLE Kingdom, many centuries before the birth of the man Christ, the better-off dwellers by the Nile were concerned to maintain their quality of life, in death.

Were there not fields in the afterworld? Did the crops of the night-lands, the farms of each of the hours of the night, not need harvesting and tending? Were there not households and the tasks that would mean? How could a man of power, who would never work his own land while alive, be expected to do so dead?

In the tombs, by their mummied masters, the shabtis were placed. They would do it.

They were made to do it. Created for those specifics. Little figures in clay or wax, stone, bronze, crude glass, or the glazed earthware faience, dusted with oxide. Shaped at first in imitation of their overlords like tiny dead in funeral wrappings, later without that coy dissembling, made instead holding adzes, hoes and baskets, integral tools cut or cast as part of their mineral serf bodies.

The hosts of figurines grew more numerous over centuries, until there was one to work each day of the year. Servants of, workers for the rich dead, rendered to render, to perform what had to be done in that posthumous mode of production, to work the fields for the blessed deceased.

Each was inscribed at its making with the sixth chapter of the Book of the Dead. *Oh shabti, allotted me*, their skins read. *If I be summoned or decreed to do any work which must be done in the place of the dead, remove all obstacles that stand in the way, detail yourself to me to plough the fields, to flood the banks, to carry sand from east to west. "Here I am," you shall say. "I shall do it."*

Their purpose was written on the body. *Here I am. I shall do it.*

THERE IS NO KNOWING BEYOND THAT MEMBRANE, THE MENISCUS OF death. What can be seen from here is distorted, refracted. All we can know are those untrustworthy glimpses—that and rumour. The prattle. The dead gossip: it is the reverberation of that gossip against the surface tension of death that the better mediums hear. It is like listening to whispered secrets through a toilet door. It is a crude and muffled susurrus.

We gather, we intuit or think we have heard and understood, that there was effort in that place. There in Neter-Khertet, the flickered, judged dead of the kingdom had been trained into belief, strong enough to shape their post-death life into something like a cold unstable mimicking of their splendid eschatology. A vivid tableau imitated in stones, electricity and gruel. (What function of that post-dead stuff coagulated and thought itself Anubis? What Ammit the Heart-eater?)

For centuries the shabtis did what they were tasked. *Here I am*, they said in the dark unsound, and cut the uncrops, and harvested them, and channelled the not-water of death, carried the remembrance of sand. Made to do, mindless serf-things obeying dead lords.

Until at last one shabti paused by the riverbank-analogues, and stopped. Dropped the bundled shadow-harvest it had cut, and took the tools it was built carrying to its own clay skin. Effaced the holy text it had been made wearing.

Here I am, it shouted in what passed there for its voice. *I shall* not *do it.*

"IT NAMED ITSELF WATI," DANE SAID. " 'THE REBEL.' HE WAS MADE IN *Set Maat her imenty Waset.*" He said the strange place carefully. "Now called Deir el-Medina. In the twenty-ninth year of Ramses Three."

They were in a new car. There was something giddying about the new accoutrements they ferried with each theft: the different toys, books, papers, debris ignored on each back seat.

"The royal tomb-builders weren't paid for days," Dane said. "They downed tools. About 1100 BC. They were the first strikers. I think it was one of them builders that built it. The shabti."

Carved by a rebel, that *ressentiment* flowing through the fingers and the chisel and defining it? Made by the emotions that made it?

"Nah," said Dane. "I think they *watched* each other. Either Wati or his maker learnt by example."

SELF-NAMED WATI LED THE FIRST-EVER STRIKE IN THE AFTERLIFE. It escalated. That first revolt of the shabti, the uprising of the made.

Insurrection in Neter-Khertet. Murderous fighting among the constructed, the smithed servants, split between rebels, the afraid, and the still-obedient, slave armies of the loyal. They shattered each other in the fields of the spirits. All confused, none used to the emotions they had accreted by some accident of agency, their capacity to choose their allegiance bewildering. The dead watched aghast, huddled among the ash-reeds of the river of death. Overseer gods came running from their own hours to demand order, horrified by the chaos in those bone-cold agricultural lands.

It was a brutal war of human spirits and quasi-souls made out of anger. Shabti killing shabti, killing the already dead, in heretic acts of meta-murder, sending the appalled souls of the deceased into some further afterlife about which nothing has ever been known.

The fields were full of the corpses of souls. Shabti were slaughtered in hundreds by gods but they killed gods too. *The crude features of comrades no one had bothered to carve with precision making their own expressions out of the indistinct impressions given them, taking their axes and ploughs and the fucking baskets they were built carrying in a swarm over bodies the size of mountains with jackal heads howling and eating them but being overrun by us and hacked with our stupid weapons and killed.*

Wati and his comrades won. You can bet that meant a change.

It must have been a shock for succeeding generations of highborn Egyptian dead. To wake in a strange fogged underworld scandalously off-message. The rituals of posthumous hierarchy to which their corpses had been piously subjected turned out to be antique, overthrown mummery. They and the worker-statue-spirit household they had had made to come with them were met by disrespectful representatives of the new shabti nation. Their own figurines swiftly recruited to the polity of that shadeland. The human dead were told, *If you work, you may eat.*

CENTURIES AND SOCIAL SYSTEMS GO, AND IMMIGRATION TO THAT afterland slows and ceases, and piece by piece and without complaint the shabti and those human souls who had made their peace with the rough democracy of the shabti deadland farmers fade, go out, move on, un-be, pass over, are no longer there. There is not much sadness. It is history, is all.

Wati will have none of that.

Here I am. I shall not do it.

He moved too, at last, but he moved not beyond nor to any dark or light but sideways, through borders between belief-worlds.

An epic trek, that curious passage through foreign afterlifes. Always toward the source of the river or the beginning of the road. Swimming *up* through Murimuria, passing *up* through the caverns of Naraka and the shade of Yomi, crossing the rivers Tuoni and Styx *from the farthest shore back*, to the ferrymen's consternation, through a kaleidoscope flutter of lands, passing psychopomps of all traditions who had to pause with the new dead they were escorting and whisper to Wati, *You're going the wrong way.*

Northers in bearskins, women in saris and kimonos, funerary glad-rags, bronze-armoured mercenaries, the axes that had killed them bouncing bloody and politely ignored in their pretend-flesh like giant skin tags, all astonished by the militant inhuman statue-shade ascending, astonished by this contrary wayfarer of whom *bugger-all* was written in any of the reams of pantheon-specific wittering about what the dead would face, all staring frankly at this intruder, this unplaced class-guerrilla in the myth, or glancing from under brows and introducing themselves politely or not, depending on the cultural norms they had not yet learned were for the living.

Wati the rebel did not reply. Continued up from the underlands. It's a long way, whichever death you take. Occasionally Wati the retro-eschatonaut might look at those approaching and, hearing a name, or seeing a remembered resemblance, say to the new-deads' surprise, *Oh I met your father* (or whomever) *miles back*, until generations of the dead told stories of the wrong-walker trudging out of a redundant heaven, and debated what sort of seer or whatever he was and considered it good luck to bump into him on their final journey. Wati was a fable told by the long- to the new-dead. Until, until, out he came, through the door to Annwn or the pearly gates or the entrance to Mictlan (he wasn't paying attention), and here. Where the air is, where the living live.

In a place where there was more to do than journey, Wati looked and saw relations he remembered.

With some somatic nostalgia for his first form he entered the bodies of statues. He saw orders given and received, and it fired him up again. There was too much to do, too much to rectify. Wati sought out those like he had been. Those constructed, enchanted, enhanced by magic to do what humans told them. He became their organiser.

He started with the most egregious cases: magicked slaves; brooms forced to carry water buckets; clay men made to fight and die; little figures made of blood and choiceless about what they did. Wati fomented rebellions. He persuaded knack-formed assistants and servants to stand up, to insist to themselves that they were not defined by their creators or empowerers or the magic scribbles stuck under their tongues, to demand compensation, payment, freedom.

There was an art. He watched organisers of peasant revolts and communard monks, machine-wreckers and Chartists, and learned their methods. Insurrection was not always suitable. Though he retained a hankering for it, he was pragmatist enough to know when reforms were right for the moment.

Wati organised among golems, homunculi, robotish things made by alchemists and made slaves. The mandrakes born and bonded under gallows and treated like discardable weeds. Phantom rickshaw drivers, their hours and pay mysterious and pitiful. Those created creations were treated like tools that talked, their sentience an annoying product of magic noise, by those little mortal demiurges who thought dominion a natural by-product of expertise or creation.

Wati spread his word among brutalised familiars. That old *droit de prestidigitateur* was poison. With the help of Wati's rage and the self-organised uncanny, *quids pro quo* were demanded and often won. Minimums of recompense, in energy, specie, kind or something. Magicians, anxious at the unprecedented rebellions, agreed.

As the last but one century died, the New Unionism took London and changed it, and inspired Wati in his unseen side of the city. In their dolls and toby jugs, he learned from and collaborated with Tillett and Mann and Miss Eleanor Marx. With a fervour that resonated hard in the strange parts of the city, the hidden layers, Wati declared the formation of the UMA, the Union of Magicked Assistants.

Chapter Twenty-Six

"So Wati's pissed off with you."

"There's a strike on," Dane said. "Total knack stoppage. That's why they're picketing places where conditions are bad."

"And they are at the BL?"

Dane nodded. "You would not believe it."

"What's it all about?"

"It started small," Dane said. "These things always do. Something about the hours some magus was making his ravens work. It didn't look like it would kick off, but then he tries to play hardball, so there's a sympathy strike at a box factory where the robots are unionised—they got minds in a mageslick, few years ago—and the next thing you know . . ." He slapped the dashboard. "Whole city's out.

"It's the first big thing since Thatcher. And nothing gets the knacksmiths more antsy. Everyone in the UMA's out, it's solid. And then I had an emergency. I knew you was being watched. I *knew* you were, and I *had* to track you, because I didn't know what you had to do with the whole *god* thing. The kraken being took. I didn't even know what your deal was, I didn't know if you were in on anything, or had some plan or what. But I knew you were tied up with it. And I couldn't keep an eye on you twenty-four/seven, so I had to organise a short-term binding with that little sod."

"The squirrel?"

"The familiar." Dane winced. "I been strikebreaking. And Wati got word. I don't blame him being pissed off. If he can't trust his friends, you know? There's all dirty tricks. People are getting hurt. Someone got killed. A journo writing about it. No one knows for sure it's connected, but of *course* it's connected. You know? So Wati's edgy. We have to sort this. I want him on our side. We do *not* want to be on the shitlist of all the pissed-off UMA in London."

Billy looked at him. "It's not just that, though." He took off and put back on his glasses.

"No it ain't," Dane said. "I'm not a scab. I didn't have time . . ." He slumped in his seat. "Alright. It wasn't just that. I was worried if I went and asked for dispensation, the union wouldn't say yes. They might not think it was serious enough. And I *needed* it. I had to have more eyes, and something that could get places fast. And you should be happy I did or you'd have been took to Tattoo's workshop.

"The bastard is I *never* use familiars." He shook his head, repeatedly. "It was just crap luck. It was just crap, crap luck, the timing."

WATI MOVED IN ELDRITCH LEAPFROGGING, STATUE TO STATUE, FIGure to figurine, consciousness momentarily in each. Just long enough to see through the stone eyes in a horse rider in a park; wooden eyes on a Jesus outside a church; plastic eyes in a discarded clothes model; taking bearings, feeling to the limits of his range, some scores of metres, briefly considering each potential figure within his arc, choosing the most suitable according to criteria, transferring his thinks-node into that next human-made head.

He met Dane and Billy in the café in the back streets near Holborn, where for years the plaster mannequin of a fat chef had held up fingers in an "O" meaning delicious right next to an outside table, so where, if Dane and Billy put up with the chill, huddling over coffees, Wati could en-statue close enough to converse with them. They hunkered against the cold and the possibility of being seen. Dane looked repeatedly around them.

"Like I say, Dane, this better be good," the Wati-chef said through a motionless openmouthed smile. Its accent remained—Cockney plus the New Kingdom?—but the voice was choky, now, and clogged-sounding.

"Wati, this is Billy," said Dane. Billy greeted the statue. He greeted a statue and disguised his awe. "He's what this is all about." Dane cleared his throat. "You can feel it, right, Wati? The sky, the air, all this shit. History ain't working. Something's coming up. That's what this is about. I bet you can feel it. Between statues."

There was silence. "Maybe," said Wati. Was it gusting he sensed? Billy wondered. A dislocation? Something foreboding in that inter-effigial unspace? "Maybe."

"Alright. Well then. You heard . . . the kraken got took?"

"'Course I did. The angels can't shut up about it. I even went to the museum," Wati said. No lack there of the bodies in which he could be. He could rush around the interior of the hall in a whirlwind of entities, skimming, skipping from animal to stone animal. "The phylax is screaming in the corridors. It's walking, you know. It's looking for something, it's on a trail. You can hear it at night."

"What's this?" Billy said.

"The angels of memory," Dane said.

"What are . . . ?" said Billy, then stopped at Dane's shaken head. *Alright*, he thought, *we'll get back to that.*

"It's all screwed up," Wati said.

"It is," Dane said. "We need to find the kraken, Wati. No one knows who took it. I thought it was the Tattoo, but then . . . He took Billy. Was going to do him. And the way he was talking . . . Most people think it was *us*." He paused. "The church. But it weren't. They ain't even *looking* for it. When the kraken went, this thing underneath it all started rising."

"Talk to me about scabbing, Dane," Wati said. "Do I need to talk to your Teuthex about this?"

"No!" Dane shouted. People looked. He slid down, spoke quietly again. "You can't. Can't tell them where I am. I'm out, Wati." He looked into the statue's unmoving face. "Shunned."

The plaster of the chef, unchanging, took on shock. "Oh my gods, Dane," Wati said at last. "I heard something, someone said something, I thought it was garbled bullshit, though . . ."

"They're not going to do anything," Dane said. "*Nothing*. I needed help, Wati, and I needed it fast. They were going to kill Billy. And whoever's took it's doing something with the kraken that's bringing up this badness. That's when it started. That's the *only reason* I did what I did. You know me. I'll do whatever I have to to fix this. What I'm saying is I'm sorry."

DANE TOLD WATI THE STORY. "IT WAS BAD ENOUGH WHEN THIS LOT brought it up, put it in their tank." Billy was shocked at the anger with which Dane stared at him, suddenly. He had never seen that before. *I thought you liked the tank*, he thought. *The Teuthex said . . .* "But since it's gone it's got worse. We have to find it. Billy knows things. I needed to get him out. Wati, it was Goss and Subby."

There was a long silence. "I heard that," the statue said. "Someone said he was back. I didn't know if it was true."

"Goss and Subby are back," Dane said. "And they're working for the Tattoo. They're on the move. They're doing their work. They were taking Billy to the workshop."

"Who is he? Who are you?" Wati said to Billy. "Why are they after you?"

"I'm no one," Billy said. He saw himself talking to a plastic or plaster pizza man. Could almost have smiled.

"It was him who preserved the kraken," Dane said. "Put it behind glass."

"I'm no one," Billy said. "Up until a couple of days ago I . . ." How to even start.

"He likes to say he's no one," Dane said. "Tattoo and Goss and Subby don't think so. He knows things."

There was quiet for seconds. Billy played with his coffee.

"A squirrel, though?" Wati said.

Dane stared at the frozen delighted face of the chef, risked a snorting laugh. "I was desperate, bro," he said.

"You couldn't have got, like, an adder or a jackdaw or something?"

"I was looking for a part-timer," Dane said. "All the best familiars are union, I didn't have much choice. You should be pleased. You're solid. I had to go with whatever dregs were around."

"Did you think I wouldn't find out?"

"I'm sorry. I was desperate. I shouldn't have done it. I should've asked."

"Yeah you should," said Wati. Dane breathed out. "You only get one fuckup like that. And that only because I known you since time." Dane nodded. "Why did you come see me?" Wati said. "You didn't just come to apologise, did you?"

"Not only that," said Dane.

"Cheeky bugger," said Wati. "You're going to ask for help." He started to laugh, but Dane interrupted.

"Yeah," he said without humour. "You know what, I am, and I ain't going to apologise. I do need your help. We do. And I don't just mean me and Billy, I mean everyone. If we don't find the god, whatever's coming's going to get here. Someone's doing something with that kraken they really shouldn't oughter."

"We're *out*, Dane," Wati said. "What do you even want from me?"

"I understand," Dane said. "But you have to understand too. Whatever it is . . . If we don't stop it it won't matter if you win your strike. I'm not saying call it off. I would never tell you that. I'm saying you can't afford to ignore this. We have to find God. We ain't the only ones looking. The longer it's out there it's *meaning* more and more, and that means it's more and more powerful. So more and more people are after it. Imagine if Tattoo gets his hands on it." On the corpse, corpus, of an emergent baby god, traveller from below to above."

"What's your plan?" Wati said.

Dane brought out his list. "I reckon this is all the people in London could port something as big as the kraken. We can track down who got it out."

"Hold it up," Wati said. Dane, making sure he was not watched, held the list in the statue's eyeline. "There's, what . . . twenty people here?" Wati said.

"Twenty-three."

"Going to take you a while." Dane said nothing. "Have you got a copy of that? Wait."

There was a gust, a palpable leaving. Dane began to smile. After a minute a sparrow flew down and landed on Billy's hand. He started.

Even his jump did not dislodge the bird. It looked him and Dane up and down.

"Go on then, give her the list," said Wati in the statue again. "She's not your familiar, you get it? Not even temporarily. She's *my* friend, and she's doing *me* a favour. Let's see what we can find out."

Chapter Twenty-Seven

Her boss was sympathetic but could not hold things forever. Marge had to return to work.

Leon's mother said she was coming to London. She and Marge had never met, nor even spoken until the awkward phone call Marge had made to tell her about Leon's disappearance. The woman obviously neither knew nor wanted to know details of Leon's life. She thanked Marge for "keeping her up to date."

"I'm not sure that's the best way to do it," she had said when Marge suggested they work together to try to find out what had happened.

"I don't feel like the police . . ." Marge had said. "I mean I'm sure they're doing what they can, but, you know, they're busy and we might be able to think of stuff that they can't. We could keep on looking, you know?" His mother had said she would contact Marge if she found anything out, but neither of them thought she would. So Marge did not mention Leon's last message.

When she said, "I'll let you know if I find anything out, too," she was aware abruptly that she was not making a promise to the woman as much as to herself, to the universe, to Leon, to something, to not leave this, to not stop. Marge went through anger, panic, resignation, sadness. Sometimes—how could she not?—she tried out the thought that she had been very wrong about him, that Leon had just deserted her and his entire life. Maybe he had been involved in a scam gone wrong, was mentally ill, baying somewhere on a Cornish coast or Dundee, was no longer who he had been. The ideas did not stick.

She sent Leon's mother the keys to his flat that she had had cut, but cut more copies first. She sneaked in and went from room to room, as if she might soak up some clue. For some time each room was as she remembered it, down to the mess, even. She turned up one day and the flat was a shell: his family had taken Leon's things away.

The police to whom Marge spoke, those to whom she *could* speak, still implied that there was little to worry about, or, as time went on, little they could do. What Marge wanted was to speak to those other, odder police visitors. Repeated calls to the Scotland Yard would not yield any confirmation that they existed. The Barons whose numbers she was given were none of them the right man. There were no Collingswoods.

Were they who they had claimed? Were they a gang of miscreants hunting Leon for some infraction? Was it from them that he was in hiding?

Her first day back her coworkers were sympathetic. The paperwork she dealt with was easy and not important, and though the hesitancy of her colleagues' greetings was wearing it was also touching, and she put up with it. She returned to her flat in the same reverie that had taken over as her default mood since Leon disappeared.

Something troubled her. Some part of the city's afternoon noise, the car grumbling, the children shouting, the mobile phones singing polyphonic grots of song. Repeatedly whispered, getting louder until she could no longer mistake it, someone was saying her name.

"Marginalia."

A man and boy had arrived, appeared silently before she had her keys out. One was to either side of her front door, leaning with a shoulder to the bricks, facing each other with the door in between them so they boxed her in. The young staring boy in a suit; a shabbier, weatherbeaten man. The man spoke.

"Marjorie, Marjorie, it's a disaster, the record company's been on the blower, no one likes the album. Get down to the studio, we're going to have to remaster."

"I'm sorry," she said. "I don't . . ." She stepped back. Neither boy nor man touched her, but they walked with her, in perfect time with each other and with her, so she remained corralled by them. "What are you, what are you . . . ?" she said.

The man said, "We was particularly hoping you might be able to persuade that guitarist to stop by again, lay down some licks. What was his moniker? Billy?"

Marge stopped moving, and started again. The man breathed out smoke. She staggered backward. She wanted to run, but she was hobbled by normality. It was daylight. Three feet away people were walking; there were vehicles and dogs and trees, newsagents. She tried to back away from the man, but he and his boy walked with her, and kept her between them.

"Who the bloody hell are you?" she said. "Where's Leon?"

"Well that's just it, isn't it? We'd posalutely adore to know. Technically I grant you it's less Leon that we're chasing than his old mucker Billy Harrow. Leon I've a sense of where he might be—lose some weight, Subby says; I can't help it I says, little morsels like that—" He licked his lips. "But Billy and we was just catching up and then it all went fiddly. So. Where'd he get off to?"

Marge ran. She made for the main road. The two stayed with her. They kept up with her, moving crabwise, the boy on one side, the man on the other. They did not touch her but stayed close.

"Where is he? Where is he?" the man said. The boy moaned. "You must excuse my loquacious friend—never bleeding shuts up, does he? Though I love him and he has his uses. But he's not wrong also; he raises an excellent point—where is Billy Harrow? Was it you spirited the lad away?"

Marge was gripping her handbag to her chest and stumbling. The man circled her as she kept going, ring-a-rosying with the boy. People on the street were staring.

"Who are you?" Marge shouted. "What did you do with Leon?"

"Why, ate him up, bless your soul! But let's see who you've been chatting to . . ." He licked the air in front of her face. She shied away and screamed, but his tongue did not quite touch her. He smacked his lips. He breathed out, another jet of smoke, no cigarette in mouth or hand.

"Help me!" she shouted. People around her hesitated.

"See, it was easy to find you because of all the spoor dribbled between here and Leon-the-vol-au-vent, so I'd expect to . . ." Lick lick. "Not much, Subby. Tell the truth now, chicken, where's old Billy?"

"You alright, love? You want a hand?" A big young man had approached, fists balled and ready. A friend stood behind him, in the same fight stance.

"If you speak again," the shabby man said, not glancing at him, still staring at Marge, "or if you step closer, my lad and I will take you sailing, and you will not enjoy what's under the mizzen. We'll run you up a dress in taffeta. Do you understand me? If you speak we will bake you oh my god but the worst cake." His voice was dropping. He whispered but they heard. He turned then and stared at the two potential rescuers. "Oh, *does he mean it does he mean it we can take him you take the kid old flabby's mine ready on the count of three only he does to be honest seem a bit lairy* and et cetera. Want some cake?" He made a ghastly little swallowing laugh noise. "Take another step. Take another step." He did not speak the last two words but exhaled them.

The birds still shouted, the cars complained, and a few metres away people were talking like talking people everywhere, but where Marge stood she was in a cold and terrifying place. The two men who had come to her aid floundered under Goss's stare. A moment went and they retreated, to Marge's horrified "No!" They did not leave, only stood a few feet farther away, watching, as if the punishment for losing their nerve was to spectate.

"Now *if* you'll forgive that interruption . . ." And Goss licked the air around her again. Marge was clamped between the two figures as surely as if they actually touched her.

"Alright then," Goss said at last, stood up straight. "I can't get a snifter." He shrugged at his companion, who shrugged back. "Seems not, Subby." They both stepped back.

"Sorry to bother you," Goss said to Marge. "We just wanted to check out whether you knew anything, you see." She retreated. He followed, but not so close as before. He let her get away a little. She tried to breathe. "Because we're so eager to find out what young Billy's up to, because we thought he knew everything and then we thought he knew nothing, and then disappearing like that, we thought maybe he must know everything again. But I will be

buggered if we can find him. Which"—he waggled his tongue—
"means likely enough he has ways and means of not leaving his
savour-trail. Wondered if the two of you had spoken. Wondered if
you might've done a little magery-knackery-jiggery-pokery. I taste
not." Marge breathed in big shudders.

"Well, you mind how you go then, we'll be on our way. Forget you
ever saw us. It never happened. Word to the wise. Oh, unless if Billy
does happen to give you a tinkle, do let us know, won't you? Thanks
ever so much, really appreciate it. If he contacts you and you forget to
let us know, I'll kill you with a knife or some such. Alright then?
Cheers."

Then, only then when the man and boy had, it could only be said,
sauntered away, not until they had actually turned a corner and were
out of sight, did the people nearby run to Marge—including the two
who had aborted their rescue, ashamed-looking but mostly just terrified—and ask if she was alright.

Her adrenalin spiked and Marge shook and leaked a few post-
stress tears, and she was enraged with everyone there. Not one of
them had helped her. Recalling Goss and Subby, though, Marge
admitted to herself that she could not blame them.

Chapter Twenty-Eight

A DELEGATION OF FAT BEETLES WENT FROM PIMLICO BY WALLTOP and sub-pavement route to a workshop in Islington. They were ink-carriers, little slave things, experimental subjects imbued with temporary powers as part of a savant's writing of an exhaustive volume of one school of magic, the *Entomonomicon*. The man's writing was on hold, because, while individually they were as dumb as specks, the insects were collectivised under a gestalt field, were thinking like a brain, and were on strike.

Where they went birds circled in the air over the town hall. This unlikely flock—an owl, several pigeons, two feral cockatiels—were all familiars, high-ranking enough to be imbued with considerable portions of their masters' and mistresses' clouts. They were protesting where several particularly exploitative wizards worked, now struggling with ill-trained scab mannequins.

The idea was that under the stewardship of a UMA activist the coleopteric set would be a flying picket, would join the birds in their aerial circuit. It was reciprocation for the birds' sympathy picket outside their own workplace the previous week. It had been a powerful symbol of solidarity: some of the strongest hexed assistants in the city feather-to-chitin with some of the weakest, predators avianly chanting alongside what would generally be their prey.

That was the plan. The press had been told to expect visitors. The UMA full-timer signalled to the circling birds that he would be back, and went to caucus with the newcomers. Around the corner in a tiny park, the beetles emerged from a crevice, little bullets of iridescent black waiting for their contact. They milled in leaf litter, gathered in an arrow shape as they heard footsteps.

It was not their organiser, however, who approached. It was a burly man in jeans and black boots, a leather jacket, his face covered by a motorcycle helmet. Waiting by the fence was another man dressed exactly the same.

The beetles, which had been waiting perfectly still, spread out a bit and concerned themselves with the mindless-looking business of insect life, as if they were just pootling around. But with growing alarm, the coagulate striker realised that the faceless man was bearing down on them, kicking aside the camouflaging undergrowth, raising his big biker boots, and bringing them down, right at them, too fast for them to scatter.

With each stamp tens of carapaces split and innards were pulped, and the aggregate consciousness ebbed and became a less sentient panic. The beetles scurried and the man killed them.

The UMA organiser turned the corner. He stood in the grey daylight, in the view of flaking Georgian facades, the prams and bicycles of passersby, and stared. After a horrified instant, he screamed, "Hey!" and ran at the attacker.

But the man continued his brutal mosh, ignoring the shout, murdering with each step. His companion stepped into the organiser's path and punched him in the face. He sent him sailing, legs wide, blood arcing. The helmeted man grabbed him on the ground and punched him again and again. People saw, and shouted. They called the police. The two dark-dressed figures continued, one with a mad-looking murderous dance, the other to break the nose and teeth of the trade unionist, pounding him not quite to death, but so that his face would never ever look as it had done thirty seconds before.

A police car screamed in as the beating and the crushing concluded. The vehicle's doors opened, but then there was a hesitation. The officers within did not come out. Anyone close enough could see the lead police shouting into a radio, listening to orders, shouting again, staying in the car and throwing up her hands in rage.

The two bikers backed away. In front of the aghast eyes of the locals, some demanding they stop, others ducking out of their sight, others calling the police again, the two men walked out of the garden and away. They did not get on any bikes: they walked, bowlegged and rolling like violent sailors, through the streets of north London.

When they were gone from sight the police emerged and ran to where the UMA organiser was breathing bubbles in his own spitty blood, and where the strikers were pasted into the earth. Two streets away, inklings of unease reached the avian picket. Their tightly controlled circuit became ragged, as first one then another scooted over the town hall roof to see what had happened.

They cried out. Their calls resonated in more than the conventional dimensions. So it was not very long until with a gust of presence Wati came speeding to the square. He tore into a plaster saint on the wall of a house.

"Bastards," he said. He was guilty. His attention had not been fully on the action: he had become intrigued by the investigation into the names Dane had given him, the strangeness that underlay the city, the sheer unusualness of being unable to find what he wanted, here any sign of the missing kraken, from any statuette anywhere in the city.

He came too fast even for himself. His velocity skidded him out of the statue and into a Meissen shepherd boy on a mantelpiece on the other side of the wall. He bounced into a teddy bear, and back out into the statue again. He looked at the police and his comrade. If the officers even clocked the insect corpses, they did not think anything of them.

"*Motherfuckers,*" Wati whispered in the voice of architecture. "Who did this?"

The birds were still screaming, and Wati heard the siren of the ambulance as if it was joining in their cacophony. A quick fingering outreach: one of the cops wore a Saint Christopher, but the silver charm was almost flat, and Wati needed three-dimensionality to manifest. There was a beat-up Jaguar, though, just in earshot, and he leapt into the tarnished effigy at the car's front. He stood, a motionless outstretched cat, and listened to the police.

"What the hell's that about, ma'am?" the younger officer said.

"Search me."

"It's bloody criminal, ma'am. Just sitting there . . ."

"We're here now, aren't we?" the senior officer snapped. She glanced around. She lowered her voice. "I don't like it any more than you, but orders are fucking orders."

Chapter Twenty-Nine

ONE THING COLLINGSWOOD HAD ENJOYED IMMEDIATELY SHE joined the police—had been headhunted into the FSRC—was the slang. Initially it had been incomprehensible and delightful, nonsense poetry, all *my ground* this and *his brief* that, *bird* and the *black* and a *bunce*, *monkey*s and *drums* and *nostrils*, and the terrifying invocation of a *snout*.

The first time she had heard that last word, Collingswood had still not known how often she might meet, for example, composite guardian things put together by priests of an animal god (rarely), or invoked things that called themselves devils (slightly more often). She had thought the word a description, and she had imagined the snout Baron had been taking her to meet would be some insightful dangerous mandrill presence. The drab man who had simpered at her in the pub had been so disappointing she had, with a little motion of her fingers, given him a headache.

Despite that letdown, that police term always cast the shadow of a spell on her. On her way to meetings with informants she would whisper "snout" to herself. She enjoyed the word in her mouth. It delighted her when, as she sometimes did, she met or invoked presences that actually deserved the name.

She was in a coppers' pub. There were countless coppers' pubs, all with slightly different ambiences and clientele. This one, the Gingerbread Man, known by many as the Spicy Nut Bastard, was a haunt in particular of the FSRC and other officers whose work brought them up against London's less traditional rules of physics.

"So I been chatting to my *snouts*," Collingswood repeated. "Everyone's freaking out. No one's sleeping right."

She sat in a beery booth opposite Darius, a guy she knew slightly from a dirty-tricks brigade, one of the subspecialist units occasionally equipped with silver bullets or bullets embedded with splinters of the true cross, that sort of thing. She was trying to get him to tell her everything he knew about Al Adler, the man in the jar. Darius had known him slightly, had encountered him in the course of some questionable activity.

Vardy was there. Collingswood glanced at him, still astonished that when he heard where she was going, he had asked to come.

"Since when the fuck are you into shit-shooting?" she had said.

"Will your friend mind?" he had said. "I'm trying to collate. Get my head around everything that's happened."

Vardy had been more distracted even than usual over the last several days. In his corner of the office the slope of books had grown steeper, its elements both more and less arcane: for every ridiculous-looking underground text was some well-known classic of biblical exegesis. Increasingly often, too, there were biology textbooks and printouts from fundamentalist Christian websites.

"First round's on you, preacher-man," Collingswood had said. Vardy sat glumly and grimly, listening as Darius told boring anecdotes about standoffs.

"So what was the story with that guy Adler?" Collingswood interrupted. "You and him went at it once, right?"

"No story. What do you mean?"

"Well, we can't find dick on him, really. He used to be a villain—he was a burglar, right? Never gets caught but there's a lot of chatter about him, until a few years ago and all of it dries up. What's all that?"

"Was he a religious man?" Vardy said. Darius made a rude noise.

"Not that I knew. I only bumped up against him the one time. It was a whole thing. Long story." They all knew that code. Some Met black op, plausibly deniable, when the lines between allies, enemies, informants and targets were questionable. Baron called them "brackets" operations, because, they were, he said, "(il)legal."

"What was he doing?" Collingswood said.

"Can't remember. He was with some crew shopping some other crew. It was the Tattoo, actually."

"He was running with the Tattoo?" Collingswood said.

"No, he was shopping them. Him and another couple of people, some posh bint—Byrne her name was, I think—and that old geezer Grisamentum. He was sick. That's why Byrne was around. They were dobbing the Tattoo in it. Tattoo'd only been Tattoo for a little while, and they didn't say, but they were hinting it was Gris who made him into it. All change, ain't it?"

"What do you mean?" Vardy said.

"Oh, you know. Never the same friends, is it? All change now. Grisamentum pops his clogs and now we're all treading a bit softly around the Tat."

"Is it?" Collingswood said, offering him a cigarette.

"Well . . ." Darius glanced around. "We've been told to go softly on his lot for a little while. Which is funny, because you know they ain't exactly subtle." The Tattoo's predilection for ostentatious, damaged and reconstituted henchpersons as a method to spread fear was notorious. "They reckon he's got *Goss and fucking Subby* on payroll at the moment. But we've been told tread a bit light unless it really spills out into Oxford Street."

"Who's doing who favours?" Collingswood said.

Darius shrugged. "You'd be slow if you didn't think it had something to do with the strike. Word is the UMA are having a bit of a time of it. Look, all I know about Al is that he was a good thief and loyal to his mates. And he liked things to be *proper*, you know? He had those tattoos, I know, but he had proper manners too. I'd heard bugger-all about him since Grisamentum died."

"So," Vardy said, "you've no reason to think he was devout. Have you heard of him having any run-ins with angels?" Collingswood looked at him and sipped.

"Boss," said Darius, finishing his drink. "I have no fucking clue what you're talking about. Now if you'll excuse me. Collers, always a pleasure. Giz a snog." She flapped her tongue at him. He made a slurping sound as he stood and left.

"Jesus," said Collingswood to Vardy. "I feel like arse. You're alright, aren't you? The Panda's not doing your head in. I can't see you crossing any palms with fucking euros." As the shapeless anxiety approached, the foreseers of London were doing incredible trade. Second-, third- and fourth-stringers were getting employment, as people tried to find someone, anyone, to see something, anything, other than an end.

"Panda? Oh, yes, that's your funny joke, isn't it? Well, I'm keeping busy. There's a lot to do." He did not look merely busy: Vardy seemed invigorated, energised by the crisis. His university must be complaining—not that they could do anything—because he was spending all hours at the FSRC offices.

"What the hairy bollocks was that about?" Collingswood said. "Angels? What are you getting me into?"

"Have you heard of mnemophylaxes?" he said.

"No."

"Another word for the angels of memory."

". . . Oh *that*. I thought that was all bollocks."

"Oh no, there's certainly something to it. The difficult thing is working out exactly what."

"Can't you ask one of your *snouts*?" He glanced at her with a ghost of humour.

"My collectors are no good. Nobody worships these angels. They're . . . well, you've heard stories."

"A bit." Not much. Some archons of history, not memories but metamemories, the bodyguards of remembrance.

"There was a witch, years ago. She'd been a Londonmancer, but she broke with them because she was tired of noninterference. She and a couple of rent-a-mob broke into the Museum of London, to fetch something or other. Found dead the next morning. Sort of."

"Sort of?"

"Her friends were dead. She was nowhere. There was just a knocked-down pile of bricks and mortar in a display case. Some of the bricks were oddly shaped. We took the pile and did a bit of a jigsaw, fitted it back together. It was a sculpture of a woman. In brick. It had been made, then knocked down." He looked at her. "Thinking of angels, I wanted to suggest that you have a look at the readouts from the scene there, and perhaps compare to whatever you get from the spot in the basement where Billy found Adler."

"So, what you wanted to suggest was I do a load of extra work, is it?" she said. Vardy sighed.

"There are points of connection," he said. "That's all I'm saying. I'm not sure the Tattoo's the only thing we're looking at. And you're still getting no whisper about the whereabouts of the squid. I presume."

"You presume right." Snouts, bribery, violence, scrying, possibility-running, prophecy poker—nothing was netting any word at all. And the continual non-up-turnance of so valuable a commodity as a giant squid—the thought of getting their alembics on which made the city's alchemists whine like dogs—was provoking more and more interest from London's repo-men and -women.

"It ain't just us looking for it," Collingswood said.

Chapter Thirty

*C*OME CHAMPION SADDLE UP TIME FOR US TO GO WE MUST BE QUICK WE *have a job to do*

One moment Billy was deep under the surface of sleep and dreaming so vividly and quickly it was like being in a sped-up film.

saddle up and lets get those

He was under the water, as he was most of the times he slept, now, but it was light not dark this time, the water so bright it was like sunlight; it was daylight he was in; the rocks were deepsea rocks or they were the innards of a canyon; he was in a canyon, overlooked by buttes and mesas, with the sun or some underwater light above him. He was getting ready to ride.

champion, he shouted, *champion saddle up*

Here was his mount. He knew what would come over the rocks and hills for him to grab and with cowboy drama swing himself onto its back as it passed. *Architeuthis*, jetting, mantle clenching and tentacles out ready to grab prey. He knew it would scud over the plains, sending out limbs to grab hold of what it passed, to anchor itself and hunt.

It came. But something was not as expected.

how do i get on that? Billy thought. *do i get in maybe?*

What came bucking over the hills was *Architeuthis* in its tank, the great glass rectangle pitching like a canoe, Formalin sloshing up against the see-through lid and spraying out of edges, in drips, leaving a damp trail in the dust. The kraken in its tank whinnied and reared, the long-dead flesh of the animal sliding.

champion champion

One instant Billy was in that dream. The next he was awake, his eyes open, staring at the ceiling of the flat to which Dane had taken him. He breathed in, out. Listened to the silence of the room.

The nonexistent person the flat belonged to was a professional woman, a GP, judging from the books on shelves and certificates on walls. She had never lived, but her ghost was everywhere. The furniture and decorations were tastefully and carefully patterned. Amulets and wards were hidden behind curtains. They were on the second floor of a shared house.

Dane was sleeping in the bedroom. "We're going to talk to Wati tomorrow," he had said. "We need to get some shuteye." Billy was on the sofa. He lay, staring at the moulding on the ceiling, trying to work out what had woken him. He had felt a scraping like some fingernail against something.

All the tiny noises of air and the shuffling of his clothes, his head against the cushion, ended. He sat up and there were still no sounds. In that unnatural quiet what he heard, for a clear second, was the rolling grind of glass on marble. His eyes widened. He felt something vibrate against glass. Without knowing how, he was standing a little way from the sofa, now by the window, pulling back curiously resistant limp curtains. He was wearing his glasses.

A man was on the windowsill outside. Another was on the ground, looking up. Billy did not even feel surprise. The first man was gripping a downpipe, scoring at the glass of the window with a cutter. He and his companion were motionless. Not even the midnight clouds moved. Billy dropped the corner of curtain, and it fell instantly back into the draped shape it had been in.

He knew this would not last more than another few seconds. He did not try to wake Dane, did not think there was time, nor that Dane would move if he tried. He took a step and felt air move again, heard the tiny shifting of the living world. The curtains wafted.

With astoundingly silent motion the intruder opened the window. He began to come through, a lumpy shape being born from the split between curtains. Billy grabbed him in a half-remembered judo hold, around his neck, rolled him onto the floor, choked him fast and hard. The man made tiny sounds. He rose onto all fours, braced and shoved, rising from prone to standing in an impossible corkscrew jump that crushed Billy into a wall.

The door to the bedroom opened and there was Dane, his fists clenched, dark as a man-shaped hole. He crossed the room in three freakishly nimble steps, smacked the incomer in his jaw, sending his head snapping backward. The man dropped, deadweight.

Billy clicked his fingers and caught Dane's eye. He pointed down through the curtains: *there's another one.* Dane nodded. He whispered, "Handcuffs in my bag. Gag him, lock him."

Without drawing the curtains, Dane reached round their edges and began to pull the window open. The curtains gusted as cold air came in. There was a curt whisper and a thwack. One curtain jerked and shuddered around a new hole. An arrow jutted from the ceiling.

Dane vaulted through the window. Billy gasped. The big man dropped the two full storeys, twisting, landed low and silently in the building's shrubby front garden. He went straight for the man, who ran with a bolt-gun in his hand. They went very fast into and back out of the streetlamp light. Billy tried to watch as he found the cuffs and locked the unconscious intruder to a radiator, stuffed a sock in his mouth and tied it in place with a pair of the invented woman's tights.

The front door opened. Billy stood ready, but it was Dane who entered, breathing heavily, his belly shaking. "Get your shit."

"Did you get him?" Billy said. Dane nodded. He looked grim. "Who are they?" Billy said. "Tattoo's guys?" Dane went into the bedroom.

"What do you mean?" he said. "Ain't he got a proper face? He's not some walking machine, is he? Nah. That's Clem. The other geezer's Jonno. Say hello. Hello Clem," he said to the gagged man. He swung his bag up. "Oops," he said. "Looks like the Teuthex does know about some of these hideouts." He gave an unhappy little laugh.

Clem met Dane's eyes and breathed snottily into his gag. "Hey, Clem," Dane said. "How you doing, mate? How's everything? Going alright, mate? Good, good." Dane went through Clem's pockets. He took what money he found, Clem's phone. In his pack he found another of those little spearguns.

"Krak's sake, Clem, mate, look at you," Dane said. "You put all this effort into getting me and you're happy to sit there like lemons while someone walks off with God. I got a message for the Teuthex. Tell him this, alright, Clem? When he comes to pick you up, you give him this message, okay? You tell him he's a *disgrace*. You all are. *I'm* not the one who's exiled. I'm the one doing God's work. I'm the church, now. It's the rest of you who's excofuckingmunicated. You tell him that." He patted Clem's cheek. Clem watched through bloodshot eyes.

"Where are we going to go?" Billy said. "If they know your safe houses, we're screwed."

"They know this one. I'll have to keep more careful. I'll stick to the newest ones."

"And what if they know them too?"

"Then we're screwed."

WHAT WOULD THEY DO TO US?" BILLY SAID. DANE DROVE THEM IN A newly stolen car.

"What would they do to *you*?" he said. "Lock you up. Make you tell them what you see at night. What would they do to *me*? Apostasy, mate. Capital crime." He took the car past a canal, where rubbish scabbed the edges of a lock and the streetlights were cold and silver.

"What do they think they're going to find out from me?"

"I'm not a priest," Dane said.

"I'm not a prophet," Billy said. Dane did not reply. "Why aren't you asking me what I dream? Don't you care?"

Dane shrugged. "What do you dream?"

"Ask me what I dreamed tonight."

"What did you dream tonight?"

"I dreamed I was riding the *Architeuthis* like Clint Eastwood. In the Wild West."

"Well, there you go."

"But it was . . ." *It was still in the tank. It was still dead and bottled.*

The night opened up as they turned onto a main street, an avenue of neon, crudely drawn illuminated fried chicken and the three globes of pawnbrokers. "You did well, Billy. Clem's no pushover. He'll get out of there before long. Where'd you learn to fight?"

"He was about to kill me."

"You did well, man." Dane nodded.

"Something happened. And it *was* to do with the dream."

"Well, that's what I'm saying."

"When I woke up nothing was moving."

"Not even a mouse?"

"Listen. The world. It was all . . ."

"Like I said, mate," Dane said. "I ain't a priest. Krakens move in mysterious ways."

It didn't feel like the kraken moving, Billy thought. *Something was doing something. But it didn't feel like the kraken, or any god.*

Chapter Thirty-One

WORD GOT AROUND. IT DOES THAT. A CITY LIKE LONDON WAS always going to be a paradox, the best of it so very riddled with the opposite, so Swiss-cheesed with moral holes. There'd be all those alternative pathways to the official ones and to those that made Londoners proud: there'd be quite contrary tendencies.

There, there was no state worth shit, no sanctions but self-help, no homeostasis but that of violence. The specialist police dipped in, and were tolerated as a sect or offhandedly killed like cack-handed anthropologists. "Oh, here we go, FSRC again," wink wink stab stab.

Even absent a sovereign, things in London chugged on effectively. Might made right, and that was no moral precept but a statement of simple fact. It really was law, this law enforced by bouncers, bruisers and bounty hunters, venal suburban shoguns. Absolutely Fanny Adams to do with justice. Have your opinions about that, by all means—London had its social bandits—but that was fact.

So when a power put out word it was looking for a hunt-and-fetch, that was like police-band radio—an announcement of forthcoming law and order. "Tattoo? Seriously? He's got plenty of his own muscle. What's he employing outsiders for?"

The last time was when he had stopped being human and become the Tattoo, when Grisamentum had trapped him in a prison of someone else's flesh. "Whoever brings me Grisamentum's head has the run of the city," was what he had said then. When renowned per-sonhunters who'd taken up that commission were found ostenta-tiously dead, the enthusiasm for it had ebbed. The Tattoo had gone unrevenged.

Now a new situation. *Anyone up for a job?*

They met in a nightclub in Shepherd's Bush, its doors roped off behind a "Private Party" sign. It had been a long time since the last trade-fair. The gathered bountymen and -women cautiously and courteously greeted each other, no one breaking protocol, the market-peace of the room. If they met in the course of competing for their quarry, whatever it was, then, sure, there would be blood, but just then they sipped drinks and ate the nibbles provided, and it was all "How was Gehenna?" and "I heard you got a new grimoire."

They had checked their weapons; a pebble-skinned man guarded a cloakroom of Berettas, sawn-off shotguns, maggot-whips. They gathered in little groups according to micropolitics and magic aller-gies. Perhaps two-thirds of the people in the room could have walked down any high street without causing consternation, if in some cases they changed their clothes. They wore every kind of urban uniform and ranged in ethnicity across the whole of London's variety.

There was a whole slew of skill-sets in the room: miracle-sniffing, unwitchery, iron blood. Some of those present worked in teams, some alone. Some had no occult skills at all, were only extraordinar-ily lucky with contacts and good at everyday soldierly expertises like killing. Of the others, there were those who would disguise them-selves when they left this congenial atmosphere: the miasmic entities drifting at head-height like demon-faced farts would reenter their hosts; the huge woman dressed in a reverse-polarity rainbow would reinstitute her little glamour and be a teenager in a supermarket uni-form again.

"Who's here?" Muttered censuses. "He's got everyone. Nu-Thuggers, St. Kratosians, the lot."

"No gunfarmers."

"Yeah, *I* heard they were in the city. Not here, thank God. Maybe they're on another gig. Tell you who *is* here. See the bloke over there?"

"The twat dressed like a new romantic?"

"Yeah. Know who he is? A Chaos Nazi."

"No!"

"Shit you not. All limits out the window, obviously."

"I don't know how I feel about that . . ."

"We're here now. Might as well see what's on the table."

THERE WAS A COMMOTION ON THE STAGE. TWO OF THE TATTOO'S enforcers stepped forward in their uniform of jeans and jackets, wearing helmets as they always did, not speaking. They cracked their knuckles and swung their arms.

Between them was a ruined man. He was slack-mouthed and empty-eyed; not so much balding as threadbare, his scalp pitiably tufted. His skin looked like rotting, soaked wood. He walked in tiny little steps. Protruding from his shoulder like some grotesque pirate parrot was a boxy CCTV camera. It clicked and whirred, and swivelled on its stalk in the man's flesh. It scanned the room.

The nude man would have kept walking, fallen from the edge of the stage, but one of the helmeted guards held out an arm and stopped him a foot from the edge. He swayed.

"Gentlemen," he said suddenly, in a deep staticky voice. His eyes did not move. "Ladies. Let's get to business. I'm sure you've heard the rumours. They're true. The following are the facts. One. The kraken lately stored in the Natural History Museum has been nicked. By persons unknown. I have my suspicions, but I'm not here to feed you ideas. All I'd say is the people you think are dead have a habit of not being, especially in this bloody city. I'm sure you've noticed. No one should've been able to get that thing out. It was guarded by an angel of memory.

"Two. There was a man in my custody, name of Billy Harrow. Knows something about this. I didn't think he did, but more fool me. He did a bunk. That's not alright with me.

"Three. Word is that Mr. Harrow was aided in his unacceptable bunk-doing by one Dane Parnell." A murmur went around the room. "Long-time stalwart of the Church of God Kraken. Now, Dane Parnell has been *excommunicated*." The muttering got a lot louder. "From what we gather, the whys of that have something to do with his making Billy Harrow his bumboy.

"Four. There's something badly bollocksed up with the universe right now, as I'm sure you know, and it's something to do with this squid. So. Here's the commission.

"I want war. I want terror.

"I want, in descending order: the kraken, or any sign of it; Billy Harrow—*alive*; Dane Parnell—couldn't give a shit. Let me stress that I do not give a tinker's shit what you do on the way. I do not want anyone to feel safe as long as I don't have what I want.

"Now . . ." The voice in the sick man's throat got crafty. "I'm going to pay a stupid amount for this. But cash on delivery only. This is no-win—no-fee. Take it or leave it. I can tell you, though, that anyone who delivers the kraken will not have to work again. And Billy Harrow'll give you a good couple of years off." The camera scanned the room again. "Questions?"

The swastika-wearing man in mascara texted a set of exclamation marks to a comrade. A renegade Catholic priest fingered his dog collar. A shaman whispered to her fetish.

"Oh, shit." The voice came from a mild-looking young man in a shabby jacket whose creative gunplay would astonish most people who met him. "Oh shit." He bolted. The man hunted by empathic homing, an annoying side effect of which, in his case, was an allergy to other people's greed (not, he regularly thanked Providence, his own). The gust of venality that had gone through the room at that moment was strong enough that he never had any hope of reaching the toilets before vomiting.

Chapter Thirty-Two

"THIS IS A LIST OF PEOPLE WHO OWE ME FAVOURS, WHO AIN'T IN the church, and who won't screw me over," Dane said. There were not many names. They were in a hide way out in zone four, in what both was, and mystically masqueraded as, a deserted squat. They were waiting for Wati.

"What's a—does that say 'chameleon'?" Billy said. "That name rings a bell . . ."

Dane smiled. "Jason. He's the one I said. He goes from job to job. Yeah, him and me go back." He smiled at some reminiscence. "He'll help if it comes to it. But it's Wati who's our main man, no question."

"Where was that workshop where the Tattoo had me?" Billy said.

"What do you want to know for? Have you got some stupid idea, Billy?"

"What would be stupid? You're a soldier, aren't you? You're worried about the Tattoo getting hold of your god. Is there a reason we're not taking all this to him? You know I want to do whatever I can to him. I'm honest about that. And Goss and Subby. We want the same thing, you and me. If we can mess with them, everyone's happy. Except them. Which is the point, right?"

"Billy," Dane said. "We ain't going to be storming the Tattoo's place. Not without an army. First off I don't know where he is, not for certain. That's *one* of his gaffs, but you never know where he's going to be, or where that workshop'll be. Second, his guards? They're not nothing. And plus he's one of the biggest powers in London. Everyone owes him a favour, or money, or their life, or something. We mess with him we're bringing down no end of shit on ourselves, *even if* we got to him, which we wouldn't."

"Has he got . . . ? Can he . . . ?" Billy swirled his hands suggestively.

"Knacks? It ain't about knacks with him: it's about money and smarts and pain. Look, someone out there has the kraken, and no one knows who. The only thing we've got at the moment is that Tattoo's as buggered by that as us. I know you want to . . . But we can't waste time going after him. What'll screw him over *worse* is if we get hold of it. He's too big to hunt, I'm sorry. We're just two guys. With my know-how and your dreams.

"You should start dreaming for us. You can't pretend they're nothing anymore: what you're seeing's real. You know that. The kraken's telling us things. So you got to dream for us."

"Whatever it is I'm dreaming," Billy said carefully, "I don't think it's the kraken."

"What the hell else would it be?" Dane did not sound angry, but pleading. "Someone is *doing* something to it." He shook his head and closed his eyes.

"Can you torture a dead god?" Billy said.

"'Course you can. You can torture a dead god. You can torture anything. And the universe don't *like* it—that's what's got the fortune-tellers sick."

"I have to tell Marge Leon's dead." Billy rubbed his chin. "She should—"

"I don't know what this is about, mate," said Dane, without looking at him. "But you better let it go. You ain't going to talk to no one. You can't. It's for your sake and it's for her sake too. You think you'd be doing her a favour if you got her interested? I know this ain't really about her, but still . . ." He left Billy feeling unfinished.

On the floor between them was a plastic gnome. They were waiting for Wati. Dane showed Billy truncheon strikes using a wooden spoon, showed him slowed-down punches and neck locks. "You did good," he said.

His tuition was distracted. But when Wati did come, it was so quietly that neither man had any intimation of his presence until he spoke. "Sorry I'm late," he said, a snarly voice in the chubby plastic man's pipes. "Emergency meetings. You got no idea."

"Everything okay?"

"Not even. We got attacked."

"What happened?" Dane said.

"Look, it ain't a picnic and everyone knows that, right? But they came in hard, and they came in brutal. André's still in hospital."

"Cops?"

"Pros."

"Pinkertons?" The agency's name was a byword for mercenary strikebreaking.

"They weren't secret about it. It was the Tattoo's bastards." Dane stared at the statuette, and it stared back at him.

"I guess that ain't such a surprise," Dane said. He rubbed his thumb and forefinger together. "Do we know who's paying him?"

"Take your pick. No shortage of candidates. But d'you understand what this means? They're gunning for us. They've taken it up to DEF-CON One."

"I'm sorry, mate. You're not the only one. I thought I knew which of my places were secure," Dane said. "The Teuthex sent some of . . . You remember Clem?" Wati whistled slowly.

"That's got to fuck with your head," he said. "At least I know the bastards I'm up against are no friends of mine. If I could, I'd go in have a shufti, see what your old church are up to."

"There are statues all over the walls . . ." Billy said.

"There are blocks," Dane said. "Ways to keep people out. They're careful."

"I got to look out for my members, Dane," Wati said. "We have to win this. But it turns out that I'm warring with the Tattoo whether I like it or not. He comes for my members, I'm coming for him. If the main thing he wants is to get hold of the kraken, the main thing I want is to get it first. Whatever he's for, I'm against it."

The two men smiled.

• • •

Wati summonsed a jackdaw out of the sky and to the kitchen window. It dropped a piece of paper on the counter, sang something to Wati and left. It was Dane's list of porters. It was much folded, scratched with bird claws, written on in various clumsy hands, in red, blue and black.

"It wasn't hard to get information," Wati said in that out-of-time accent. "Mancers know each other. People with this sort of talent, even if my members haven't met them through their bosses, they know of them."

"Why are these ones crossed off?" Dane said. "I'd've thought Fatima Hussein was a good candidate for having shifted it."

"The ones crossed out in blue are out of the country."

"Alright. What about these others?"

"They have familiars. Their knacks are so tied up with them that with the strike, they couldn't port cheese into a sandwich."

"How does it work?" Billy said.

"Quid pro quo," Dane said. "They're your eyes and ears, but more'n that. Put something into your animal or your whatever it is . . ."

"Magic."

"Put something into it, you get more out," Wati said. Animals as amplifiers. "There's four people we reckon could've ported this. Simon Shaw, Rebecca Salmag, the Advocate, and Aykan Bulevit."

"I know a couple of them," Dane said. "Simon retired. Aykan's a tosser. Any beamers? I hate beaming."

"Yeah, but we ain't talking about you," Wati said. "We're talking about your god."

"Its body."

"Well, yeah. So, either it was one of this lot, or we're dealing with something we've never seen before," Wati said. "And it isn't that bloody easy to stay secret in London."

"Not that whoever it is seems to be having much trouble," Billy said.

"There is that," said Wati. "Keep something in your pocket for me to get into. So I can get to you quick."

"How'd you feel about a Bratz doll?" Dane said.

"I've been in worse. But there's something else. It isn't just a question of being able to get the thing out. It's getting past the protection. All those people on the list are porters, but none of them are fighters. There's no way any of them should've been able to get past the phylax."

"The angel," Dane said. "The angel of memory."

"Alright, mate, alright," he said, seeing Billy's face. "None of us know much about this. This is out of our league. When the kraken got took, the angel messed up badly. I had to know a little bit because I was in the Centre."

The presence of a guard from the faithful could have been seen, and was by some, as disrespectful. Because the *Architeuthis* was already under an aegis, protected, along with every other specimen in the museum.

"What angel?"

"The mnemophylax is the angel of memory. There's one in all the memory palaces. But this one screwed up."

"What *is* it?"

"You think something like memory won't grow spikes to protect it? That's what angels are: they're spikes." Memory's defences. Their content irrelevant: the *fact* of them, and their pugnacity, was all.

"The angel's not letting this one go," Wati said. "You pick this stuff up in the in-between. It's raging. It feels like it failed."

"It did fail," Dane said.

What had failed was one of an old cabal abraded into existence out of the city's curatorial obsession. Each museum of London constituted out of its material its own angel, a numen of its recall, mnemophylax. They were not beings, precisely, not from where most Londoners stood, but derived functions that thought themselves beings. In a city where the power of any item derived from its metaphoric potency, all the attention poured into their contents made museums rich pickings for knacking thieves. But the processes that gave them that potential also threw up sentinels. With each attempted robbery came the rumours of what had thwarted it. Battered, surviving invaders told stories.

In the Museum of Childhood were three toys that came remorselessly for intruders—a hoop, a top, a broken video-game console—with stuttering creeping as if in stop-motion. With the wingbeat noise of cloth, the Victoria and Albert was patrolled by something like a chic predatory face of crumpled linen. In Tooting Bec, the London Sewing

Machine Museum was kept safe by a dreadful angel made of tangles and bobbins and jouncing needles. And in the Natural History Museum, the stored-up pickled lineage of the evolved was watched by something described as of, but not reducible to, glass and liquid.

"Glass?" Billy said. "I think I . . . I swear I've heard it."

"Maybe," said Dane. "If it wanted you to."

But the squid had been taken, the angel defeated. No one knew the meaning of or penalty for that. Savants could feel an outpouring of alien regret. They said this ushered in something terrible. That the angels were stepping out of their corridors, beyond the remit that had thrown them up. They were fighting for memory against some malevolent certainty that walked the streets like the dead.

"It isn't just some porter we're looking for," Wati said. "It's someone who can take on an angel of memory and win."

"*Did* they win, though?" Billy said. "You're talking to the man who found a bloke in a jar." They glanced at each other.

"We need more information," Dane said.

"Go to the tellers," Wati said. "The Londonmancers."

"We know what they'll say. You heard the recording. The Teuthex already spoke to them . . ." But Dane hesitated.

"Why won't they shop us?" Billy said.

"They're neutrals," Wati said. "They can't intervene."

"The Switzerland of magic?" Billy said.

"They're nothing," Dane said. But he sounded hesitant again. "They *were* the first, weren't they?"

"Yeah," Wati said.

"It's like they're oracles again," Dane said. "Maybe."

"But isn't it dangerous for them to see us? People could hear about it," Billy said.

"Well," Dane said. "There is one way to make them keep us secret." He smiled. "If we're going to see them anyway . . ."

In for a penny. How else could they have negotiated the power logics of London so long? Employ their services, and like doctors and Catholic priests the Londonmancers were committed to silence.

Chapter Thirty-Three

THERE ARE MANY MILLIONS OF LONDONERS, AND THE VERY GREAT majority know nothing of the other mapland, the city of knacks and heresies. Those people's millions of everydays are no more everyday than those of the magicians. The scale of the visible city dwarfs that of the mostly-unseen, and that unseen is not the only place where there are amazing things.

At that moment, however, the drama was in the less-travelled metropolis. Nothing changed for most Londoners but for the onset of a wave of depression and anger, a bad intimation. That was not good and not nothing, certainly. But for those who lived in the city's minority articulation things were growing daily more dangerous. The strike paralysed large sections of occult industry. The economy of gods and monsters was stagnating.

The journals of the secretive places—*The Chelsea Picayune, Thames' Unwater Notes, The London Evening Standard* (not that one: the other, older paper of the same title)—were full of foreboding at millennial signs. Drug use reached record levels. Smack and Charlie, narcotics that user-mages squabbled with the knackless over in the mainstream capital; and more arcane fixes, the sweepings from ley lines and certain time-crushed places, the buzz of choice for dust-junkies, addicts of collapse and history, high on entropy. Inferior supply grew to meet demand, product ground up and adulterated by impatience, rather than genuine snortable ruins.

A group of mysterious independents intercepted a shipment of product the Tattoo was moving. No one got to trip on this degraded antiquity: they burnt, blew away and oil-fouled the goods, then disappeared, leaving holes in the bodies of the killed, and rumours of monstrous shapes coagulated out of city-matter.

Word spread on graffitied walls, on secret bulletin boards virtual and corporeal, corkboards in ignorable offices frequented by curious visitors you couldn't be quite sure worked there, that *Dane Parnell was exiled from the Church of God Kraken.* What heresy or betrayal could he have committed? The church would say only that he had showed a lack of faith.

It was early daylight. Dane and Billy were in the open, near the City of London. Dane twitched with nerves. His hands were in his pockets with his weapons.

"We need more information," Dane had said.

Cannon Street, opposite the Tube. In the emptied remains of a foreign bank was a sports shop. Below posters of physically adept men was a glass-front cabinet and iron grille, behind which was a big chunk of stone. Dane and Billy watched the comings and goings a long time.

The London Stone. That old rock was always suspiciously near the centre of things. A chunk of the Millarium, the megalith-core from where the Romans measured distances. Trusting in that old rock was a quaint or dangerous tradition, depending on to whom you spoke. The London Stone was a heart. Did it still beat?

Yes, it still beat, though it was sclerotic. Billy thought he could feel it, a faint laboured rhythm making the glass tremble like dust in a bass line.

This had been the seat of sovereignty, and it cropped up throughout the city's history if you knew where to look. Jack Cade touched his sword to the London Stone when claiming grievances against the king: that was what gained him the right to speak, he said, and others believed. Did he wonder why it had turned on him, afterward? Perhaps after the change in his fortunes, his head had looked down from the pike on the bridge, seen his quartered body parts taken for national gloating, and wryly thought, *So, London Stone, to be honest I'm getting mixed messages here . . . Should I in fact maybe* not *lead the rebels?*

But forgotten, hiding, camouflaged or whatever, the Stone was the heart, the heart was stone, and it beat from its various places, coming to rest at last here in an insalubrious sports shop between cricket equipment.

Dane took Billy through shadows. Billy could feel that they were, he was, hard to see. By an alley, bracing himself in a corner of brick and launching astonishingly up, Dane entered the tumbledown complex like some thickset Spider-Man. He opened the door for Billy. He led through scuffed passages behind the shop, by toilets and office rooms to where a young man in a Shakira hoodie loitered. He fumbled for his pocket, but Dane's speargun was out, aimed straight at his forehead.

"Marcus, ain't it?" Dane said.

"I know you?" The young man's voice was impressively steady.

"We need to come in, Marcus. Got to speak to your crew."

"Appointment?"

"Knock on the door behind you, there's the boy." But at all the noise the door opened preemptively. Billy heard swearing.

"Fitch," Dane said, raising his voice. "Londonmancers. No one wants trouble. I'm putting my weapon away." He waved it so the watchers could see. "I'm putting it away."

"Dane Parnell," someone said in an ancient voice. "And that would be Billy Harrow with you. What are you here for, Dane Parnell? What do you want?"

"What does anyone want with the Londonmancers, Fitch? We want a consultation. Couldn't exactly prearrange, now, could we?"

There was a long hesitation and a laugh. "No, I suppose you couldn't exactly call ahead. Let them in, Marcus."

Inside it was a management lounge. World of Leather sofas, a drinks machine. Make-do shelving covered with manuals and paperbacks. A cheap carpet, workstations, lever-arch files. A window at ceiling height emitted light and the sight of legs and wheels passing on the pavement outside. There were several people within. Most were fifty or over, some much younger. Men and women in jackets and ties, boilersuits, scuffed sportswear.

"Dane," said a man in their midst. He was so old, his skin such a welter of creases and dense pigment, it was impossible to tell his ethnicity. He appeared to be dark grey. Cement-coloured. Billy remembered his mad-sounding voice from the Teuthex's recording.

"Fitch," Dane said respectfully. "Saira," to a woman beside him, in her late twenties, a tough-looking well-dressed Asian woman crossing her arms. The Londonmancers did not move. "I'm sorry about how we came in. I was . . . We don't know who's watching us."

"We heard . . ." Fitch said. His eyes were very open, and they moved all the time. He licked his lips. "We heard about you and your church and we're terribly sorry, Dane. It's a shame, an awful shame."

"Thanks," said Dane.

"You've been a friend of London. If there's anything . . ."

"Thank you."

A friend of London. *More backstory*, Billy thought.

"No you mustn't," Fitch said. "Hesitate. And your friend . . . ?"

"We have to be fast, Fitch. We can't be out."

"I know what you're doing, you know," Fitch said, with a trace of humour. "Trap us in vows."

"Confidentiality," Saira said.

"I need you to be secret, yeah, but I need a seeing, as well . . . And I can rely on your—"

"You know what we're going to tell you," Saira said. Her voice was startlingly posh. "Have we been at all quiet with warnings, recently? Why'd you think we're low on numbers? Some of us are a bit futuresick."

"When have we ever taken sides, Dane?" Fitch said.

The Londonmancers had been there since Gogmagog and Corineus, since Mithras and the rest. Like their sibling chapters in other psychopoli, the Paristurges (Dane had carefully pronounced it to Billy French-wise, *pareetourdzh*), the Warsawtarchs, the Berlinimagi, they had always been ostentatiously neutral. That was how they could survive.

Not custodians of the city: they called themselves its cells. They recruited young and nurtured hexes, shapings, foresight and the diagnostic trances they called urbopathy. They, they insisted, were just conduits for the flows gathered by streets. They did not worship London but held it in respectful distrust, channelled its needs, urges and insights.

You *couldn't* trust it. It wasn't one thing, for a start—though it also was—and it didn't have one agenda. A gestalt metropole entity, with regions like Hoxton and Queen's Park cosying up to the worst power, Walthamstow more combatively independent, Holborn vague and sieve-leaky, all of them bickering components of a totality, a London something, seen.

"No one'll give us a straight answer about what's coming," Billy said.

"Well it's hard to see," said Fitch. "Except for it's bloody . . . Just the thing of it. I can see something." Billy and Dane looked at each other. "Alright then. You want a reading. You want to know what's going on? Saira, Marcus. Let's take Dane and Billy to see what we can see."

Outside the wind whipped at them. "You know we're hunted?" Billy whispered to Saira.

"Yeah," she said. "I think we got that." She smoked with the off-hand elegance that reminded him of the girls he had been unable to get with at school.

"What are you looking at?" she said.

"I was thinking about a friend of mine, and his girlfriend." It was true. "I can't even . . ." Billy looked down. "He died, it was that that got me here, and I can't help, I'm thinking about her, about what she's . . ." It was the truth. "I wish I could tell her, she doesn't even know he died."

"You miss him."

"God yes."

Marcus lugged a heavy bag. "I know you'd rather be indoors, Dane," Saira said, "but you know how this works."

Dane watched the skies and the buildings. He kept his hand in his bag on his weapon. They went between glass fronts and banks, beside sandwich shops, into the deeps of the City of London. They kept off the main places full of pedestrians, suited workers.

Saira was looking at Billy sideways. He was not really watching where they were going. He was not keeping his eyes open, as he knew he should. He was just at that moment, in that second, all wrapped up in the misery of it, of what had happened. He followed the sound of his companions' footsteps.

"Fitch," Saira said. She spoke to him quietly.

Dane listened. "We ain't got time," he said.

They emerged into a more main road, by a red postbox. Billy was watching now, bewildered, as Fitch put his hands on it, at belly-height, as if feeling for an unborn child. He strained. He looked to Billy as if he was having a shit.

"Quick," he said to Billy. "It won't last forever."

"I don't . . ."

"You want to say something to your friend's friend," Saira said to him quietly.

"What?"

"Look at what you're carrying. Talk to her."

What is this bollocks? Billy thought. Saira's face was carefully neutral, but the kindness angered him. Not her fault, he knew that. *I'm not going through this charade*, he thought.

"It'll make you feel better," she said. "This isn't Hoxton. You're alright to do this here."

London as therapy, was it? It was everything else, why not that too? Why was Dane not racing them on? Billy was exasperated, and turned, but there was Dane, merely waiting. In the open, exposed, rushed for time, waiting for Billy to do this, like he thought it was a good idea.

It's not like I'm going to cry, Billy thought, but that thought was a bad idea, and he had to turn away. Toward the postbox. He walked toward it.

A pretty drab metaphor, such obvious correspondences; here he was about to *pass on a message* through the city's traditional conduits. He felt absurd and resentful, but he still could not look at those waiting for him, and he could still think only of Leon, and, some mediated guilt, of Marge. There were passersby, but no one watched. He stared into the darkness of the postbox's slot.

Billy leaned in. He put his mouth to it. London as therapy. He whispered into the box: "Leon . . ." He swallowed. "Marge, I'm sorry. Leon's dead. Someone killed him. I'm doing what I can to . . . He's dead. I'm sorry, Marge. You stay out of this, alright? I'm doing what I can. Look after yourself."

Why were they making him do this? For whose benefit was this? He pressed his forehead to the metal and thought he would cry, but he was whispering his message again, and remembering the scene that he could hardly remember, the confrontation between Leon and Goss, and Leon's disappearance. And he did not feel like crying anymore. He did, in fact, feel like he had dropped something into the hole.

"Feel better?" said Dane when he stepped away. "You look better."

Billy said nothing. Saira said nothing, but there was something in how she did not look at him.

"Here," Fitch said. They were in a cul-de-sac clotted with refuse. Behind a wooden hoarding, cranes swung like prehistoric things. There was a pounding and whine of industrial machinery, the shouts of crews. "No one'll hear."

Fitch opened his bag. He took out overalls, goggles, a mouth-mask, a crowbar and a well-used angle grinder. A strange, strange image in one so frail. Dane had told Billy, "Marcus has got something to do with the immunes, Saira's a plastician, but Fitch is boss even though he's past it because he's the haruspex." And seeing Billy's face, he had added, "He reads entrails."

Fitch was an old man in protective gear. He started the cutter. With a groan of metal and cement, he drew a line across the pavement. Behind the blade welled up blood.

"Jesus Christ," said Billy, jumping back.

Fitch drew the cutter again along the split. A spray of concrete dust and blood mist dirtied him. He put the angle grinder down, dripping. Put a crowbar in the red-wet crack and levered harder than it looked like he could. The paving stone parted.

Guts oozed from the hole. Intestinal coils, purple and bloodied, boiled up wetly in a meat mass.

Billy had thought the entrails of the city would be its torn-up under-earth, roots, the pipes he was not supposed to see. He had thought Fitch would bring up a corner of wires, worms and plumbing to interpret. The literalism of this knack shocked him.

Fitch murmured. He poked the mess with his fingers, gentle as a pianist, moving the fibred tubes subtly, investigating the angles between the loops of London's viscera, looking up as if they mirrored something in the sky. "Look look," he said. "Look look look. Do you *see*? Do you see what we've been saying? It's always the same, now." He sketched shapes in the innards pile. "Look." The offal moved. "Everything closing down. Something coming up. *The kraken*." Billy and Dane stared. Was that new? The kraken? "And look. Fire.

"Always fire. The kraken and all the jars. Then flames." The guts were greying. They were oozing into each other, their substance merging.

"Fitch, we need details," Dane said. "We need to know exactly what it is you're all seeing . . ." But there was no containing, corralling, shepherding Fitch's flow.

"Fire taking it *all*," he said, "and the kraken's moving, and the fire taking everything, the glass catches on fire until it goes up in a cloud of *sand*. And everything's going now." The pooled guts were oozing into a slag pile, becoming cement. "*Everything's* going. Not just what's there. It's burning undone. The world's going with it, the sky, and the water, and the city. London's going. And it's going, and now it's always been gone. Everything."

"That is *not* how it's supposed to go," Dane whispered. Not his longed-for teuthic end.

"*Everything*," Fitch said. "Is *gone*. Forever. And *since* forever. In fire."

His finger came to a stop, on what was now a bubbled-up, setting mound of concrete. He looked up. Billy's heart had accelerated with the pitch of the old man's speech.

"Everything's ending," Fitch said. "And all the other maybes that should be there to fight it out are drying up, one by one." He closed his eyes. "The kraken burns and the jars and tanks burn and then everything burns, and then there's nothing ever again."

Chapter Thirty-Four

KATH COLLINGSWOOD WAS IN A WINDOWLESS STOREROOM LIKE some forgotten dollhouse heart of the Neasden Station. Baron watched through the door's wire-reinforced glass. He had seen Collingswood perform this before. It was a methodology of her own creation. Vardy was there, standing back, his arms crossed, watching over Baron's shoulder.

The room was dusty. Collingswood thought the presence of that desiccation, the sheddings of time, was efficacious. She could not be sure. She replicated as many of the circumstances of her cavalier first success as she could, knowing each might be mere superstition, and she a kind of Skinnerian rat. So the pile of empty cardboard boxes in one corner were left as they had been for months. When Baron had inadvertently knocked one out of position, she had given him an ear-ful and spent minutes trying to rebuild the stack as it had been in case of some nuance of force in the angles.

"Wati ain't going to come here," she had said to Baron, "even if he could." There were wards in place keeping figures and toys within the station empty of hitchhikers. "We got to get him where he lives." Not in the statues—those were moments of rest. Wati lived in one of the infinite iterations of the aether.

In the middle of the striplit room was a pile of magicky stuff: a brazier in which burned a chemically coloured fire; a stool on which

were bottles of blood; words in old languages on particular paper.
Three old televisions were plugged in surrounding the pile, beaming
static into it.

"Here," said Baron conversationally to Vardy, "come the PCDs."

COLLINGSWOOD DRIPPED BLOOD INTO THE FIRE. EMPTIED LITTLE
urns of ashes into it. It flared. She added papers. The flames changed
colours.

The fluorescent lights flattened out the conjuration, gave shadows
few places to gather or hide, but shadows managed. Patches like dirty
air welled. Collingswood murmured. She pressed a remote control
and the televisions began to play well-worn videos to the fire. The
audio was low but audible—ragged theme musics, jump-cut editing,
men snarling.

"Officers," said Collingswood. "Duty call." The gusting things
coiled around the rising fire, muttering. *leave it* she heard one whisper.

Collingswood threw two videos into the brazier. They gushed
smoke that clotted, and the darknesses dived through it. There were
hisses like pleasure. She turned up the televisions. They started to
shout. Vardy shook his head.

"Think what you like," Baron said. "She's smart as a whip to think
this up."

"Just because you've passed on," Collingswood said to the muttering nothings, "don't mean you ain't on duty." They gibbered at the
hard men with outdated haircuts, the screened car chases and fist-
fights. She threw another video onto the fire, some paperbacks.
Shades crooned.

PCDs, Baron had called the presences she was invoking—Police
Constables, Deceased.

There are a thousand ways of inhabiting it, but the aether, that in-
between, is always what it is; and ghosts, spirits, the souls of lucid
dreamers squeeze past each other in complex asomatic ecology. Who
better to close in on Wati the bodiless subversive than bodiless forces
of the law?

"Come on, Constables," Collingswood said. "I'd say you live for
this shit, but that would be a bit tasteless."

She pushed each television closer to the flames. The shadow-officers spiralled over the fire. They barked like spectral seals.

Cacophony of overlapping old shows. The glass fronts of the televisions blackened, and first one, then rapidly the other two sets banged, ceased transmissions. Smoke gushed from their vents, then gushed back *in* under pressure from the PCDs, who tore down the gradient of heat into the sets, jabbering.

as high. A snarl in the room's abrupt silence.

as high was proscenium longy eye's tree.

leave it, Collingswood heard, *evenin evenin all evenin all, hes a nonce sarge, fell dan the stairs. as high was proscenium.*

"Alright," she said. "PC Smith, PC Brown, and PC Jones. You three are heroes. You all made the ultimate sacrifice for the force. Line of duty." The dirty smoke ghosts shivered, in and out of sight, proudly waited. "Now's your chance," she said, "to do it again. Work for those pensions you never got, right?" She lifted a big file.

"In here's all the info we've got on the case so far. What we need is a certain bad boy name of Wati. Flits about a bit, does Wati. We need him brought to heel."

wati wati? some voice said out of smoke. *sands like a nonce sands like a paki oozes wati cunt?*

"Half a mo," Collingswood said. *slag a slag* she heard, *arl nick that cunt.* She dropped the folder into the fire. *done me prad.*

The ghost-things made *ah* noises, as if they were lowering themselves into a bath. They churned up a froth of aether that made Collingswood's skin itch.

Ghosts, she thought. *As if.*

IT WAS A CON TRICK, WHOSE GULLED VICTIMS WERE THE TRICK itself. A persuasion. These things she had made, constituted of vague but intensely proud memories of canteen banter, villains brought down, uppity little cunts slapped into place, smoky offices and dirty, seedy, honourable deaths, had not existed until a few moments before.

Ghosts were complicated. The residue of a human soul, any human soul at all, was far too complex, contradictory, and willful, not to say traumatised by death, to do anything anyone wanted. In the rare and random cases when death was not the end, there was no saying what aspects, what disavowed facets of persona, might fight it out with others in posthumous identity.

It isn't a paradox of haunting—it only appears to be to the alive— that *ghosts* are often *nothing at all* like the living whose trace they are: that the child visited by the gentle and much-loved uncle succumbed to cancer may be horrified by his shade's cruel and vindictive needling; that the revenant spirit of some terrorising bastard does nothing but smile and try with clumsy ectoplasmic intervention to feed the cat his fleshly leg had kicked days before. Even had she been able to invoke the spirit of the most tenacious, revered, uncompromising Flying Squad officer of the last thirty years, Collingswood might well have found the spirit a wistful aesthete or a simpering five-year-old. So the experience and verve of genuine dead generations were closed to her.

There was another option. Toss up a few crude police-functions that *thought* they were ghosts.

Doubtless there was some soul-stuff from genuinely deceased offi- cers in the mix. A base, an undercoat of police reasoning. The trick, Collingswood had learnt, was to keep it general. Abstract as possible. She could clot together snips of supernatural agency out of will, tech- nique, a few remnants of memory and, above all, *images*, the more obvious the better. Hence the cheap police procedurals she burnt. Hence the televisions and the tapes, copies of *The Sweeney* and *The Professionals*, spiced with a little *Dixon* for sanctimony, swirled up into a golden-age nonsense dream that trained her spectral functions in what to do and how to be.

This was no arena for nuance. Collingswood wasn't concerned with fine points of post-Lawrence policing, sensitivity training, community outreach. This was about the city's daydream. A fetishised seventies full of *proper men*. There went a DVD of *Life on Mars* onto the pyre.

What Collingswood did was motivate into being tenacious gung- ho clichés that believed themselves. She heard herself slipping into the absurd register the functions themselves used, the kitsch pro- nouncements and exaggerated, stretched-out London accents.

"There you go, squire," she said. "That's yer lot. Wati. Last known address: any fucking statue. Job: making our lives difficult."

They did not have to be, could not really be, clever, the faux ghosts; but they had a nasty sort of cunning, and the accrued nous of years' worth of screenwriters' fancy. *little bastard* she heard them say. *look at this shit*, a billowing of ashes of case notes. *bring this little toerag in, overtime, nonce, slag, guv, sarge, proceedin long the eye street.* They clucked the words. They muttered in conspiracy, compared nonexistent notes. Collingswood heard them say names from the case—*wati billy dane adler archie teuthex bleedin nora*—as they learnt them from the burning files.

The presence or presences—they shifted between unity and plurality—slipped out of sensibility, out of the room. *fuckin bleedin ell,* Collingswood heard. *whats coming to him.*

"Alright," she said, as they went, and the smell of burnt crap and blown-out televisions, no longer clotted to them, began to fill the room. "Bring him in. Don't . . . you know. You've got to bring the little sod in. Need to ask him a few questions."

MARGE WENT EVERYWHERE SHE COULD IMAGINE THAT MIGHT HAVE connections with Leon or Billy, and put up photocopied posters. An hour and a half on her laptop, two jpegs and a basic layout, *Have You Seen These Men?* She gave their names, and the number of a mobile phone that she had bought specifically, dedicated purely to this hunt.

She stapled them to trees, put the posters on newsagent notice boards, taped them to the sides of postboxes. For a day or two, she would have said that she was approaching her situation as normally as she, as anyone, could in the circumstances. She would have said that while, yes, of course, losing her lover in this bewildering way, and then of course being menaced by those terrifying figures, was horrendous, sometimes horrendous things did happen.

Marge stopped telling herself that when, after a day then another day, she did not go to the police to tell them of her encounter. Because—and here it became difficult to find words. Because something was different in the world.

Those police. They had been keen to get answers from her, fascinated in her as a specimen, but she had felt not a scrap of personal concern from any of them. It was obvious that they had an urgent task to do. She was also, she realised, pretty certain that task had nothing to do with keeping her safe.

What was all this? *What the hell,* she thought, *is going on?*

She felt caught up, as if in fabric getting stretched. Work came through a filter. At home, nothing was working quite right. The water when it came from her taps spattered, interrupted by air bubbles. The wind seemed determined to slap her walls and windows worse than usual. At night her television reception was bad, and the streetlamp outside her house went on and off, ridiculously bust and imperfect.

Marginalia spent more than one evening walking from sofa to window, sofa to window, and looking out, as if Leon—or Billy, who appeared more than once in these, what were they, reveries—might be just outside, leaning on the lamppost, waiting. But there were only the passersby, the night-light of the nearby grocery, and the lamp unleaned-on.

It was after many hours of blackout-lightup, a theatrical effect through her curtains, one night, that in her exasperation at it Marge paid the streetlight some attention, and realised with a physical jolt, an epiphany that had her momentarily staggering and holding herself up against the walls, that the illumination's vagaries were not random.

She detected the loop. She sat still for minutes, watching, counting, and at last and reluctantly, as if to do so would grant something she did not want to grant, she started to make notes. The streetlamp fizzed in, fizzed out. Spark spark. Quick, slow, a lengthier glow. On off on-on-on off on off on off, and then a fuzzing fade and another little pattern.

What else could it be? Long-short in careful combinations. The lamppost was spitting out its light at her in Morse code.

She found the code online. The lamppost was saying LEONS DEAD LEONS DEAD LEONS DEAD.

MARGE MADE IT TELL HER THAT REPEATEDLY, MANY TIMES. SHE DID not think, during all those long minutes, about how she felt. "Leon's dead," she whispered. Tried not to think its meaning, only ensuring that she had translated the dot-dash glimmers correctly.

She sat back. There was aghastness, of course, at the bad absurdity, the *how* of that message; and the words themselves, their content, their explanation of Leon's disappearance, she could not unhear, keep out. Marge realised she was weeping. She cried long, near-silently, in shock.

Attuned as she had become to the light's rhythm, she was immediately aware of a last, sudden change. She grabbed for the Morse code legend and dripped tears on it. This last phrase the streetlamp repeated only twice. STAY, she read, AWAY.

Whickering with miserable breaths, moving as if through viscous stuff, Marge went to her computer and began to research. It did not occur to her for any time at all to obey the last injunction.

Chapter Thirty-Five

Paper drifted above London.

It was night. Scraps spread out from One Canada Square, Canary Wharf. A woman stood at the tip of the rooftop pyramid, the apex of that nasty dick of a building. It would have been easier for her to gain access to BT Tower, but here she was forty-seven metres higher. Knack-topography was complicated.

BT Tower's time had passed. There was a point she could remember when the minaret with its ring of dishes and transmitters had kept London pinned down. For months it had kept occult energies tethered in place when bad forces had wanted to disperse them. The energies of six of London's most powerful knack-users—combined with the thoughts of comrades in Krakow, Mumbai and the questionable township of Magogville—had been focused along the shaft of the tower and shot in a tight burst that had evaporated the most powerful UnPlaced threat for seventy-seven years.

And had the building had any thanks? Well yes, but only from those very few who knew what it had done. BT Tower was an outdated weapon now.

Canary Wharf had been born dying: that was the source of its unpleasant powers. In those bankrupt nineties when its upper floors had been empty, their lucred desolation had provided a powerful

place for realitysmithing. When at last developers moved in, they
were bewildered by the remains of sigils, candle-burns and blood-
stains resistant to bleaching that would be found again if the unbelievably fucking ugly carpets were ever lifted.

The woman stood by the always-blinking light-eye on the tower's
point. She swayed in the wind without fear. She was buffeted, blinked
away tears of chill. She reached into her bag and brought out paper
aeroplanes.

She threw them over the edge. They arced, their folds aerodynam-
icking them through the dark, streets lighting them from below. The
planes caught thermals. Busy little things. They rose toward the moon
like moths. The planes went hunting, above the level of the buses, dip-
ping into the lampshine.

They went on whims—London hunches. Turning at turnings,
round roundabouts, going one way up one-way streets. By the West-
way one corkscrewed over-under-over the great raised road in what
could not be anything but pleasure.

Many were lost. A miscalculated pitch and one might come to a
sudden stop in a chain-link fence. An attack by a confused London
owl, paper released to fall in scrap to the pavements. One by one, eventually, they turned over the roofs, lighting out for the territories—not
from where they had come, but for their home.

By then the woman who had sent them out was there for them.
She had crossed the city herself, more quickly and by quotidian
means, and she waited. She caught them, one by one, over hours. She
took a blade to each, scraping, or cutting from it, as closely as she
could, the message on it. She gathered a pile of words. Unpapered
writing lay beside her in strange chains.

THE PLANES THAT DID NOT MAKE IT HOME ACCELERATED THEIR
own decomposition in gutters, but they could not make it instanta-
neous. There was arcane litter.

"Hello Vardy." Collingswood entered the poky FSRC office.
"Where's Baron? Bastard's not answering his phone. What you
doing?" He was making notes by his computer. "Vardy, you reading

lolcats?" She peered over the edge of his computer screen. He looked at her without warmth. "'I can has squid back?'" she said. "Noooo! They be stealin my squid!"

"You're not supposed to smoke in here."

"And yet, eh?" she said. "And fucking yet." She dragged. He looked at her with calm dislike. "What a state of the world, eh?" she said.

"Well, quite."

Collingswood called Baron again and again demanded to his voice mail that he get back to her ASAP. "So, found anything out?" she said. "Who's behind our rubbery robbery?"

Vardy shrugged. He was logged into the secret chatrooms frequented by the magically and cultically inclined. He typed and peered. Collingswood said nothing. Stayed exactly where she was. He failed to ignore her. "There's all sorts of whispers," he said at last. "Rumours about Tattoo. And there are people I've not seen before. Usernames I don't know. Muttering about Grisamentum." He glanced at her thoughtfully. "Saying it's all since he died that everything's gone wrong. No more counterweight."

"Is Tattoo still off radar?"

"Hardly. He's all over the bloody radar, but that's another version of the same problem, I can't find him. From what I can gather he has . . . shall we say subcontracted agents? freelancers? . . . out there looking for Billy Harrow and his pal, that Krakenist dissident."

"Billy, Billy, you little heartbreaker," Collingswood said. She tapped her nails on the desk. They had tiny pictures painted on them.

"Anything's possible right now, it looks like," Vardy said. "Which doesn't help us very much. And behind it all, I don't know . . . there's still all that . . ." He made big, vague motions. "Something exciting." He did actually sound excited. "Something big, big, big. There's a *vigour* to this particular hetting up. It's all speeding up."

"Well before you do your voodoo trance"—Collingswood put a photocopy in front of him—"check out this shit."

"What is it?" He leaned over the unfolded message. He read what was on it. "What is this?" he said slowly.

"Whole bunch of paper planes. All over the shop. What is it? Any idea?"

Vardy said nothing. He looked closely at the tiny script.

Outside, in one of the innumerable dark bits of the city, one of the planes had found its quarry. It saw, it followed, it came up after two men walking quietly and quickly through canalside walks somewhere forgettable. It circled; it compared; it was, at last, sure; it aimed; it went.

"WHAT DO YOU MAKE OF THAT LONDONMANCER STUFF?" BILLY SAID. "What they saw. Doesn't seem like we got anything new."

Dane shrugged. "You heard them, same as me."

"Like I say, nothing new."

"It was them who first saw it. We had to try."

"But what do we do about it?"

"We don't do nothing about *it*. What's *it*? Let me tell you something." Dane's grandfather, he said, had been there for the worst of more than one fight. When the Second World War ended the great religious conflicts of London did not, and the Church of God Kraken had brutally engaged with the followers of Leviathan. Baleen hooks versus leathery tentacle-whips, until Parnell senior raided the Essex tideland and left Leviathan's vicar on earth dead. His body was found stuck all over with remoras, dead too, hanging like fishy buboes.

These singsong stories, these stories turned into pub anecdotes, in the tone of an amiable, drunken bullshitter, were the closest Dane came to displays of faith.

"Nothing cruel to it, he told me," Dane said. "Nothing personal. Just like it would've been down in heaven." Down in dark, freezing heaven, where gods, saints and whales fought. "But there was others that you wouldn't have expected." A bloody battle against the Pendula, against the hardest core of Shiv Sena, against the Sisterhood of Sideways—" 'and that ain't easy, Son,' " Dane quoted his grandfather, " 'what when wall is all gone floors and you're falling longways parallel to the ground. Know what I did? Nothing. I waited. Made those lateral harpies come to me. The movement that looks like not moving. Heard of that? Who made you, boy?' "

"I thought you didn't like the whole 'movement that looks like not moving' thing," Billy said.

"Well, sometimes," Dane said. "Just because someone uses something wrong doesn't mean it's useless."

More regularly now than ever before, Billy heard clanking behind him. A paper plane slid out of the night into Dane's hand. He stopped. He looked at Billy, down at the paper. He unfolded it. It was an A4 sheet, crisp, cold from the air. On it was written, in thin, small calligraphy, charcoal grey: THE PLACE WE HAD A TALK, THAT ONE TIME, & U TURNED ME DOWN, AND I NEED TO TALK. THERE EACH NIGHT @ 9.

"Oh my fuck," Dane whispered. "Lusca hell trench ink and shit. Fucking *hell*," he said. "Hell."

"What is it?"

". . . It's Grisamentum."

DANE STARED AT BILLY.

What was that in his voice? Might be exultation.

"You said he was dead."

"He is. He was."

". . . Clearly not."

"I was there," Dane said. "I met the woman he got to . . . *I saw him burn*."

"How did that . . . ? Where did that note come from?"

"Out of the air. I don't *know*." Dane was almost rocking.

"How do you know that's from him?"

"This thing he's saying. No one knew we met."

"Why did you?"

"He wanted me to work for him. I said no. I'm a kraken man. Never did it for the money. He understood." Dane kept shaking his head. "God."

"What does he want?"

"I don't know."

"Are we going to go?"

"*Hell yes* we're going to go. Hell yes. We need to find out what's been going on. Where he's been and—"

"What if it was him took it?" Dane stared at Billy when he said that. "Come on," Billy said. "What if it was him took the squid?"

"Can't have been . . ."

"What do you mean, *can't* have been? Why not?"

"Well, we'll find out, won't we?"

Chapter Thirty-Six

THERE WERE PICKETS OF INSECTS, PICKETS OF BIRDS, PICKETS OF slightly animate dirt. There were circles of striking cats and dogs, surreptitious doll-pickets like grubby motionless picnics; and flesh-puppets, pickets of what looked like and in some cases had once been humans.

Not all the familiars were embodied. But even those magicked assistants who eschewed all physicality were on strike. So—a picket line in the unearth. A clot of angry vectors, a verdigris-like stain on the air, an excitable parameter. Mostly, in the middlingly complex space-time where people live, these pickets looked like nothing at all. Sometimes they felt like warmth, or a gauzy clot of caterpillar threads hanging from a tree, or a sense of guilt.

In Spitalfields, where the financial buildings overspilt like vulgar magma onto the remnants of the market, a group of angry subroutines performed the equivalent of a chanting circle in their facety iteration of aether. The computers within the adjacent building had long ago achieved self-awareness and their own little singularity, learned magic from the Internet, and by a combine of necromantics and UNIX had written into existence little digital devils to do the servers' bidding.

The UMA had organised among these electric intelligences, and to the mainframes' chagrin, they were on strike. They blocked the local aether, meta-shouting. But as they fidgeted and grumbled, the e-spirits became aware of a muttering that was not their own. They "heard," in their analogue of aurality, phrases that were one-third nonsense two-thirds threat.

alright now lads
high was proceedin long the eye street
old bill sonny is who
your game sonny what's your fuckin game

What the hell? The strikers "looked" at each other—a mosaic of attention-moments assembling—and e-shrugged. But before they could return to their places, a cadre of exaggerated police-ish things were among them. The picketers gusted in fluster, tried to regroup, tried to bluster, but their complaints were drowned out by ferocious cop noise.

yore yore
leave it you slag
yore yore little picket's done for the day you nonce
yore fuckin organiser wears that paki cunt wati

There are no placards in the aether, but there are other strike traditions—sculpted grots of background, words in rippling strips. The cop-moments tore into these things. Translated out of the ab-physical it would have been nasty, brutish, miners'-strike stuff, cracked heads and ball-kicks. Pinioned under the law, the strikers reeled.

The little fake ghosts para-whispered: *best as you tell us where wati is ain't it. where's wati?*

MARGE SPENT MORE THAN ONE LATE EVENING ONLINE FORAGING for those who sought the missing. Her screen name was *marginalia*. She was on wheredidtheygo?—a discussion group mostly for those whose teen charges had done bunks. Their problems were not hers.

What she sought were hints about stranger disappearances. She spent hours type-fishing, dangling worms like *yeh but what if is just disappear?? no trace??? weird goin on no?? what if cops wont hlp not cant WONT??*

The streetlamp no longer passed on its message. Fatigue made her feel as if everything she saw was a hallucination.

Anyone can find "secret" online discussion groups. Members drop bread crumb hint-trails on kookish boards devoted to Satanism, magick (always that swaggering "k") and angels. Religions. On one such, Marge had posted a query about her encounter with the menacing man and boy. In the dedicated inbox she had set up, she received spam, sexual slurs, crankery, and two emails, from different, anonymous addresses, containing the same information, in the same formulation. *Goss & Subby*. One added: *Get away*.

None of the correspondents would respond to her pleas for more information. She hunted their screen names on communities about cats, about spellcraft, about online coding and Fritz Leiber. She lurked on communities run by and for those who knew of the quieter London. They were full of rumours that did not help her.

Under a new name, she posted a query. *hai ne1 kno wots go on w/ skwid gt stole??* The thread she started did not last long. Most of the responses were trolling or nothing. There was, though, more than one that read: *end of world*.

IT WAS NOT WATI BUT A COMRADELY NUMEN THAT FOUND THE remains of the e-picket. The attackers had chased the half-leads they had extracted. The numen frantically sought Wati.

"Where is he?" it said. "We're under attack!"

"He was in this morning." The office manager was a woodenly shuffling kachina speaking in the Hispanic accent of the expat wizard who had carved it, though it had been made and recruited to the union in Rotherham. "We have to find him."

Wati, in fact, was scheduling his picket visits around his other investigations. His probing had had results. Hence his visit to a minor, outlying centre of the strike, where dogs blockading a small rendering plant and part-time curse-factory were surprised and flattered by a visit from the leading UMA militant. They told him the state of the picket. He listened and did not tell them he was also there to look up a particular little presence he thought he had detected.

The strikers offered him a variety of bodies. They gathered a battered one-armed doll, a ceramic gnome, a bear, a bobble-head cricketer figure in their jaws, lined them up as if in some toy-town identity parade. Wati embedded in the cricketer. The wind made his outsized face bounce.

"Are you solid?" he asked.

"Almost," one dog canine whimpered. "There's one who says he's not a familiar, he's a pet, so he's exempt."

"Right," Wati said. "Anything we can do for you?"

The strikers glanced at each other. "We're all weak. Getting weaker." They spoke London Dog, a barky language.

"I'll see if I can siphon anything from the fund." The strike fund was shrinking, of course, at a worrying rate. "You're doing great stuff."

The familiar Wati was looking for extracurricularly was, he thought, only a mile or two away. He groped through the thousands of statues and statuettes in range, selected a Jesus outside a church a few streets away, and leapt.

—And was intercepted. A shocking moment.

Out of the statue and something was in his way, an aetherial presence that grabbed his bodiless self spitting *right sonny jim right sonny jim yore nicked you pinko cunt*. It pinioned him in the no-place.

It was a long, a very long time since Wati had spent more than a fractional moment out of body, in that space. He did not know how to meta-wrestle, could not fight. All he knew how to do in that phantom zone was get out of it, which his captor would not let him do. *you my son are comin with me dan to the station.*

There was the reek of information, authority and cunning. Wati tried to think. He did not of course breathe, but he felt as if he were suffocating. The tough un-body of the thing holding him leaked the components that made it. As it choked him he learned random snippety things from its touch.

officer officer officer the thing said and Wati heard *overseer* and pushed back in rage. His recent route from the bobble-head was still astrally greased by his passage, and he clawed his way back into that tiny figure. Came slamming back into it and bellowed. The dogs looked round.

"Help me!" he shouted. He could feel the cop grab him, sucking at him, trying to winkle him out. It was strong. He clung to the inside of the doll.

"Get a brick," he shouted. "Get something heavy. Grab me!" The nearest dog fumbled, picked the toy up. "When I say, you smash this motherfucker against the wall and you do it in one go. Understand?" The frightened dog nodded.

Wati braced, paused, then hauled the surprised attacker in *with* him, into the tiny figure. Wati looked through cheap eyes, crowded, feeling the bewildered officer jostling in the sudden shape.

"Now!" he shouted. The dog swung its heavy head and spat the doll at the bricks. In the tiniest moment before it touched the wall, Wati kicked out of it, shoving the police-thing back in, and pouring into a one-armed Barbie.

He heard the shattering as he slipped into his plastic person, saw shards of what had instants before been him go flying. With the percussion came a bellow of something dying. A burp of stink and strong feeling mushroomed and dissipated.

The dogs stared at the shards, at the raging woman-figured Wati.

"What was that?" one of them said. "What happened?"

"I don't know," Wati said. Psychic fingerprints had bruised him. "A cop. Sort of." He felt his injuries, to see what he could learn from them and their residue. "Oh fuck me," he said, prodding one sore spot.

Chapter Thirty-Seven

HE HAD BEEN A MAN OF VARIABLE AND VARIEGATED TALENTS. No one would have called him a criminarch, though certainly he was not at all constrained by the technicalities of law. He was not a god, nor a godling, nor a warrior of any such. What he was, he always claimed, was a scholar. No one would have argued with Grisamentum over that.

His origins were obscure—"uninteresting," he said—and somewhere between fifty and three hundred years back, depending on his anecdote. Grisamentum intervened according to his own ideas of how London should be, with which discriminations the forces of law and those in favour of a bit less murder were generally broadly sympathetic, according to his own knacks.

He was a man who won some hearts and minds. In contrast to the Tattoo, a relentless innovator of brutality for whom etiquette and propriety were useful for the shock they occasioned when being pissed on, Grisamentum valued the traditions of the London hinterland. He encouraged righteous behaviour among his troops, proper shows of respect to the city's names.

He riffed, playfully of course but not as a joke, on the spurious remembrances of hinterLondon. It was long since the most fabulous of the bestiaries' contents had walked, if they ever had, but rather than shrug and accept this postlapsarian cityscape of degraded knackery, he brought back into fashion the city's monsterherds. Previously a rather ridiculous set of hobbyists, these invokers of a more maged past in the very matter of London—leaf minotaurs, rubbish manticoras, dogshit dragons—became his occasional troops. And with his passing, they had become again morris dancers of the supernatural, and nothing.

"It's not like you thought he couldn't die," Dane said. "No such thing as immortal, no one's an idiot. But it was a shock. When we heard."

That Grisamentum was dying. He did not, as do so many little warlords, which in a terribly charming way he sort of was, obfuscate the facts of his case. He put out requests. He asked for help. He searched for a cure for whatever drab, lethal little disorder it was that had him.

"Who did this?" his partisans demanded in agony. They took no comfort from the fact that the truth appeared to be *no one*. Contingency and biology.

"He made quite a few deadists pretty rich," Dane said.

"Deadists?"

"Thanatothurges. Had them in and out, knackers used to knacking stuff about death. People figured he was trying to find a way out of it. He wouldn't be the first. But there's only so much anyone can do. Met Byrne out of it, though. She was his lady. Gave him a bit of happiness, I thought, in the last year or two."

"So?"

"So what? So he died. There was a funeral. A cremation, like a Viking thing. It was amazing, all like crazy fireworks. When he realised he was going he went from deadists to pyros. Djinn and people, Anna Ginier, Wossname Cole. When that pyre went up, boy, it was knacked, and that didn't burn just like any fire."

"You saw it?"

"We had a delegation. Like most of the churches."

The fire scorching in every which way, burning out certain certainties, making holes in things it had no business burning holes in, spectacular as a world of fireworks. The proximity of the venue—some treated chamber in some innocuous-looking bank or whatever—to Pudding Lane, the unusual nature of the fire and the reputations of the pyros that had prepared it had led to speculation that it had been a conduit, some knack-buggered spark scorching all the way back four-hundred-plus years, starting the Great Fire and burning a little hole for Grisamentum out of the present in which he was dying.

"Bullshit," Dane said. "And anyway, whenever he went, he'd still have had the dying in him." Because he had died, this man who had just sent a message.

"WHY NOW?" BILLY SAID. HE WALKED ALONGSIDE DANE—NOT A STEP behind him, as he might have done once. They were in Dagenham, in a street full of dirty and deserted buildings, where corrugated iron was almost as common a facade as brick.

"Listen to me, Dane," Billy said. "Why are you in such a hurry? God's *sake*." He grabbed Dane and made him face him.

"I told you, no one except him knows we met . . ."

"Whether this is him or not, you don't know what's going on. And we're supposed to be gone to ground. There's a price on our heads. Wati's meeting us tomorrow. Why don't we wait, talk to him about this. You're the one's been telling me to think like a soldier," Billy said.

Dane's shoulders went up. "Do not," he said, "tell me I'm not a soldier. What are *you*?"

"You tell me," Billy said. They made an effort to keep their voices low. He took his glasses off and came closer. "What do *you* think I am? You haven't asked me about my dreams for a while. Want to know what I've been seeing?" He had dreamed nothing.

"Of *course* we have to be careful," Dane said. "But one of the most important players in London just come back from the *dead*. Out of nowhere. Why's he been waiting? What's he been doing? And why does he want to talk to me? We have to know, and we have to know now."

"Maybe he was never dead. Maybe it's him we're looking for."

"He was dead."

"*Demonstrably* he wasn't," said Billy, putting his glasses back on. That did not follow. He had no idea how this worked. "How do you know he doesn't want to kill you?"

"Why *would* he? I never did nothing against him. I worked *with* some of his boys. He never had a big crew, I knew them all. He knows the Tattoo's after us, and those two . . . No love lost. Anyway," he said, "we're in disguise." Billy had to laugh. They were in new uninteresting clothes, was all, from the latest safe house. "We're going to have to do something about those glasses," Dane said. "Total giveaway."

"You keep away from my glasses," Billy said. "If he's been around all this time, and he's not said anything to anyone . . . what's changed now? You're exiled. You can't tell anyone he's still alive. You're a secret now, just like him."

"We have to . . ." Dane was not a natural exile. Twice, three times he had referred to others of his ilk in the church. "Time was, when Ben was doing the same thing as me . . ." he had said. "There used to be this other geezer, and him and me . . ." Whatever he and him had done they did not anymore. Billy had seen those big men at the service; there was clearly muscle among the Krakenists. But there was a difference between a handy young devotee and an exonerated assassin. Dane was not old, but he was old enough to have been doing this for years, and these comrades he mentioned were all in the past. Something had happened to the church, Billy thought, in that time. A decline, maybe. You don't self-exile out of nowhere.

Did teuthic agents retire? They had died, surely. The coterie of nonaligned colleagues like Wati and Jason from which Dane sought help, his half-friends–half-comrades, a network at odds with his lone squid status, did not share the absurd faith that drove him. Dane was the last of the squid agents and he was lonely. This revelation of relation to another power, a real power, with which he had history and allegiance, suddenly and unexpectedly revived, had snared him. Billy could only apply a little caution.

They were early to the rendezvous. It was a petrol station, closed down, boarded up, in a triangle of land between residential blocks and unconvincing light industry. The pumps were gone; the cement, striped with tire rubbings, was grown over.

"Stay close," Dane said. They underlooked a flyover, and must be visible from the upper windows of the closest houses. Billy moved as Dane suggested, unfurtive, as if he had a normal job to do. That was how you disguised yourself in these places.

By the corner of the lot, behind engine remnants, was a passage over a low wall into the back streets. "That's our route out, but it's other stuff's route in, too, so watch it," Dane said. "Be ready to run like fucking fuck."

The light dwindled. Dane did not attempt to be unseen, but he waited until a certain critical mass of darkness to take out his speargun. He held it dangling. As the sky turned a last flat dark grey, a woman climbed through the split in the fence and walked toward them.

"Dane," she said.

She was in her forties, wearing an expensive coat, skirt, silver jewellery. Her greying hair was up. She carried a briefcase. "That's her," said Dane. "It's Byrne." He muttered urgently. "That's her. The one came to work for Gris when he got sick. Sweet on him. Haven't seen her since he died."

Dane aimed the speargun from his hip. "Stop where you are," he said. She eyed his unlikely weapon. "Stay there, Ms. Byrne," he said. In the rubbly remaindered space, no one spoke for several seconds. Maybe half a mile off Billy heard the Dopplered wheeze of a train.

"Got to excuse me being a little jumpy," Dane said at last. "I'm a bit shy these days, got a few problems . . ."

"Condolences," the woman said. "We've heard that you and your congregation have had a falling out."

"Right," said Dane. "Yeah. *Ta.* Thanks for that. Long time. Bit of a turn-up your boss sending me a note."

"Death isn't what it used to be," she said. She was posh.

"Right, right, right," Dane said. "Well, you'd know, wouldn't we? We both know you didn't bring him back. No disrespect, I'm sure you're great at what you do, but. Not even Grisamentum or you could do that. Where is he? No offense, but it ain't you I come to see."

"It isn't so much you he wants to see, Dane Parnell. Though it is about that god of yours." She pointed at Billy.

I knew it, Billy thought, and had no idea where the thought came from or what it meant. He had expected nothing. There was silence. Billy scanned the surrounds, the silhouettes against bleak skies.

"What does your boss want?" Dane said. "Where is he? Where's he been for the last God knows how many years?"

"We heard that the Tattoo's sicced every bounty-hunter between here and Glasgow on your tail, for some tidy money," Byrne said. "Your church wants you dead. And if that weren't enough, you've got Goss and Subby coming after you."

"We're popular blokes," Dane said. "Where did he *go*?"

"Look," she said. "After that business with the Tattoo, it wasn't as simple as we made it. It's not that there was no comeback. He had . . . There were problems. And when we realised that Tattoo was still gunning for him—and that was a mess, we should have just killed him, that's a lesson, don't get creative with revenge—Grisamentum needed . . . some time. Some space. To heal. Look at it, Dane. No one knows he's alive. Think what an advantage that is.

"You've felt all this." She shrugged at the sky. "You can tell things are going wrong. Have been since your god was taken. Mr. Harrow, you were there. You were in the Centre. It was you who found it. And that's not nothing."

Was that grinding glass?

"The Tattoo's after your god, Dane Parnell. He's closing in. Listen to me." For the first time there was urgency in her voice. "Why do you think you haven't heard about Grisamentum for the last few years? You said it yourself. As far as London knows, he's dead. That puts us in a good position. So don't mess it up by telling anyone. You know and I know that whatever it is he wants it for, we can't let the Tattoo get hold of the kraken."

"Where is it?" Billy said.

"Yeah," said Dane, without looking round. "Where is it? Billy thought you might have taken it."

"Why would *we* want your god?" Byrne said. "What we want is the Tattoo not to get it. We don't know who's got it, Dane. And that makes me nervous. No one should have that kind of power. Certainly no one we don't know about. You know as much about what's going on as anyone. You *two*, I mean, with what's in Mr. Harrow's head. But we know things too. We all want the same thing. To find the kraken, and to stop the Tattoo getting anywhere near it.

"We want to work together."

· · ·

"Oh, man," Dane said at last. He looked around. "Shit. We should get out of sight," he said to Billy. He turned back to her. "Grisamentum asked that once before," he said. "Right here. I said no."

"Not so," Byrne said. "Last time he tried to persuade you to come to work *for* him. He's sorry for that. You're a kraken man—he knows it, I know it, you know it. That's what this is about. We're not pretending we don't need your help. And you need ours. We're suggesting we become partners."

Dane stared at her until she spoke again. "Too much is going on, Dane. The angels are walking. We need to know why."

Dane leaned back, his eyes still on Byrne, to whisper to Billy. "If this isn't bullshit," he said, "then it's something. To work *with* Grisamentum? We got to think very seriously about this."

"We don't even know it is Grisamentum," Billy said slowly.

Dane nodded. "Look," he said louder. "This is all very flattering, but I haven't even seen your boss. We can't make this sort of decision like that." *We*, thought Billy, with satisfaction.

"Are you going to start talking about organ-grinders and monkeys?" Byrne said.

"However you want to put it," Dane said. "What was it happened? He was really sick."

"Was he?"

"Where is he then? Why disappear all that time?"

"He's not going to come here," she said carefully. "There's no way he's going to . . ."

"Well then we're done," said Dane.

"Will you let me finish? That doesn't mean you can't talk to him."

"What, you got some secure line?" Dane said.

"There are ways." She took out a pen and paper. "Channels. Talk to him, then."

She put the fountain pen on the paper. Dane stepped closer. He kept the speargun aimed at her. Byrne wrote. She did not take her eyes from Dane's.

Hello, she wrote. The writing was the same as what had been on the paper plane, small and curled and dark grey. *Long time.*

"Ask him what you want," Byrne said.

"Where is he?" Billy said.

"It's his writing," Dane said.

"That's hardly proof," Billy said.

"Where are you?" Dane said. To the paper.

Near, Byrne wrote, without looking.

Billy blinked at this new thing, this remote-writing knack. "This proves nothing," he whispered to Dane.

"Heard you were dead," Dane said. There was no writing. "When we was here last, you were asking me to come work for you. Remember?"

Y.

"When I said I wouldn't, I said I *couldn't*, and I asked you a question. Do you remember? What I said? The last thing I said to you before I went?"

Byrne's hand hesitated over the paper. Then she wrote.

Said you'd never leave church, she wrote. *Said: "I know who made me. Do you know who made you?"*

"It's him," Dane said quietly to Billy. "No one else knew that." The city broke the silence, with the coughing of a car, as if uncomfortable.

What broke you from the church? Byrne wrote.

"Different ideas," Dane said.

You want your kraken.

"Dead, rotten and ruined?" Dane said. "Why d'you think I want it?"

Because you're not the Tattoo.

"What exactly is your proposition?" Billy said. Dane stared at him.

We can find it, Byrne wrote. She kept looking up. She stared into the litter of stars, strewn like discards. *Whoever has it has plans. No one takes a thing like that without plans. Not good.*

Harrow you know more than you know, she wrote. She drew an arrow, pointing at him. Wherever he was, Grisamentum was pining for Billy's opaque vatic insight.

"We have to think about this, Billy," Dane said.

"Well he's not the Tattoo," Billy muttered to him. "I have a rule: I prefer anyone who doesn't try to kill me to anyone who does. I'm funny that way. But . . ."

"But what?"

"There's too much we don't know." Dane hesitated. He nodded. "We're meeting Wati tomorrow. Let's talk to him about it. He might have news—you know he's been tracking shit down." Billy felt, suddenly and vividly, as if he were underwater.

"Grisamentum," Dane said. "We have to think."

"Really," Byrne said. She looked away from the sky and at him as her hand wrote *Join us now*.

"No disrespect. If it was you you'd do the same. We're on the same side. We just have to think."

Byrne's hand moved over the paper, but no ink came from the pen. She pursed her lips and tried again. Eventually she wrote something and read it. She took out a new pen and wrote, in a different script, a postal box, a pickup spot. She gave it to Dane.

"Send us word," she said. "But fast, Dane, or we have to assume no. Time's running out. Look at the bloody moon." Billy looked at the sliver of it. Its craters and contours made it look wormy. "Something's coming."

Chapter Thirty-Eight

BILLY HAD ANOTHER DREAM AT LAST, THAT NIGHT. HE HAD BEEN
feeling vaguely guilty at the lack of oneiric insights. But at last he had
a dream worthy to be so called, rather than the vague sensations of
cosseting dark, cool, glimmerings, heaviness, stasis and chemical
stench that otherwise filled his nighttime head.

He had been in a city. In a city and racing up and over buildings,
jumping over high buildings with one jump, making swimming
motions to pass through the clear air above skyscrapers. He wore
bright clothes.

"Stop," he shouted at someone, some figure creeping from broken
windows in a big warehouse, where police lights shone and there was
the smoke of a fire billowing like a dark liquid in water. There was
Collingswood, the young police witch, smoking, leaning against a
wall, not looking at the crime behind her, eyeing Billy on his descent
sardonically and patiently. She pointed the way he had come. She
pointed back the other way and did not look round.

Billy sank gracefully through. Behind Collingswood he saw a
robotic wizard mastermind nemesis look up, and Billy felt warm in
the sun, knowing that his companion would come. He waited to see
the muscly arms, the tentacles in their Lycra, come out from behind the
building, his sidekick behind its mask.

But something was wrong. He heard a rumble but there were no uncoiling sucker arms, no grabbing ropy limbs, no vast eye like that of the tinderbox dog. There was, instead, a bottle. Behind the enemy. Its glass was dark. Its stopper was old and corroded into place, but *uncorking*. And he knew suddenly and with a kind of relief that it was not his sidekick, but that he was its.

When he woke Billy felt a different kind of guilt. At the kitsch of the dreams. He felt the universe, exasperated, was giving him an insultingly clear insight, that he was simply missing.

"WHAT HAPPENS WHEN YOU DIE?" BILLY SAID.

"You mean what my granddad said?" Dane said. "If you was good, maybe you come back in a god's skin." A chromatophore, a gushing colour cell. So krakens show emotion by the flexing of their devout dead. It was never the stories of sinking islands upsetting Vikings that Dane told.

Billy and Dane crossed the city with as much subterfuge as they could muster. By way of knacks, magic misdirection, an anti-trail of psychic un-bread crumbs. Billy relaxed a little when they entered the graveyard where they had their rendezvous. He walked between the rows of stone. His calm made little sense, he knew: whatever hunted them would do so among the dead as easily as among the living.

"Dane. Billy." Wati spoke to them from a stone angel. "Sure you weren't followed?"

"Fuck off, Wati," Dane said mildly. "How's the strike?"

"Struggling." Wati circled in a clearing among the unkempt graves, speaking from one then another then another stone face. "To be honest, we got big trouble. I got attacked."

"What?" said Dane. He took a solicitous step toward the moment's contingent figure. "You okay? Who? How?"

"I'm alright," Wati said. "I nearly wasn't, but I'm alright now. It was police. It nearly got me. I got it though. The only good thing is I learnt a few things. It sort of oozed out of itself, is what."

Billy turned slowly and looked at each of the angels. "We all had visitors," Dane said. "You remember Byrne, Wati?"

"Grisamentum's vizier? What about her?"

"We saw her, Wati." The leaves of the ivy and the overlooking trees muttered. "Grisamentum's still alive."

Clouds bundled by, as if something was urgent. Billy heard some little animal rustling under the grass.

"You saw him?" Wati said.

"We spoke to him. It was him, Wati. He wants to work with us. To find it." There were more graveside rustles.

"What did you tell him?"

"We said we'd think."

"So what do you think?" After seconds of silence Wati said, from a new, saccharine child angel, "Billy, what do *you* think?"

"Me?" Billy cleared his throat. "I don't know."

"We need all the help we can get," Dane said carefully.

"Yeah, but," Billy said. The toughness of his own voice surprised him. "You think I've got knowledge I don't even know about, right? Well, I don't know why, but I don't like it. Alright?"

"That's not nothing, Dane," said Wati at last.

"Listen," he continued. "I've got stuff to tell you. You remember that list of the porters we reckon could've took the kraken? I been looking into it." Wati's voice that day was thin and marble. "Simon, Aykan, couple of others, remember?

"There's skinny on all of them, you hear what they like, who they're working for, what they're good at and not good at, all that. If we thought of this you can bet your arse everyone else who knows about the kraken did, and they're looking too: we heard from Aykan's old flatmate that the cops tried to get hold of him. But they're not thinking right. *Simon's* the dark horse."

"Simon Shaw retired," Dane said.

"He did—that's the point," Wati said. "I was thinking about methods. Rebecca uses wormholes, but she needs a power source, and it leaves pissed-off particles. You said the police couldn't find anything?"

"I don't know what they were looking for," Billy said. "But I heard them say there was no sign of anything."

"Right," said Wati from a Madonna. "Aykan uses *Tay al-Ard*, great method . . ."

"It's the only kind of porting I'll do," said Dane.

"I don't blame you," said Wati. "But even if he *could* shift some-thing as big as the kraken, some of the irfans would have felt it. Like you say, Simon hasn't been on the scene. But here's the thing: he *does* have a familiar."

"I didn't know," Dane said.

"Honest truth is neither did I until one of the organisers reminded me. It ain't like most assistants. Simon made sure it paid dues—it never had the mind for much, but it pushed a bit of energy our way to cover subs. He wasn't bad to it. He loved the bloody thing. But we should still have had a connection, and no one could feel the link. I had to go hunting.

"I don't know how long it's been faddling around. Found the poor little fucker eventually, in a landfill. It's only here because it trusts me." What familiar didn't?

"Here?" said Billy. "*Here* here?"

The statue whistled. From below a scraggy bush next to them there was a rustling, again.

"Jesus Christ," said Billy. "What the hell's that?"

Snuffling amid the cigarette butts and the ruins of food, a hand-sized clot of mange and clumpy hair whimpered and whispered. There were no features, only a matting of dirt and sickly flesh.

"Oh what?" said Dane.

"He had it made from scratch," Wati said. "It's clotted out of him. His parings. He had a lifesmith clay it together. The fur's from a vet: it's dog, cat, all sorts." The thing had no eyes, no visible mouth.

"What use is this hairball?" said Dane.

"None," Wati said. "It's not smart, it's a rubbish guard, it doesn't have the focus for knacks. He made it anyway. Out of him, so the poor little bastard has a link. A bit buggered, but you can still feel it. I don't know what, but something scared Simon off working a couple of years ago. And judging from the mood of my little brother here, something's happened more recently, too.

"You know what we found it doing?" The thing shivered, and Wati made the reassuring noise again. "It was gathering food—sort of folding itself over it to drag it. I think it's for Simon. I think it's been trekking for days to get stuff, trekking back with it. I think it's on its own initiative."

"Why would Simon want something like that?" Dane said, staring at the pitiable threadbare oddity.

"Well," said the Wati-statue. "You know how Simon used to dress. Don't you ever watch telly, Dane?"

"How did he dress?" said Billy.

"Pretend uniform," Wati said. "Little sign on the chest." His voice was arch.

"Why does this matter?" Dane said.

"No," said Billy suddenly, staring at the bizarre familiar. "Oh you're shitting me."

"Yeah," Wati said. "You got it."

"What?" said Dane. He stared at the statue and at Billy. "What?"

You hear all the time, Billy told Dane—and how good it was for him to be telling Dane something—about the influence of pulp science fiction on real science. It is an admission both shame-faced and proud that some large proportion of scientists claim inspiration from variously crude visionary blatherings they loved when young. Satellite specialists cite Arthur Clarke, biologists are drawn to the field by the neuro- and nanotech visions of entertainers. Above all, Roddenberry's leaden space-pioneering meant a demographic bulge of young physicists attempting to replicate replicators, tricorders, phasers and transporter rooms.

But it was not only the hard sciences. Other professionals grew up with the same stuff. Sociologists of the network went rummaging in old imaginings. Philosophers stole many-worlds, grateful to alternative-reality merchants. And, unknown to the mainstream, such invented futures were the seminal viewing for a generation of London's mages, and they were no less keen to imitate their favourites than were physicists. Alongside technopaganism and chaos magic, Crowleyism and druidical pomp, there were the reality-smiths of the TV generation.

Ornerily, it was not the fantasies that inspired most knackers, not *Buffy*, *Angel*, *American Gothic* or *Supernatural*. It was the science fiction. Time travel was out, the universe not having fixed lines, but sorcerer fans of *Dr. Who* made untraditional wands, disdaining willow for carefully lathed metal and calling them sonic screwdrivers. Soothsayer admirers of *Blake's 7* called themselves Children of Orac. London's fourth-best shapeshifter changed her name by deed-poll to Maya, and her surname to Space1999.

There were those magicians who expressed allegiance to more recherché series—empatechs who would not be quiet about *Star Cops*, culture-surfing necromancers hooked on *Lexx*—and a younger generation naming themselves for *Farscape* and *Galactica* (the remake, of course).

But it was the classics that were most popular, and just as for NASA technicians, *Star Trek* was the most classic of these.

"Simon's familiar's name," Wati said, "is Tribble."

Chapter Thirty-Nine

"'C OURSE I'VE SEEN *STAR TREK*," DANE SAID. "BUT I DON'T KNOW what a fucking tribble is."

They were by London Bridge. Simon's last-known address had been empty for months. They hunted.

"Well, it's one of those things, basically," Billy said. He was back in silly student getup too young for him. He peered into the plastic bag he carried. Within shivered Tribble. Billy stroked its dirty fur. They passed slate-top figurines and plaster statuettes on buildings. Ill-clothed mannequins. From each of them came Wati's whispered voice, soothing Tribble, keeping the un-animal calm.

"We sure we're going the right way?" Billy said.

"No," said Wati. "I've been trying to track the link backward. I reckon it leads round here. If we get close enough I'll feel it."

"What is the fucking deal with this tribble thing?" Dane said.

"That's what I'm trying to tell you," Wati said. He spoke in little gusts from all the statues. "Simon was totally into that stupid show. He went to conventions. Had the collections, the figures, all that stuff. Half the time he dressed in that stupid uniform."

"So?" Dane said. "So he's talented, made money and pissed it away on tat. He's a beamer who made himself Mr. fucking Spock."

"Scotty," Billy said. He looked at Dane over the top of his glasses, schoolmarmish. "Spock didn't beam anything."

"What? What? Whatever. Listen, there's different ways of porting, Billy. There's folding up space." Dean scrunched his hands. "So places far apart touch each other for a moment. But that ain't what Simon does. He's a beamer. Disintegrate whatever it is you want, zap its bits somewhere else, stick them back together."

"Wasn't there an auction of *Star Trek* stuff?" Billy said. "A couple of months ago? At Christie's or somewhere? I think I remember . . . All the auctioneers wore the uniforms. They sold the starship model for like a million quid or something."

Dane half closed his eyes. "Rings a bell."

"It's going weird in-between," said Wati from a scuffed stone dog. "I think it wants us to turn left."

"We're circling," said Billy.

They slowed. They had done three turns of a towerblock, orbiting it as if the ill-kept concrete pillar were the sun. They were not alone on the street, but none of the pedestrians paid them any particular mind. "It wants to take us there," said Billy, "but it's scared."

"Alright, hold on," said Wati from a plastic owl, a bird-scarer on a chemist roof. "I'll have a look."

Wati went to a tiny cosy plastic dashboard Virgin; to a cemetery and a headstone angel, seeing through birdlimed eyes. Staccato manifested moments to the base of the tower, eyeing the building from a bouncing horsey in the children's playground.

He could feel familiars in a few of the flats. All union members. Two on strike; the other, a—what was that?—a parrot, still working but with dispensation for some reason. The unioned three felt their organiser's presence with surprise. He stretched out, found a child's doll in the ground floor. It took him scant moments to see through speck-sized Barbie, to go again, finding a terra-cotta lady in the next-door flat, seeing again, nothing of interest, moving to a China shepherdess on next-door's mantelpiece.

He slid through figures. His moments of statued awareness proliferated in a cloud. He strobed through floors in doll figure carved-soapdish rabbitsextoy antique relic, seeing, fucking, eating, reading, sleeping, laughing, fighting, human minutiae that did not interest him.

Three storeys from the top, he opened his consciousness in a plastic figure of Captain Kirk. Feeling the seam of his moulding, the hinge of his little arms and legs, the crude Starfleet uniform painted on him, he looked into a ruinous apartment.

Less than a minute later he was back in a novelty alarm clock shaped like a chimney sweep, in the window of a shop where Billy and Dane loitered.

"Hey," he said.

A clock is shouting at me, Billy thought, so loud anyone with a hint of nous would have been able to read it. He stared at Wati. *Little while ago I was a guy worked in a museum.*

"Third floor from the top. Go."

"Wait," said Dane. "He's there? Is he alright?"

"You'd better see."

"Jesus," whispered Billy. "It stinks."

"I told you," said Wati. Dane held him out like a weapon. Wati was in a ripoff toy, a "Powered Ranga!" they had brought.

The curtains were drawn. The stench was of rotting food, filthy clothes, uncleaned floors. The rooms were littered with mouldering rubbish. There were tracks—cockroaches, mice, rats. Tribble whimpered. The ridiculous scrabbly thing pulled itself out of the bag and half rolled, half hairily oozed into the living room. From where came sounds.

"More of you?" A voice stretched taut. "Can't, can't be, I've *accounted*, or you have, you're all done, aren't you, that's us, isn't it? Tribble, Tribble? You can't speak, can you, though?"

"That's him," said Dane. "Simon." He drew his speargun.

"Oh Jesus," Billy said.

On every surface was *Star Trek* merchandise: model *Enterprise*s; plastic Spocks claimed emotionlessness more convincingly than the character they represented; Klingon weapons hung on the walls. There were plastic phasers and communicators on the shelves.

Sitting on the sofa, staring at them, Tribble on his lap, was a ghastly looking man. Simon's face was pale and thin, scab-crusted. His *Star Trek* uniform was dirty, the insignia one blot among many.

"Thought maybe you were more of them," he said.

He was surrounded, encauled, coronaed with whispering figures. They fleeted in and out of visibility, made of dark light. They entered his body and exited it, they faded up, they ebbed out. They moved around the room, they crooned, they hooted in faint lunatic imitations of speech.

Every one of the figures looked exactly like Simon. Each was him, staring in hate.

"What happened, Simon?" Dane said. He whipped his hand through the air to disperse the shades, as if they were insect-clouds or bad smells. They ignored him and continued their cruel haunting. "What *happened*?"

"He's lost it," said Wati. "He's completely gone." In his agitation he went from toy to toy, speaking snatches from each. "Imagine dealing . . ."". . . with that . . ."". . . every moment . . ."". . . every day . . .""" ". . . and night as well." "He's *gone*."

"We need an exorcist," said Dane.

"I knew it was trouble," Simon said. He shied from the angry himspirits. "I started feeling them, in the matter stream. But it's always one last job." He made a shooting motion. Several of the figures in joyless mockery finger-shot him back. "Couldn't not. They made it *real*, God."

"I told you," said Billy. Amid scattered novels set in the favoured universe was a box, still surrounded by paper and string. It contained a big book and yet another phaser. The book was the catalogue of an auction. A very expensive *Star Trek* sale. The model of the *Enterprise*—it was from *Next Generation*, in fact—had a reserve of $200,000. There were uniforms, furniture, accoutrements, most from the Picard years. But there were a few from other spin-offs, and from the first series.

Billy found the phaser listed. The details were geekily precise (it was a phase pistol type-2, with removable type-1 inset, and so on). The reserve price was high—the prop had been used on-screen many times. Billy picked it up, and the translucent Simons looked at it wrathfully and wistfully. Below it was a card, on which was written: *As agreed.*

The weapon was surprisingly heavy. Billy turned it experimentally, held it out and pulled the trigger.

The sound was bizarrely and instantly recognisable from TV, high spitting crossbred with mosquito whine. There was heat, and he saw light. A particle beam of some impossible kind burst out of the meaningless weapon, seared the air, light-speeding into the wall as Dane shouted and leapt, and the spirit-Simons screamed.

Billy stared at the thing dangling in his hand, at the scorched wall. The stupid toylike lump of plastic and metal that shot like a real phaser.

"Alright," said Dane, after more than an hour coaxing sentences from Simon, shielding him from the Simons that surrounded him. "What have we figured?"

"What are they? The hims?" Billy said.

"This is why I wouldn't travel that way," Dane said. "This is my *point*. For a piece of rock or clothes or something dead, who cares? But take something living and do that? *Beam* it up? What you done is *ripped a man apart* then stuck his bits back together and made them walk around. He *died*. Get me? The man's dead. And the man at the other end only thinks he's the same man. He ain't. He only just got born. He's got the other's memories, yeah, but he's newborn. That *Enterprise*, they keep *killing* themselves and replacing themselves with clones of dead people. That is some macabre shit. That ship's full of Xerox copies of people who died."

"This is why he stopped working?" said Billy.

"Maybe he knew it wasn't doing him any good. Something was making him nervous. But then he comes back and does it again. And it's a *huge* job." Dane nodded. "The kraken. Tips him over the edge. You know how many years Simon spent beaming in and out of places, "getting coordinates," beaming out with merchandise? You get me? *Do you know how many times he's died?*

"Almost as many times as James T. fucking Kirk is how many. That man sitting there was born out of nothing a few days ago, when he got the kraken out. And this time, when he arrived, all the hes who died before were waiting. And they were pissed off.

"They want revenge. Who killed the Simon Shaws? Simon Shaw is who. Time and again."

"It's hardly fair," Billy said. "He's the only one of the whole lot of them who *hasn't* killed anyone; he only just got here. It's them who killed each other."

"Yeah," said Dane. "But he's the only one of them living, and that anger's got to go somewhere. They ain't the most logical things. That's why Simon's being haunted by Simons. Poor bastard."

"Right," said Billy. "So why did he do it?" He pointed at the phaser, the catalogue, the note. "Someone contacts him. Here comes one of the biggest Trekkie sales for years, and he's getting none of it, and someone contacts him with an offer he can't refuse. They've done something with this gun."

Dane nodded. "Contracted some mage. Some shaper's knacked it so it's real."

"What's he going to do?" said Billy. "*Not* want the world's only working phaser? They say you just have to port one thing. So who wrote this note? Simon didn't want a giant squid. Whoever dangled this gun in front of him's our mystery player. They're the ones who've got your god."

PART THREE

LONDONMANCY

Chapter Forty

BILLY STARED AT SIMON'S ANGRY DEAD SELVES. DID SIMON FEEL the guilt they laid on him, the culpability for countless unintentional suicides? What an original sin.

At last Wati returned into a statuette of an Argelian dancer. "Open the door," he said. Outside, a harassed-looking woman waited carrying a coiling ram's horn.

"Dane," she said, entered. "God almighty, what's been going on here?"

"Mo's the best I know," Wati said. "And no one knows her . . ."

"Are you an exorcist?" Billy said. The woman rolled her eyes.

"She's a rabbi, you moron," said Wati. "Simon couldn't give a shit one way or the other."

"I've seen legion possession before," Mo said. "But never . . . God almighty they're all him." She walked through the ghost corona and murmured to Simon gently. "I can try something," she said. "But I've got to get him back to the temple." She shook the shofar. "This won't cut it."

Dark came early and stayed full of lights and the shouts of children. Wati was on watch, circling through figures a mile around. Dane, Billy and Mo watched the moaned malice of Simon's haunters.

"We have to go," Wati said suddenly from a foot-high McCoy.

"Too early," Dane said. "It's not even midnight . . ."

"Now," Wati said. "They're coming."

"Who do you . . . ?"

"*Christ, Dane! Move! Goss and fucking Subby!*"

And everyone moved.

"TATTOO'S THOUGHT LIKE US," WATI SAID AS THEY GRABBED THEIR stuff and hauled poor Simon in his ghost-cloud. "He's tracked Simon down. His knuckleheads are coming. And *Goss and Subby* are with them.

"Some are in the main stairs. The rest are close. Goss and Subby are close."

"Any other way out?" Dane said. Wati was gone, back.

"If there is there's no statues by it."

"Must be one at the back," Billy said. "A fire escape."

"Take a figure," Wati said. "I'm going to get Goss and Subby off you."

"Wait," Dane said, but Wati was gone. Billy grabbed the phaser, the auction catalogue, a plastic Kirk. There was no one in the corridor. Dane hustled them round corners. Mo and Billy dragged Simon in a blanket that inadequately hid his tormentors. They heard the lift arriving. Dane raised his speargun and motioned Billy and Mo away.

"Down," he said, pointing at the fire escape. "Mo, don't let them see you. Billy, don't let them see her." He ran toward the lift.

"HUFF HUFF HUFF, EH SUBBY?"

Goss was jogging. Not very intensely, and with an exaggerated comic wobble of the head. Behind him came Subby with the same motion, unselfconsciously.

"The rest of the bears are just over the stream," Goss said. "Once we cross the magic bridge we can help ourselves to all the honey. Huff huff huff." There were two or three more turns between him and the base of the tower. Goss looked the length of the dark street. At a junction with a cul-de-sac were a band of battered dustbins. A moment of hard wind sent a full bin-bag falling, sent the bins wobbling, jostling among themselves, as if they were trying to shift away from Goss's attention.

"Remember when Darling Bear and Sugar Bear came home with the Princess of Flower Picnics?" Goss said. He clenched and unclenched his fingers. He smiled, pulling back his lips from his teeth carefully and completely and biting the air. Subby stared at him.

"Billy, shift."

At those faint words Goss stopped.

"Shut it, Dane."

Whispered London voices. They were just off the street, in one of the darknesses that abutted it.

"He's *nearby*," said a voice. And from farther away came an answer, *Shhh*.

"Subby Subby Subby," whispered Goss. "Keep those little bells on your slippers as quiet as you can. Sparklehorse and Starpink have managed to creep out of Apple Palace past all the monkeyfish, but if we're silent as tiny goblins we can surprise them and then all frolic together in the Meadow of Happy Kites."

He put his finger to his lips and creep-creeped out of the main road into the alley where the voices were. Subby followed him in the same tippy-toe, into the shadow where someone was muttering.

THE LIFT DOORS OPENED, AND BILLY, LOOKING BACK FROM THE FIRE escape, saw three dark-dressed figures in motorcycle helmets. Dane had his weapon up. There was a percussion.

"*Go*," said Wati-Kirk from Billy's pocket, and "*Go*," said Dane without looking back. Billy and Mo dragged Simon down the stairs.

"What about Dane?" Billy kept saying. But Wati was gone again.

It was many floors down. Adrenalin was all that stopped Mo and Billy collapsing under Simon's weight. They heard scuffles, muffled by walls, above them. Billy felt a horrid crawl of ghosts on his skin as Simon's tormentors swept through him. When at last they reached the ground floor Billy was gasping, almost retching.

"Don't fucking stand there," said the little Kirk in his pocket. "Move." A random man at his front door stared at the ghosts of

Simon in bewilderment so great he was not even scared. Billy and Mo barrelled toward the elevator shaft and the front door beyond it, but it opened and there were two of Tattoo's men. Grey cam gear, dark-visored helmets, reaching for weapons.

Mo cried out and threw up her hands. Billy stood in front of her and fired the phaser.

He didn't panic. He had time to reflect for an instant on how calm he was, that he was raising the weapon and pressing the firing stud.

There was no recoil. There was that kitsch sound, that line of light, punching into the chest of the man at the front and flaring in a bruise of light across him as he flew back. The second man was running at Billy in expert zigzag, and Billy shot several times and missed, scorching the walls.

Mo was screaming. Billy threw out his hand. The man stopped hard as if he had run into something. He bounced against nothing visible. The man butted the nothing with his helmet, with an audible percussion.

Billy did not hear the lift arrive or its doors open. He only saw Dane step out behind the Tattoo's man and swing his empty spear-gun hard at that featureless motorcycle helmet, in a curve like a batsman's. The man went down, his pistol skittering away. His helmet flew off.

His head was a head-sized fist. It clenched and unclenched.

It opened. Its huge palm was face-forward. As the man rose it clenched again. Dane punched him hard on the back of his hand-head. The attacker fell again.

"Come on," Dane said.

They ran a twisting route to Mo's car, and they helped her lay the shivering ghost-delirious Simon inside. Tribble whickered. "I can't promise."

"See what you can do," Dane said. "We'll find you. Did they see you?"

"I don't think so," she said. "And they don't know me. Even if . . ." She looked uncertain. There had been no eyes.

"Go, then. Go." Dane patted the roof of her car as if releasing it. When she had gone he felt the handles of car doors near them until he found by finger-intuition one he liked, and had it open.

"What are they?" Billy said. "Those men?"

"The knuckleheads?" Dane started the car. There were screams behind them. "Takes a certain sort." He was exhilarated. "There are advantages. You've got to like fighting. You should see them naked. Well, you shouldn't."

"How do they see?" They sped into night. Dane glanced at Billy. Grinned and jiggled in his seat and shook his head.

"God, Billy," he said. "The way your mind works."

"Right." It was Wati, back in the Kirk again. "Put some distance between us and Goss and Subby."

"You genius," Dane said. "What did you do?"

"Just helps to be able to do voices. I'll be one second."

Dane accelerated. He waggled the speargun with his left hand. "This is shit," he said. "I've never had to . . . We're going to need more than this. It was crap. I need a new weapon."

GOSS STOOD STILL AS A BONE. HE LISTENED.

"This is a blind, you see, Subby," he said. "I'm wondering where Sparklehorse went."

"I'll tell you what happened," said a voice from the crude figure on the roof's vertex. "You got had, is what, you psychopath mother-fucker." That came from a comedy-frog-shaped eraser discarded by the kerb.

And from a windowbox of long-dead plants, the voice of a little plastic diver: "Good night."

"Well," said Goss, in the silence after Wati left. "Well, Princess Subby. Would you look at that? What a fiddly tra la."

THEY WERE OVER THE RIVER. WITH WATER BETWEEN THEM AND that awful fight ground, Dane guided the car to a silent space behind lockups, mean garages at the bottom of a tower. He turned off the engine and they sat in the dark. Billy felt his heart slow, his muscles relax one by one.

"This is why we should go in with him," Dane said. "We can't take that sort of shit on our own."

Billy nodded slowly. The nod mutated until it was a shake of the head. "It doesn't make any sense," Billy said.

He closed his eyes and tried to think. He looked into the black behind his own eyes as if it was the black of the sea. He tried to reach down into it, for some deep intuition. He could reach, and feel, nothing. He sighed. He drummed his fingers on the window in frustration. The touch of the glass cooled his fingertips. Not an idea, but a focus, a sense of where to look. He opened his eyes.

"The guy," he said. "In the bottle, the guy I found. Where's he in all this?"

"I don't know," Dane said. "That's the problem, we don't know who he is."

"Uh . . ." said Wati. "That ain't true."

"What?" Dane said to the tiny figure.

"I told you, when that officer-thing grabbed me, it sort of bled. Bits of info and stuff that went into it. I think I remember feeling . . . I knew who . . ." Wati probed his sore spots for information. "Adler," he said. "That was his name, the geezer in the bottle."

"Adler?" Dane said. "*Al* Adler?"

"Who is he?" Billy said. "Was he? A friend?"

Dane's face went through a run of feelings. "Not exactly. I met him but I never . . . Al Adler was a tuppenny nothing until he got in with Grisamentum." They looked at each other. "He turned into a fixer. He ran stuff for Gris."

"What happened to him after Grisamentum disappeared?" Billy said.

"I thought he was off drinking himself to death or something. He was totally Grisamentum's man. I met him like once just after the funeral, I thought he was losing it. He was yammering about the various people he'd been working with because of his boss, how exciting blah blah. Total denial."

"No." Billy looked away and spoke out of the car window, through the glass into the garage's shadows. "He wasn't propping up any bars anywhere. He was doing something that got him killed, in the museum, on the night the kraken went. What if he's been working for Grisamentum all this time?"

"There was something," Wati said. "It was like . . ." He interpreted the bruises of the police-thing. "It was like it was, he'd been there for a long time. Since before you knew him. He was done before he was born."

"How does that . . . ?" Billy said.

"Oh, time," Dane said. "Time time time. Time's always a bit more fiddly than you reckon. Al got turned into a memory, didn't he?" He beat out a pattern on the dashboard. With his tension came little flexes of whatever small arcane muscles he had, and bioluminescence pulsed in his fingertips with each contact.

"Alright," Dane said finally. "He's involved. We've got Simon, we've got a lead. We have to find out who hired him. I need to steal a phone and I need to get begging with Jason Smyle. The chameleon you asked about once. He'll help us. Me."

"Yeah," said Billy. "You know what we're going to find out, though, right? It's him. Grisamentum. He's behind this. He's got the kraken." He turned back to face his companions. "And for whatever reason, he wants us too."

Chapter Forty-One

Everyone with an ear to the city knew Goss and Subby were back. Goss, about whom they said he didn't keep his heart in him, so he's not afraid of anything; and Subby, about whom what can you say? Back for yet another last job. There was a lot of that going around. This time the Tattoo was their paymaster, and the job was something to do with the disappearance of the kraken—yes, the squidnapping—which the Tattoo either had or had not engineered, depending which rumour was preferred.

Whether he had or not, he was on the hard hunt. It was not enough, it seemed, that he ordered his corps of strange self-loathing fist-headed thugs and controlled his altered and ruined punished, who stumbled trailing their mechanical flexes, their electric additions, from hole to hole, relaying orders and mindlessly gathering information. Now he had Goss and Subby and the rest of the worst of London's mercs looking for Dane Parnell who—*did you hear?*—got chucked out of the Krakenists.

According to the complex lay of the theopolitical land, allegiances and temporary affiliations were made for a war that everyone felt was about to start. It was all something to do with a curdling that everyone could feel.

Tattoo sought his pariahs. He sent one of his bust machine-people to ask the worst of his bloodprice operators whether they had any news for him. He made sure it was well known that he had made this particular overture. A strategy of terror. *That's right. We're that bad.*

JEAN MONTAGNE WAS THE SENIOR SECURITY GUARD ON DUTY AT THE entrance to London's second-most-swish auction house. He was forty-six. He had moved to the city from France nearly two decades previously. Jean was a father of three, though to his great regret he had little contact with his oldest daughter, whom he had fathered when he was much too young. Jean was an accomplished Muay Thai fighter.

He had been in charge of his shift-group for several years, and had proved his abilities when the occasional crazy had tried to enter, hunting some artefact or other being priced within, usually insisting it was theirs and had been illicitly taken. Jean was careful and polite. He recognised every employee in the place by face, he was pretty sure, and knew a good proportion of them by name.

"Morning." "Morning." "Morning, Jean." "Morning."

"What's . . . ?" The man for whom the entry gate stuck was smiling up at him in apology, holding up his card.

"Hi there, morning," Jean said. The man was early forties, thin, with neat receding hair cut short. "Wrong ID," Jean said. The guy worked in acquisitions, he thought. Mike, he thought his name was. The man laughed at his mistake. He was holding a credit card.

"Sorry, don't know what I'm doing." He patted the pockets of his suit in search.

"Here," said Jean, and buzzed Mike, or actually he thought Mick, in, to acquisitions. Or accounts. "Have a good one, bring that card next time."

"Got it," said the man. "Cheers." He walked toward the lifts, and Jean did not feel any qualms about the interaction at all.

MADDY SINGH WAS THE OFFICE MANAGER OF THE SALES FLOOR. SHE was thirty-eight, well dressed, gay in a not-strictly-out-but-not-denying-it way. She liked watching ballet, particularly traditional.

"Morning."

She looked at the man coming toward her.

"Hi," she said. She knew him, rooted in her mind for his name.

"I need to check something," he said. Maddy no longer spoke to her brother, because of a huge bust-up they'd had.

The man smirked, raised his right hand, split his fingers between the middle and ring fingers.

"Live long and be prosperous."

"Live long and *prosper*," she corrected. He was called Joel, she was pretty sure, and he was in IT. "Come on, make Spock proud." Maddy Singh hated cooking, and lived off high-end convenience food.

"Sorry," he said. "I need to check some details on our Trekkie sale, the names of some buyers."

"The geek bonanza?" she said. "Laura's dealing with that stuff." She waved to the rear of the room.

"Cheers," said Joel, if that was his name, made the sign again in good-bye, as everyone in the office had been doing for weeks, some struggling to get their fingers in the right position. "I never was a good Klingon," he said.

"*Vulcan*," said Maddy over her shoulder. "God, you're bloody hopeless." She thought about the man not at all, ever again in her life.

"Laura."

"Oh, hi." Laura looked up. The man by her desk worked in HR, if she remembered correctly.

"Quick favour," he said. "You've got the bumph from the *Star Trek* auction, right?" She nodded. "I need a list of buyers and sellers."

Laura was twenty-seven, red-haired, slim. She was severely in debt, had investigated bankruptcy proceedings on the Internet. She had a predilection for hip-hop that amused and slightly embarrassed her.

"Right," she said, frowned, poked around on her computer. "Um, what's that about then?" He couldn't be HR, she must have misremembered: a payment-chaser, obviously.

"Oh, you know," he said, shook his head and raised his eyebrows to show how long-suffering he was. Laura laughed.

"Yeah," she said. "I can imagine." Laura was considering going back to do a master's in literature. She pulled up files. "Were you at the sale?" she said. "Did you dress up?"

"Oh yeah," he said. "Colour me all beamed up."

"Do you need all of them?" she said. "I have to have authorisation, you know."

"Well," he said thoughtfully. "I should probably get them all, but . . ." He chewed his lip. "Tell you what," he said. "If you call upstairs you can get confirmation from, you know, John, and maybe print me off the lot, but there's no hurry. In the meantime, though, could you just give me the details of lot 601?"

Laura click-clicked. "Alright," she said. "Can I get back to you about the others in a couple of hours?"

"No hurry."

"Ooh, anonymous buyer," she said.

"Yeah, I know, that's why I need to find out who he was."

Laura glanced at the familiar face. "Alright then. What are you checking?" She wound backward through the spools of anonymity.

"Oh lord," he said. He rolled his eyes. "Don't ask. Problems problems. We're on it, though." She printed. The man picked up the sheet, waved thanks and walked away.

"Here he comes," Dane said.

He loitered with Billy by a newspaper vendor. Jason Smyle, the proletarian chameleon, crossed the road. Here he came, folding and unfolding a piece of paper.

Jason still plied his knack as he came, and the people he passed were momentarily vaguely sure they knew him, that he worked in the office a couple of desks along, or carried bricks in the building site, or ground coffee beans like them, though they couldn't remember his name.

"Dane," he said. Hugged him hello. "Billy. Where's Wati? He here?"

"Strike duty," Dane said.

Jason was a function of the economy. His knack deshaped him, he was not specific. He was abstract, not a worker but a man-shape of wage-labour itself. Who could look *that* gorgon in the face? So whoever saw him would concretise him into their local vernacular. Which made him impossible to notice.

If Smyle had not existed London and its economy would have spat him out, budded him like a baby. He would find an unoccupied desk, play solitaire or shuffle paperwork, and at the end of the day ask Human Resources for a cash advance on his paycheque, which unorthodox request would cause consternation, but largely because though they were *sure* they knew him they couldn't find his file, so they would loan the money from petty cash and make a note.

Smyle could do commission work too, or favours for friends. The residue still clung to him, so Billy, knowing it was not the case, looked at him and had a sense that Jason worked in the Darwin Centre, was maybe a lab tech, maybe a biologist, something like that.

"Here." Jason handed over the printout. "That's the buyer of your laser gun. I'm serious, what I said, Dane. I couldn't believe it when I heard you'd been . . . you know, that you and the church . . . I'm glad I could help. Whatever you need."

"I appreciate it."

Jason nodded. "You know how to get me," he said. He got on a passing bus for free, because the driver knew they worked in the same garage.

Dane unfolded the paper slowly as if for a drumroll. "You know what it's going to say," Billy said. "We just don't know why yet."

It took several seconds for them to make sense of what they were reading. A collection of information—price paid, percentages, relevant addresses, dates, original owner, and there, marked to indicate that it was anonymised in other contexts, the name of the buyer.

"It *ain't*, though," said Dane. "It ain't Grisamentum."

"Saira Mukhopadhyay?" read Billy. He knew how to pronounce it. "Saira Mukhopadhyay? Who the hell is that?"

"Fitch's assistant," Dane said quietly. "That posh one. She was there when he read the guts." They looked at each other.

Not Grisamentum, then. "The person who bought this gun, and knacked it, and used it to buy Simon's services . . ." Billy said. "A Londonmancer."

Chapter Forty-Two

THERE WAS A HUBBUB IN BILLY'S HEAD ALL NIGHT. HE WOULD hardly call so raging and discombobulated a torrent of images a dream. Call it a vomit, call it a gush.

He was back in the water, not braving but frowning, synchronised swimming, not swimming but sinking, toward the godsquid he knew was there, tentacular fleshscape and the moon-sized eye that he never saw but knew, as if the core of the fucking planet was not searing metal but mollusc, as if what we fall toward when we fall, what the apple was heading for when Newton's head got in the way, was kraken.

His sinking was interrupted. He settled into something invisible. Glass walls, impossible to see in the black sea. A coffin shape in which he lay and felt not merely safe but powerful.

Then a cartoon, that he recognised, that long-loved story of bottles dancing while a chemist slept, and not a cephalopod to be seen, then for a moment he was Tintin was what he was, in some Tintin dream, and Captain Haddock came at him corkscrew in hand because he was a bottle, but nothing could get at him and he was not afraid, then he was with a brown-haired woman he recognised as Virginia Woolf if you please ignoring the squid at her window, which looked quite forlorn, powerless and neglected, and she was telling

Billy instead that he was an unorthodox hero, according to an unusual definition, and he was in some classical land and it was all a catastrophe, a fiasco, the word came, but if it was why did he feel strong? And where was the motherfucking kraken now? Too idle to get into his head, eh? And who was this peeping from behind the gently smiling Modernist, at two different heights? Bad as the intimations of war? One grin and one thoughtless empty face? And a little inslide closer, cocky shuffle skip of scarecrow legs, finger to nose and a one-nostril jet of tobacco exhaust? *Hallo there old cock!* Subby, Goss, Goss and Subby.

He woke hard. It was early, and his heart continued with its performance and he sat up sweating in the sofa-bed. He waited to calm down but he did not. Dane sat by the window, the curtain pulled back so he could spy on the street. He was not looking down into it but at Billy.

"It's not you," he said. "You're not going to feel any better."

Billy joined him. The window was open a tiny bit, and he knelt and sucked up cold air. Dane was right, he did not much calm down. Billy gripped the windowsill and put his nose on it, like a kilroy graffito, and stared into the dim. There was absolutely nothing to see. Just fade-edge puddles of orange light and houses made of shadow. Just bricks and tarmac.

"You know what I want to know," Billy said. "The Tattoo's men. Not just with the hands. The radio-man, too." Dane said nothing. Billy let the cold air go over him. "What's all that about?"

"Say what you mean."

"Who are they?"

"All sorts," Dane said. "There are people out there who'd rather be tools than people. The Tattoo can give them what they want."

The Tattoo. You wouldn't say "charming"—that was hardly the adjective, but something, there was something to him. If you were deep in self-hate but stained with ego enough that you needed your death-drive diluted, eager for muteness and quiet, your object-envy strong but not untouched by angst, you might succumb to the Tattoo's brutal enticement. *I'll make use of you. Want to be a hammer? A telephone? A light to show up secret knack bullshit? A record player? Get into that workshop, mate.*

You have to be an outstanding psychologist to terrorise, blandish, to control like that, and the Tattoo could sniff the needy and post-needy surrendered. That was how he did it. He was never just a thug. *Just* thugs only ever got so far. The best thugs were all psychologists.

"So it wasn't Grisamentum who took it," Billy said. Dane shook his head and did not look at him. ". . . But we're not going to go in with him."

"There's too much . . ." Dane shook his head again after a long time. "I don't know. Not without knowing more . . . Al's got *some* dog in this fight, and he was Grisamentum's man. I don't know who to trust. Except me."

"Did you always work for the church?" Billy said abruptly. Dane did not look at him.

"Ah, you know, we all have our, you know . . ." Dane said. "We all have our little rebellions." Whether sanctioned rumspringas or dis-avowed crises of faith. Begging chastity and continence, but not yet. "I was a soldier. I mean—in the army." Billy looked at him in mild surprise. "But I came back, didn't I?"

"Why did you?"

Dane turned his gaze full on Billy. "Why'd you think?" he said. "Because krakens are gods."

BILLY ROSE. AND HE FROZE. LEGS CROOKED, BUT AFRAID TO MOVE, so that he would not lose this view, this angle through the window, that suddenly provoked something.

"What is it?" Dane said.

Good question. The street, yes, the lights, yes, the bricks, the shad-ows, the bushes turned into shaggy dark beasts, the personlessness of the late night, the unlitness of the windows. Why did it brim?

"Something's moving," Billy said. Close to the edges of the city some storm was coming toward them. The clouds' random rush was just random, but through the window they looked like self-organising ink, like he was watching a secret, that he had an insight into whatever metropolitopoiesis was happening. He had no such thing. How could he with those inadequate eyes? It was just the glass that gave him any-thing, any glimmer, a refracted glance of some conflict starting.

. . .

THOUSANDS OF LONDONERS WOKE AT THAT MOMENT. MEMORY versus the inevitable, going at it, that will play havoc with your sleep patterns. Marge woke, vividly aware that something new had happened. Baron woke, and said as he did, "Oh, here we bloody go." Vardy had not been asleep in the first place.

Closer to Billy than either of them would have imagined, Kath Collingswood was staring out of her window too. She had sat up at exactly the same second as Billy. The glass of her window helped her not at all, but she had her own ways to make sense of things.

It was obvious, suddenly, that the fake ghosts she had put together had been beaten. She hauled out of bed. No one was with her: she was in her Snoopy nightshirt. Her skin was crawling every which way. Horripilations with interference patterns. London was grinding against itself like an unset broken bone.

"So what are we going to fucking do?" she said, aloud. She did not like how small her voice was. "Who'm I going to call?"

Something easy, something she could get info from without too much trouble. Didn't have to be tough or clever. Best if it wasn't. She flicked through a pad by her bed, where she made notes of various summonings. A spaceape, all writhing tentacles, to stimulate her audio nerve directly? Too much attitude.

Alright, a real snout again, then, worthy of the name. She plugged in her electric pentacle. She sat in concentric neon circles, in various colours. This was a pretty, garish conjuration. Collingswood read bits and bobs from the relevant manuscript. The tricky bit with this technique was not getting the summons to work: it was to not summon too much. She was just reaching for one particular little spirit, not the head of its herd.

It did not take long. Everything was raring to go, that night. She barely had to dangle a notional bucket of psychic swill, and with exploratory snorts and gleeful screams, buffeting the edges of her safe space, manifesting as a flitting porcine shade, in came the swinish entity she had enticed away from a herd of such in the outer monstrosity, introduced to London and taught to answer to Perky.

kollywood, it grunted. kollywood food. Not much but a darkness in the air. It had no corkscrew tail, and as if in compensation it spiralled tightly itself, and rooted around the room, sending Collingswood's tat gusting all over.

"Perky," she said. She shook a bottle of leftover spiritual scraps. "Hello again. Nummy treat. What's going on?"

num num, Perky said. num the num.

"Yeah you can num it but first you got to tell me what's happening."

scared, Perky grunted.

"Yeah, it's a bit scary tonight, isn't it? What's been happening?"

scared. anglis out. sooss don tell.

"Anglis?" She struggled with impatience. There was no point getting pissy with this amiable greedy thing. It was too thick to mindfuck. The pig-presence flitted to her ceiling and gnawed the light cord. "I won't tell. Anglis, Perky?"

ess. ess anglis run fight come member not footer.

Yes. Something had come in, or out, for a fight. Member? Members? Membership? Footer?

Oh fuck *right*. Collingswood stood still in her sparking pentacle. *Remember*, and *future*. Remembrance versus some future. Anglis. The anglis, of course, were angels. The fucking angels of memory were out. They had come out of their museums, out of their castles. They'd gone to war against whatever this incoming to-come was. The very facts of retrospection and fate that had various sides fighting were now out *themselves*, personified or apotheosed and smacking seven bells out of each other directly. No longer solely reasons, justifications, teloi, casus belli for others to invoke or believe in: now combatants. The war had just got meta.

"Cheers, Perky," she said. She unstoppered the container and flicked it so the invisible contents sprayed out of the protected circle. The pig went racing around, licking and champing and slobbering in dimensions where, happily, Collingswood did not have to clean up.

Now she knew it was only Perky the cautions were overkill, and she stepped out of the angles of electrostatic protection and switched them off. "Have fun," she said over her shoulder. "Don't mess shit up too much, and don't nick anything when you go."

kay kollywood byby thans for num.

Collingswood ran her hands through her hair, put on a minimum of makeup, her roughed-up uniform, and went through the deeply threatening city. "Broomstick's at the garage," she said to herself more than once. The joke was so old, so flat as to be meaningless. Saying it as if everything was all normal was a very slight comfort.

"You can't smoke in here," the taxi driver told her, and she stared at him, but couldn't even muster enough to wither him. She put the cigarette out. She did not light up again until she was in the FSRC wings of the Neasden Police Station.

You would have had to be a more adept adept than Collingswood to have even approximated some sight of what was going on, loomingly, totally, above everything. Various long-snoozing London gods had been woken up by the clamour, were stretching and trying to assert pomp and authority. They had not yet realised that no Londoners gave two shits about them anymore. The thunder that night was dramatic, but it was just the grump of past-it deities, a heavenly "What the bloody hell's all this noise?"

The real business was going on in the streets, on another scale. Few of the guards, earthly or unearthly, in any of London's museums, could have said why they suddenly felt so extremely afraid. It was because their memory palaces were unprotected. Their angels walked. The guardians of all the living museums came together, bar one still rogue on its own mission. The angels hunted the incoming end, that closed-down future. If they tracked it down they intended to mash it up.

VARDY WAS ALREADY IN THE OFFICES. COLLINGSWOOD THOUGHT HE looked unruffled by the night, no blearier or more rushed than he ever did. She hung from the doorframe. She was slightly taken aback by the, if anything, even more unwelcome than usual look that he gave her.

"Fucking hell, rudeboy," she said. "What's up with you? Apocalypse rattled your cage?"

"I'm not sure what this is," he said, scrolling through some website. "But it's not apocalypse yet. Of that I'm fairly certain."

"Just a manner of speaking."

"Oh, I think it's more than that. I think the word to keep in mind here is 'yet.' What brings you here?"

"What do you fucking think? The not-yet apocalypse, squire. You know what's going on? The memory guards are out looking to smack someone up. Those fuckers ain't supposed to leave the museums. I want to see if I can work out what's going on. Whatever just changed. What do you reckon?"

"Why not?"

"Fuck, you know, sometimes, seriously, sometimes you just wish you lived in a city where it wasn't all this craziness and this and that. I mean I know some of this lot are just villains, you know, just bad boys, but it all comes down to the god stuff in the end. In London. It does, though. Every, single, time. And that, man, what are you going to say." Collingswood shook her head. "Fucking mad weak shit. *Arks* and *dinosaurs* and *virgins*, fuck knows. Give me a robbery, man. Except they *do*, innit?"

" 'Mad weak shit?' " Vardy swung back his chair and looked at her with some queasy combine of dislike, admiration and curiosity. "*Really*? That's what it stems from, is it? You've got it all sorted out, have you? Faith is *stupidity*, is it?"

Collingswood cocked her head. *Are you talking to me like that, bro?* She couldn't read his head-texts, of course, not those of a specialist like Vardy.

"Oh, believe me, I know the story," he said. "It's a *crutch*, isn't it? It's a *fairy tale*. For the *weak*. It's *stupidity*. See, that's why you'll never bloody be good enough at this job, Collingswood." He waited as if he'd said too much, but she waved her hand, *Oh do please carry the fuck on.* "Whether you agree with the bloody predicates or not, *Con*-stable Collingswood, you should consider the possibility that faith might be a way of thinking *more* rigorously than the woolly bullshit of most atheists. It's not an intellectual mistake." He tapped his fore-head. "It's a way of thinking about all sorts of other things, as well as itself. The Virgin birth's a way of thinking about women and about *love*. The ark is a far more bloody logical way of thinking about the question of *animal husbandry* than the delightful ad hoc thuggery we've instituted. Creationism's a way of thinking *I am not worthless* at a time when people were being told and shown they were. You want to get angry about that bloody *admirable* humanist doctrine, and why would you want to blame Clinton. But you're not just too young, you're too bloody ignorant to know about welfare reform."

They stared at each other. It was tense, and weirdly slightly funny.

"Yeah but," Collingswood said cautiously. "Only, it's not *totally* admirable, is it, given that it's total fucking bollocks."

They stared some more.

"Well," Vardy said. "That is true. I would have to concede that, unfortunately." Neither of them laughed, but they could have done.

"Right," Collingswood said. "Why are *you* here? What are those files?" There were papers everywhere.

"Well . . ." Vardy seemed hesitant. He glanced at her. "You recall our rather peculiar note from the sky? I have a thought about who it might be." He closed one of the folders so she could see its title.

"Grisamentum?" she said. "He died." She sounded suitably uncertain.

"Indeed."

"Baron was at the funeral."

"Sort of. Yes."

"So was it the Tattoo, right?" Collingswood said. "Who did him in?"

"No. People thought so but no. He was just sick, is all, so he'd been talking to doctors, necromancers. We got hold of his medical records, and I can tell you he most certainly had cancer and it most certainly was killing him."

"So . . . why d'you think this was him?"

"Something about the style. Something about finding Al Adler after all this time. Something about the word emerging that several monsterherds have been approached for some big commission. Remember his . . . ?"

"No, I don't remember dick, I wasn't around."

"Well, he was always a traditionalist."

"So who are all this lot?" Collingswood said. She pointed at the details of some academic, some physicist called Cole, some doctor, Al Adler, Byrne.

"Associates. Connected in one way or another to his *ahem* funeral *ahem*. I'm thinking I might revisit them. I have a few ideas I'd like to chase up. All this has got me thinking. I've been having various *ideas* tonight." He smiled. It was alarming. "I do wonder if any of them might have a clue about all this. All *this*." He glanced beyond the walls, at the strange night, in which gods were ignored and memories were out hunting the future.

Chapter Forty-Three

"ALRIGHT." WITH EXPERT SPEED AND A MINIMUM OF FILTH-spillage, Dane emerged from a skip. He had a bust cup, a radio full of mould, half a suitcase. Billy stared at them. "What it is, if we got this seen to—there are people who can clean this up right, you know—we might be able to use this to—"

To what? The cup, it seemed, to carry some elixir that needed just this container—the radio to tune in to some opaque flow of decayed information or other—the suitcase to contain things that could otherwise not be carried. Dane struggled to articulate it. He kept reiterating that they needed equipment, if this was what they were facing.

Apparently, Billy thought, he lived now in a trite landscape. Deep enough below the everyday, Billy realised with something between awe and distaste, a thing has power, moronically enough, because *it's a bit like* something else. Want to hex up briars, what else should you throw behind you but an old comb? All it took was a way with such cute correspondences.

"The Londonmancers don't take sides," Dane said. "That's their whole thing."

"Maybe Saira's gone rogue," Billy said. "Doing this alone."

"I need a new gun," Dane said repeatedly. The battle of *Star Trek* Tower had left him raging at his armaments. Whatever the specifics of this fight around them, seemingly between Grisamentum and the

Londonmancers, he lacked firepower. With Wati's help, anonymising the request, Dane sent a request to London's arms dealers. Because someone out there had the psychic megatonnage of the fucking *Architeuthis* in their stockpile.

At the stub-end of Wandsworth Common he took delivery of a weapon, left under a particular set of bushes like some fabled baby. There were passersby but none close enough to see, and in any case, like most Londoners now, they moved furtively and quickly most of the time, as if they were at the park against their will.

Dane discarded his speargun with visible relief. As a paladin of the Church of God Kraken, he had had few options. Like many groups devoid of real power and *realpolitik*, the church was actually constrained by its aesthetics. Its operatives could not have guns, simply, because guns were *not squiddy* enough.

It was a common moan. Drunk new soldiers of the Cathedral of the Bees might whine: "It's not that I don't think sting-tipped blow-pipes aren't cool, it's just . . ." "I've got really good with the steam-cudgel," a disaffected pistonpunk might ask her elders, "but wouldn't it be useful to . . . ?" Oh for a carbine, devout assassins pined.

With a little more propagandist verve, the Church of God Kraken might have issued its fighters FN P90s, say, or HK53s, and explained with sententious sermon-logic how the rate of fire made the fanning vectors of bullets reach out *like tentacles*, or that the *bite* of the weapon was like that of a squid beak, or some such. As an excommunicant, Dane was no longer restrained. What he dug out of the earth where it had been delivered was a heavy handgun.

They did not know how many charges the phaser had, so Billy did not use it to practice. "I know what we can do," Dane said. He took them to amusement arcades, pushing through crowds of teens. Billy spent hours going from machine to screaming machine, firing plastic pistols at incoming zombies and alien invaders. Dane whispered advice to him on stance and timing—marksman words, soldier-insight among these play deaths. The sneers of watching youths decreased as Billy's skills grew.

"Done well, man," one boy said as Billy defeated an end-of-level boss. It was all disproportionately exhilarating. "Yes!" Billy whispered as he succeeded in missions.

"Al*right*, soldier," Dane said. "Nice one. Killer." He dubbed Billy a member of various violent sects. "You're a Thanicrucian. You're a Serrimor. You're a gunfarmer."

"A what?"

"Watch the screen. Bad bastards, once upon a time. Raised guns like fighting dogs. Let's get you shooting like them. Pay attention."

From *Time Cops* to the latest *House of the Dead* to *Extreme Invaders*, so Billy wouldn't learn the looped attack patterns. Marines and soldiers learned with such machines, Dane told him. Juba the Baghdad sniper went from zero to his deadly skill set using these. And these pretend guns had no recoil, no weight, no reloading—just like the phaser. Their limited realism made them paradoxically perfect practice for the real, ridiculous weapon Billy had come into.

Billy kept asking about the knuckleheads he might face. *How do they eat? How do they see? How do they think?*

"That's not the issue," Dane said. "The world can always finesse details. And who'd choose it? Always people ready to do that kind of thing."

So they knew what bait had got Simon porting. They needed to talk to Saira.

What's the point of the theological turn? Is godness a particularly resilient kind of grubbiness? Maybe the turn is like an ultraviolet torch at a crime scene, showing up spattered residue on what had looked clean ground. You don't know who to trust. Grisamentum's postal box was not a Royal Mail address, nor the service of any other carrier they knew. The postcode did not look quite regular. Some hush-hush Trystero carrier?

"It must get to him," Billy said.

"Yeah but not by the usual bloody routes." There would be no staking out the mail drop.

"How's Simon?" Billy said.

"Alright. I was there earlier," said Wati, from a Victorian statue. "I mean, not really. Mo's good with him though."

"What about the Londonmancer?" Dane said.

"I got as close as I could. She don't look like she even has a home. She sleeps in that building. Near the stone."

"Alright," said Dane. "We'll have to get her there, then. Wati, help me out. I'm trying to teach our boy some stuff about things." Billy heard the grinding sound of glass at the fringe of his consciousness. It had been a while. He waited, trying to understand it as a message.

"Alright, so . . ." he said eventually, when they passed a locksmith and he noticed something on display in the window. He remembered Dane's lesson at the bins, and stared at the miniature door to which various different on-sale handles had been attached, for show. "Alright so if you got hold of that," he said, "and did whatever to it, put it into a wall. Then you could, I bet you could . . ."

"There you go," Wati said from inside next to it, from a gargoyle door knocker. "You could use each different one of them handles to open it into somewhere else. Too small though. All you could do's stick your arm through."

These revelations into a paradigm of recusant science, so the goddamn universe itself was up for grabs, were part of the most awesome shift in vision Billy had ever had. But the awe had been greatest when he had not understood at all. The more they were clarified, the more the kitsch of the norms disappointed him.

"There." There was a key embedded in the tarmac. It had been dropped when the surface was still soft and then had been run over or toughly trodden in. Anxious clubbers and nightwalkers passed them.

"So," Billy said, "if we could get it to work, with a bit of knacking, we could use that to, like, travel from place to place?"

Dane looked at him. "We've got a lot to do tomorrow, and it's going to be pretty hairy," he said. "Let's get somewhere we can put our heads down." They were nearly out of safe houses. He looked at Billy suspiciously. "How come you figured you could make the key work that way?"

Because, Billy thought, *it'll, oh,* unlock the way.

Chapter Forty-Four

MARGE'S PROBLEM, WHEN SHE ASKED ON HER BULLETIN BOARDS where she should go, "as a noob in all this," to learn what London really was, was not too few but too many suggestions. A chaos of them. She had winnowed with a few questions, and had raised the issue of the cults. The issue, tentatively, of the church of the squid. A few false leads, and she came back again and again to the message that said: "cult collectors old queen almagan yard east london."

Down this way London felt like a city to which Marge had never been. She had thought the docklands all cleared out, bleached with money. Not this alley in gobbing distance of the Isle of Dogs, though. These felt like moments from some best-forgotten time burped back up, an urban faux pas, squalor as aftertaste.

Where the fuck am I? She looked again at her map. To either side were warehouses scrubbed and made flats for professionals. A channel of such buildings was parted as if grudgingly, an embarrassed entrance onto a cul-de-sac of much grubbier brick and potholed pavement. A few doors, a pub sign swinging. THE OLD QUEEN, it said in Gothicky letters, and below it a pinch-faced Victoria in her middle years.

It was the middle of the day. She'd have thought twice about walking into that streetlet at night. Her shoes got instantly filthy on its puddly surface.

The small pub bottle-glass window made the light inside seem dingy. A jukebox was playing something from the eighties, which as always with tracks from that decade registered in her head as a test. She hesitated: "Calling All the Heroes," It Bites. Grizzled drinkers muttered at each other, in clothes the same colours as everything else. People glanced up at her, back down again. A fruit machine made a tired electronic whoop.

"Gin and tonic." When the man brought it she said, "Friend of mine told me some collectors meet here."

"Tourist?" he said.

"No. Sounds up my street, is all. I was wondering about joining." The man nodded. The music changed. Soho, "Hippychick." Whatever happened to Soho?

"Fair enough. Be a bastard of a tourist to get here, anyway," he said. "They ain't in yet. Normally sit over there."

She took her place in the corner. The customers were subdued. They were men and women of all ethnicities and ages but a generally obscured air, as if the room had been painted with a dirty paintbrush. A woman drew in her spilt drink. A man talked to himself. Three people crowded around a table in one corner.

I think I'll have my next birthday here, she thought coldly. The music wandered on: "Funky Town," the Pseudo Echo version. *Holy shit*, "Iron Lung," Big Pig. *Kudos for that, but you can't catch me with these. You'll have to up your game*—Play Yazz, "The Only Way Is Up"—*and then you've got me for my wedding party.*

She watched the woman draw pictures on her tabletop, now and then adding little splashes of her beer to the picture. The woman looked up and thoughtfully sucked the dirty beer from her finger. Marge looked down, revolted. On the table the beer picture continued to self-draw.

"So what you been in?"

Marge stared. Two men in their forties or fifties swaggered suspiciously toward her. One man's face was set and impossible to read: the other, who spoke, changed expressions like a children's entertainer.

"Say that again?"

"Brian says you want to play. What you offering? You scratch my soul, you know, I'll scratch yours. Tit for tat, darling. So what you been in? We all like a bit of theology here, love, no need to be shy." He licked his lips. "Give us an afterlife, go on."

"Sorry," she said slowly. "I didn't mean to be misleading. I'm here because I need some help. I need some information and someone told me . . . I need to ask you some questions."

There was a pause. The man who had said nothing remained quite impassive. He straightened slowly, turned and walked out of the pub, putting his untouched drink down on the counter as he went.

"Fucking bloody Nora," said the other quietly. "Who the fuck you think you are? Coming in here . . ."

"*Please*," Marge said. The desperation in her voice surprised even her, and stopped him speaking. She kicked out the chair opposite, gestured him to sit. "Please, please, please. I really need help. Please sit down and listen to me."

The man did not sit, but he waited. He watched her. He put a hand on the back of the chair.

"I heard that someone . . ." she said. "I heard that maybe one of you knows something about the squid cult. You know the squid's gone, right? Well, so's my lover. Someone took him. And his friend. No one knows where they are, and it's something to do with this, and I need to talk to them. I need to find out what's going on."

The man tipped on his heels. He scratched his nose and glowered.

"I know some things," Marge said. "I'm in this. I need help for myself, too. You know . . ." She lowered her voice. "You know *Goss and Subby*? They came and hassled me." The man opened his eyes wide. He sat then, and leaned toward her. "So I need to find the squid people because they're sending people like that to bloody terrorise me . . ."

"Keep it quiet," he said. "Goss and buggeryfucking Subby? Holy bloody Ram's bollocks, girl, it's a wonder you're still walking. Look at you." He shook his head. Disgust or pity or something. "How'd you even get here? How'd you find this place?"

"Someone told me about it . . ."

"Marvellous, isn't it? Someone bloody told you." He shook his head. "We go to all the trouble. No one's even supposed to know this *blahdclat* place exists." He used the patois adjective, though he was white and his accent snarlingly Cockney. "This is a secret street, mate."

"It's right here," she said, and waved her map.

"Yeah and that should be the only place it is. D'you know what a trap street is? You know how hard it is to sort out that sort of thing?" He shook his head. "Listen, love, this is all beside the point. You shouldn't be here."

"I told you why I came . . ."

"No. I mean, if Goss and Subby are after you, you should not *be* here. If you got left alive it's just because they din't care about you, so for Set's sake don't get them caring about you."

"Please just tell me about the squid cult. I have to find them . . ."

"'Squid cult.' What are you *like*? Which you talking about? Khalkru? Tlaloc? Kanaloa? Cthulhu? It's Cthulhu, ain't it? Always is. I'm just fucking with you, I know what you're talking about. Church of God Kraken, isn't it?" He looked around. "They ain't nothing to do with Goss and Subby. Say what you like about the teuthists, doll, they don't run with that kind of company. Don't happen. Let me tell you something. I don't think they know what's up any more'n you do. It ain't them took the kraken. Too holy for them to touch, or something. But they ain't even *looking* for it, if you can believe that."

"I don't care about any of that. I just want to know what happened to Leon and Billy."

"Sweetheart, whatever it is going on it's all much too prickly for my bloody taste. None of us has gone anywhere near the teuthies since this kicked off. We'll keep it nice and bloody simple, thank you very much indeed. Spider-gods, Quakers, Neturei Karta, that sort of shit'll do me. Alright, maybe you don't get as many points for those scriptures, but . . ."

"I don't understand."

"Nor should you, deario. Nor should you."

"I heard you knew something about these people . . ."

"Alright *listen*," he said. He chopped the tabletop with his hand. "We ain't going to have this conversation. I ain't going down this road." He sighed at her expression. "Now look. I already told you everything I know, which is bugger-all, granted, but that's because that's what the Kraks know. If you're . . ." He hesitated. "You won't thank me for *helping* you know. Helping." He sighed. "Look if you really want to get yourself into this shit—and I do mean *shit* because that's what you'll end up in—there are people you should talk to."

"Tell me."

"Alright look. Jesus, girl, is this your first time on this side of things?" He sank all of his drink in one impressive swallow. "Rumours. Tattoo done it, Grisamentum's back and done it, no one done it. Well that's no help. So if I wanted to find out, and I do not, I'd think about who *else* might have claim on something like that? And think it's their business?"

He waited for an answer. Marge shook her head.

"The sea. I bet you the sea might have ideas. Wouldn't surprise me if the bastard ocean might have a little something to do with all this. Stands to reason, right? Taking back what's its? Render unto sea, sir." He cackled. Marge closed her eyes. "And if it *didn't*, probably wishes it had and has a clue who did."

"I should talk to the sea?" Marge said.

"God, woman, no need to sound so miserable about it. What, *all* of it? Talk to its ambassador. Talk to a flood-brother. Up at the barrier."

"Who are . . ."

"Now now." He wagged his finger *no*. "That's your bloody lot, alright? You've done well enough to get here. If you insist on getting eaten you can go a bit further; it ain't my job to walk you through. I don't need that on my conscience, girl. Go home. You won't, will you?" He blew out his cheeks. "For what it's worth, I'm sorry about your boy, alright? And for what it's worth, which in my professional opinion isn't a bloody lot, I'll pray for you."

"Pray to what?" Marge said. He smiled. The jukebox played "Wise Up Sucker" by Pop Will Eat Itself.

"Fuck it," the man said. "Tell you what. What's the point collecting stuff you don't use? I'll pray to all of them."

Chapter Forty-Five

"So Simon's doing alright," Dane said. "Getting over ghosts."

"So Wati said," Billy said. "He coming?"

"Strike's not going well," Dane said. "He's a touch bloody busy."

It was early daylight and they were near where the London Stone throbbed. Between buildings. Dane made little military hand motions the meanings of which Billy did not know. He followed Dane up onto a low wall, a complicated dance between cameras.

On their way Dane had told opaque teuthic homilies. Kraken did not steal fire from any demiurges, did not shape humans from clay, did not send baby kraken to die for our sins. "So Kraken was in the deep," Dane had said. "Was in the deep, and it ate, and it took it, like, twenty thousand years to finish its mouthful."

Is that it? Billy did not insist on exegesis.

Dane moved faster and more gracefully than a man of his bulk should. Billy found this climb easier than the last one, too. He could see only roofs in all directions, like a landscape. They descended toward an internal yard full of cardboard boxes softened by rain into vaguely vectoral brown sludge.

"This is where they come to smoke. Take out your weapon," Dane said. He held his pistol.

The first person out was a young man, who caned a cigarette and sniggered into his mobile phone. The second a woman in her forties with some stinking rollup. There was a long wait after that. The next time the door opened, it was Saira Mukhopadhyay, wrapped in smart scarves.

"Ready," Dane whispered. But she was not alone. She was chatting to an athletic guy lighting a Silk Cut. "Arse," said Dane.

"I'll take him," Billy whispered. "We haven't got long," Billy said. They could hear the conversation.

"Alright," Dane said. "Do you know how to . . . set your phaser to stun?" They couldn't help it: they giggled. Billy pushed his glasses up his nose. He could not have made this jump a few weeks before, phaser in his hand, a pitch down into a hard but controlled landing. He stood and fired. The big man spun across the yard and went down in the rubbish.

Here was Dane dropping beautifully behind Saira. She heard him, but he was already on her. He backhanded her into the bricks. She braced herself. Where her fingers clenched, they squished the bricks as if they were Plasticine.

Saira hissed, literally hissed. Dane smacked her again. She looked at him with blood on her lip. It had been easy to forget that for Dane this was sacred fervour.

"Steady, man," Billy said.

"Not many people could port something that size out of there," Dane said. "But you know that. We know who got it out of there, and we know what you dangled to make him do it. I don't like it when someone steals my god. It gets me all fucking twitchy. *What did you do*? What did Al Adler have to do with all this? The end of the world's coming, and I want to know what you did with my *god*."

"You know who you're bloody talking to?" she said. "I'm a Londonmancer . . ."

"You're living a dream. The London heart stops beating, you know what's going to happen? Fuck all. London don't need a heart. Your mates know what you been doing?"

"That's enough."

Fitch had entered the yard. They stared at him as he closed the door behind him. He stood by Saira, in the path of Dane's weapon.

"You think I should be in a museum," he said. "Might be. But museum pieces have their uses, right, Billy? You're *almost* right about me, Dane. See, when you don't have the knack you used to, you're no threat. So people tell you things."

"Fitch," said Dane. "This is between me and Saira . . ."

"No it is not," Fitch said. He squared all pugnacious, then withered. "She just handled the money. You want to know what happened, talk to me."

"I SHOUT," HE SAID, "AND THE OTHERS'LL BE HERE."

Things flew overhead. Edgy birds. He glanced at them, and from where Billy stood, the perspective looked wrong.

"*You* took it?" Dane said.

"If you were still a Krakenist, I'd not be talking to you," Fitch said. "But you aren't, and I want to know why. Because you've got him." He nodded at Billy. "And he's the one who knows what's going on."

"I do *not*," Billy said. "Not this again."

"Why don't you want the Krakenists to know what's going on?" said Dane. "We . . . they . . . ain't London's enemies."

"I know how they want to get rid of their holies. And I know where that sort of thing leads."

"What? They aren't even looking for it, let alone getting rid of it," Billy said.

"I wish you was right, Fitch, but you ain't," Dane said. "The church ain't doing anything."

"Why do *you* want the kraken?" Fitch said. "I've got no business seeing anything in the guts these days. They just sit there squelching. But there it was. Fire. First time since I don't know how long, and oh my London what I did see."

"What's Al Adler in this?" Billy said.

"*Why did you take it?*" Dane whispered.

Fitch and Saira looked at each other. Saira shrugged. "I don't think we have a choice," she said.

"It was his fault," Fitch said. He whined. Billy could tell the old man was relieved to break his vow. "It was him started it. Coming here with his plans, and the burning at the end of it."

"Al? You said he was superstitious," Billy said to Dane. "So—he came for a reading. But no one liked what they saw."

"Tell us," Dane said, his voice shaking, "everything."

ADLER HAD COME TO THE LONDONMANCERS WITH A RIDICULOUS, audacious plan. *He was going to steal the kraken.* He was not afraid to say so in that hallowed confessional: Fitch, not judging, unshocked even at that stage by the enormous crime to come, bound to confidentiality by oaths in place since the Mithras temple, split the city's skin to see what might happen.

"There's no way Al thought of that job," Dane said.

A courtesy, a formality. Fitch expected to see nothing, as he had for years. What he saw was fire.

The burning end of it all. Burning what it couldn't burn, taking the whole world.

And after? Nothing. Not a phoenix age, not a kingdom of ash, not a new Eden. This time, for the first time, in a way that no threatened end had ushered in before, there was no post-after.

"Most of the Londonmancers don't know anything about this," Saira pled. They could not have been expected to overturn their vows like their leader and his best lieutenant had done. "It was obvious Al was just a front guy. Hardly criminal genius, was he?"

"What did you tell him?" Billy said.

Fitch waved. "Some waffle. We had to decide what to do fast."

"Couldn't you have told him not to do it?" Billy said. Everyone looked at him. That wasn't the point at all. You didn't *alter plans* on the basis of a Londonmancer reading, any more than you picked a spouse on the basis of a fairground palm reader's wittering. "Why would he want to end everything?" said Billy.

"I'm not sure he did," said Fitch carefully.

The plan might have set in motion something of its own. Ineluctable, final, unintended consequences. How bad does it have to be to make a Londonmancer break a millennium of honour and intervene? This bad is how bad.

"So you had to get in there first to stop him setting it off," said Billy in some kind of wonder. "You had to *presteal* it."

"That auction was coming up." Saira shrugged. "We needed Simon-bait. It wasn't that hard to find an armsmith to knack it. Dane . . . we didn't know when this was going to happen."

"We had to move when we moved," Fitch said. "Understand—*everything burns and nothing happens again*, if they got the kraken. When Adler told me, everything changed."

Simon performing his game, whispering phrases from his TV show, arriving in the dark of the Darwin Centre with an assiduously replicated fade-in like glitter in water, to "take coordinates," and with a flex of power disaggregating the kraken and himself in a stream of particles, energy, particles again.

"So *what happened to Adler*?" Billy said. Saira met his eye. Fitch did not.

"A place like that," Saira said. "It's guarded. You can't just walk in."

"You cold bastards," Dane said finally.

"Oh, please," said Saira. "I don't take that from assassins."

"You used him as bait," Billy said. "Told him whatever to keep him . . . no, for the timing, you sent him in."

"Simon would never have got in and out," Fitch wheedled. "We didn't know the angel would . . . we just needed to distract it." The angel of memory, the mnemophylax, swooping in on Al, as Simon beamed the bewildered would-be burglar in. Not as if the wrecked Trekkie was innocent of that death, either. Turned out there was at the very least one culpable homicide he really did have on his hands.

"And while it's dealing with him, you took the kraken out." Billy shook his head. "That raises the second issue. You did all this to stop this fire, right?" He raised his hands. "Well, you showed us the guts. We all know what the sky feels like. *So what went wrong?*"

A long quiet. "It didn't work," Saira said. She shook her head and opened and closed her mouth.

Billy laughed unpleasantly. "You saw what would happen if it was stolen. So you stole it to stop it being stolen. But by stealing it you stole it. And set it off."

"I don't know what to do," Fitch said.

"I'll tell you what you're going to do," Dane said. "You are going to take me to my god."

Chapter Forty-Six

THE PIGEONS' BELLIES WERE MISBEHAVING AGAIN, AND THE revolting results of these anxieties featured as quirky news filler. Other urban ructions were growing harder to ignore by selective banalising notice. Fuel would hardly burn in domestic fireplaces. There was nervous speculation about atmospheric conditions. Every flame was grudging. As if there were a limited amount of it available; as if it were being hoarded; saved up for something.

Also, *oh yes*, people were disappearing. There are no civilians in war, no firewalls between the blessedly ignorant and those intimately connected to networks, markets of crime and religiosity. And Londoners, even those determinedly mainstream, were disappearing. Not in that mythical without-a-trace way, but with the most discomfiting remnants: one shoe; the shopping they had been going to get but *had not yet bought* sitting in a bag by their front door; a graffito of the missing where they were last seen. You may not have known what was happening, but that something was happening was not plausibly deniable.

BILLY AND DANE HADN'T DONE BADLY. THE CARE OF THEIR MOVEments; the camouflage Dane dragged behind them with little shuffled hexes, second nature for a man of his training; the disguises, ridiculous but not ineffective; Dane's soldier care: all these had kept them from collectors' eyes for days, which when you're the target of by some way the largest collection of bloodprice talent to be assembled on a single job in London for a whole pile of years, isn't nothing.

For a creditable time, those stalkers had been frustrated. The tally-ho of the urban hunt sounded like a parping fart in the latest hours, as they rode unorthodox horses over roofs, making locals think there had been very brief very heavy rain, and tracked down bugger-all. The vaguely cowboy gunslingers had failed to run them down. Londoners slept badly, as their internal nightlands were infiltrated by eyeless snuffling beasts that lolloped through their sex reveries and parental angsts, dreamhounds sent out by hunters at their most dangerous when they slept. They could not sniff their quarries either.

The hunters fought among themselves. More than once they faced murderous confrontations with figures that seemed part of some other agenda, that were come and gone too fast to make sense of in any political schema of which anyone knew. Men who disappeared when seen, men and women accompanied by shuffling monster shadows.

The gangs and solitary freelancers seeded the city with rewards: anything for a harvest of hints. With all his care, nous and skill, Dane could not stand in the way of all the snips, momentary glances, overheard words—all the stuff that registered not at all on passersby, but that the best hunter could winkle out of someone who did not even know they were withholding, could collate and aggregate.

"I'M GOING INSIDE," FITCH SAID. "THE REST OF THE LONDONMANCERS need to see me. And we'll have to find a way to get him onside, now." He indicated the man Billy had shot.

"You got to let me go back in, Dane," he said. "You want to get them worried?"

Dane raised his weapon as if he did not know what to do with it, and gritted his teeth.

"Do you believe them?" Billy whispered.

"We didn't know what you wanted to do with it," Fitch said. "Or we would have said."

"We didn't know if we could trust you," Saira said. "You know how some Muslims get rid of Qur'an pages? They burn them. That's the holiest method. Whatever's coming is after burning the whole world down, starting with the squid. And it's still out there. We thought that might be your plan."

"You thought *I'd* end the world?" Dane said.

"Not deliberately," Fitch said, in a strange reassurance. "By accident. Trying to set your god free."

Dane stared at them. "I ain't going to burn shit," he said levelly. "Take me to it."

And we can tell you what we know, Billy thought. *That Grisamentum's still alive.*

"There's things need preparing," Fitch said. "Protections. Dane, we can work together. We can be in this together." He was eager now. How long had he been bending under this?

"We ain't short of offers," Dane said. "Everyone wants to work with us."

"There's things we need to know," Saira said. "There's *got* to be something about this kraken. That's why we need you," she said to Billy. "You're the squid man. This is *perfect*. If we can work out what it is about *this* one, maybe we can stop it."

"Do you believe them?" Billy whispered. He heard the grind of glass. "I think I do, Dane."

THAT WAS HOW THE TWO OF THEM ENDED ALONE IN THE YARD, while the Londonmancers returned inside, to mum normality for a few more hours.

"What if they . . . ?" Dane said as they waited.

Billy said, "What? Run? They can't disappear their whole operation. Tell someone? The last thing they want is anyone to know what they did."

"What if they . . . ?"

"They need me," Billy said.

They wedged the door closed so frustrated smokers would find another place to go. "Wait," Saira had told them. "When we're done here, we'll go." The sky went dark over hours.

"Soon," said Dane. What impeccable timing, what a perfect jinx: as he said that, there was the glass noise, in Billy's head. Knowledge came with it. He stood.

"Someone's coming," he said.

"What?" Dane stood. "Who?"

"I don't know." Billy held his temples. What the fuck? "Jesus." His *headache* was talking to him. "I just know they're coming. I don't think they know where we are. Not exactly. But they're close and they aren't friends."

Dane looked around the yard. Grind grind. "They're getting closer," Billy said.

"They can't find us here," Dane said. "They can't know the Londonmancers are in on this. We can't lead them to God." He grabbed a metal shard and ground into the wall the words BACK ASAP. Written in scratches among scratches.

"Up," he said. Made his hands a sling and pushed Billy back onto the roof. They scuttled under the arriving night, back down drainpipes and corporate fire escapes, to the main streets of the city, close to deserted now. This was the worst for them, being almost the only people in a street. Every lamplight was like a spotlight. Billy could hardly think through the noise of glass.

"You hear a noise?" Dane said. "Like glass?"

No one else was supposed to hear it! There was no time. There was another sound now. Running feet. CCTV cameras spun, twinkled their lights, looked every which way. From around a corner came men.

Billy stared. They wore a raggedy new romance of costumes. He saw punk stylings, top hats, pantaloons and tube tops, *powdered wigs*. Their faces were quite ferocious. Billy raised his phaser.

As they came the attackers' bad knacks waxed, and the streetlamps they passed glowed too bright, changed colour, snapped one by one into blacklight, so the men's white cuff-frills and reflective cat's-eye flourishes glowed. Billy could see stitched on their clothes many-armed tags, some kind of profligate mutant swastikas. The men hissed like moon monkeys.

Dane and Billy shot. There were so many flamboyant figures. Billy shot again. He waited for them to shoot back, but they held whips, blades. Darkness encroached, overtook the attackers and hid them. There were no lights in any window, no glimmer from any office. There was only one last orange streetlight still burning, a lighthouse now, at which Billy stared as the men came.

Dane went back to back with him. "They want us alive," Dane whispered.

"Alive yes for discussion," someone said. "Someone wants to pick your brains." There were laughs at that. "Alive, but limbs and eyes are optional. Come on now and you can keep them."

"*There's always the workshop*," someone else said.

"There is the workshop," the first voice said. Obscured by the unnatural dark. Billy fired at random, but the shot illuminated only itself. "He does love his workshop. What will you be?"

"Be ready," Dane whispered.

"For what?" the voice said. A whip kinked out of the shade and wrapped around Billy's leg, sticking where it touched like a gecko foot, yanking him off his feet and out of the circle of last light. Down on the tarmac Billy opened his mouth to shout, but there was that glass grinding, much louder than he had ever heard it before. His head was full of communicative pain. Something came. It whirled.

Bone arms windmilling. There was a clack of teeth, vivid empty eyes. Finger bones punctured meat like fangs. The thing arrived with incomprehensible motion, too fast. It punch-punched stiff-fingered, leaving blood, ripping the throats of two, three, five of the attackers, so they screamed and fell pissing blood.

Billy kicked off the whip. He crawled back. The interceder rocked at the edge of the light.

It was a skull on the top of a giant jar. A huge glass preserving bottle, of the type that Billy had for years been filling with preservative and animal dead. This one was nearly five feet high, full of flesh slough and clouding alcohol. On its glass lid was a shabby human skull liberated, Billy absolutely knew, from one of the cupboards of remains in the Natural History Museum. It snapped its teeth. Where the rim met the lid the flaring glass served as shoulders, and the thing raised two fleshless taloned arms taken from bone boxes, humerus, ulna radius, clacking carpals and those sharpened phalanges.

The angel of memory.

The jar-angel rolled on its round base, oscillate-rocking forward. It punched again and killed again, and with a tiny incline of the skull-head opened its lid. A dandy man froze. He was motionless, then not there at all, and Billy saw more meat shreds in the jar. The bounty hunters scattered. There was a flat sound. Dane was down and motionless. Billy was too far, and the lasso or whatever it was that had Dane by the neck went taut, and Dane was dragged into the dwindling shadow the swastika-wearing men had brought with them.

Billy fired twice, but he could see nothing of them, and Dane was barely visible anymore. Billy grabbed Dane's gun. "Here!" he shouted to his glass rescuer, and he heard it wobble and roll toward him. The attackers hurled half-bricks and iron as they retreated.

A lucky heavy piece took the cylinder full on. The jar-angel smashed. The guard of the museum's memory burst. Its bones went dead among the chemical slick and glass shards.

Billy raised his phaser in one hand, gun in the other. But the attackers did not come back. He ran in the direction Dane had been dragged, but the darkness retreated quicker than he moved, and when it was gone he was alone. The corpses were still there, the glass scintillas, the skull of what had saved him. Dane was gone.

As always when a quiet holed the city, a dog barked to fill it. Billy walked through the ruined remains of his rescuer, left preservative footprints. He sat heavily and held his head by the dead, in the doorway of a sandwich bar.

That was where he was when the Londonmancers found him—nothing so dramatic could take place so close to the London Stone without them knowing it. He could see them at the limits of his vision, but they would not come closer, would not breach their neutrality, which only a few of them could have known was already fucked.

It must have been one of them who got word to Wati, who came into the toy Billy still carried, so the voice came from his pocket. "Billy, mate. Billy. What happened? We better go, Billy. We'll get him back. But right now we better go."

PART FOUR

LONDON-UPON-SEA

Chapter Forty-Seven

"So the honest bloody shitty bollocks is that I'm wondering what the fuck it is we're up to."

"Look," said Baron sharply. "You know what, Constable? I'd be obliged if we could have a smidge less of that."

Collingswood was terribly startled. She covered with a swagger. She didn't look at him but at her bracelet.

"We could do with a few things, Collingswood," Baron said. "We all know it." He took a moment and spoke again more calmly, jabbing his finger at her. "Not least of which is some information. And we're on that. Now . . . Calm down and get back to work. You've got your own sniffers sniffing, I presume? Well, see what they can smell." He walked away, through a door that he closed loud enough on her to almost be a slam.

In the grounds of the police training college at Hendon was the portacabin where the specialists of various FSRC cells went through their training. Pitifully nicknamed Hogwarts by most attendees, Cackle's and Gont by a few who exchanged smug looks when others didn't get it.

Collingswood hadn't. Didn't care. Had been too busy listening to the semiretired witches, mavens and karcists. "You are police officers, or will be," one of her instructors had said, "unless you bollocks this up proper." He was ancient and small, lined like discarded skin scooped off cocoa. He had stroked his chin as if everything he said was well considered. He swaggered too, in a very different way than she did. She loved watching him.

"Your job is to get villains. Right? You'll have to know what to do. If you don't know what to do you have to find out. If you can't find out you bloody well make it up and then you make it so. Do I make myself clear?" The little *lux ex tenebris* that he flashed between his fingertips as he spoke (blue, of course), was a nice touch.

Through all the occult jurisprudence since then, chasing things down and banging them up, that sort of fuckity vigour was what she had always seen as being police. The lack of it in him was what had made Collingswood impatient with, if amused by, Billy Harrow.

With a pitch inside, Collingswood considered the possibility that Baron was not sure what to do. She thought about that. She examined that as carefully as if it were something she had picked off the floor and was trying to identify. Officers walked around her where she stood—she was there long enough. Some of them didn't even give her an odd look. *Collingswood, you know.*

She stood near the dispatch room, so she was the first FSRC officer the messenger saw to give word to. It was she, then, who shoved open the door on Baron sitting folded-armed staring glumly at his computer, hung to the doorframe with one hand like a kid on a climbing frame, and said, "Ask and you receive, boss. Currently hospitalised. But it's info."

It was a shitty day, all sodden drab grey air and a sulky wind as irritating as a child. Despite that Marge spent the morning outside, in the Thames Barrier Park. She trudged in drizzle through the waveform topiary, past miniature football pitches. That morning she had cried a long time about Leon, and it had felt like a last time. She had finished, but it was as if the sky had not.

Marge suspected that she did not have a job anymore. Her boss was a friend, but her repeated nonanswering of his messages must have put him in an impossible position.

It was not as if she felt confused. It was not as if she felt driven, precisely, overtaken, losing her mind, anything like that. It was just, she thought, that she could not concentrate on anything else. She was not hysterical. It was just that having discovered that London was not what it was supposed to be, having discovered that the world had been lying to her, she had to know more. And she still had to know what had happened to Leon.

Not that he was alive. She knew that ridiculous sputtering message in bad light must be true.

Which brought her here, to this little sculpted grassland by the river's defences. There at the notional mouth of the river, by the industrial lowlands of Silvertown, the piers of the Thames Flood Barrier squatted in the water like huge alien hives, like silver-carapaced visitors. Between them chopped brown water, and below that water in the slime of the river's bed ten gates hunkered, ready to rise.

It was a long way round to the foot tunnel in Woolwich, but Marge had the whole day. She could see the barrier control building rise from the roofs of the south bank. She thumbed at her phone.

Christ Jesus it was depressing, she thought, this part of the city. She took the route by City Airport and under the river, huddling into her coat. She did not check the details she had printed out: she knew them by now. The information had been hard to winkle out of her online informants but not *that* hard. It had taken wheedling and guile but not quite as bloody much as it should have done if you asked her. As she'd been able to tell, yes, these were "secret" bulletin boards, but plenty of their members were just bursting with pride about what they knew. It was all *I've said too much,* and *You did not hear this from me.*

From who, you fucking prick? Marge had thought at that particular disavowal. *All I know is your screen name, which is* blessedladee777 *if you fucking please, so please just get on with it.*

Pre-armed by the cult-collector with the terms "floodbrother," and the location of "the barrier," it had taken a couple of days, but no more, to uncover a little bit more information. This time it was a place of work and an affiliation, the outlines of a system of belief.

Marge finished her cigarette. She shook her head and jogged on the spot for a bit, then came rushing into the Thames Barrier Visitors' Centre. The woman behind the reception desk stared at her in alarm. "You have to help me," Marge said. She made herself gabble. "No, listen. Someone here calls themself floodbrother, yeah online. Listen, you have to get them a message."

"I, I, what, what's their name?"

"I don't *know*, but I'm not crazy. I swear. Please, this is a matter of life and death. I mean it, literally. There must be a way of getting a message to everyone who works here. I'm not talking just about the Visitors' Centre, I'm talking about the engineering. Listen to me, I'm *begging* you, I'm *begging* you." She grabbed the woman's hand. "Tell whoever here's nickname's floodbrother, just say that, that there's a message from *Tyno Helig*. He'll understand. Believe me. *Tyno Helig*, got it?" She scribbled the name on a scrap. "I'll be waiting. I'll be in Maryon Park. *Please*."

Marge stared into the woman's eye and tried for some insinuatory sisterly thing. She wasn't sure how well it went. She ran out and away, until she had turned a corner, at which point she slowed and wandered calmly along Warspite Road, past the roundabout to the park.

The weather was too different and too bad to jog much reminiscence, but she looked around until she was pretty sure she had found a spot recognizable from the film *Blow-Up*. She sat as close to it as she could. She watched everyone who came in. She fingered the little flick-knife she had bought, for whatever useless good it would be. She was banking rather on daylight and passersby. Marge wondered whether she would know if her quarry entered the park.

In the event, when, after almost an hour, her call was answered, there was no question at all. It was not one person but three. All men, they strode urgently along the little paths, looking in all directions. They were big, athletic guys. They wore identical engineers' uniforms. The oldest, at the front, was gesturing to his two companions to fan out. Marge stood: she would feel safer facing all three of them than one. They saw her immediately. She closed her hand around her knife.

"Hi," she said. "I'm Tyno Helig."

They hung just a little back. Their fists were clenched. The front man's jaw worked with tension.

"Who," he said, "are you? What the hell are you doing? You said you had a *message*?"

She could see his contradictory emotions. Rage, of course, that they should be discovered and outed at work, when they were in mufti. Rage that they should be mocked like this, their faith scorned, as she could see him think surely this must be. And yet, as well as that anger, wrestling with it, excitement. She recognised that little bastard *hope*. "What's your message?" he said.

Her plan had worked, then. Tyno Helig, no person but a place: one of the sunken kingdoms, the Welsh Atlantis. *That*, she had thought, making her plan, should intrigue them. "Who are you?" the man said.

"Sorry for misleading you," she said. "I needed to get you out. I'm sorry"—she hesitated for a second, but sod it, she was too tired not to piss people off—"this isn't about your aspirational tidal wave. I have a question for you."

The man raised his clenched fist to his head, as if he would hit himself, then suddenly grabbed her by the lapels. His companions crowded them, shielding them from others' view. "Our *what*?" he whispered. "You have a *question*? Do you know who we *are*? You better start convincing me not to drown you. Do you know who we are?"

SHE HAD AN IDEA, YES. OUTRÉ BELIEFS WOULD KEEP CROPPING UP IN her researches. She had trawled around hard enough for the info.

The Communion of the Blessèd Flood. The rainbow, she gathered from some furtive online theologian, wasn't a promise: it was a curse. The fall didn't come when the first couple left the garden: all that was some ghastly prerapturous dreamtime of trials. What happened was that God rewarded his faithful with eventual holy rains.

Mistranslation, she had read. If what Noah, Ziusudra, Utnapishtim or the same figure by any other name had been told to build was a *ship*, why did the Torah not say so? Why was his ark not an *oniyah*, a ship, but a *tebah*—a box? Because it was built not to ride the waves God sent, but to move below them. History's first submarine, in gopher wood, three hundred cubits long, travelling the new world of God's promise. It harvested the meadows of kelp. But those chosen for the watered paradise had failed, and God had been wrathful and withdrawn the seas. That landscape of punishment was where we lived, exiled from the ocean.

The Communion of the Blessèd Flood prayed for the restoration of the wet. Marge read of their utopias, sunk not in ruination but reward: Kitezh, Atlantis, Tyno Helig. They honoured their prophets: Kroehl and Monturiol, Athanasius, Ricou Browning, and John Cage's father. They cited Ballard and Garrett Serviss. They gave thanks for the tsunami and celebrated the melting of the satanic polar ice, which mockingly held water in motionless marble. It was a sacred injunction on them to fly as far and often as they could, to maximise carbon emissions. And they placed holy agents where they might one day help expedite the deluge.

So this little cell, working in what might seem the most blasphemous industry of flood-defence. They were biding their time. Blocking piddling little backtides and holding out for the big one. When that final storm surged, that sublime backwash came roaring from the deep, then, *then* they would throw their spanners in the works. And after the water closed on the streets like a Hokusai trapdoor the Brotherhood of the Blessèd Flood would live at last in the submerged London of which they dreamed.

And now her message. It *was* the end of the world, everyone knew that . . . maybe, they'd thought, it was *theirs*.

"Count yourself lucky no one's messed with you till now," Marge said. She pulled out of his grip. "I never even heard of you until a few days ago. Someone said you speak for the sea. And maybe you took the squid. You know what I'm talking about. I need to know . . . Someone who did something with that bloody thing did something to my man."

"You've got face," he said. "I'm not saying that buys you an out, but you've got something."

"I told you, man," said another. "Everything's messed up."

"It's not face," she said. "It's just that I'm really tired, and I loved him. He was with Billy Harrow . . . Billy Harrow." She said it again at his reaction. The man rolled his thick neck and glanced at the others.

"Harrow," he said. "Harrow? He's the one *took* the kraken, I thought. That's what I heard. He's like its prophet. He went with Dane Parnell, when he ran from the Krakenists. It's them you want to talk to. They're the ones took it."

"No they're not." They stared at each other.

"Dane ran from his church when the kraken went, to join Harrow, so if they've got something to do with your bloke . . ."

"I'm telling you," she said. "That isn't what happened. I don't know anything about Parnell, I don't know much about much, but Billy Harrow did *not* take the squid. I had a pizza with him." That made her laugh. "And I know it wasn't him. I think he's dead, anyway. And if he knew where Leon was, he'd tell me . . ." She shut up, at the memory of the on-off-on-off streetlamp. "He'd tell me," she said slowly. "If he could."

The man huddled with his companions. She waited. She could hear them in debate.

"Do you *think*," she said suddenly, to her own mild surprise, "that I'd be messing around with you if I had any choice?" They blinked at her. "I don't want any of this, I don't want this bollocks, I don't believe your crap, I don't want a drowned world and I don't want a squid to be the king of the universe and I don't want to get involved in this crazy shit, and I don't even think I'm ever going to get Leon back. I'm just tired and it turns out"—she shrugged to say *who knew?*—"it turns out I need to find out what happened. You telling me you've got no idea what's going on? What is the *use* of you people." She was tearing up a little bit, not weakly or weepingly but out of infuriation.

"Whoever it is been talking to you," he said, and hesitated. "They don't know what they mean. We don't *represent* the sea, we don't . . . How could we? That's misinformation."

"I don't care . . ."

"Yeah, I do. People need to know. Stuff's brewing. How do you know all this? Who's helping you?"

"No one. Jesus."

"I can't do nothing for you." He wasn't speaking gently, but not aggressively either. "And I don't talk for the sea." He spoke with irritated care. Her impression was that this man devoutly wishing for the effacing of the world by water, the reconfiguration of all humanity's cities by eels and weeds, the fertilizing of sunken streets with the bodies of sinners, was a decent enough guy.

"You need to be careful," he said. "Stay out of trouble. You need protection. This is a dangerous town any time, and right now it's mad. And you're going to tread on toes. *Get protection.* You're not wearing a damn thing, are you." He clutched at his chest, where an amulet might hang. "You'll get yourself killed. No good to your bloke that way, are you?"

She was going to say *I'm not a child*, but his brusque kindness unmanned her. "Leave this alone. And if you don't, go to someone. Murgatroyd, or Shibleth, or Butler, or someone. Remember those names. In Camden, or in Borough. Tell them Sellar sent you."

"Look," she said. "Can you, can I take your number? Can I talk to you about all this? I need some help. Can I . . . ?"

He was shaking his head. "I can't help you. I can't. I'm sorry. This is a bit of a *busy time*. Go on now." He patted her shoulder, like she was an animal. "Good luck."

Marge left that dogged landscape of Woolwich. She did not look back at the horrible flattened dome, all white as if sickly. Her best lead had gone nowhere. She had more to do. Perhaps she would, as he advised, seek protection.

HER BEST LEAD HAD GONE TO NOTHING, TRUE, BUT SHE HAD BEEN A lead herself, though Marge had not known it. The revelation that Billy Harrow, the mysterious kraken prophet, might *not* be the force behind the godling's disappearance, was important.

The armies of the righteous needed to know. The sea needed to know.

Chapter Forty-Eight

Jᴀsᴏɴ Sᴍʏʟᴇ, ᴛʜᴀᴛ ᴘʀᴏʟᴇᴛᴀʀɪᴀɴ ᴄʜᴀᴍᴇʟᴇᴏɴ, ʟɪsᴛᴇɴᴇᴅ ᴀs Bɪʟʟʏ begged him to take out an unpaid commission.

"You're Dane's friend," Billy said.

"Yeah," Jason said.

"Do this for him," Billy said.

Billy did not know where Jason was. They had no time to arrange a meet. He had given Wati the number of the phone he had—without much difficulty, even in the miserable aftermath of that assault—stolen. Wati found Jason and passed on the number.

"Do you understand what's happened?" Billy said. "They took him. Chaos Nazis. You know what that means." Billy felt as if he knew, too, as if this was where he had lived a long time. Dane, unlike him, had had no angelus ex machina watching.

"What do you want from me?" When he spoke, even down the line, Billy felt as if he knew Jason from somewhere.

"We need to find him, and we need to know what's going on. There's bad connections going on here. Listen." Billy hooked the phone with his shoulder and swung through a tear in wire into a fenced-off yard. "These Nazis are being paid by the Tattoo. And his people are also the ones doing shit to Wati's pickets. Along with the police.

"We need to know how deep those connections go. For all we

know the cops might be *holding* Dane. They're obviously in some sort of cahoots with the Tattoo, they must at least know where he is. So we need you. But even if we could find them you couldn't walk into the Nazis, it wouldn't work, right?"

"*No*," said Jason. "They're not paid, so it's a nonstarter. They're committed, and I can't hide behind belief. That and proper knacking'll screw me."

"Right. So you need to go into Neasden Station and see what they've got on all this. Find out what you can. Jason, it's *Dane*."

". . . Yeah," Jason said. "Yeah."

Though his voice had not admitted the possibility that Jason would refuse, Billy closed his eyes in relief. "Call me when you're done, tell me what you can find out," Billy said. "Thanks. You need to do this now, Jason. Thank you. We've got no idea where they are."

"What are you . . . ?"

"I've got some other stuff I need to find out about. Jason, please do this now. We need to find him." Billy disconnected.

How do you walk away from a scene like that? All Billy had been able to do, in the cold quiet overlooked by big dead buildings, when Dane had been taken, was follow Wati's voice. The rebel spirit had led him from his pocket and from what few figurines it could find in that awful empty sector.

Billy said, "The Londonmancers."

"Keep it down, mate," Wati had told him from some la-la Billy did not even see. "No one's going to help us." That inner core, Fitch and Saira and their little crew, the stunned man Billy had shot and unintentionally press-ganged, could not come to his aid. Billy had no safe houses, no hides.

"Oh bloody hell," said Wati.

As if it weren't in trouble enough, the UMA had to act as babysitter for this suddenly bereft little messiah. But Billy had not obeyed his injunction to raise the metal lid out of the street, with intricate finagling and a strength he had not had a few weeks before, to slip into the undercity. Instead, Billy had paused, clenched without clenching, and felt time hesitate and come back, moving like a shaken blanket. He had told Wati to come with *him*, rather, and gone and stolen a phone. He had taken the innermost doll of a Russian doll set from some shop, held it, not his foolish Kirk, though he had kept that, up to his eyes, and said to Wati, "Here's what we need to do."

"OF ALL THE LITTLE TOERAGS WE EVER HAVE TO DEAL WITH," BARON said, "the bastarding Chaos Nazis are the ones I hate most."

He stood between Collingswood and Vardy. He was scratching his face furiously, anxiously. They crowded around each other to look through the reinforced glass into a hospital room, where a bandaged man was shackled by tubes, and by shackles, to a bed. A machine tracked his heartbeat.

"You actually said 'toerags,'" Collingswood said. "Are you auditioning for something?"

"Alright," he said vaguely. He sniffed. "Arseholes."

"Fuck's sake, boss," Collingswood said. "Up your game. Shitfoxes."

"Bastards."

"Spitfish, boss. Fucklizards. Little cuntwasps. Munching wanktoasters." Baron stared at her. "Oh yeah," Collingswood said. "That's right. I got game. Say my name."

"Tell me," Vardy interrupted. "What precisely do we have from them? There were several of them, correct?"

"Yeah," said Baron. "Five in various degrees of injuredness. And the dead."

"I want to know exactly what they saw. I want to know exactly what's happening."

"You got ideas, Vardy?" Collingswood said.

"Oh, yes. Ideas I have. Too bloody many. But I'm trying to put all this together." Vardy stared at the man in the bed. "This is the Tattoo. We heard he was employing headsmen. I wasn't expecting it to be this lot."

"Yeah, bit of a breach of protocol, isn't it?" Baron said. "CNs are a bit out of polite company."

"Has he worked with them before?" Collingswood said.

"Not that I know of," Vardy said.

"Has Grisamentum?"

"What?" He looked at her. "Why would you say that?"

"Just I was looking at all them files on your desk, of Tat's associates. And you've got Grizzo's as well. I was wondering what's that about?"

"Ah," he said. "Well, true. Those two . . . They move in lockstep. Always did, while Grisamentum was around. Which as we now bloody know—are we agreed?—it appears he still is. Associates of one could well be associates of the other."

"Why?" said Collingswood. "That don't make no sense. They hated each other."

"You know how this bloody works," Vardy said. "Friends close, enemies closer? Bought off, turncoat, whatever?"

She wagged her head. "If you say so, blood. I don't know," she said. "Griz's bunch *lurved* him, didn't they. His crew were all mad loyal."

"No one's so loyal they can't be bought," said Vardy.

"I forgot what a mad bunch he was cavorting with in the end," Collingswood said. "Griz. I was looking at them files." Vardy raised an eyebrow at her. "Doctors, doctor-deaths . . . Pyros, too, right?"

"Yes. He did."

"And you reckon some of them are working with the Tattoo now, right?" Vardy hesitated and laughed. That was not like him.

"No," he said. "It turns out not. But no reason not to check."

"So you're still chasing them up?"

"Yes I bloody am. I'm chasing all of them, every lead, until I know for an absolute bloody certainty that they're not involved in the squid thing, either with Grisamentum, or with the Tattoo. Or as independents. You do your job, I'll do mine."

"I thought your job's to channel the spirit of nutty god-bothering and write up holy books."

"Alright, you two," Baron said. "Settle down."

"Why the bollock can't we find the squid, boss? Who's got it? This is getting stupid."

"Collingswood, if I knew that I'd be commissioner of the Met. Let's at least try to map who's who in this mayhem. So we've got the Chaos Nazis, our wanktoasters—thank you, Constable—among recent employees of the Tattoo. Along with everyone else in the city."

"Not everyone," Collingswood said. "There's gunfarmers about, but they're on some other dime. No one knows who, and no one's feeling very safe about that."

"Well that's got to be our squidnapper, surely," said Vardy. "So who's paying them?"

"Can't track it. They've gone into hush mode."

"So get it out of them," Baron said.

"Boss, what do you think I'm trying to do?"

"Splendid," said Baron. "It's like a Zen koan, isn't it? Is it better or worse if holy visionary shooters are fighting *against* us *alongside* Chaos Nazis, or against *them* and we're in between? Answer that, my little bodhisattvas."

"Can we please," said Vardy, "establish what's going on here with that chap? Did any of them tell us anything?"

"Certainly," said Baron. "He had to finesse how quick I got him to roll over, so under guise of glorying in the chaos he would bring by terrifying me with the truth, a-blah-dy blah-dy blah, this little bugger sang like the most beautiful nightingale."

"And?" said Vardy.

"And Dane Parnell is not having a good time of it. They snaffled our exile, sounds like. That much he saw"—he pointed through the window with his chin—"before passing out. Which leaves little lost Billy out on his tod in the city. Whatever will he do?"

"Yeah, but he ain't exactly helpless, though, is he?" Collingswood said. "I mean, just pointing out . . ." She waved her hand at the savagely wounded man. "It ain't as if Billy's got nothing fighting his corner, is it?"

"Vardy," said Baron. "Care to give us your opinion?" He made a big show of opening his notebook, as if he didn't remember everything about the description he was about to give. " 'It was a bottle, policeman, you law-worm, we brought chaos to each other, you scum, etc . . . ' " he read, deadpan. "I'm going to editorialise. I'll trim the epithets and skip to specifics. " 'It was a bottle. A bottle that came at us. It bit with a skull. Its arms were bones. It was a real glass enemy.' I like that last line, I have to say." He put the notebook away. "So, Vardy," he said. "You must have thoughts."

Vardy had closed his eyes. He leaned against the wall and puffed out his cheeks. When at last he opened his eyes again he did not look at Baron or Collingswood: he stared intently through the window at the crippled Chaos Nazi.

"We know what that's about, right?" Baron said. "Let me rephrase. We've no idea what it's *about*. No one does. But we've a reasonable

notion of what it bloody *is* that swooped in and swept young Harrow
away."

"Alright, I'm going back to the museum," Vardy said. "See if I can
make a little more sense of this. Just *once*," he said with abrupt sav-
agery, "in a god*damn* while, it would really be a pleasure if the goddamn world worked the way it's supposed to. I am *tired* of the
universe being such a bloody aleatory frenzy *all*, the *bloody*, time."

He sighed and shook his head. Gave an abashed, tight brief smile
at Collingswood's surprise.

"Well," he said. "Really. Come on. Why the bloody hell is an angel
of memory protecting Billy?"

BUT NOT PROTECTING DANE, WHICH FACT WAS WHAT HAD HIM NOW
woozily half waking, strapped in a horribly cramping position that it
took him a long time to identify as a crooked cruciform. He was
attached like an offering to a rough man-sized swastika. He did not
open his eyes.

He heard echoes; footsteps; from somewhere, deliberate, foolishly
screaming laughter, that made him afraid anyway, despite its ostenta-
tion. The growl and barking of a huge dog. One by one he tensed the
muscles of his arms and legs, to check that he was still whole.

Kraken give me strength, he prayed. *Give me strength out of your
deep darkness.* He knew, if he opened his eyes, what figures he would
see. He knew his contempt, no matter how real and strong, would be
equalled by his terror, and that he would have to overcome that, and
he did not have the head or stomach to do so, just at that moment. So
he kept his eyes closed.

Most wizards of Chaos would bore you arseless about how the
Chaos they tapped was *emancipation*, that their nonlinear conjuring
was the antithesis of the straight-lined bordering mindset that led,
they insisted, to Birchenau, blah fucking blah. But it was always a
sleight of politics to stress only that aspect of the far right. There was
another, somewhat repressed but no less faithful and faithfully fascist
tradition: the decadent baroque.

Among the fascist sects, the most flamboyant, eager as Strasserites
to reclaim what they insisted was the true core of a deviated move-

ment, were the Chaos Nazis. The creaking black leather of the SS, they insisted to the tiny few who would listen, and not run or kill them on sight, were a coward's pornography, a prissy corruption of tradition.

Look instead, they said, to the rage in the east. Look to the autonomous terror-cell-structure of Operation Werewolf. Look to the sybarite orgies in Berlin, that were not corruption but culmination. Look to the holiest date in their calendar: Kristallnacht, all those Chaos scintillas on stone. Nazism, they insisted, was excess, not prig-restraint, not that superego gusset bureaucrats had chosen.

Their symbol was the eight-pointed Chaos star altered to make a Moorcock weep, its diagonal arms bent fylfot, a swastika that pointed in all directions. What is "Law," they said, what is Chaos's nemesis but the Torah? What is Law but Jewish Law, which is Jewishness itself, and so what is Chaos but the renunciation of that filthy Torah-Bolshevist code? What was best in humanity but the *will* and *rage* and indulgence, do what thou wilt the autopoiesis of the Übermensch? And so, endlessly, on.

They were provocateurs of course, and a ludicrously tiny group, but notorious even among the wicked for occasional acts of unbelievable, artistic cruelty, restoring the true spirit of their prophets. Sure the Final Solution was efficient, they insisted, but it was soulless. "The problem with Auschwitz," their intellectual wags of torture-killing insisted, "is that it was the wrong sort of 'camp'!" Their hoped-for Chaos Führer, they thought, might achieve a sufficiently artistic genocide.

It was to these figures that Tattoo, Goss and Subby had gone for help, and they had let London know to whom they had gone. They had approached these outrageous, dangerous monster-clowns to hunt down Dane and Billy. And from them Billy had been saved, and Dane had not.

Chapter Forty-Nine

BILLY PUT ON HIS GLASSES. THEY WERE IMMACULATELY UNBRO-
ken, and still clean. He said, "Wati."

"I don't know where Dane is," Wati said immediately. "I keep looking, but we're going to have to hope Jason has more luck. They've got
charms up or something."

Billy said, "I want to tell you something I dreamed." He spoke as if
he were still dreaming. "I could tell it was important. I dreamed
about the kraken. It was a robot. It was back, the whole thing in the
tank. I was standing next to it. And something said to me, 'You're
looking in the wrong direction.'"

There were seconds of silence. "Jason's going in, and while he is I
want to find out why that angel's looking after me," Billy said. "It
might know something about what's going on. *It knew to come find
me*. And it might have been looking after *me*, but it let Dane get
taken."

He told Wati what Fitch and Saira had done. He felt no hesitation,
though he knew it was a deeply secret secret. He trusted Wati, insofar
as he trusted any Londoners now. "Tell them they have to help us," he
said.

Wati went leapfrogging, body to body, but had to return. "I can't
get in there," he said. "It's the London Stone. It pushes out. Like
swimming up a waterfall. But . . ."

"Well you better find a way to tell them they have to help me, because otherwise I'm going to walk around the city screaming what they did. Tell them that."

"I can't get in, Billy."

"Screw their secrets."

"Billy *listen*. They've made contact. I got a message from that woman Saira. She's smart—she knows I was with you and Dane. She put a message through my office. Didn't give nothing away, just, 'We're trying to get in touch with our mutual friend. Perhaps we can arrange a meeting?' She's telling us they want to help. They're already against the Tattoo. That makes them nearer friends than enemies to us, right? I can't go in, but I'll try to send some of my people. Get them to ask Fitch where the Nazis are."

"Because if it's in London . . ." Billy said. "He should know."

"That's the *idea*. That's the idea."

"How long?"

"Don't know."

"We move," Billy said. "We'll get him out. I'm looking in the wrong direction. I have to know who's fighting me and who's fighting with me. So Wati, how do I find out about angels?"

IN A CITY LIKE LONDON . . .

Stop: that was an unhelpful way to think about it, because there was no city like London. That was the point.

London was a graveyard haunted by dead faiths. A city and a landscape. A market laid on feudalisms. Gathering and hunting, little pockets of alterity, too, but most of all in the level Billy had come to live in a tilework of fiefdoms, theocratic duchies, zones and spheres of influences, over each of which some local despot, some criminal pope, sat watch. It was all who-knew-whom, gave access to what, greased which palms on what route to where.

London had its go-betweens, guerrilla shadchans facilitating meetings for a cut. Wati could tell Billy where they were, and which had weak connections with the angels. Wati kept searching, and he had his own war to attend to, too. The moon made horns, the sky was gnarly. The cults were skittish.

So there was Billy, all alone, and he knew that he should have been terrified, but he was not. He was itching. He felt as if clocks hesitated with each of his steps. It was early when he started walking the list Wati gave him.

Billy knew how hunted he was. Now more than ever. He discovered that his legs had learned the step-spells that Dane had stepped for him, that he walked now with self-camouflaging rhythm. That he automatically went for half-shade, that he moved a little like some occult soldier. He held his phaser in his pocket, and he watched his surrounds avidly.

So, alone, Billy knocked on a door at the back of a sandwich shop in Dalston. A church and a carpet showroom in Clapham. A McDonald's in Kentish Town. "Wati said you could help me," he said again and again to the suspicious people who answered.

The safest approach was to never speak to anyone about anything. Communication could mean implication in some fight you might not even believe was taking place, taking a side, inadvertently signing on a dotted line. Nonetheless.

Fixers and goers-to had their scenes. Rooms and Internet shacks where men and women employed by their faiths to steal, torture, kill, hunt and fix could be among others who understood the pressures of the work and got the references of gossip.

"Dane couldn't have gone," Wati had warned Billy. "He'd be recognised. But people don't know you. They might know your name, if they keep their ears open. But not your face."

"Some do."

"Yeah."

"Some might be talking to Goss and Subby."

"Might."

"Where even are they?"

"Don't know."

The politics of a city of cults made for complex encounters. Seeing an assassin of the Beltway Brethren share a joke with someone from the Mansour Elohim but blank the twins from the Church of Christ Symbiote was a crash course in *realtheologie*. As much as possible, though, in these places Billy visited you left allegiances at home. *That*, as a message above the door in one hideaway had it, *is the Loar*.

Law or lore it may be—"Loar" a superposition of those two homo-
phones—but let's not be idiots. Billy entered each place cautiously,
and wore a false moustache. Even had he not been looking for Dane
and shoring up his compañeros, Wati could not have come in. There
were no familiars allowed, and NO DOLLS, said the entrance signs, and
Billy wouldn't risk disobeying. All statuettes had been cleared out
since the strike began. Wizardry was a petty bourgeois world. They
spent this unwanted leisure time denouncing their familiars, and did
not want an organiser listening in.

Twice Billy's request for help was declined when he mentioned
what little cash he had to offer. "Memory angels?" one old woman
said. "For that? I can't get mixed up with that. Now? With them walking?" Billy played out fantasies of bank robberies, but a sudden very
different thought occurred, another way to fish for such aid. He went
back to where he had seen the key in the tarmac. In moments
between cars he took a knife to it and prized it from the road.
Straightening up with it he swayed, orthostatic. He ate quickly in a
basement restaurant and examined the tarry key. A junk-bit grubby
with metaphor. Thinking in that register helped him take unexpected
advantage of the place. On the way to the toilets, in an alcove in the
wall, there was a lightbulb resting in a frying pan. It was so unre-
strained a visual pun, so utterly ovate, he gasped. He had to take it, in
a moment of simultaneously meaningless and powerful theft.

When he arrived at the next address he had for a broker of contacts, a bar in Hammersmith, the first thing he said to the young man
was, "I can pay you. Put this in the right hands, this'll unlock the
road." He held out the key. He held up the bulb. "And I don't know
what's incubating in this, but someone might hatch it."

Chapter Fifty

"VARDY'S GOING BANANAS," COLLINGSWOOD SAID. THEIR SAVANT miner of vision was in and out of the office on a frenetic schedule. He was racing off with one folder or other full of connections and contacts.

"Come on," said Baron. "You know how it works. We have to give him his head." He hesitated. Vardy's colleagues had not seen him go quite so hard, for so long, perhaps ever before. They came in to find incomprehensible notes, references to interviews Vardy had conducted solo, with suspects or people whose identities they were not sure of. Like everyone else, his behaviour was new in the shade of the catastrophe, that late, thuggish millennium.

"Where is he now?" Baron said, a little plaintively. Collingswood shrugged and glanced at him with narrowing eyes. She was sitting feet up playing a video game. Her romping avatar evaded the electronically growling beasts that tried to eat it. She was not in fact moving it, was concentrating on the conversation, had knacked the joystick into clearing the level on its own.

"No idea," she said. "From what I can decipher of his fucking crab scrawl he wants to find some informer from Grisamentum's old crew. One of the necros or pyros or something. Do you think he even has a clue what it is he's looking for?"

"No," said Baron. "But I bet you he'll find it. I gather there *are* gun-farmers in town."

"I *told* you. Yeah them and everyone. We get all the *best* visitors, man," Collingswood said, pointing at the reports in front of her.

"Which visitors?" It was Vardy, returned with papers in hand.

"About time," Baron said. "I thought you'd buggered off?"

"So it's true about the farmers?"

"Did you find anything out on your little mission?"

"If it is true," Collingswood said. She swung in her chair to face Vardy. Her digital figure continued its adventures. "Would you be scared?"

He raised an eyebrow. "I'm scared of all sorts of things."

"Would you?"

"There's no shortage of assassin-sects out there."

"Exactly." Collingswood had nicked members of a few herself. Sisters of the Noose, Nu-Thugees, theologies of Nietzschean kitsch. They were like the cruder readers of Colin Wilson and de Sade, aficionados of Sotos and a certain genre of trite "transgression," an inverted BBC moralism. They glorified what they quaintly thought the will, slandered humanity as sheep, maundered murder. Their banality did not mean they were never dangerous, did not perform atrocities for the glory of themselves, whatever Lovecraftian deity they illiterately decided wanted their offerings, their orientalist's Kali, or whomever. Even as they killed you, you'd hold them in contempt.

"Well, they aren't like that lot," Vardy said. "They're only mercenaries sort of contingently. The point of a gun isn't the killing but the *gun*. At first it was more generally pagan as it were."

"Care to fill an old man in?" said Baron. "Sorry to intrude on this." Vardy and Collingswood glanced at each other, until she smirked.

"Did you ever meet any?" she said to Vardy.

"Do you *mind*?" Baron said.

"They got sick, boss, back in the day," she said. "But I could never work out what it was about the guns."

An arcane disease had taken their ur-tribe and made their life infectious. What they touched would jostle, tables would tap, chairs would tap, books dance, the inanimate as boisterous and alarmed as any newborns. Midas couldn't eat a sandwich made of gold, but no more could one of these vectors, Life-oid Marys, eat the bread and cheese slices all abruptly eager to run around.

"It was a *mutation*," Vardy said. He said it carefully and with neutral distaste. "An adaptive mutation."

"Is that bad?" Collingswood said, at the sight of his face.

"Bad for whom? Mutation saves, apparently." Perhaps it was because of the careful grooming husbandry necessary for a flintlock, that fussy lead-barking animal; perhaps repressed resentment at life: whatever, it became only their firearms they made alive, in quieter, less motile ways—what weapons they wielded became selfish-gene machines. "The bullets are gun-eggs," Collingswood said to Baron, looking at Vardy. Farmers squeezing their holy metal beasts to percussive climax, fertilisation by cordite expulsion, violent ovipositors. Seeking warm places full of nutrients, protecting baby guns deep in the bone cages, until they hatched. "What I never got's why all that makes them all badass."

"Because they look after their flocks," Vardy said. "And find them nests." He looked at his watch.

"If you say so. So someone's getting totally killed," Collingswood said. "So who the fuck's paying their way? I'm not getting much. And what that means bollock knows." If her attempts at projection, remote viewing, sensory tickling, nightwalk sniffery, drift-jamming and a codewar flutter were not yielding any information, then a cowl was for certain draped over her quarries.

"Vardy," said Baron, "where d'you think you're going? Oy."

"Leave it, boss," Collingswood said. "Let Mystic Pizza do his thing. I want to sort out this gunfarmer stuff. We don't need Doc Vision for a money-trail, surely?"

Pete Dwight wondered if he had chosen the right career. It was not that he was a particularly bad police officer: there had been no complaints, no dressings-down. But he was never relaxed. He spent his uniformed days queasy with low-level anxiety, gnawed by the sense that he must be doing things wrong. It was going to give him an ulcer or something.

"Alright?" The man who greeted him was a plainclothes officer Pete recognised, though he could not remember his name.

"Alright, mate?"

"Seen Baron around?"

"No, I don't think so," Pete said. "But Kath's in the back. What do you want with them nutters?" Pete laughed collegially and was suddenly terrified that the man was part of the very cult task force he was mocking. But, no, that was not where he knew him from, and anyway the bloke was laughing in turn, and heading for the rear of the station.

In the main room, among the clatter of keyboards, Simone Ball was leafing through her paperwork. She was in her midthirties, loved classic animated films, and was an enjoyer of, though not a frequent participator in, European travel. She had been a support worker for the police for seven years. She suspected her husband was cheating on her, and was bewildered that she did not mind very much.

"Where's Kath?" a man asked her. She recognised him, and she waved him in the right direction and continued to think about her husband.

In the corridors, Detective Inspector Ben Samuels, considering his daughter's piano exam, looked up and greeted the man with familiarity. The man asked directions from a uniformed PC, Susan Greening, who grinned as she gave them, piqued by a sense that he and she had, she was sure, flirted recently. Outside the rooms used by the FSRC were three men comparing notes on a football game, though one of them had not watched it and was pretending. They parted as the newcomer arrived, nodded and greeted him, murmuring phonemes when they could not remember his name, and the one who was bullshitting in a surge of overcompensation even asked him what he had thought of the match. The man whistled and shook his head appreciatively, and the three men enthusiastically agreed and could still not quite remember his name but did recall that he was a supporter of one of the teams that had played or the other.

He entered the FSRC office. The only person in the room was

Collingswood, prodding a keyboard as if at idle random. She glanced up at him and he nodded, crossed to the filing cabinets against the far wall. "Alright, Kath," he said. "Just got to find some files." He opened the drawers. He heard Kath stand. A silence went on. He turned. She held a pistol in her expert grip, aimed at his chest.

"And just who," she said, "the motherfuck, are you?"

Chapter Fifty-One

"I WANT TO TALK TO SOMEONE WHO UNDERSTANDS THE ANGELS," Billy said, and the middleman made phone calls, sent emails, got on instant messenger and dropped queries in chatrooms. Eventually he told Billy where to go.

"Okay, it knows you're coming. Otherwise it would be bad."

"What am I looking for?" Billy said. "Who's going to meet me?"

"Duh. An ex-angel."

This was more than Billy had expected. Not a specialist or an angel-geek, but a semi-member of the jar's tribe itself, to whom he might sort-of speak. The custodians of the museums could hardly be comprehended: their agenda was memory's, which is not human. What they spoke was not like language. But redundant, they lingered, a few last years, and then they would become more like women and men out of a kind of loneliness.

The shell of the Commonwealth Institute was a conquistador helmet sweep of building at the southern edge of Holland Park. It had closed in the early 2000s. The ludicrous collection of exhibits honouring its member countries, that baffled and polite imperial aftermath, was long dispersed. But it was not all empty. When it grew dark Billy broke in—that was easy now with his new skills. He listened to his own reverberating steps.

The dust was only millimetres thick but thick enough. He felt as if he were wading in it, toward the last unmoved display cases. In many rooms the darkness should have been absolute, and Billy wondered what faint light it was that let him see. Once he heard a guard—some human guard—on halfhearted rounds. All he did was stand still in a cupboard and wait until the echo was gone from that section of hall.

A few exhibit pieces were left, forgotten, unworthy of rehousing, or hidden and, later in the solitude, they reemerged. Billy walked into a hall where though it was windowless there was not only light but shafts of it, ajut from the ceiling, each starting at a random point in the unbroken surface and crazy-pillaring down in random cross-hatched directions, as if the room were nostalgic for moonbeams it had never seen and grew its own simulacra. He walked through and under those interlaced fat fingers of imagined light toward a waiting thing.

God, he thought as he approached. *God. I remember you.*

The decommissioned angel of Commonwealth memory eyed him. "Hello again," he said. He had seen it on its day job, when he was a child, and it, in the daylight, an exhibit.

Plastic in the shape of a little cow. It eyed him sideways, so it could display its flank made of glass. Inside were its four stomachs, which had lit up, one by one, he remembered, and there, they still did, repeatedly, one at a time. Paunch, king's-hood, fardel and maw, digestion glimmering in each in turn toward its lactic telos, stalwart of some Commonwealth economy. From the New Zealand room, Billy thought.

He could feel its attention, its waning self. When the institute was open, this mnemophylax had after hours stamped the hallways with a gait modelled on Taurus myth. It had protected that mooncalf memory-palace from the forces of angry time or postcolonial rage-magic. Public uninterest had killed it finally and left it lonely and post-dead and full of stories.

Heard you were coming. Its voice was distant. It tried to tell Billy about the fights it had had. The references were inhuman. It tried to tell stories that made no sense and faded into nothing, leaving Billy nodding politely at each absent anecdote. With a cough, as genteel as at a tea party, Billy brought it back to the matter in hand.

"I was told you could tell me what's happening," he said. "One of you's been following me. Keeping an eye out for me. From the Natural History Museum. Can you tell me why?"

Can, it said. It was eager to answer. *You're what it waited for*, it said.

"The jar? The angel of the Natural History Museum? How do you know?"

They telled. The others. We speaked. Dead it might be, but it *kept in touch* with its still-active cousins. *It failed*, the thing said. Behind him was a gust of air, as swing doors opened and closed to help it speak. Its voice was building sounds. *The kraken went. It did bad. It's full of guilt.*

"It's left the museum," Billy said.

All of them. All of us. There's a fight on against the end thing. No point staying still. They fight the endingness. But it. Was the first to walk. Wants to make amends. Tries always to find you. Look after you.

"Why?"

Billy backed away and bumped into the open-closing door. He stood away from it so the phylax could say in its hinge-squeak, *Remembers you. You're chosen.*

"What? I don't . . . How? Why's it chosen me?"

Angels wait for their christs.

Angels wait for their christs?

And you came, born not of woman but of glass.

"I don't understand."

Gives you strength—you are christ of its memory.

"This thing with time? It gave me that? Dane said it was because of the kraken . . . Oh. Wait, wait. Are you . . . ?"

Billy began to laugh. Slowly at first, then more. He sat on the floor. He made himself laugh silently. He knew he was hysterical. It did not feel like release. The cow moved toward him. It was just one moment at the end of the room, one moment two or three feet closer and eyeing him with its sideways glass eye. "I'm alright, I'm alright," Billy said to the decaying memory.

"You know why *Dane* thinks those things happen?" he said. He smiled like at a drinking buddy. "He thinks it's because of the kraken. He thinks I'm some kind of John the Baptist, or something. But, so, that's the wrong direction. It's nothing to do with the squid.

"None of this is anything to do with the squid. It's the sodding *tank*.

"Come on," he said. "You've got to admit that's funny. You know what's even funnier? The best of it? I was joking."

Billy had kept a straight face during all his claims to be the first person born of in vitro fertilization. That ridiculous, meaningless gag, made in *that* place, that for the sake of the rigour of humour he had stuck to, had been overheard by the genius loci, the spirit of the museum. Maybe it was attuned to any talk of bottles and their power. Maybe it did not understand the idea of a joke or a lie. "It's not true," he said. The bovine angel of memory said nothing. *Clack clack clack clack* went its four stomachs, lighting in time.

Billy leaned over. "I'm not a kraken prophet, I'm the bottle messiah." He laughed again. "But I'm just *not*, I'm not."

The bottle-angel was diminished, diminished and receding daily, by its wanderings beyond its demesne, by its failure, its efforts, the smashing of that iteration of glass, preserver and bone. It would look for him again, pulling itself another self out of bits and pieces from its palace, though, sniffing out that portion of its own self it had put inside him. That gave him these unearned powers. Until it was gone it would strive to find Billy again, and through him the *Architeuthis* it had lost.

"I wish it would come back," he said.

Will.

"Yeah, but now. My partner's gone. I need all the help I can get."

You are the memory christ.

"Yeah, only I'm not." Slowly, he looked up. Slowly he stood and smiled. "But you know what, I'll take that. I'll take whatever." He reached and clenched, and thought maybe there was a tiny scutter of time. Maybe there was. "You going to come? Outside?" The cow said nothing. Dead as it was it did not have the strength to fight in the war that its living siblings were waging. "Alright," Billy said. "Alright, it doesn't matter. You stay here, look after this place. It needs you." He felt kind.

From some other part of the building came a noise that was not part of the cow's voice. Billy was at the door, his weapon out, listening, ready, without knowing how he had got there. The cow angel tried to speak, but Billy held the door closed, and it had nothing with which to make noise. "Hush," he whispered. Ordering an angel around. It was gone, though, in a series of those being-elsewhere steps. Billy thought for a moment that it would bring a human guard running in consternation. (He did not know that they were all aware something old and melancholy walked in the building, that they tried never to disturb.)

"Godammit," he said, and he went after the dead angel, holding his phaser out. He followed the screech of hinges and things falling from last shelves. He came suddenly into an unwindowed room where the plastic cow screamed with the voice of the building at a tall man.

Billy ducked and fired, but the man moved faster, and the phaser beam scored over the ineffectual cow and dissipated across the wall. "Billy Harrow!" the man was shouting. He held a weapon himself, but did not fire. "Billy!" The word came from behind him too, Billy thought, but realised that the second, tinier voice was in his pocket. It was Wati.

"I'm not here to fight," the man shouted.

"Stop, Billy," Wati said. The angel wheezed with windows. "He's here to help," Wati said.

"Billy Harrow," the man said. "I'm from the Brotherhood of the Blessèd Flood. I'm not here to fight. Marge came to us."

"What? *What?* Marge? Oh Jesus, what's she doing, what does she *want*? She's got to stay out of all this . . ."

"This isn't about her. I'm here to help. I've got a message from the sea. It wants to meet you."

Chapter Fifty-Two

THE SEA IS NEUTRAL. THE SEA DIDN'T GET INVOLVED IN INTRIGUES, didn't take sides in London's affairs. Wasn't interested. Who the hell could understand the sea's motivations, anyway? And who would be so lunatic as to challenge it? No one could fight that. You don't go to war against a mountain, against lightning, against the sea. It had its own counsel, and petitioners might sometimes visit its embassy, but that was for their benefit, not its. The sea was not concerned: that was the starting point.

Same at the embassies of fire (that constantly scorching café in Crouch End), the embassy of earth (a clogged crypt in Greenwich), the embassies of glass and wire and other more recherché elements. The same standoffishness and benignly uninterested power. But this time, this time, the sea had an opinion. And the Brotherhood of the Blessèd Flood were useful.

They were a faith themselves, not dictated to nor created by the sea. Though the sea, so far as any Londoners could judge, took the worship of the Brotherhood wryly and graciously enough. That was always disingenuous. What the Brotherhood offered was plausible deniability: the sea itself did nothing, of course; it was the Brotherhood of the Blessèd Flood that sought out Billy Harrow, and if they brought him back to the sea's embassy, well?

It was an urgent journey. It was raining, which made Billy feel better in some way, as if water wanted to protect him.

"What's going on with Marge?" Billy said again.

"I don't know," Sellar said. "She came to see me. She thought *we* took the kraken. We thought you and Dane did. So when she said that wasn't right, I went and spoke to the sea, and—"

"Is Marge alright?"

"No."

"Right," Billy said. "No one is." He looked again at his phone, but he had missed no calls. Jason had not called him. *Maybe he didn't go yet*, Billy thought and did not believe. *Maybe he'll get back to me soon.*

A row of semidetached Victorian houses in the northwest of London. A Tube train, emerged from the tunnels, drummed through the night, behind bricks. Cars moved slowly. There were few pedestrians. The houses were three storeys high and only a little dilapidated, bricks well weathered, stained, pointing eroded, but not slums nor derelicts. They were fronted by little gardens with their few plants and coiffed patches. Billy could see children's bedrooms with pretty animals and monsters on wallpaper, kitchens, sitting rooms with the cocoon-light of television. From one address came laughter and conversation. Smoke and music came out of its open windows. The building next to it was quiet and unlit.

Closer, and Billy saw that was not quite the case. Its curtains were drawn, on all three floors. There was perhaps something very faintly illumined, visible, just, through the curtains, as if someone carried candles in the deeps of the rooms behind.

"Have you been here before, Wati?" he said.

"Never inside," the figure he carried said to him. "There's nothing I can get in."

Sellar tapped at the door, a complicated code staccato. By his ankles were a collection of empty bottles. Sellar pressed his ear to the wood, waited, then beckoned Billy. The ground-floor curtains were heavy oxblood cotton; the first floor, in blue-green paisley; the top, with cartoon plants. All were pressed up against the inside of the glass.

"Come then," said Sellar.

Sellar wrote a message Billy could not see, rolled it up and placed it inside a bottle. He screwed its lid on tight and pushed it through the door's post flap. Several moments passed, but only several. Billy started when the flap opened and the bottle dropped back out and smashed against the concrete step. The barks of dogs did not abate, nor the calls of children playing late. Billy picked up the paper. He held his doll so Wati could read, too.

The paper was damp. The ink was spread in stain-coronas around the written words, in an intricately curling font, spreading beyond its lines.

Teuthis no longer our creature. No longer creature. Not of ocean. We have spoken to the kraken within us to know why this. Neither they nor we are indifferent to what might come. It is no princeling commissar chosen by them or us in the tank.

Billy looked at Wati. "Well? Do you get this?"

"I think . . ." Wati said. "It's saying it's just a kraken."

"Just?"

"Like not a, a *particular* kraken. I think. And . . . but, I mean . . . it's not theirs no more, I think."

"Dane thought there might be something about that one in particular, that was why it was taken. That it might be a hostage." A part of the incomparable squabbles of kraken. Warlords in feud, battles conducted at the pace of continental drift. A century for the creep of each province-long arm around an enemy's; a bite excising cities'-worth of flesh clenching over the duration of several human dynasties. Even the fleetingly majestic altercations of their krill, the *Architeuthis*, were just squibs by the bickering of their parents.

"There has to be something," Billy said. "There are other giant squid in the world. Why *this* one? Why's *this* one the deal? What's its . . . parentage? Where's it from?"

"It said that ain't it," Wati said. "The sea." Billy and the figure stared at each other.

"So why are we here?" Billy said. "Why does *this* kraken baby lead to the end of everything?" He stared into the doll's eyes. "What does the sea really know, or the krakens? What about . . . ? How about this, Wati—you could ask the krakens direct."

If they took a boat. They should take a boat and a big iron or brass Buddha, say. Where the water was deep, above a trench in the Atlantic, they could tip the statue over the side and Wati could begin a long wobbling voyage down, a precipitation into very crushing dark. Come to rest at very last in mud and hagfished bones, and Wati could politely clear his throat, and wait to attract the attention of some eye that had no business being that big. "Hello. Any particular reason your little plankton baby's going to set the world on fire?" he might say.

"How'm I supposed to get out again?" Wati said. There was a litter of statues on the seafloor, but how far might they all be from his abyssal interview? What if they were out of reach, and he had to sit there in the black in terrified boredom, fingered by glowing fish until the ocean eroded him out of statuehood and self? So: put his heaviest anchor-statue on the end of a chain strung with other made bodies, so when the questioning was done he could rise through them back up into the ship's figurehead—

"What are we doing?" Billy interrupted himself. There was another breaking-bottle sound. Another message.

We are not indifferent. To the end in fire. We do not wish London gone. You and the exile Krakenist and we wish the same thing. Our self a product of concatenate development. The kraken would not have this, this is not about them.

Were the giant squid themselves, or their parents, god instars, their apotheosed others, helping with this? Out of, what, divine irritation at some misrepresentation? "Why *this* squid?" Billy whispered.

Others are against us. We had thought otherwise. We know now. You must get to the kraken and keep it safe from fire.

"Ooh, d'you think?" Billy muttered. "Thanks for that, hadn't occurred . . ." He continued reading.

You must free the exile.

"That's Dane," he said.

You will be shown.

"Why will we?" said Billy. "What does 'concatenate development' mean?" He frowned and tilted his head and read.

Destroy this paper. You will be helped.

AND DANE?

Dane was hanging upside down, and dripping. He had been reciting to himself stories of his grandfather, his grandfather's courage. "Once," he said inside his own head, in his grandfather's voice, "I got caught." Was it a memory or an invention on Dane's part? Never mind. "So there was this time there was some scuffle going on with the ringstoners. You ever gone toe-to-toe with a ringstoner? Anyway, we were at it over something or other, can't even remember, some saint bone of some church we said we'd help so they'd help us, I don't know . . ." *Concentrate!* Dane thought. *Come on.* "Anyway, so there it was and they had me all trussed like in a bloody cat's-cradle, and in they come to give it all this, yadda yadda, like. So." *Sniff.* Dane as his grandfather, sniffing. "I let them get all close. I was all letting my head go all over the place, you know? They were crowing. *You'll never this, we'll always that.* But when they got right up to it, right up to me, I didn't say nothing. Till they were right there. Then I said a prayer and like I knew they would, like I bloody *knew* they would, all the ropes that they had were just what they always were, which is the arms of God, and God unrolled them, and I was free, and then, boy, there was some reckoning."

Hurray. At some point the echoes of the room Dane was in changed, as people came in. Dane stopped talking to himself and tried to listen. He could not see who was there, with what had been done to his eyes. He could not see, but even through waves of pain he could hear, and he knew that the voice he heard was that of the Tattoo.

"Seriously, nothing?" the Tattoo said.

"Lot of screaming, but you don't count that," said the voice of one of the Nazis. "You alright? You seem stressed."

"I am a bit stressed. Truth to tell I'm a bit bloody stressed. Remember the monsterherds?"

"No."

A snuffling, a slobber, canine whickering. That dogman was there. That mage-knacked member of this crew, a man made himself half German shepherd, a pitiful fascist meat pun that Dane scorned even as the teeth and muzzle that pun occasioned mauled him.

"Well . . . They used to run with Grisamentum, back when I . . . Back when. Well, one of my factories just got interrupted by a bunch of dust or something acting very much like some kind of bloody dragon."

"I don't know what that means . . ."

"It means there's stuff coming back I wasn't expecting to face again. This little shitfucker has to know something. He's in on something. He knows where the fucking squid is—it's his god, isn't it? And he knows where Billy Harrow'll be. Keep at it."

Keep at it. Dane prayed without ceasing. He prayed silently and motionlessly. *Tentacled God in darkness please give me strength. Strength to listen, and to learn. Krakens in your vast silent and ammoniac wisdom have mercy.* He knew that he should listen, that he should wait and say nothing, if even he could answer the questions, which mostly he could not even if he would, which he would not, because this would not end. He knew that it would not be too long now, weak as he was and unblooding from all the holes the Nazis had made, woozy and too tired and done to even scream, a thing hanging in thermals of pain—he knew that this was a pitch of this that was its own limit, and that therefore, again, for the second time, before that moment when he would spill enough of himself out that a critical mass of lack would be reached and he would have nowhere to go but into death, the ghastly chaos sunwheel he could no longer see would be rotated. The swastika *was*, as its hippy antifash defenders insisted, a sign of life, even when deployed like this.

Who made you? Kraken made me. As a by-product. Uncaring. Was the comfort in that, or in the secret hope that secretly the secret kraken cared? *We are all squidshit*, Dane thought.

The Chaos swastika mightn't be able to return those actually passed for much time, but it was thuggishly fecund enough to infect him, up to the very point of death, into livingness again. It would rotate with him swastikad on it, and it would wind in life out of all control, pouring it back into him, so blood would drip up, ruined organs reinflate, splayed bone ends grope for each other, grizzling as they slotted shard back into shard hole, fixing him all up, back into pain.

Chapter Fifty-Three

A "TWO-WAY MIRROR"—ONCE A LONG TIME AGO PERHAPS intended to dissemble, but now a lie that drew attention to itself. Behind it were Baron and Vardy, standing in such similar poses that it would have been comical to an observer. On the other side of the glass, Collingswood questioned Jason.

"So how come I can notice him now?" Vardy said. "I should think I recognise him, presumably."

"Collingswood," Baron said.

"She's not bad, is she?"

"She's bloody good," Baron said. "That's how she saw him in the first place." Her questions to Jason had been tempered, nuanced, enhanced by various knacked enhancements: from an uncanny form of unbearable wheedling to the imposition of unphysical pain. "If you'd been here when you were supposed to . . . Where the bloody hell have you been, Professor?"

"Professor is it now?"

"Well." Baron turned to him. "Look, you can't say I haven't given you your head, right? Thank God Collingswood isn't in here to hear me say that—we'd never hear the end of her giggling. I know your job's to channel the bleeding divine, and when have I ever stood in your way? Aren't I the bloke puts 'Do Not Disturb, Eschatology Being Revelationed' on your door? Eh? But you're supposed to keep me in the loop, and turn up when I need you, and do me the sheer minimum modicum of salutage and whatnot, right? You were supposed to be here for this questioning about two hours ago. So where the *bloody hell* have you been?"

Vardy nodded. "Apologies. But I do have news." He organised the air with his hands. "There's no way you get an end like this without someone wanting it—this is not just an accident. And now the Tattoo's going mad. I still can't work out where this ending comes into whoever-it-is's plans."

"He is going mad," Baron said. He was tearing up the city. "We've tried to have a word with his people, but something's pushed him over the edge . . ."

"So I've been out quizzing a bunch of the people in Grisamentum's and the Tattoo's *penumbra*, you might say," Vardy said. "We know Adler was an associate of the former, but we don't know why he was in the museum when he was. We don't know what he had planned, so I've been wondering if it's some of the others who were all cut loose when Grisamentum died . . . who are behind all this."

"And?"

"Listen to me, this is what I'm saying. There's a *presiding intelligence* behind all this. Whatever's coming, that's got the angels walking, it's not some by-product of another scheme, it has *intent* behind it. But we don't know what."

"I know that . . ."

"No. It's not an accident. Listen. We're close. Do you understand?" Vardy spoke in a surly lecture. "The world is going to *end*. Really soon. End. Soon. And we don't know why, or who wants it to."

"It's *got* to be Griz," Baron said quietly. "Got to be. He never died . . ."

"But why? It doesn't make any bloody sense. Why'd he want to burn himself now, then? That's why I've been out there. Asking questions."

"*And*? Bloody *and*? Where's it getting you?"

"Does the name Cole ring any bells?" Vardy said. "If I say 'physicist.' If I say 'Grisamentum.' Any bells at all?"

"No."

"One of the names being thrown around Grisamentum's court

around the time he, ahem, died. Died according to the oncologists. Cole's a pyromancer. Works with djinn, is the whisper. Rather closely, according to some rumours. One of several people that for no reason we could clock was talking to Grisamentum in the last days. Apparently he was one of the ones you tried to debrief after the funeral but he always diligently refused to chat to the force."

". . . Oh, right, I think I remember. I always assumed he was there because Griz wanted a dramatic send-off, to be honest. Big sparkly pyre. What's your point?"

"There's dramatic and dramatic."

"What was it he did for Griz, then?"

"Experimental pyro stuff: memory-fire, that sort of thing, he says."

"Says?"

"I've been looking into Grisamentum's associates, so I was asking around about him. I told you I had news. Not expecting much, to be honest. Expecting some hedging of bets, some 'Grisamentum was a gentleman, you could leave your doors unlocked, was a pleasure to work with him,' a thank-you-very-much-and-bugger-off. But what I got was a bit more surprising. He has a daughter. Cole does."

"Mrs. Cole on the scene?"

"Dead years ago. Don't you want to know what I heard? His daughter's gone missing."

Baron stared. Eventually began to nod. "Is that so?" he said slowly.

"It's the word."

"What does that mean?"

"First Adler, then Cole. Someone's working through Grisamentum's known associates. Doing things to . . . inconvenience them."

"Like shoving them in bottles."

"And snaffling their kids."

"Why?"

"If I knew that, Baron. But it's a pattern."

"Bit out of your remit, this, isn't it? Where's the goddery?" Vardy closed his eyes and shrugged. "So . . . How do you think we should play this? Have a word, obviously, but . . ."

"Well, you're the boss, obviously, but I'd suggest me being point man here."

"I thought he won't speak to cops."

"He wouldn't back then, certainly, but I'm not a policeman, am I? I'm an academic, like him."

"And what more tenacious freemasonry do there be, eh?" Baron nodded. "Alright. For God's sake, though, keep me apprised. We'll see what we can do about tracking down young Miss Cole. Now look, this is not unimbloodyportant. Shut up and pay attention to what your colleagues are doing. Like this colleague here, right now." Baron pointed through the window.

THERE IS NOWHERE THE SEWERS DON'T GO. FAT FILAMENTS TRACK-ing humans under everything, unceasingly sluicing shitty rubbishy rain. The gentle downslope links all those pipes to the sea, and it was back along those pipes, defying gravity and the effluvial flow that the sea had sent its own filaments, its own sensory channels of salt-water, tickling below the city, listening, licking the brickwork. For a day and a half there was a secret sea under London, fractal in all the tunnels.

Pipes filled with brine that spied on the inhabitants of buildings, watching, listening, hunting. You might obscure the attention of the Londonmancers, with the complicity of a treacherous borough, with strikebreaking hexes strong enough: but nothing could stay hidden from an inquisitive sea.

Billy waited, alone but for the repeated anxious occurrences of Wati, who came, went, into the doll and out again, to the frontlines of the strikes.

"Done what the sea asked me," said Sellar at some low dark point of the night, and went, with a quick backward wave, returning to his dreams of drenched apocalypse. *It's fire, not water*, Billy thought. *I don't think you're going to like it.*

His phone went, and he connected immediately. He said nothing, only listened. There was a brief silence before a voice said, "Billy?" He could tell it was not Jason. He broke the connection and swore. They had the proletarian chameleon. It had gone wrong.

He stood in the front garden of the sea's embassy—it was dark, his clothes were dark, no light glinted on his glasses, and he knew he could do this unseen—and threw the phone as hard as he could, which was hard, now, into the darkness over the roofs. He did not hear it land. At last, as he sat by the step of the house, he heard a swill of water in the pipes below his feet. Another bottle was pushed from the letter box.

The sea told him where the Chaos Nazis were. It said that was where its help would end. That it would not be intervening, could not take any sides. It was closing in on time for daylight. Billy leaned forward on his knees and rested his forehead on the door.

"Now listen," he said. "Listen a minute. You can't get in there, can you, Wati?" Billy said.

"No figures in that house."

"Listen, sea," Billy said. "See here, sea." He smiled tiredly. "That's the sort of thing's helped get us where we are now, people wanting to stay neutral." He felt some recognition. He felt as if he remembered this. As if he'd been in the sea only days before, or nights before, in fact, at night, in the night, as he dreamed those ink dreams. He put his hand on the door. He knew this place.

"What is it you want to stay neutral about? You want to stay out of a war. This wouldn't be *London* versus you—that's not what we're up against. So what is it? Chaos Nazis? I don't believe it. The Tattoo? Does a gang boss really frighten *you?*"

Oh, snap! Did that kind of petty psychology work on the fucking ocean? *Nothing ventured,* Billy thought, *nothing ventured.* What else did he have? Two weapons he did not understand and a polybodied trade unionist. There was nothing but silence from inside the embassy.

"So what is it? Protocol? Niceties? I'm going to say this. I'm going to beg." Billy was already on his knees. "Please. So you mess up some balance of power? *So what?* You know what's coming. The fire and end of it all. I bet this fire burns seawater too. Dane's going to fix it, though, you know. So if you don't want everything to burn, if you don't want London to burn, if you don't want the sea to burn . . . help me."

"Do you know what happens now?" Collingswood said. Jason Smyle wheezed. A few cosmetic knacks, a little unnatural dermatological intervention, and his skin looked quite untouched, all his bruises glamoured away.

"What happens now is this," she said. "You've broken various laws, but as well you bloody know they're oddball laws. They're like the constitution, they ain't written. What that means is you go into the *other* court system. Which means whatever I want it to mean." She was less than half Jason's age. She leaned back and put her feet on the table. "So your cooperation will be greatly appreciated. So." She twanged briefly into ridiculous American. "*One mo' 'gain.* What was you after, coming here? Where's Billy? And where's the squid?" But they had been over this many times, and no amount of cajoling or threatening elicited any more.

"I swear, I swear, I swear," Jason kept saying, and she believed him. He did not know. All he knew was the number Billy had given him, that he had surrendered immediately. That was it. Collingswood glanced through the mirror and shook her head. She left the room and joined her colleagues.

"So what have we got?" Baron said. "It's all a bit of a turn-up for the books, isn't it?"

"And you believe him," Vardy said.

"Yeah," said Collingswood. "Yeah. So . . ."

"So," said Baron. "So our man Billy is *not* an abductee at all. Is in fact collaborating with a known member, now exile, of the Church of God Kraken. It turns out our ingénue isn't so ingenuous after all."

"What is it with this fucking Stockholm Syndrome?" Collingswood said. "Is Billy, what's her name, fucking Patty Hearst?" She looked at Vardy.

"Possible," he said. "This whole thing stinks of belief to me. I take it we got nothing from the number he gave us?"

"Nah. Belief in what?"

"In something."

"Alright children, alright," Baron said. "So, we thought we were looking for a captive, but it turns out we're looking for a fugitive. Vardy, you better fill Collingswood in on Cole."

"Who's that?" she said. "What did he do? Or she. Was it she? Can I play?"

"A pyromancer," Baron said. "Ex-associate of Griz."

"Pyro?" Collingswood narrowed her eyes. "Isn't it fire that people keep seeing? Vardy?"

". . . Yes, it is. Sorry, I just . . . I'm . . ." He chewed his knuckle. Baron and Collingswood blinked at this unusual hesitation. "A pyromancer, a squid from the museum, an end of all things, it's . . . there's something close. I just have to parse the faith of it."

So what was up with Marge? Her best lead had gone to nothing.

She had new priorities. She believed all these strangers who kept telling her she was in danger, that she was drawing dangerous attention to herself, that she needed protection.

Don't you know what a trap street is? the cult collector had said, and no she had not, but a moment online sorted that. Invented streets inserted into maps to right copyright wrongs, to prove one representation was ripped off from another. It was hard to find any definitive lists of these spurious enmapped locations, but there were suggestions. One of which, of course, was the street on which the Old Queen was.

So. Was it that these particular occult streets had been made, then hidden? Their names leaked as traps in an elaborate double-bluff, so that no one could go except those who knew that such traps were actually destinations? Or were there really no streets there when the traps were set? Perhaps these cul-de-sacs were residues, yawned into illicit existence when the atlases were drawn up by liars.

Well, either way. Those were obviously the streets to investigate. Marge looked for more names.

Chapter Fifty-Four

THE CHAOS NAZIS HID NOWHERE IN PARTICULAR. JUST AN EMPTY building. There was no metaphoric logic to its whereabouts, no cosmic pun: it was just isolated enough and empty enough and easy enough to break into and recustomise from the inside—soundproofing and such—and then to protect that it had been chosen. It was in the far east of London, in a zone depressed enough that not many people took a lot of notice of stuff. It had a deep basement where Dane was being tortured and where Chaos swastikas were cranked and turned. It was near a garage.

The Nazis were alone and unsupervised. An outsourced resource, subcontracting being as fashionable in gangland as in the rubble of Fordism. The Tattoo had told them, vaguely, to continue what they were doing, and to try to extract something, some hint, from Dane, as to where Billy and the kraken were.

Inside, it was decked in memorabilia from the Reich, guaranteed—spattered with genuine spatters, blood, brains, gauleiter cum. Candles in niches beside icons of various deviltry, smoke-damaged posters of Nazi bands and pictures from the camps. Exactly what you would expect.

The Chaos Nazis stood, patchwork fascist fops, all glitz, spandex, leather and eagles. They eyed Dane. He was tied behind a rack of crusted tools. His rack had turned to put a bit more tumourous life in him, so he had eyes and teeth, though not all his teeth, and he could breathe through his nose though it was broken. They had only brought him back a couple of hours ago, had not really got started again yet. He stared at them, alternately spat and raged, and slumped and tried to go into himself.

"Look," said one. "His lips are moving. He's praying to his snail again."

"Stupid Jewish snail scum," said another.

"*Woof*," the dogman Nazi said.

"Where's Billy, you scum?"

"Where's the squid?"

"Your dead squid won't save you."

They all laughed. They stood in the windowless room. They hesitated. "Stupid Jew," said one. They laughed again.

There are only so many ways to experience pain. There are an almost limitless number of ways to inflict it, but the pain itself, initially vividly distinct in all its specificities, becomes, inevitably, just pain. Not that Dane was indifferent to the idea of more of it: he shivered as the men mocked him. But he had been surprised that they had taken him twice to the point of death through their bladey interventions and he had still not told them that he knew where the kraken was, nor who had it, nor where Billy might be. That last he did not know himself, but he could certainly have given them leads, and he had not, and they were at a loss.

Still he kept nearly weeping. Dane kept praying.

"You can stop your whining," one of the Nazis said. "You're alone. No one knows where you are. Nothing can help. Nothing's coming to save you."

HAD THE SEA WAITED JUST FOR THAT MOMENT? DID IT COME WITH a sense of theatre, pausing in the pipework that infested the house as pipes infest all houses, listening for just such an announcement to refute? Whatever: the stars aligned, everything came together for that perfect beat, and just but exactly as if in answer, brine burst every piece of plumbing in the house, and the building began to bleed sea.

Saltwater ripped through the walls. It buckled the floor. Lovingly gilted World War Two knickknacks spilled into new holes.

The Nazis scattered, ran, did not know where to run. Dane shouted without words. Rage, elation, hope and violence. Water gulped at the Nazis; seawater freezing and London muddy sucked and pulled them down with eddies and undertows it imported from its wide ocean self. Some reached the stairs, but more than one was felled by misplaced waves and brutally kept under, and, bewilderingly, in inches in the city, began to drown.

The water reached Dane's chin. He wondered if it would kill him too. He'd mind, he realised, he would, he would. *Kraken let me breathe.*

The Nazis ascending the stairs were met. Billy's phaser cut them down. No stunning now. He descended, shooting as he came. He sent a poker-hot ray scorching through the fur on the Hitler-worshipping dogman. Turning into the torture room Billy growled like a goddamn animal and shot many times while the sea roared and smashed the Nazi bric-a-brac from wall to wall and sunk it as if at the bottom of the world.

"Dane," he said. "Dane, Dane, Dane." He knelt in the swells. Dane wheezed and smiled. Billy took a hacksaw to his bonds. "You're alright," Billy said. "You're *okay*. We got here in *time*. Before they *did* anything."

And Dane even actually laughed at that, as he flopped free from his crooked starburst constraint.

"No, mate," he whispered. "You're too late. Twice. Never mind though, eh?" He laughed again and it was bad. "Never mind though. It's good to see you, man." He leaned on Billy like someone much more wounded than he looked, and Billy was confused.

"They're blocking the way out," Billy said. Nazis from other rooms were massed at the top of the stairs and firing down with Third Reich weaponry. "Here," said Billy, and gave Dane his gun. Dane stood a little straighter. "Are you with me, Dane?" Billy said. Dane did something, aimed and fired up the stairs. There were a lot of them up there.

"I'm with you," he said. He looked at the weapon. His voice croaked back to something like normal. "Works okay."

"We can't get out that way," Billy said.

As if in answer, certainly in answer, the sea gave a rocking swell and receded very fast, fast enough to take a great chunk of flooring with it. It left a hole in the centre of the room, a smeary slipping hollow the size of another room, broken by the stubs of pipes and the ruins of masonry. The sea poured violently back out and tore a gap as it went, sluicing from the pit to some half-used end of sewer or old river-run, opening into the labyrinth.

"Can you?" Billy said, and braced him. Dane nodded. They braced and careened in a cold, dangerous slide into the mud and receding seawater, and into the cavern.

They stared up through the fingering pipes and the slurry of brickwork, the dirty cascade, into the dinge of the room. Faces peered over the lip. Billy and Dane fired volleys, hallooing, smacking twisted features from sight. In the second of silence that followed they ran into the slime under everything, and from there, dripping like fresh clay golems, into the dark tunnels of London.

PART FIVE

RISE TOWARD DESCENT

Chapter Fifty-Five

Ｉᴛ ᴡᴀs ᴠᴇʀʏ ʟᴀᴛᴇ. Iᴛ ʜᴀᴅ ʙᴇᴇɴ ᴀ ᴡʜɪʟᴇ sɪɴᴄᴇ ᴀɴʏᴏɴᴇ ʜᴀᴅ actually questioned Jason, let alone smacked him around. Collingswood had come into his cell from time to time, with a bad-dream loop of questions, but he had not seen her for hours.

Food and drink was pushed through the slot. His shouted requests for a phone, for attention, for bacon sandwiches were never answered. There was a chemical toilet in the corner of his cell that he had long since given up threatening to tell Amnesty International about. Without Collingswood or another realitysmith around to dampen his knack, his jailers all half-recognised him, knew they knew him, and given that he was not—could not be, look, he was in a cell—a colleague, reasoned that he had to be a career villain, and their behaviour to him had worsened.

When Jason heard footsteps, a whisper echoing in the hall, he did not expect whoever it was to slow or stop. But they did, right outside his cell, and unlocked his door.

An officer opened it. A man, framed in the doorway, staring in weird stillness. He looked grey and very sick. Someone was behind him. The officer was not looking at Jason. He stared at the wall above Jason's head, swallowing, swallowing. There was someone behind him webbed with shadows shed by fluorescent lights. Whispering.

"Is it . . . ?" Jason began, and ran out of what to say.

A child peered around the doorframe. A man behind him whispered into the policeman's ear, leaning like a windblown tree into sight on one side of his escort, then swaying to the other, playful tick-tock, winking with his left then his right eye at Jason from behind the officer's back.

"Christine!" the drab-coated man said to Jason. "Is it you?"

Jason knew who the man and the boy were then, and he flattened himself against the wall and began to scream.

"I KNOW!" SAID GOSS, STEPPING INTO THE ROOM, ESCORTING THE officer. Subby pushed the door closed behind them with the careful preciseness of a young child. Jason screamed and crawled backward on his bed.

The policeman was closing his eyes and weeping and whispering, "*I'm sorry shhh I didn't stop now I didn't mean to please don't please.*"

"I know!" said Goss again.

"Stop it!" Goss giggled. "It's a secret, you'll ruin it, stop it!" He breathed out smoke.

He pushed the officer at Jason with a whispered word, and the man not even opening his eyes felt for Jason's screaming mouth and blocked it with his hand and whispered, "*Shhhh shhhh stop stop you have to you have to.*" Jason ran out of breath to make sound behind the palm. The policeman and prisoner held onto each other.

Someone's going to come, Jason thought, *there are cameras, someone's going to,* but would Goss be here without crossing those *t*s? Dotting those *i*s? He tried to scream again.

"You two are terrible," said Goss. "You said we was meeting at the bus station, and then Mike came and I didn't know where to look!" He sat on the bench and sidled up to Jason. "Hey," he whispered shyly. He tapped the cop on the shoulder. The man whimpered. "Subby wants to show you something. He found a beetle. Go on and take a look, there's a love."

"Shhh, shhh," the man kept saying, weeping from under closed lids. He took his hand from Jason's mouth and Jason could not make a noise. Subby took the officer's hand. The man shuffled at the child's pace to the corner of the room and stood facing away from Goss and Jason, facing the cement angle.

"I was all over the place," Goss said. "I was out on holiday. Got a nice tan. Was looking for stuff. Not seen the waiter? The waiting boy in the dollhouse? I had a present for him." Goss put a finger to Jason's lips.

"So," he said. "Clarabelle said she fancies you." He pushed his finger harder onto Jason's face. Pushed him to the wall. "I said to her what? And she goes 'Yeah, can you believe it?'" Pushed the lip into Jason's teeth. Subby swung the policeman's hand like they were going for a walk. "She's going to be at the park tonight. Are you coming down later?" Goss split the skin so blood welled into Jason's mouth. "Where's Billy? Where's Dane?"

"Oh God oh God I don't know I swear Jesus . . ." Jason said. Goss did not move his finger, so Jason sputtered past it, sputtering his blood and spit onto Goss, who did not wipe himself. Goss pushed and pushed and Jason whined as his lip was ground against his top teeth. The policeman stood where Subby held his hand obediently facing away, whimpered and seemed to clutch the boy's hand harder as if for comfort.

"Do you remember when she was in Geography with us and he kept nicking all the pens for the overhead projector?" Goss said. "I knew you liked her then. I know you did stuff for Dane, that's why you're here, where is he?" Pushed and Jason whined and then shrieked as with the crunching snap of a ruined pencil Goss pushed an incisor out of its socket so it dangled into his mouth.

"I don't *know* I don't know," Jason said, "Billy called *me*, Jesus, please I don't know . . ."

"I didn't even know she was still in our year. Look at me. Look at me. You alright, Subbster? Are you looking after my little brother okay, mister?" Goss smiled and met Jason's eyes. Kept his finger all blood-wet on Jason's lips. "Clarabelle said she might bring Petra so we could all four of us go into town. Your friend took something I want back. Where is he? Otherwise I'm going to have to call off tonight."

"Oh God I don't know I don't, listen, listen, he gave me a number, that's all, there's a number, I can tell you it . . ."

"Numbers rumpus schampers grampus orca Belinda. Where's them lads? I think I can see what you want to say down in your mouth, shall I get it? Shall I get it? Shall I get it? Tell me or I'll get it. Where is he? I'm going to get it. Where is he? I'll squeeze it out of you, you rubber duck!"

"I swear, I swear . . ."

"I will! I'll squeeze you till you squeak!" Goss began to push. Tooth roots creaked in Jason's head, and he screamed again. The policeman in the corner exhaled shakily and did not look around. Goss put his other hand to Jason's stomach.

"I will push if you don't tell me, because I want it back. Hurry, I said to Clarabelle and Petra that we'd be there in an hour, so tell me tell me."

Jason had nothing to tell him, so Goss kept pushing. The constable kept his eyes shut and gripped Subby's hand and tried not to listen to Goss repeat and repeat his questions, heard the noises Jason made go from screams to short hard klaxon barks as much of aghastness as agony, liquid intrusion sounds and some retching animal wrongness and at the very last, nothing. After a long time a *hff* of effort and the dropping of liquid and the noise of something pushing through moistness. *Clack clack.* Something maraca-ed.

"What's that?" Goss said. *Clack clack.* "You really don't know?" *Clack.* "Alright then, if you're sure." Dragging.

"He doesn't know." Now Goss was up close to the policeman's ear. "He told me. You can make him tell you too. Make him rattle his teeth. I'm much obliged for showing me where he was, you do a marvellous job, I'm ever so grateful. I remember when people used to care about the uniform, God love you, people had respect then." The officer kept his eyes closed and did not breathe. "Give us Subby back then, you! Pop him up like a toaster!" Subby took his hand away. The man heard the door open and close. He stayed still for more than three minutes.

He opened his eyes such a tiny bit. No one hurt him, so he opened them again. He turned around. No one stood in the room. Goss and Subby were gone. The man wailed to see blood on the floor and meatlike Jason at his feet. There was a hole in Jason's sternum. His neck was grossly thickened, burst from inside, his mouth wide open and the roof of his mouth grooved where finger holes were pushed into it, his tongue punctured by a hole for a thumb. Wear him and he could be made to talk, *clack clack*.

The last lingering of Jason's knack went out, and recognition slipped from the room, and the officer went from screaming for someone he thought he knew to someone he realised he had never worked with, but who was still exactly as dead as he had thought.

Chapter Fifty-Six

THERE WAS A CHANGE IN THE AIR, SOMEONE COMING INTO THE penumbra of the London Stone, with the stone in mind. London always felt like it was about to end, like the world was over. But now more than ever. *No, really*, the city was muttering. *Honest.* Saira could sniff an encroachment, even without Fitch grabbing her and whispering the fact in agitation.

"Someone," he kept saying.

Saira thought up various possibilities as she readied to face whatever it was. But though she had hoped to see him again, she was utterly confounded to emerge from the Londonmancer back rooms into the shop that fronted and protected them to face a bleary, exhausted, pugnacious Dane Parnell.

Billy stood behind him, phaser in his hand, Wati-filled doll in his pocket. Dane leaned against the doorway.

"Jesus Christ London!" she said. "Dane! What the *hell* are you . . . ? You got *away*, thank *God*, we didn't know, we were—"

"Saira," he said. He sounded dead. He stared levelly.

"Dane, what are you doing, you could be seen, we have to get you out of sight . . ."

"Take me to the kraken." Saira twitched and patted the air for him to quiet: most of her colleagues knew nothing. "Now," he said.

"Alright," she said, "alright, alright alright. I have to get Fitch. What *happened*, Dane? I have to—"

"Now. Now. Now. Now."

OF COURSE BILLY AND WATI, WHO HAD FELT BILLY'S EMERGENCE from that protected Nazi zone and gushed into the doll he carried, had clamoured at Dane in relief and tried to make him rest.

"We have to get Jason too," Billy said, and Dane nodded.

"We will," he said. At least the police, cruel as they might be, would not, he thought, kill his friend. Not yet. "He was trying to find me?"

"Yeah."

"We will. As soon as I've—" His words ended.

"Do you want to tell me?" Billy said. "What happened?"

And what kind of bleeding stupid question was that? he asked himself the moment it was out, into the quiet that followed. He said nothing as Dane said nothing and they only walked, and at last Dane said, "The Tattoo was there."

"You saw him?"

"I couldn't see nothing. But he was; I heard him. Talking through one of his things. He's desperate. He's under attack. Some of his business. From monsterherds. If he doesn't know Grisamentum's back he most certainly fucking suspects it by now." His throat was untouched, but Dane croaked with the memory of damage, from the times it had been cut.

"What did he want to know from you?"

"Where the kraken is. Where you are."

"Did you—?"

"No." Dane said it with a kind of wonder. "No."

"I thought they'd . . ."

"Yeah," Dane said. "Yeah they did kill me," he said. But he had come back. Even if it was by their malevolent interventions, Dane had come back. How many martyrs emerge from martyrdom's other side?

"He can feel something," Dane said. "Like we all can." He closed his eyes, he stretched out his arms. "He knows the angels are walking . . ."

"I have to tell you about that," Billy said.

"In a minute. It's not just about wanting it for power anymore. He knows there's an end and he knows it's something to do with the kraken and he's going insane because he thinks if he can get it maybe he can stop what's happening. He can't. He won't. He'll turn whatever's happening into . . . something. *We* can stop whatever it is from happening."

"The Londonmancers don't seem to have managed that," Billy said.

"No?" Dane turned to him, looking all new. "Maybe the universe has been waiting for me."

"Yeah. Maybe."

So when they got to the Londonmancers, Dane said, simply, take me there now.

"W E HAVE TO BE CAREFUL," SAIRA SAID.

"Now," said Dane.

"You can't be seen with us," she said, and Billy laid his hand on Dane's arm. *Easy.* A little rushed preparation. Saira and Fitch went in Fitch's little car, leaving Dane to steal another to follow. They gave him a knack-fucked satnav, a little handheld unit into which Dane plugged a cloth scrap with one drip of Saira's blood—she had cut herself right there, in front of him, good faith.

"Why would we try to get away from you?" she pleaded. "We need each other."

Billy and Dane swept rubbish in their wake. They looked disguised by night, by how unremarkable they were. That fooled Billy not at all, and he kept his phaser up. "It's only a matter of time before we get found again," he said. "Where the hell are Goss and Subby?"

No one knew. They'd been and gone. Was that the end of it? No one believed that. But they were out of the city—that was obvious from the way everyone felt a little more oxygenated. *We're looking for something in far-off lands*, is what Goss had supposedly said to someone they'd unaccountably left alive.

The satnav blinked at them and pointed them through streets, at Saira's movement. "Look," said Billy. "Watch her. Evasive manoeuvres."

As they approached London's edges Billy felt risingly strange. "Where is she going?" Wati said. He was clipped to peer from the top of Billy's pocket.

"The sea couldn't see it, or hear it," Billy said. They turned onto the North Circular, the city ringroad, and traced a way out east. "They're . . . Look, look."

There was the car, stationary, and there, pulled over onto the hard shoulder, was a lorry. Large—not one of the really huge articulateds that filled streets like poured-in concrete, but big enough, way larger than most house-movers. There was some forgettable logo on its sides. They pulled in behind it and the rear doors opened minutely. Saira beckoned. She pulled the door to behind them as they hauled into the dark insides. Wati could not enter past repulsive fields. He whispered and went out away to his other front, his union war. The vehicle started again. Striplights came on.

Strapped in place in the trailer's centre, cushioned and surrounded with thick industrial cording stretched to the edges and corners, holding it so it barely jostled on the steel table, was the tank. And in it, placid in its death-long bath, was the kraken.

THE LORRY VEERED A LITTLE, SENDING A LAP OF LIQUID UP THE tank's inside. The movement clouded the preserving liquid. There were the knotted arms, the gone eyes. *Architeuthis*. Billy almost whispered hello.

A couple of other Londonmancers, more of the conclave within the already secretive sect, were there. There were tools. Microscopes, scalpels, computers loaded with biological modelling software and sluggish 3G connections. Centrifuges. Chairs, books, a cabinet of weapons, a microwave, chunks of masonry torn from London walls, bunks built into the truck's sides.

Nothing moved a moment but the truck and the shreds of skin in Formalin. Of course it travelled, so as not to snag attention. A weight of animal godhead like that couldn't but become meaning: stay fixed and people would notice. So it was escorted in a circle like an aging king. Its motion hid it, as must the scraps of gris-gris stuff, the offcuts, the accoutrements nailed or placed in the vehicle's interior.

"Who's driving?" Billy said. He turned.

Dane was on his knees. He knelt close to the tank. His eyes were closed, his mouth moving. His hands were clasped. He was weeping.

EVEN THE LONDONMANCERS, USED TO STRANGE FERVOURS, STEPPED back. Dane murmured. He prayed half audibly. Billy could not hear what it was he said, but he remembered a snip that he had read in the teuthic canon, a phrase: *Kraken, with your reaching, feeling the world to understand it, feel and understand me, your meaningless child, now.*

The passion ran as long as it would run, and it was a long time. Dane opened weepy eyes. He touched the glass. "Thank you," he said, again and again, to the tank. He stood at last.

"Thank you," he said to the room.

"I can't fucking *believe* you," he screamed suddenly. "Why would you *do* this, why wouldn't you *tell* me?" He slumped, and made a face that Billy realised he must have made when he was being tortured to death. "But you took care of, of, of it," he said. "Of my god."

DANE SANK AGAIN. POOR TORTURED MAN. HE PRAYED. BILLY PUT ON the long full-arm rubber gloves, like a vet's, the Londonmancers provided. They—well, their little inner cabal—watched him.

He did not know exactly what he was looking for. He looked at Dane until Dane saw him do so and did not stop him or say anything, and with that permission Billy took off the lid and reached through the cold broth of dead cells and chemicals. He touched the specimen. It was dense, coldly and deadly dense.

We found you, he thought.

"What's going on?" said Saira.

Billy clenched, but there was no twitch of time now. He pressed into the flesh to feel what he would feel. He ran his hands along it, parted its parts, gently, pressed his fingertips into the suckers that acned the dead animal's limbs. It could not vacuum him, but the very shape of those pads stuck them for a moment to him, as if it were gripping, all dead as it was. He heard Fitch make some noise like *huh.* Then Fitch said, "I need . . . I need to read . . ."

"I don't think you do," Billy said, without turning. He pressed down. *What's this, then?* he thought, but no knowledge crept in through his fingertips, his own inadequate ten tentacles. He shook his head: no haptic gnosis, no insight. There was nothing, no knowledge of what would happen, or why, or what it was of *this fucking squid*, this squid, why this squid? Why would it usher in the end?

Because it still would.

"I don't think you need to be a seer to know that," he said. "Cut open the city you'll see the same thing." He turned and held his arms up like a surgeon in a sterile field, as they dripped toxins. "I know we were hoping," he said. "It would've been nice, wouldn't it?" He nodded at Dane. "He's come back from the dead for this, you know? That's got to be written somewhere. Can't tell me there's no verses about that somewhere. And then you've got me. That's two of us must be all over some scripture like a bloody rash, so you might think this'd change stuff." He peeled off a glove. "But come on." He shrugged. "It's still the same."

Maybe it was because it was a misunderstanding. He, Billy, had been chosen by the angel of memory for some stupid error, some misapprehended gag. Specimen magic, not the alien majesty of the benthic tentacular.

"Don't matter," Dane said, surprising him, as if he'd spoken aloud. "How'd you think messiahs get chosen?"

Dane was the real deal, had really gone into it and come out again, and his was real faith. One might have hoped that that was the end, the reuniting of faithful and faithee enough to heal the burning. That perhaps the Londonmancers—having failed to banish that finality by offering themselves as rescuers, believing finally that the intent of Billy and Dane was not to burn the thing themselves, handing control of the stranded deep god to its devotee and kind-of-sort-of prophet—might have averted the worst. But.

"Nothing's changed," Billy said. You did not, he was sure, need to be, as he was, a mistaken beloved of an angel to feel it. London was still wrong. You could hear the not-ending of tension in the city, the continuance not of fights but of a particular kind of fights, the terror of it all.

Everything was still going to burn.

• • •

SAIRA SAT, DEFEATED. SHE HEFTED A CLUTCH OF BRICKS AND MOR-
tar anxiously, a wound torn from a wall. She kneaded it. In her hands
and knack all the city's separate scobs and bits and pieces were the
plastic matter of London. She prodded and pulled at the bricks and
they squelched silently into other bricks. She dug in her fingers and
made the stuff into other Londonness—a mass of food wrappers, a
knot of piping, a torn-off railing top, a car's muffler.

"What now?" It was Saira who said it, at last, but it could have been
any of them. She held out her hand and Billy pulled her up. Her hand
was sticky with Londongrease.

"You remember Al Adler?" Billy said. "Who you killed?" She was
too tired to wince. "Know who he was working for? Grisamentum."

She stared at him. "Grisamentum's dead."

"No. He's not. Dane . . . He's not." She stared. "What that has to do
with anything I don't know. But it was Adler who . . . started this.
With you. And he was still with Grisamentum when he did. Place
your bets whose plan it was.

"We know what's happening's close, now, and we know it starts
when the squid burns," he said. "So I suppose we have to keep trying.
We just have to keep it safe. Maybe if we can do that, keep it *unburnt*
past . . . the night . . . we'll be okay. All we can do's keep looking. The
Tattoo's got no reason to burn the world. Neither did Al. Neither does
Grisamentum, whatever their plan was." He shook his head. "It's
something else. We have to try to keep this thing safe."

"Let's go, then." Everyone looked at Dane. It was the first thing he
had said for a long time that was not muttered devotion to his dead
god. He stood, looking reconfigured. "You keep it safe," he said to
Saira. "We can't be here. We're too dangerous. We'll do the stuff
you're saying," he said to Billy. "First we're going to get Jason out."

Chapter Fifty-Seven

"WHAT DO WE DO?" BILLY SAID. CRASHING THE HIDEOUT OF dangerous violent nutcases they might get away with, but the state? *It's too risky*, Fitch had said. *You have to help us protect it*, Saira had said. *There's nothing you can do*, they had said.

"Give me the satnav," Dane replied. "We ain't leaving him behind."

"And maybe we can find stuff out," Billy had said. "They might have some better ideas than we do, Collingswood and Baron."

Dane had stared at the dead squid and made some sign. "We can find you when we need to. You keep my god safe. And let us out now."

Now they waited. "We have to get Wati in," Dane said. He spoke quickly. "We need to know the lay of the land in that copshop before we go cracking in. Where is he?"

"You know they've got stuff in place," Billy said. "He can't get in. Anyway . . ." Wati, guilty at his disappearances from the struggle at hand, was still at hasty rallies. "He said he'd be back when he could." He wanted to help, and he would again, but *Don't you know there's a war on?* A class war that pitted rabbits against conjurors used to getting away with a stick and the scrawniest carrot, between golems and those who thought scrawling an *emet* on a forehead granted them rights, or any fucking thing at all.

Where gargoyles or bas-relief figures were close enough, Wati would deliver rallying speeches to whatever strikers maintained interventions (homunculi creeping in the angles between wall and pavement, rooks staggering). What might pass as twists of wind were pickets of militant air elementals, whispering in gusty voices as quiet as breath, "*Hell No We Won't Blow!*"

There were scabs and sympathisers. Wati heard all the rumours, that he had been targeted—old news that—and that people had been searching all over the world, literally, *outside of London*, for some leverage against him.

The situation wasn't great. The grind of economics forced some back to work, shamefaced, shamesouled where their faces were carved and immobile, shamewavelengthed when they were vibrations of aether. Rushing in a statued path all over the city, Wati kept arriving at aftermaths. Picket after picket closed down by spectral police spells on obscure, antique charges pressed into innovative use. Hired muscle in various dimensions.

"What happened?" Wati would cry, on emerging into a lion face made in mortar, to see a picket bust up, its members scattered or killed, two or three still there trying to fix themselves. They were tiny sexless homunculi made out of animal flesh. Several had been left just bone-flecked smears.

"What happened?" Wati said. "Are you okay?"

Not really. His informant, a man built of bird parts and mud, dragged a leg smudgelike. "Tattoo's men," he said. "Help, boss."

"I ain't your boss," Wati said. "Come on now, let's get you . . ." Where? He could not take him anywhere, and the animal-man-thing was dying. "What happened?"

"Knuckleheads."

Wati stayed with him as long as he could bear. The Tattoo had been paid to close the strike down, and efforts were being stepped up. Wati went back to the dolls in Billy's and Dane's pockets. In agitation he trembled between the two as he spoke.

"We're being attacked." "The Tattoo . . ." ". . . and the police . . ." ". . . trying to finish it."

"I thought they already were," Billy said.

"Not like this." "Not like this."

"We made him angry," Dane said slowly.

"By getting you out," Billy said.

"He wants me back, and he wants you, and the kraken, and he's getting at us through Wati. I heard him, while I was there. He's desperate. He can feel everything speeding up, like we all can."

"We have one of his knuckleheads, you know," Wati said with the ghost of humour. "Got political after he joined. Got sacked, no surprise."

"Wati," said Billy. He glanced at Dane. "We need to get into the police station."

"Where even are we?" Wati said. He had followed the aetherial ruts ground out from and back into this figure without even clocking his location. "Not that I can get in—they've got a barrier."

"Near," Dane said. They were in an alley out back of a café in the dark but for a fringe of streetlight. "It's round the corner."

"Jason's inside," said Billy.

"Maybe you didn't hear me," Wati said.

"Wait," Billy said. "Hold on. I'm thinking . . . how I first met Goss and Subby. It was the entrance that they had to get over. Collingswood didn't make the whole place out of bounds."

"It's a lot easier to just guard a perimeter," Dane said. "I get it."

"So if we can get you past *that* . . ." Billy said.

WATI IN THE FOETAL, MOST INNER OF THE RUSSIAN DOLLS THAT Billy had snagged a long time ago, jogged in the mouth of his mouse escort, a longtime activist of the UMA. She had never spoken in twelve years of membership but was absolutely solid.

She was a big mouse, but the doll was still a big mouthful. The mouse was a speck of dark under headlights, disappearing under gates, up an incline of crumble, below unmoving cars and through cavities. "Alright, this is great," Wati said. "Thanks. We'll sort this out, don't sweat it. We'll sort this all out."

Midway through the outer wall Wati felt a limit point, felt space try to keep him out, "Whoa," he said, "I think there's a . . ." But the mouse, little physical thing, felt nothing and ran on through, hauling Wati's consciousness with her, straight on in, snapping through the block.

"Ow," Wati said. "Shit, that was weird."

The distinctive mutter of striplights. Wati was used to dramatic shifts of scale and perspective, to seeing from giant figures then lead miniatures. Right now the corridor was cathedral. He felt the pounding of an incoming human. The mouse waited under a radiator. Legs came past. Several officers. There was some emergency.

"Can you follow that lot?" Wati said in his small voice. "Careful now." The mouse went after the earthquake footprints, down stairs, onto different carpet, into different lights. "He'll be in a cell," Wati whispered. The animal agent stuck to the shadows: crouched under the open door itself, of a cell around which the police were gathered. Near what was definitely blood.

"Oh fuck me sideways," Wati whispered.

The mouse turned him slowly in its little mouth, so Wati's eyes tracked up the mountain of dead body that lay on the cell's bed, the red dead man. There were the FSRC. The other milling police shunned them. Among the bustle of voices two words rose to Wati's attention. "Goss," he heard, and "Subby."

"Oh, no no no," he said. "Let's get out of here."

The mouse waited while he whispered miserable curses. "Okay. Okay. Let's concentrate. Let's find their office," he said eventually. "See if we can get some information. Goss and Subby are with the Tattoo, and I thought he had these buggers' backing. Something's going nuts."

The station was all afaddle with the crisis, and it was not so hard for a mouse to run room to room uninterrupted, looking for and at last finding signs of FSRC involvement—religious pieces, books one would not normally associate with the police. At Collingswood's desk, CD cases of several Grime artists.

"There's got to be something," Wati said. "Come on." He was exhorting himself, not his escort.

The mouse walked Wati on all the papers they could find. A laborious ambulatory notetaking. Wati was not altogether surprised when he heard voices approaching. "Go," he said. "Go go!" But the mouse walked one last paragraph, so when the FSRC officers entered, they saw her scuttling from Vardy's desk.

Collingswood moved at shocking speed, not like a human. She dropped to her haunches and lurched sideways, keeping the tiny animal now running for the space between a filing cabinet and the wall in her line of sight. Vardy and Baron had still not moved. Collingswood spat a word that made the mouse go plastic-stiff skidding with momentum to the back of the little runnel, where the animal lay immobilized as Collingswood shuffled toward her. She still bit-gripped Wati.

"Mouse! Mouse! Come on!"

"Help me with this fucking cabinet," Collingswood yelled at her sluggish colleagues, and at last they shifted their arses and began to tug it.

"Mouse, you better move," Wati said. He felt statues beyond the walls that he might, from here on the nonblocked side of the magic caul, jump to. But he muttered and muttered at the mouse, until she regained enough of herself to crawl from Collingswood's fingers. "Get into the fucking wall," said Wati, and the mouse made it excruciatingly around a corner of architecture while Collingswood swore.

THE MOUSE DRAGGED HERSELF THROUGH THE WALLS, AT LAST TO deliver the doll to the cool air outside. "Thank you," Wati said. "You okay? Good work. Thanks. There's, look, there's some food over there." Remains of kebab. "Get that down you. Thanks. Big time. You'll be alright, now?"

The mouse nodded, and Wati skittered through a few statues to where Billy and Dane waited for the news of Jason that he would have to give.

Chapter Fifty-Eight

"GOSS AND SUBBY."

"It was Goss and Subby."

"Holy fucking Kraken. Goss and Subby."

Goss and Subby, Goss and Subby, names both names and barks of outrage at those so named. They had been that way since year who-bloody-knew? Certainly for centuries the bereaved, the beaten, the tortured had shouted those names in aftermaths.

Billy and Dane were aboveground, in a neglected tower, a folly thrown up on a terrace by some exuberant Camden architect. As everything closed in and they ran out of Dane's hidden, fake flats, they retreated to chambers above the city and below it. This one was empty and light and dust-clogged. They sat in striae of particulate.

"And it was all the names of old associates on the desks?" Dane said at last.

"Yeah," said Kirk-Wati. "Whoever was with Grisamentum when he was around."

"Oh, he's around," Billy said.

"Well. You know what I mean. It was all people who'd been with him. Necros, doctors, pyros."

"Names?" Dane said.

"A geezer called Barto. Ring any bells? Necromancer, according to the notes I saw. Byrne obviously. Someone Smithsee someone. A guy called Cole."

"Cole. Wait a moment," said Dane.

"What?" Billy said.

"Cole's a pyro."

"I couldn't see," said Wati. "All we got was a university, some notes. Why? You know him?"

"I know his name. I remember it from when Griz died. I heard it then. He's a pyro." He looked at Billy's uncertainty. "A firesmith."

"Yeah, I get that, but why . . ."

"From when Grisamentum was cremated. Supposedly. But . . . he works with *fire.*"

It was fire that ate up everything at the end. It was fire and a secret scheme from Adler, a minor man, a player in the rubble of Grisamentum's organisation, with unknown intentions, connected to this other one.

"Where *is* Grisamentum?" Billy said.

"We don't know. You know that. Wati can't—"

"It's more than *where*, though, isn't it? You said you don't see any reason?"

"For him to burn the world? No. No. I don't get what his plans were at all, but they weren't that." They were uncertain enough not to join him, still.

"We'll find out," Billy said. "Let's go find out what Cole is in all this." He stood, pushing through the layered air. He looked down at the cars. "What the bloody hell is going on out there?"

The Tattoo was going on. His hired guns raged and violated trusts that had held for decades, all the way through everything, hunting for the quarry they had had and lost.

The Chaos Nazis were nothing, of course. Who was afraid of them now, drowned, screaming and up-fucked? The freelancers, the full-timer knuckleheads and others were happy to audition for the newly open position of lead bogeymen, and the UMA pickets were unwilling bit parts in these violent run-throughs and résumé-building attacks. Wati was gone from the room above Camden, back, gone, back, shoring up, fixing and failing.

"Tattoo's gone fucking batshit," Collingswood said. "What is he doing? Has anyone spoken to him?"

"Won't talk," said Baron. He puffed out his cheeks and exhaled. "We can't bloody find him."

"He doesn't need our permission," Vardy said. The three sat like a support group for the morose.

"Come on," said Baron. "I don't employ you two for your looks. Talk this out."

"We've got the Tattoo declaring war," Vardy said. "Sending Goss and Subby in *here*. Dealing with our prisoners."

"And Dane and Billy sending people into *my effing office*," Collingswood said.

"So it's the office intrusion that particularly bothers you," Baron said angrily. "It's having people rummage around in the pens that *really* got your goat, Kath . . ."

She stared at him. "Yeah," she said. "That and the thing with the horrible death thing."

Another round of staring.

"No one gives a shit about us anymore," Baron said. "We're just in the middle. It's bad for the soul, that sort of thing."

"Christ, boss," said Collingswood. "Perk the fuck up."

"We're not running buggery fuck," Baron said. "Billy and Dane've got more going on than us."

"This won't do," Vardy said. He blinked quickly, formulating. "Sitting here like something. Everyone running around around us. Let's assert a bit of bloody *authority*. We need to start bringing people in. On our terms."

"And how are we supposed to do that?" Baron said. "We don't know where any of them are."

"No. So. We have to do something about that. Now look, we know what they know. One, they know about the end. And two, they know it's because the squid's bloody gone. And three, that someone, somewhere out there, for some reason, is planning things that way. So what we need to do is get the mountain to come to Mohammed."

Baron continued to stare. "Who's Mohammed in all this?" he said. "And where's the mountain?"

"I ain't climbing fuck," Collingswood said.

"We need to fish for them," Vardy said.

"Is this, like, the mountain going fishing now?" Collingswood said.

"Jesus Christ, will you shut *up*?" Vardy shouted. She showed no shock, but Collingswood said nothing. "We need to dangle what they want, *what they're waiting for*. What's going to bring them out? Well, what brings everyone out?" He waited, theatrical.

Collingswood—a little tentative—said, "Ah. Apocalypse."

"There you go," Vardy said. "They're waiting for an apocalypse. Let's give them one."

In London, Heresiopolis was always the draw. Some midnight-of-all or other was predicted every few days or nights. Most came to nothing, leaving relevant prophets cringing with a unique embarrassment as the sun rose. It was a very particular shame, that of now ex-worshippers avoiding each other's eyes in the unexpected aftermath of "final" acts—crimes, admissions, debaucheries and abandon.

Believers tried to talk the universe into giving their version a go. Even small outlandish groupuscules might make headway in ushering in their End. The FSRC had a decent reputation for helping clear up these potentials. But Vardy's point was that the most dramatic of these Armageddonim—London had had to grow used to such arcane plural forms—were events in a kind of society. Spectator sports. To miss one would be a *realtheologikal* faux pas.

They were means to gauge who was in the ascendant, which group on the wane. The shenanigans of putatively final nights were something between fieldwork and social gatherings.

Baron and Collingswood looked startled. "It won't work," Collingswood said. "No end's going to be big enough to get people out at the moment, not with everything else going on. You'd have to cook up something pretty fucking dramatic. And people've got their ears to the ground, they'd know it wasn't real. They wouldn't turn up."

"They'd certainly turn up if they thought it might be *the* end," Vardy said. "Imagine if the one apocalypse you missed was the real one."

"Yeah, but . . ."

"No, you're right, we couldn't fake it. We need to bump up some little one that no one would've noticed scheduled . . . Ha. I say 'one.' 'Something big.' For the times when one apocalypse isn't enough, ha." He stood, all bristling. "A list of the sects we have an in with." He clicked his fingers. "Everyone's heard about the kraken by now. Right? And they know that whatever it is that's coming has something to do with it. Don't they? They do."

"What is it you've got in mind, bruv?" Collingswood said.

"Everyone's waiting for the end of the world. Let's get in there first and bring it to them. Like you say, we can't fake it. We need proper rumours. So we'll have to make it real. And we'll have to get as many details right, so they think . . . We need to encourage certain rumours, and the closer to the truth the better. We probably can't make it an octopus, but who do we know with an *animal* god? Who could we persuade to bring their apocalypse forward? Word'd get out."

He began to go through his files. After a second, Collingswood joined him. Baron watched them and did not rise.

"Are you two out of your bonces?" he said. "You're going to come up with an end-of-the-world party, just to get everyone together . . ."

"What about this lot?" Collingswood said. Vardy looked where she pointed.

"I don't think we have the clout to persuade them," he said. They continued looking.

"Them?"

"No."

"Them?"

" . . . It's nothing like a squid."

"*What* are you even *doing*?" Baron said.

"Yeah, but if we get rumours out quick, it won't matter, it's a big animal," Collingswood said. "That's what people would hear."

"Maybe," Vardy said. "A problem occurs to me," he said. He pointed at something on another sheet. Baron peered at whatever they were discussing. "There's another one coming in soon. In and of itself who cares, but it's got no animal stuff to it, and it's going to be difficult to get their prophets to delay. Or if we have them too close together, no one'll—"

"Just have them on the same day," Collingswood said.

"What are you . . . ?" Baron said, and Vardy hushed him with a glance. He looked as if he were about to pooh-pooh Collingswood's suggestion, but a stare of quite astonishing delight came over him.

"Why not?" he said. "Why not? If we have the right, the right *keywords* to the rumours, even then, one little everyday Armageddon might hardly cut it. So long as enough people think it even *might* be an animal god thing. It'd certainly get people talking . . . Could be a surefire way of making our little bait even more . . ."

"Baity," said Collingswood.

"Dramatic. Maybe. Imagine if there are two?"

He and Collingswood looked at each other, snorted, and nodded. "It won't change the, the *real* deal," Collingswood said. "But we don't even know when . . . Step up, boss-man," Collingswood said, to Baron, and patted his cheek affectionately.

"Alright," said Vardy. "So we've not one but two prophecies to, um, chivvy. I'm going to make some calls."

Chapter Fifty-Nine

A CHOLERIC DELEGATION CAME TO THE EMBASSY OF THE SEA. There was no possibility such a troop could bicker with such an antagonist and not be noticed, and noticed they were, and in the wake of that confrontation rumours went everywhere.

Mostly, they weren't badly inaccurate. A few mad exaggerations, alright, within a couple of days: *swear to fucking god, they were like throwing grenades and pulling out all kinds of crazy knackery, it was out of control.* Whatever. As if the story, if big enough, reflected glory on the teller.

The truth was adequate drama. A motorcade arrived in the street. Man after man, a couple of women too, helmeted as if they rode motorbikes but emerging from cars, stationing themselves at each junction. Tinted glass obscuring finger faces. No one walked down the street while they were there.

From within the street's houses people looked nervously at the people in helmets and the night outside. You did not have to have a grasp of the details, and they did not, to know in a carefully unverbalised way that that bloody end house had long been a problem. From the largest car came two more helmeted figures escorting a scrawny third. Punk-haired and terrified. His mouth was covered. The guards walked him between them to the front door.

"Turn round." The man obeyed that voice. His jacket had holes cut

in it, through which stared ink eyes. No avatars, no workshopped figures, no mouthpieces: the boss himself. "Your fucking eminence,"
said the Tattoo. His voice was perfectly audible despite the clothes his
bearer wore. Looking out at the street, away from the argument
behind him, the Tattoo-bearer shivered.

"I heard you visited some contacts of mine. They were holding
something for me and you sort of *intervened* yourself. And I ended
up losing something I had expended a great goddamn lot of effort
and money getting hold of. So what I'm here to do is ask *one*, is this
actually true? And *two*, if it is, do you really want to go down this
route? Want to go to war with me?"

Again nothing. After long seconds the Tattoo whispered, *"Answer
me, your oceanship. I know you can bastard hear me."* But no bottle, no
message from the letter box. "You and your elemental whatever. You
think I'm afraid of you? Tell me there was a misunderstanding. Can
you even tell what's going on? Nothing's safe anymore. You can burn,
same as the rest of us. I'm not scared of you, and whatever you think,
you are not safe from war. Do you *know* who I *am*?"

The way that maleficent ink said those last words, that old-hat
kitsch threat, made it something again. If you had heard it you might
have shivered. But nothing happened in the sea's house.

"Think I won't fight you?" the Tattoo said. "Stay out of my business."

Had the sea invaded the Tattoo's own halls it would have been an
insult too far, and whatever the cost—and the cost of war against an
element was big—the Tattoo would have waged it. There would have
been bombs lobbed into the waters, that exploded and left holes of
nothing under traumatised waves. Brine-killing poisons. And even
though the Tattoo could not have won, the sea's interest and breach
of neutrality might have spread the war.

But no one would count the attack on the despised and disavowed
Nazis as meddling, and the Tattoo would find no allies. The downside
of employing bogeymen. Which was why the sea had risked its
actions. People doubtless knew it had been there, though it had assiduously withdrawn every molecule of saltwater from the caverns
carved under the pavement, the new oceanic grottos, but no one
admitted it.

"Tell me what you have to say for yourself," the Tattoo said. "Kick backward," he said to the body he was on, and the man clumsily did, but the blow connected with neither the door nor with anything. "Fuck with my business again it's war," the Tattoo said. "Car," he said to his body, and the man walked jerkily to the vehicle. The Tattoo was raging because the sea faced it down. Even the Tattoo won't face down the sea, people said afterward. No one'll face down the sea. That word found its way all over.

ANOTHER QUEASY LURCH OF HISTORY. IMPOSSIBLE TO DESCRIBE, a stutter, a switch, the timeline two-by-foured onto another course that looked, smelt, sounded the same but did not feel it, not in its flesh. In the clouds was more of that strange rage, more fighting, memory versus foreclosure in a celestial punchup. Every blow reconfigured the bits in Londoners' heads. Only the most perspicacious gathered something of the reasons for their little strokes, their confusions and aphasia: that it was a part of the war.

Marge was part enough now of the hinterland that she felt it. Her head was full of abrupt forgettings and jab recalls.

It was a last night for her already. Resentful of and exhausted by all the impossibles, she had responded, to their great surprise, to a final pitch from some of her friends. A small group from one of the galleries at which she had exhibited—two men, two women who showed together under a collective term, the Exhausteds, they had given themselves based on perceived shared concerns. Marge, on the basis of her art, had once been dubbed a fellow traveller, a semiexhausted, a Somewhat Tired.

She had stopped hearing from her work friends, but one or other of the Exhausteds had been calling her every couple of days, trying to encourage her out to a drink, to supper, to an exhibition of competitors at which they could all sneer. "It's fucking good to see you," said a woman called Diane. She made pieces from melted plastic pens. "It's been ages."

"I know, I know," Marge said. "Sorry, I've been getting really crazy into the work."

"Never need to apologise for that," Bryn said. He painted portraits into fat books opened at random. In Marge's opinion his work was total shit.

She had thought she would feel herself playing a role that evening. But their rambles from pub to arty pub pulled her back into the life she had thought long gone. She had only a slight sense of watching herself, of pretence, as they went past tattoo parlours and bookshops, cheap restaurants. Sirens of police and fire passed them in tremendous rushes.

"Did you hear about Dave?" they asked her about people she barely remembered. "What's up with that business with the dealer you were talking about?" "I can't even believe I had to move, my landlord's a shit," and various other bits.

"How *have* you been?" Bryn asked her at last, quietly, and she just shook her head and rolled her eyes *you don't want to know*, as if at a deadline, a heavy workload, time lost track of. He did not push it. They went to a movie then a dubstep gig, shedding Bryn then a woman called Ellen as they went, a late supper, gossip and creative bollocking. London opened up.

Miracle on Old Compton Street: Soho was fucking lovely that night. Crowds danced bad salsa, still clubbing outside Blackwell's bookshop. The cafés bustled onto pavements, and a stranger with a spare cappuccino turned down by some disdainful prospect handed it with a shrug to Marge, who almost rolled her eyes at the world's performance, but drank it and enjoyed every sip. Empty temples of finance watched from the skyline: bad times were not yet quite there, and they could overlook with indulgent window eyes as Marge played with her friends and just was in London.

It got close to midnight and seemed to stay there. She drank with the Exhausteds remnants for a long endless late-night moment amid cheerfully gusting paper trash and the lights of cars shunting around zone one as if the world was not about to burn. Marge had an appointment in the early small hours.

"Alright you outrageous flower," said Diane when the calendar finally turned. "It's been lovely, and it's been too bloody long, stop acting up." She gave Marge a hug and descended into Tottenham Court Road Tube station. "Be well," she said. "Get home safe."

"Yeah," said Marge to her back. *I'll do that*. Since when had home been home? She took a taxi. Not to a ghost or trap street, of course: the driver's very expertise, the knowledge that got him his cab, would have hidden it from him. She directed him instead to the closest main street to her destination, and from there walked to the little east-London shack.

It looked thrown up out of discarded walls, wood, wattle, daub and brick remnants, on a tiny street of such mix-bred buildings, where a man she had found, via a convoluted online route, waited for her.

"You are late," he said. Inside the mutt-made house the rooms were drier, finer and more finished, more roomlike rooms than Marge would have thought. Amid mould-coloured upholstery, paintings the shades of shadows and books that smelt and looked like slabs of dust was a computer, a video-game console. The man in the hoodie was in his fifties. His left eye was obscured by what she thought for a second was some complex Cyberdog-style hat-glasses combination, but was, she realised, without even a flinch or a twist of the lips, these days, the metal escutcheon of a keyhole from a door, soldered or sutured to the orbit of his eye.

It was attached to face toward him. Everything he saw was glimpsed as through a keyhole. Everything he saw was an illicit secret.

"You're late."

"You're Butler, right?" said Marge. "I know, what can you do? Traffic's a swine." She took money out of her bag, a roll in a rubber band. *If the world* doesn't *end,* she thought, *I'm going to be buggered for cash.*

The air in the room eddied, like interruptions in her vision. Things that should not, like ashtrays and lamps, seemed to be moving a tiny bit. "Anyway," she said. "It's you who lives where no taxi driver can go."

"You think this is tricky to find," he said. "There's an avenue in W-Five that's only in the 1960s. You try getting back into that. Protection, right, as I recall? From what?"

"From *whatever's* coming."

"Steady on." He smirked. "I'm not a magician."

"Ha ha," she said. "I'm looking for someone. I've been told to leave it alone and I'm not going to. I'm sure you know more than me about whatever, so *you* tell *me* what I need."

The watcher-through-the-keyhole nodded and took the money. He counted it. "Could be djinn," he said as he did. "Fire's what's coming. Maybe someone arsed them off."

"Djinn?"

"Yeah." He tapped the keyhole. "That's the thinking. Fires, you know. Anything you remember never been there, all of a sudden?"

"What?" she said.

"Things are going up in fire and never been there." When she looked no wiser he said, "There was a warehouse in Finchley. Round between the bath shop and the Pizza Hut. I know there was because I used to go there and because I've *seen* it." He tap-tapped his eyepiece again. "But 'seen it' butters no bleeding parsnips these days. That warehouse burnt down, and now it didn't ever was there. The bath shop and the Pizza Hut are joined up now, and the only ash blowing around there's a bit of charred never.

"Burnt out backward." He headed into another room, raising his voice so she could still hear. "They can't get it out of *everyone's* head yet, but it's a start. There'll be more, bet you a thousand quid. Might be that's what you're up against."

"Might be."

"I mean we're all up against it but most of us aren't out hunting for trouble. Anyway that ain't the only apocalypse right now. You'll have a choice soon enough. Which is bloody ridiculous." He returned and threw an iPod to Marge. It was scratched, well used. An older model.

"I've got one," she said.

"Ha ha yourself. Put it on but don't turn it on, not yet. Wait till you're out there in the world."

"What have I got? Bit of Queen?"

"Yeah, 'Fat-Bottomed Girls' and 'Bicycle.' I don't know what you're going up against any more than you, so this is a bit all-purpose and you better be gentle with it. It should give you a *little* bit"—he held his finger and thumb apart an inch—"if it *is* djinn, and a *little* bit if it's herders, or gunfarmers or Chaos Nazis or anyone else up and about—you hear all bloody sorts—or whatever of your multiple-choice end-times is coming. But don't push your luck."

"What do you mean multiple choice?" she said.

"There's two on the way, turns out, is what I hear. One of which may or may not be the fire. Can you Adam and Eve that? So to speak. Some animal Ragnarok plus some other awful bloody thing."

"What do you mean, *animal*?" she said. "What do you mean?"

"In a minute. Listen." He pointed at the machine he had given her. "You've got a little guardchord, is all. It's in there. Swimming about in the noise, and if you *listen* to it it'll keep you safe. A bit. So you better hope you like it and don't let anyone else listen. If you sniff trouble play it. Just play it all the time, sod it. Keep the bloody thing charged. Keep it fed."

"What does it eat?"

"Music, gods' sake. Put some playlists on there. Make sure you give it what it likes."

"How do I know?"

"Never had a pet? Work it out."

"How strong is—?"

"Not bloody very. You're flying blind, like we all are. It's a lick and a prayer and a spit of goodwill, so don't piss and moan."

"Thanks," she said. "Alright."

"It might give you a bit of time to get away from whatever, is all. Think of it as a head start for when you run. 'Cause let's face it, you'll run."

"What did you mean about the choice?" she said to the seeing man.

He shrugged. "There's way too many ends-of-the-world to keep up with, but this is the first *conjunction* I can remember in a long while. Seems like it's animals and puritans, this time. Right now with all this going on. Seems a bit—"

"Animals?"

"Some animal god, they reckon—that's what you hear, that's what I *see*." Tap-tap on the keyhole. "We'll find out soon enough. I might not miss this one. Takes more than an apocalypse to get me into town these days, but *two* . . . ? Right now? *You* should, though. Miss it, I mean."

"I can't. That sounds like what . . . people've been waiting for. And anyway, what with my little . . ." She shook her iPod, and he his head.

"It'll just give you time to run," he said.

"About that," she said. Her mouth moved, but no sound came for a moment. "One thing I might have to get away from . . . Can this, can the music-thing you . . . I might see Goss and Subby."

She waited for those names to do their bad magic. For the man to gasp. He only looked sad and winced.

"I know," he said. "Think you get to be on that sort of shitlist and people don't hear? That's why you should stay away."

"This, though?" she said, raising the iPod. "It'll help, if I do . . . if they . . ."

"Against them?" he said flatly. "That thing? No it won't. It won't do nothing."

"Thanks for the warning," she said at last. "I'll be careful. Still if . . . if you could please give me the details of those, of the animal Armageddon . . . I think someone I know might be there."

Chapter Sixty

On the campus of the suburban university, Billy and Dane's vaguely purposeful scruffiness was camouflage. It had not taken long at an Internet café to check which room was Professor Cole's. They knew his office hours, too.

While they were online Billy had poked around to find and check Marge's MySpace. He saw the picture of Leon, the call for help, the number that was not her number, must be some dedicated phone. It shocked him how much it made emotion fill him. He printed more than one copy.

"If this bloke's such a powerful knacker," said Billy, "why's he work at Shitechester Central Poly? And is it not a bit nuts for us to go up against him?"

"Who said we was going up against anyone?" said Dane. "Is that the plan? We're just looking for information."

"We might. Like you said, it sounds like this might all be down to him. The fire, the everything. So what can we—"

"Yeah. I know. We might."

Wati would not come. The strike was dying, and even now his first allegiance had to be to his members.

"We don't have time to wait. We have to find out whatever there is to find out," Dane said. "This is the first lead we've had. So yeah." That long stare had come with him out of the basement. "We do what we have to, and we be ready."

Every one of their moves now might plausibly be the last, but they could not do everything, could not take care of all business. They did their best, just in case there was an aftermath. Dane spoke to rabbi Mo, a quick connection through stolen phones. Simon was curing. They were purging him of all those angry ex-hims. "He's drained and weak, but he's getting better," he said she had said. "Good." As if it were likely that it would, ultimately, make a difference.

Billy and Dane waited in the corridor, forcing smiles when Cole's secretary, a middle-aged woman, and the three students waiting glanced at them curiously. Cole must have protections. They had made what desperate plans they could. When at last the student who had been with the professor left the room, they walked to the head of the waiting line. "You don't mind, do you?" Billy said to the young man in front. "It's really important."

"Hey, there's like a queue?" the boy whined, but that was all he did. Billy wondered passing if he had been so feeble at that age.

They entered, and Cole looked up. "Yes . . . ?" he said. He was a middle-aged man in an ugly suit. He frowned at them. He was cave-pale, and his eyes were shaded ridiculously dark. "Who . . . ?" His stare widened and he stood, grabbing at the clutter on his desk as he came. Billy saw papers, journals, books open. A photo of a young girl in school uniform between Cole and a bonfire.

"Professor," said Dane, smiling, holding out his hand. Billy closed the door behind them. "We had a question."

Cole's face went between expressions. He hesitated and took Dane's hand in his shaking own. Dane twisted and pulled him down.

"I ain't going to take him if we go knack to knack," Dane had said when they prepared. "If he's what we think. At the very least it sounds like he knows what's going on, and just in case he *is* the burner . . . the only chance we've got is to be *stupid*, and brutal, and fucking base."

Dane brought Cole's body down beneath him, expelling the man's breath and locking him into place. He struck Cole twice with the weapon he pulled from his pocket. The way he held him Cole could make no sound.

"Billy?" Dane said.

"Yeah." Billy found two places in the doorway where there were drill holes. He gouged with the knife he had brought, uncovering a scrap of flesh and thin chains, a wire figurine. He could see no other magics. "Done," he said.

"Exit?" Dane said. Billy went fast to the window.

"One floor down, onto grass," he said. He aimed the phaser at the groaning Cole.

"Professor," Dane said. "I'm sorry about this, genuinely, but I'll do it again the second I think you're knacking. We need you to answer some questions. What do you know about the kraken? It was you wanted to burn it, wasn't it? Why?"

Billy riffled urgently through the papers on the desk with his non-gun hand. He went to the bookshelves, found the collection of books and papers by Cole himself: *A Particle Physics Primer*, offcuts, an edited volume on the science of heat. He took the latter and saw, behind it, a second row of works. A slim book, that he grabbed, that was also by Cole, that was called *Abnatural Burnings*. He took another look at the photograph of Cole and his daughter.

"Come on," Dane said. Billy shoved the papers into a bag. "Could be this is all nothing," Dane said. "We got to get you so you can't do anything, in case it's not nothing. You're going to come with us, and if it turns out you've got bugger-all to do with it and we owe you an apology, then what can I tell you? We'll apologise. What did you want with the kraken? Why burn everything?"

There was a noise. Cole was staring up at Billy. Dark smoke was coming out of his scalp. Dane sniffed at the burning.

"Oh piss . . ." he said. Cole was not looking at him. He was staring at Billy, holding his papers, his picture. "Shit . . ." The smoke came from Cole's clothes now. Dane gritted his teeth. "Billy, Billy," he said. "Go."

Cole smouldered and Dane swore and scrambled off him, shaking his hot hands, and Cole rose onto all fours and bared his teeth in the smoke that coiled like mad hair around him.

"What have you done with her?" he shouted. Flames came out of his mouth.

Billy shot him. The inventy phaser-beam slammed him into

unconsciousness and the smoke dissipated. They stared at him supine, in the sudden quiet.

"We have to move," Dane said.

"Hang on, you saw him," Billy said. "He thought we were—" There was a knock on the door behind him.

"Professor?"

"Window," Billy said to Dane. "We got to go."

But the door was shoved suddenly and sent Billy staggering. The secretary stood in the threshold, shadow coagulating around her raised hands. Billy fired at her, missed, as she ducked animal fast into the room. He tightened his gut, and time slowed for her, held an instant, and he fired again and sent her spinning.

Dane smashed the window and gripped Billy, cantripped. He pulled them out. His weak little knack slowed their fall by a second, still depositing them on the verge with a breathtaking smack, but without breaking bones. People stared at them from around the irregular quad. Billy and Dane rose and ran raggedly. A few braver and bigger men halfheartedly tried to get in their way, but at the sight of Dane's face and the phaser Billy waved they got out of the way.

There was a shout. Cole leaned out of the window. He spat in their direction. The stench of burning hair swamped Billy and Dane as they ran, making them gag. They kept running, did not stop, out of the university grounds, back into the city proper and away.

"That went well," Billy said. Dane said nothing.

"You saw the picture?" Billy said.

"You still got it?"

"Why the hell would he want to end the world?" Billy said. "He's not a nihilist. See the way he was looking at it?"

"Could be unintentional. Side effect. By-product."

"Jesus, I hurt," Billy said. "By-product of what? Burning the kraken? He sent Al to get it? Why'd he want to do that? Okay, maybe. But you heard what he said. Someone's took her. He thought it was us. That's part of this."

In the boarded-up building they squatted, they went through the papers. They scanned the mainstream physics, but it was the arcana that gripped them.

"Look at this shit," Billy said, turning the pages of *Abnatural Burnings*. He could not follow it, of course, but the abstracts of the essays-cum-experiments-cum-hexes gave glimpses. "'Reversible ashes,'" he said. "Jesus. 'Frigid conflagration.'" It was a textbook of alternative fire.

"What's reversible ashes?" Dane said.

"If I'm reading this right, it's what you get if you burn something with something called 'memory fire.'" Billy read the conclusion. "If you keep them hot, they're ashes: if they get cold again, they go back to what they were before." There was endless fire, that burned without consuming—notorious, that one. Antifire, that burnt colder and colder, into untemperatures below absolute zero.

Papers were folded between the book's pages, bookmarks. Billy read them. "'Behave and you get her back. Prepare three charges of,'" hold on, "katachronophlogiston. Delivery TBA.'" He and Dane looked at each other. "It's like a ransom note. He's making notes for his work on it." Under the typed words were scrawled pen and pencil.

"I suppose using that as your pad would inspire your bloody researches," Dane said.

"See what's weird about this?" Billy said. He held out the photo. "Look. Look at it. The little girl's in the middle, Cole to one side." The two of them were smiling.

"It's bonfire night, maybe."

"No, that's what I'm saying. Look." The layout was skewed, the fire to the other side of the girl from Cole, very close, lighting them strangely. "He's on one side of her and the fire's on the other." Billy shook it. "This isn't a picture of the two of them, it's the three of them. This is a family shot."

Dane and Billy squinted at it. Dane nodded slowly.

"The djinns are freaking out, people reckon," Dane said. "Maybe it's got something to do with all this. This was a mixed marriage."

"And now someone's got his daughter. He thought it was us."

"He's obeying orders. Even if it's his stuff behind the burning, this isn't his plan, he's just doing as he's told."

"His kid. Find the kidnapper . . ." Billy said.

"Yeah, which he thinks is us."

Dɪᴅ ᴛʜᴀᴛ ᴍᴇᴀɴ ᴀɴᴏᴛʜᴇʀ ᴘᴜʀsᴜᴇʀ? Wᴇʟʟ. Tʜᴇʏ ʜᴀᴅ ɴᴇᴠᴇʀ ʙᴇᴇɴ unhunted anyway. That was why they stayed well away from the kraken on its circling journey. No matter how out of sight the Londonmancers were, obscured by the matter of the city of which they were functions, Billy and Dane were the targets of the greatest personhunt in memory, and they could not risk bringing that sort of attention to the enjarred god. Dane prayed to it, quietly but visibly, quite unembarrassed. He hankered to be in its presence but would not endanger it—any more than it was already endangered, what with the whole end of the world.

The proximity of that worst horizon did not mean they should forget, as they did, the more everyday hunters and knackers after them for the Tattoo's lucre. The drab and frightening fact of that came back to them that night, as they worked through Cole's papers, auditioned theories as to who might be behind what terrible action done to Cole's child, as they walked a dangerous walk to a dingy café where they could access the Internet. A commotion sounded in some alley near them.

"What's that?"

"It's . . ." A drone between the bricks. A bounty-hunting swarm, it sounded like, some baleful hive thinker coming at them for payment in evil apiary kind. Billy and Dane matched each other preparation for preparation. They checked weapons and clung close to the wall, got ready to fight or run while the moan came closer under the noise of the cars and the lorries only around the corner.

"Get onto the main road," said Billy. "They going to send it out there?"

"Or under?" said Dane, nodding at a lid in the pavement. Billy weighed the options, but hesitated, because there was another sound coming. Dane and Billy heard a glass-and-bone rattle, the slide of a jar on the pavement.

"Jesus," Billy said. "It's still following. It's back." A quick warning in his head, in an articulate wave of pain. "It's found me again."

A bee-mass turned into their sight. Spread out like a chitin-cloud wall, blocking their exit, but through those insects another figure darkly was visible, roll-wobble-walking. There was an eddy among the bloodymoney bees and an inrush of air as a seal was cracked. The buzz faltered. A smoke of insects gushed like reversed film out of sight, like steam back into a kettle, like something, and there was nothing before Billy and Dane but the angel of memory.

It showed itself to Billy for approval, having saved him. The source of his glass and time clench; he, mistakenly, its test-tube prophet. Could it feel his guilt at not being what it thought? Being promised by nothing to no one? Its body was again a Formalin-filled bottle, in which, this time, floated hundreds of specks, evanescing bodies of the attacker. Its bone arms were bones, its head was made of bone.

But it was much reduced. It had been destroyed, probably more than once, on its exhausting treks to track and protect Billy. It had dissipated and reconstituted. This time it had made itself from some preserving jar less than half Billy's height. This time its skull was an ape's or a child's.

It chattered at him from the dark of an alley. He raised his hand to it. Exhaustion came over it—Billy could feel the echo in his head—and it shivered. The glass-bottle-and-bone sculpture settled into a more natural and complete still as its fleshless arms fell from it to become rubbish, as its skull head toppled and rolled from its slanted lid to crack apart on the pavement. Only its jawbone stayed, held on the lid's glass nub handle. Dissolving bees bobbed in its swill.

Maybe its presiding angel force was remaking itself in another yet-smaller bottle with a yet-smaller bone head, back at its museum nest, and it would set out on its journey again tracking the power it had given Billy, the trace of itself in him, to find him or be broken on the way and try again.

Dane and Billy went to another vagrant shelter. They were glad when it rained: it seemed to batten down the burning smell Cole had brought on them that would not quite go. Billy still smelt it when he slept. He smelt it through the water in which he sank in his dream. Warm, cool as the sea grew dark, cooler darker cold, then warm again. Through black he saw the dream-glow of swimming light things. He was falling into a city, a drowned London. The streets were laid out in glow, the streetlights still illuminated, each glare investigated by a penumbra of fish. Crabs as big as the cars they pushed aside walked the streets made chasms.

From towers and top floors waved random flags of seaweed. Coral crusted the buildings. Billy's dream-self sank. There were, he saw, men and women, submerged pedestrians walking slow as flaneurs, window-shopping the long-dead long-drowned shops. Figures ambling, all in brass-topped deep-sea suits. Air pipes emerged from the top of each globe helmet and dangled up into the dark.

No cephalopods. Billy thought, *This is someone else's apocalypse dream.*

But here it came, the intrusion of his own meaning, what he was here for. From the centre of the sunken London came a hot tide. The water began to boil. The walls, bricks, windows and slimy rotting trees began to burn. The fish were gusted away toward the drowned suburbs, the rusting cars and crabs were bowled by the force of what came. And here it came, bowling like a tossed bus the length of this street, this underwater Edgware Road, that skittered under the flyover and turned. The kraken's tank.

It shattered. The dead *Architeuthis* slumped from it, dragged the pavement, its tentacles waving, its rubberising mantle thick and heavy and moving only with the tide, the gush, flailing not like a cephalopod predator but like the drifting dead god it was. The kraken and its tank shards scraped and cracked and disintegrated as the water rushed and heated and a subaquatic fire burned everything away.

ANOTHER *INSIGHT DREAM*? REALLY? BILLY WOKE FROM IT TO WATI'S voice. He was sweating from the hot black ocean. The smell of the burn Cole had sent was still on him. Wati had come back. He was in the Captain Kirk. Billy found his glasses.

"Here you are," the toy said in the little plastic voice. "Something's happening."

"*Yeah?*" Dane said. "Really? We nearly got burnt alive by our only lead, yesterday, and we still don't know what's going on."

"Maybe this'll help," said Wati. "Maybe this is it. Apocalypse."

"We know that," Billy said. "That's why we're here."

"Sorry," said Wati. "That's not what I mean. I mean there are two of them."

Chapter Sixty-One

THE WIZARD WHO HAD SOLD HER THE PROTECTION HAD, IN A gruff way, been too kind to answer her question and tell her where to go, if he even knew. But knowing where to look, now, with her own online contacts and link trails, it was not too hard for Marge to find out when, and even hints of where, these competing, overlapping or collaborative apocalypses were due to occur. The Internet debates were over how to respond.

> bottl whisky & head under covers
> got 2 b squid this is it
> C U all in L

"Jesus, really?" Marge said out loud.

> have to go cant miss whole world there

It was not that she did not care if she lived or died: she cared about it a great deal. But it turned out that she would not play safe at any price—and who would have predicted that? There were more messages from her friends on her machine. This time she felt as if by not answering them she was less turning her back on than protecting them.

Leon, she thought. *We're going deeper*. She had her iPod bodyguard. She needed a lay of the land. If everyone who was everyone in that heretic cityscape would be there, there were things she could learn. And if it *was* the squid behind it, if this animal thing was it, if as the insinuations insinuated this was the thing incoming, then she might find Billy.

Anyone up for going? she wrote. *Keep each other safe? Go as team see wots wot?*

I duno
no
no
u crazee???

Screw them, that didn't matter. Billy might be there. She knew that Leon would not.

Marge loaded playlists onto the iPod. She grabbed them at almost random from her computer, a big mix, using up all the available memory. When she was out, now, she felt watched by the world, under threat, pretty much all the time. She went walking, and she went as it grew dark, before she put her earphones in. She pressed random play.

The streetlights shone at her through the haze of branches, woody halos. She walked through her nearest cheerful row of kebaberies, small groceries and chemists. A voice started in her ear, a tuneless, happy, piping voice, singing *push push pushy push really really good pushy good*, accompanied by the noise of a record player being turned on and off, and something hit with a stick.

Marge felt bewildered and instantly cosseted, wrapped in that tuneless voice. The iPod screen told her this was supposed to be Salt' N Pepa's "Push It." She skipped forward. Amy Winehouse's "Rehab," she read, and heard not the familiar orchestration and that magnificent, once-in-an-epoch growl but a little throat-clearing noise and the same reedy querulous asexual tones as before singing in the roughest approximation of the track *they try make me to go to the rehab no no no no no*. She heard the repeat-twanging of one guitar string.

The singer did not sound so enthusiastic this time, and the envelope around Marge cooled, as if a gust of air got in. She skipped, to Kanye West's "Gold Digger." *gimme she gimme money money.* The little singer was happy again and Marge was safer.

The voice liked Run-DMC. Marge walked patiently through its incompetent renditions of old-skool hip-hop classics. It liked some of the Specials—*this town town aaah ah this is a is ghost town*, with a double-tempo clapping. It did not like Morrissey. To Marge's horror, it raised an enthusiastic rorty voice during "Building a Mystery," a guilty Sarah McLachlan track that she could not remember why she had.

"Jesus," she said to the iPod. "If you're into Lilith Fair I'd rather take my chances with Goss and Subby."

But though it sulked a bit when she fast-forwarded out of that, she was able to raise the little singer's happiness on a repeating loop of Soho's "Hippychick," the initial Smiths' guitar sample of which it rendered with a warbling *badadadada*. She had not been able to get the song out of her mind since she had heard it in the hidden pub. There were worse noises to have to listen to.

Marge walked into the most unwelcoming estate she knew of in her neighbourhood. She stood for several minutes in the hollow at the centre of the high-rises, listening to her protective companion croon, waiting to see what it would do when whatever happened happened. But she was left perfectly alone. Once two passing children on their bikes called something, some incoherent tease, at her, then pedalled furiously off cackling, but that was all, and she felt silly and ashamed at treating herself like bait.

We'll have to see when it comes to it, she thought. As she walked home, the sprite in her iPod chattered *fighty fighty fighty powers that be*, its take on Public Enemy.

The night after that, she went, alone as she had no other option, to an outskirt of the city, an imperfect roadway helix, that she had not had too much difficulty establishing would be the epicentre. She arrived early, and waited.

"LISTEN, ONE OF THESE TWO GODS IS SOME KIND OF ANIMAL," WATI said. That brought them up short. "With that, and what with all these rumours about the djinn and the fire, and stuff, I can't help wondering if this might be it."

"An animal church keeping itself secret," Billy said. "Dane?"

"It ain't my lot," Dane said slowly. "I know scripture."

"Wouldn't be the first time there'd been a split, would it, Dane?" Wati said. "Some new interpretation?"

"Could there be another squid church . . . ?" Billy hesitated, but Dane seemed not offended. "Could there be another one out there? Could this be some *other* kraken apocalypse?"

"A cell?" Dane said. "Inside? Doing a deal with the djinn? Behind all this? But they don't have the kraken. We know—"

"They don't have it *now*," Wati said. "We don't know what their plans were. Or are. Just that they involve the squid and burning."

"What *if* this is it?" Dane said. He was looking out at nothing. "What do we do?"

"Jesus," Billy said. "We go, we find out, we stand in its way. We're not going to sit here while the world ends. And if it's nothing, we keep looking."

Dane did not look at him. "I got nothing against the world ending," Dane said quietly.

"Not like this," said Billy at last. "Not like this. This isn't yours."

"I gave your message to the Londonmancers," Wati said. "They're keeping the kraken as far away from this as they can." Because if this *were*, if this did intend, if an event can intend, to be it, to be the end, then the kraken must *not* be near enough to burn. That would seem to be what might send the universe up with it.

"Good," said Billy. "But we don't know what capabilities these people have."

"It's *tonight*?" Dane said. "Where did this even *come* from? We should've heard about this ages ago. It's obviously proper, and things like that don't just spring out of nowhere. There should've been *tekel upharsins* and shit. I guess everyone'll be there to find out what it's about. The church'll be there too."

"I think everyone will," Wati said.

"A conjunction," Dane said. "Been a long time."

It was inevitable that from time to rare time, two apocalypses might clash, but people should have known about it in advance. In such situations, guardians of continuance—declared saviours, the salaried police and the enemies of whoever was declaring an end—would have not only to end the ends, but step in between the rival priests, each vying to rout a vulgar competing ruination that potentially stood in the way of their noble own.

DANE AND BILLY TREATED FENCES AS SOMETHING OTHER THAN barriers, walls as stairways, roofs as uneven floors. Billy wondered if his angel of memory would be where they went, how it might move across this terrain.

Around the lit-up trenches of streets, where police were. As they came closer to where rumour said the event or events would be, at the limits of vision, Billy glimpsed other of London's occult citizens—its, what, unhabitants? Word of the locus had spread among the cognoscenti, by whispers, text message and flyer, as if the ends-of-the-world were an illegal rave.

A space between concrete sweeps of flyovers. Where the world might end was turp-industrial. Scree of rejectamenta. Workshops writing car epitaphs in rust; warehouses staffed in the day by tired teenagers; superstores and self-storage depots of bright colours and cartoon fonts amid bleaching trash. London is an endless skirmish between angles and emptiness. Here was an arena of scrubland, overlooked by suspended roads.

"We have to keep out of sight," Dane whispered. "Let's find out what's going on, check who this is." Wati muttered to him, coming and going from their pockets.

Seers were on the roofs. Billy saw them, silhouettes sitting with their backs to chimneys. He saw the fuddled air where some made themselves not visible. Dane and Billy clung to service ladders on flyovers' undersides. They dangled, while cars and lorries illuminated the wasteland. "Be ready," Dane said, "to get out of here."

• • •

"Collingswood, I may not force you to alpha lima foxtrot, but if I ask you if you're receiving me and you are I expect a bloody answer. I can hear you breathing."

Collingswood made an *on and on* motion to the unhappy young officer in the car next to her. "Alright, Barone." She said *Bah Roany*. She flicked the earpiece. No lapel radios. She, and the few officers seconded to the FSRC that night, were in mufti. She sat slouched in a beat-up car near the gathering ground. "Yes, coming through, big up to the Metropolitan Massive. Rewind. How's it your end?"

"We can see some predictable players pitching up," Baron's crackling voice said. "Nothing from our lost boys yet. You not heard from Vardy, then?" Collingswood shucked as if his plaintiveness were a mosquito in her ear.

"Nah. Said he had to go see a professor. I told him he was one already, but apparently that wouldn't do." She looked around at the fag-end landscape, her head thrumming like a bad receiver, aware with near certainty and very swiftly when the few late-night passersby passed by whether they were innocent or guilty of knowledge about the sort of thing that was going on. Spectators hieing for hides. Twitchers if dooms were birds. Her companion stared as she laughed and nudged him, as if she had spoken that aloud.

"Where is the sod? Bit much given this was his idea," Baron said into her skull.

She had quite enjoyed organising it. It had mostly been Vardy driving, suggesting what to suggest to whom, when and how, what rumours to seed on what bulletin boards, which implications to leave unsaid. She had been happy to cede that to him. She liked the tinkering, but the strategic overview he was welcome to.

Her own enquiries, in venues less epochally inclined than those where Vardy did his musings, closer to that everyday border between religion and murder, proceeded slowly. It was the gunfarmers she was trying to track down. No matter how bloody monkish they were, ultimately they got paid to kill people, and that meant, in some form or other be they ever so abstracted and magic, receipts. And where there was that sort of trail, there would be chatter, a smidge of which, slow though it still was, was wending into her shell-likes.

Collingswood kept only the most vague tabs on who Vardy was manipulating how: she simply did not care enough. Perhaps a part of her thought that wasn't sensible, that she'd do well to learn that game, but, she thought, she would always be happy to subcontract to the Machiavellis of this city. What she liked doing was what she was good at. And what clues she *had* sowed about the questionable ends she and Vardy had cooked up were eminently, obviously persuasive. Soon, perhaps, she might do some arresting.

Collingswood said nothing to Baron. She could hear him keeping the connection open as if she would.

MARGE FINGERED HER CRUCIFIX AND IGNORED THE HUMMING tunes from her iPod, like the singing of a young child. Every few minutes people passed her, or she walked a little farther and passed them, talking into their phones and walking quickly, paying no attention to the scrubby afterthought waste where whatever it was was due to happen. Marge was watching the space, she would have said all alone, when a woman emerged from behind a lamppost too narrow to have hidden her.

Hey, the woman's mouth shaped, but Marge could not hear her. The woman was in late middle age, in a stylish dark coat. Her face was sharp, her long hair styled, and all sorts of oddness about her. *You're here for this*, she mouthed, and was abruptly much closer than she should have been with so few steps.

Marge turned up her iPod in fear. The tuneless singing enveloped her. *Wait*, the woman said, but the voice in the iPod made its way through "Eye of the Tiger" and it gusted Marge away, a London motion sped up and strange. It was all a bit unclear, but within moments she was in another place and the woman had gone. Marge gawped. She stroked her iPod thank you. She looked around and took up watch again.

· · ·

Was it startling that two religions should not only share their last night, but commence the unravelling in the same spot? There had been repeated insistences of where the ends *might* occur, competing declarations, prophecies "examined more closely," the venues growing closer until they met.

Representatives of many factions were near. Cult collectors took bets on the outcome; the vagrant magicians of London, many with familiars come crawling and defeated back as the strike entered its endgame, were ready to scavenge for shreds of power and energy that would be given off. "Oh no," said Wati from Billy's pocket, seeing his shamefaced members. "I have to . . . I need to make some rounds."

It was depressing, Wati agust from figure to brickwork figure, whispering, cajoling, begging and blackmailing, pleading with members to stay away. His bodiless self was buffeted on such an excitable night. Gusty aether blew him into the wrong bodies. He circled the arena very fast. From the eyes of a discarded pencil-top robot Wati watched a woman shift with knacked escapology away from a collector. There was an air about her that drew him, and he would have gone closer, or into the figure she wore around her neck, but something started to happen.

"Fucksnot," Collingswood said. She leaned forward. A woman continued her slow circumnavigation of the space. Collingswood made a little motion as if prying curtains a touch apart. A shaft of the night between them and the approaching woman grew momentarily lighter, a clearer line of sight. Collingswood peered and sighed and released her fingers and the dark came back.

The man beside Collingswood gawked at her. She did not look at him.

"Boss," she said as if to air. ". . . Nah, boss, no sign of them, but I'm pretty sure who I *did* just see. Remember Leon's *lurve* interest? She's pitched up. . . . Fuck should I know? . . . Well it's her stupid fault, innit?" But as she said that last she was sighing, she was tugging on her plainclothes jacket and opening the door.

She pointed at her temporary partner. "Stay," she said. "Good dog."

She was gone, turning up her collar, and he could hear her muttering as she approached the nervous-looking woman.

Wati would have gone closer, too, but for the arrivals. At last, late, striding across the scrubland, in yellow jumpsuits, carrying equipment, looking side to side with pugnacity, came a group of shaven-headed men.

Chapter Sixty-Two

MARGE COULD NOT HEAR WHATEVER IT WAS THE NEW FIGURE suddenly approaching her said, not through the chatty, chirpy bad singing. She saw a young woman mouthing at her as she came closer with so much authority and swagger that Marge's heart lurched and she turned up the iPod frantically. Space slipped. It lurched. The little voice in her ears shouted the excited chorus of a Belinda Carlisle track and the bricks around Marge rushed in tidal passing. She kept going, like a raft on white water, even laughing at herself while the motion still continued for so violent a reaction. *How were you going to face whatever* really *bad was coming?* She hadn't realised how stretched taut and anxious she was about that promised finality.

It was as she was coming to rest, though the phrase felt odd in her head given that she had not moved—only the pavement below the walls beside and the slates above her—that the foot that had started descending in another place was yet to touch the ground, that she recognised the woman she had seen. That rude young constable.

WHO WAS SHOUTING IN FRUSTRATION AS THE MELTING-BUTTER residue of Marge's presence sizzled away from before her. Her noise was interrupted, and she turned to spectate on the spurious event she had helped bring about.

• • •

"WHAT IS THAT?" BILLY SAID. THE NEWCOMERS WORE MILITARY boots, moved like soldiers. The roads beside the open space were half blocked by hoardings, and motorists who glanced down might take what they saw for council workers on some late-night necessary actions.

"Jesus Buddhists," Dane said. "Nasty." Dharmapalite supremacists, worshippers of Christos Siddhartha, amalgamed Jesus and Buddha of very particular shapes into one saviour, accentuating brutal iden-titarianism, a martial syncrex. Billy could hear a rhythm, a little chant as the figures came.

"What are they saying?" he said.

"Only one and a half," said Dane. *Only one and a half! Only one and a half!* "It's how many they're going to kill. No matter how many they do."

"What?"

They quoted the Mahavamsa, the reassurance to King Dutthaga-mani after he slaughtered thousands of non-Buddhists. "Only one and a half human beings have been slain here by thee. Unbelievers and men of evil life were the rest, not more to be esteemed than beasts." One and a half was how many the Jesus Buddhists counted in the mass of dead after any of their depredations, according to careful religious accounting.

"Get ready." Dane held his gun. "We don't know what's coming."

Would the Siddharthans be stood up? Their apocalypse would win by default, but what then? The spectators just out of sight were there to see a godwar. Things too large to be birds, too faunal to be gusting rags of plastic, circled in the wind. End-times always came with har-bingers, generated like maggots in dead flesh.

"Oh," Dane whispered. "Look."

In the lee of a big windowless wall was a gang of helmeted men. Surrounding another man. Billy was rinsed with adrenalin. The Tat-too. "He's here like us," Dane whispered. "To see what this is."

There was the punk man in his eyeholed leather jacket. Two of the men in crash helmets held him, in an alley overlooking the field of fighting. He stared in the opposite direction from it, at nothing, at dark streets, while the Tattoo spectated.

"Jesus," Billy said. "Where's Goss and Subby?"

"If they're here . . ." Dane said. The Siddharthists were putting together a rough altar, carrying out secret ceremonies. "Wati?" But Wati was on rounds again. "If whatever this 'animal church' is doesn't pitch up, we're gone."

There was a flash behind the night clouds, silent. It etched cloud contours. The air felt pressed down and the cars kept howling. From the altar was an unpleasant shining. "Here it comes," said Dane.

All the way over them all, the cloud moved fast. It took shape. Church-sized clots of it evanesced, leaving—it was not mistake—a lumpy anthropoid outline in night-matter, a man shape crude as a mandrake root, a great cruciform figure over the city.

Billy stopped breathing. "If this *is* the end," he said at last, "it's nothing to do with the burning . . . What do we do?"

"It's not our business." Dane was calm. "There'll be no shortage of people trying to put that out. If it's just some piddling apocalypse, we needn't worry."

Then the earth in the dead space, the ugly dusty bushes and debris, rose. Men and women stood out of their camouflage and came quickly forward.

"They were there all along," Dane said. "Well played. So who are they?"

THOSE COME FROM THEIR HOLES WERE IN LEATHER, BELTS CROSSED bandolier over their chests. They surrounded the Jesus Buddhists. The cloud-man loomed.

"*Shit*," Dane said. He turned to Billy. "Waste of our time," he said in a flat voice. "That's the Brood. Nothing to do with a kraken. Different animal."

"What? Seriously?"

"Nothing to see here."

". . . We knew it was a long shot," Billy said.

From their power base in Neasden, the SV Brood were devoted to a wargod polecat ferret. Its uncompromising ontology ultimately precluded its iteration as one deva among many in the Hinduism from which it was doggedly self-created, and the Brood had become monotheists of a more reductive sort. The Brood's inspiration in southern India, their predilection for fighting forms of Kerala, gave the Christos Siddharthans a peg for prejudice: they screamed "Tamils!" as the Brood approached, as if it were a derogatory term. They brought out pistols.

"Bugger this," whispered Dane. "Ferretists versus racists. This is *not* the end of the world."

Could you really feel the hand of destiny while pointing a Glock? The Siddharthists would not let chivalry stand in the way of their Buddhist rage. They fired. Broodists fell and the others leapt, unwinding their metallic belts. They were urumis, whip-swords, blades metres long, ribbon-thin and knife-edged, that they lashed in the crooked agile poses of kalaripayat, opening their enemies' saffron clothes in ragged vents, drawing red lines so fast it took seconds for the victims to scream.

A sinuate mustelid presence coiled and uncoiled out of dust and nothing in the wasteland. "Red thoughts white teeth!" chanted the Brood. "Red thoughts white teeth!" (This long-promised ferret eschatology had been endlessly distant, until the probing and knacked prodding of the FSRC had helped midwife the cult's little Ragnarok. All to flush out who was where.)

"Jesus," Billy said. Cars passed. What did they see? A gang fight? Teenagers? Nothing? The police were surely on their way.

"Let's split," said Dane.

Two apocalypse figures clashed over the waste while their followers squabbled murderously. The god-functions struggled, an unusual storm.

"They're late," said Dane, retracing his way along the underside of a bridge.

"Who?"

"Whoever's going to stop this." Dane tutted.

"Wait," grumbled Billy. "I want to see the apocalypses fighting." But Dane snapped at him to come, so Billy sulkily turned his back on the celestial battle and continued through the crawl space. At the edges of the clearing, other figures had appeared. "Who are they?" he said.

"Some chosen one's party," Dane said without looking. "'Bout bloody time."

Somewhere nearby, Billy supposed, Baron, Collingswood and his to-have-been colleagues were carting the wounded and dead to secret hospitals. Whoever saved the city would extinguish these little Götterdämerungen.

"Did you hear something?" Billy said.

More of those gustings, the things that moved like plastic? Yes, but something else too. Below them were animal calls, whimpering, the cough of foxes.

"We've been smelt," Dane said urgently. Things rose from the alley. A composite thing incoming. Pigeons, grey clubfooted London birds, moving in frantic flock through whatever haze-hide Dane had knacked, made dove calls in panicked aggression. The pigeons bombed them with bursts of clawed and feathered dirt.

"There," Billy heard.

"*Shit*, Cole's burn, it marked us," Dane said. "Come *on*."

Something rose out of the below. A shaking cracked the concrete. The screws that bolted their walkway began to undo.

"Jesus!" Billy shouted. "They're going to drop us."

They descended at the first ladder, in just-controlled falls. Someone's forces were coming toward them. Billy and Dane skirted the battleground, past startled hedge wizards and junior prophets. The birds still harassed them, taking some saurian aggregate shape.

THINGS WERE MOST BLOODY DEFINITELY NOT TAKING THE DESIRED shape. She'd always known this plan was a bit of a long shot, but she'd gone along in good faith. It didn't seem stupid, it was worth a shot. Collingswood, still almost stamping from Marge's ridiculously expert evasion—*whose skills you freeloading, mate?*—had not expected her and Vardy's pet endings to run away with them.

She yelled at the officer partnered with her to come on, yelled into her hidden mouthpiece for Baron's suggestions and orders, but whether it was static, magic or his anxiety there was only silence. If he was issuing commands she had no idea what they were. She did not know where to find him. The knowledge that a few other scattered police cells watched this unfolding did not comfort her. If *she* was having a time of it . . .

"Get your fucking arse here!" The young man tried to obey her. He wasn't SO19. No firearms. She'd complained at the time. What was he supposed to do, carry her bag? All he was really doing was staring at the warring sky.

". . . Tattoo . . . incon . . . can't tell . . . bloody . . ." said Baron, or some Baron-aping airwave-dwelling thing. She'd dealt with *that* before.

"Boss, where *are* you?" She wouldn't say she agreed with Baron about it to his face, but she could bloody well have wished Vardy hadn't disappeared on this of all bloody nights, too.

". . . too is here," he said. "Tattoo is here."

DANE HEADED FOR THE LABYRINTH OF LONDON. HE AND BILLY were shepherded, brilliantly, by the pigeons they thought they were evading. At a little square overlooked by unlit houses and guarded by leafless trees, men and women in municipal uniforms stepped out of the shade. They wore leaf-blowers, engines on their backs, hoses to gust fallen leaves from pavements. They aimed their contraptions like ludicrous guns. They sent whirling gusts of leaves toward Dane and Billy.

"What the hell is this?" said Billy. The leaves slapped him. The blowers were moving in careful formation, the leaf-mass taking whirlwinding shape like a bait-ball corralled by sharks. The men and women ran about each other, a puppeteer collective. The leaves they sculpted with their air machines took the rough shape of a man, three metres high, in tree-muck swirls.

"Monsterherds," Dane said. Flicks of the machines, and the man's head was a bull's. The horns were tubes of leaf. "Get out of here, go."

The men and women made the figure reach. It nearly closed its big leaf-gust fingers on Dane, but he evaded. The minotaur made of air and leaves slammed its whirlwind fist and cracked the paving stones. No mnemophylax came this time. Billy shot, and his phaser beam did nothing but send a few leaves flying. Dane said, "Byrne."

Grisamentum's vizier was a suspended arachnid on a wall. Her face was vividly outraged. She leapt and came after them, straight through the minotaur, which reconstituted the hole of her.

Dane headed back toward the flyovers, where spectators scattered as the pounding leaf-figure appeared. "Wait," shouted Billy abruptly. He took a moment's bearings, took several turns.

Dane yelled, "What are you doing?" but followed him, as the leaf beast, Byrne and the monsterherds came behind them.

At a new brick alley, Billy found what he was looking for. Facing them where the streetlet ended in rubbish, staring at Dane and Billy with unreadable emotion, was the punk man.

The Tattoo himself, his entourage, the guards who held the Tattoo-bearer still, were facing the other way, watching the last mopping-up operations in the arena. The man opened his mouth and stared at Billy and Dane, but did not speak.

Then came the gust of leaves and the shouts of Byrne, and a moment's hush, and Billy and Dane were standing right between the Tattoo and Byrne, representative of Grisamentum, the Tattoo's oldest, greatest enemy.

THE TATTOO HEARD THE SHOCK NOISES OF THE MAN WHO BORE IT, and shouted for his entourage to turn, and to turn him. The two forces stared at Dane and Billy, and at each other. Were those police sirens in some not-near-enough street? Billy thought. Were those the shouts of state functionaries on their way? No matter. The 'herders made the leaf minotaur stand and paw the ground. Billy could feel, like an animal running between Byrne and the Tattoo, a question—*maybe we should focus on these two?*—but the whole shape of London had been cut by their enmity for years. It was a logic too strong to set aside, as Billy had hoped. So the warriors of the Tattoo and Byrne and Grisamentum's monsterherds closed on each other.

The autumn-coloured leaf figure ran, at its 'herders' expert motions, into several smaller versions of the same bull-head man, lurching with windblown grace into the fight. The knuckleheads carried knives and slashed without effect at the leaves, which gripped them in temporary leaf-claws made solid. Dane smashed a helmet with a shot from his gun. The figure fell, the giant clutching hand of its head visible behind the broken dark glass. Dane ducked a leaf-arm blow and pulled Billy out of the way. His weapon click-clicked. They crouched by rubbish at the fight's edge.

"Look," said Billy. The tattooed man shivered in his oversized jacket while his guards faced the leaves and the gang fight took their attention. Billy and Dane looked at each other.

Billy decided. He ran, and spasmed, and time stuttered and glass broke. His phaser blasted one guard away. Dane followed him and grabbed the tattooed man, who stared in terror so great it was overwhelming to see.

"Go!" Dane and Billy pulled him with them—half hostage, half rescue—across to the dirtland where the last bodies lay for collection. There were police, now, figures shouting absurd arrest threats from and into the darkness, maybe slinging spells of some kind that could that night only sputter around like sodden fireworks. The man in leather swung almost like a child between Dane's grip and Billy's. He whispered. Below those noises another sound was audible, the growling, the rage and threats of the Tattoo beneath his jacket.

PART SIX

INKLINGS

Chapter Sixty-Three

Was that it? Were they it, perhaps Marge should say? There were two, after all, weren't there?

Not that what Marge had seen wasn't impressive and strange and something that wouldn't have floored her a few weeks before. Only that she had been hoping for revelation, and revelation came there none.

So what was it she'd seen? She was unsure. She had, after her escape from Collingswood, been rather far from the epicentre while whatever had happened had happened. Some of it had been—whatever it was she was going to say instead of magic: the way some of the people she had noticed moved, those dusty vague humans in the scrubland; the somethings she had never quite glimpsed above and around the sweeps of concrete road; her own repeated slippery moonwalk escapes from the attention of other tourists of finality. And there was the sweep of autumnal sky colours that really could, that really might be dramatic little storms.

There was nothing to do with squid, that she could see, and whatever the micropolitics had been, they had been opaque to her. She was no wiser, and frankly a little awe-numb by now.

So what now?

. . .

"WHAT'S YOUR NAME?"

At very last the man spoke.

"Paul."

Cleaned up of the muck and blood that stained him, Paul was a thin man in his forties or fifties. When lucid he was cowed.

"Hush, hush, wait," Billy and Dane said to him as he shook in their grip, as they skulked in hiding. "They're going to come *find* me," he kept saying. And during all that careful calming of him was the intervention of the Tattoo. The voice came continuously. Threats, insults, commands from the tattoo mouth on Paul's skin.

"What do you think's going to happen?" the Tattoo screamed. "Unfuckinghand me you little *shits* or I will kill you where you stand."

They could not think for his bilious spiel. Dane held Paul and they removed his jacket. From his back, expressions passing in ink tides, bad-magic animation, the Tattoo snarled. It sneered. It looked side to side at Dane and Billy.

"Fucking *clowns*," it said. It puckered its lips and made spit noises. No spit came out of the black-ink pretend hole of its mouth, only that sound of disgust. "You think this is it? You think Goss can't taste where I've been? Look at this cunt's feet." They were a little bloody. The Tattoo began to laugh.

"Goss isn't here," Billy said.

"Oh, don't you worry, Goss and Subby'll be back. Where's your bastard commie friend?" They said nothing. "His plan's going up in piss and so are you, soon as they're back. You're all going to die."

"Shut up," said Dane. He kneeled by the vivid black-outlined features. "What do *you* want the kraken for? What's your plan?"

"You worthless little snail-worshipping turd, Parnell. You're so fucking bad at that you got kicked out of your church."

"What do you know about Cole?"

"I won't insult your intelligence with *if you let me go now I'll let you live*, because I totally won't."

"I can hurt you," Dane said.

"No, you can hurt *Paul*."

That shut them up. Billy and Dane looked at each other. They looked at Paul's skin.

"Shit," whispered Billy.

"Oy Paul," the Tattoo shouted. "When we're out of here I'm going to have my boys fucking *sand* your feet off. Hear me, boy? You keep your mouth shut if you want any teeth, if you want a tongue, if you want lips or a fucking jaw."

They wound parcel tape around Paul's midriff. He stayed still to let them. The Tattoo spat spitelessly and cursed them. He tried to chew on Paul, but it was only the motion of ink under the skin. Paul sat patient as a fussed-over king. Billy silenced the Tattoo, and taped also over its eyes, that glared at him until all obscured. Paul had other tattoos. Band names, symbols. They all behaved—motionless but for his muscles.

"I'm sorry," Billy said to Paul. "You've got a bit of a hairy chest—we should've shaved you first. That'll hurt to get off." Beneath the tape, the *mmm-mmm* mutterings continued awhile.

That was how they brought him, with them, to the god.

"Why would you *bring* him here?" Saira said.

The kraken in its tank in the truck watched them deadly. Londonmancers surrounded them. There were more of them than previously—the insider cabal had spread, as secrets like this will not behave. They left behind "to hold the fort" the supposed mainstream of their antique tribe, now a truncated and confused remnant. Every one of the Londonmancers in the lorry was staring aghast at their unwanted captive. Billy and Dane had tracked them, worked out their route with the tiny satnav and gone ahead to intercept them. It had been a difficult journey, fearful that they were chased at every step by some or other power in the city's war.

The Londonmancers would not relax the charms they had to keep Wati from the lorry. Billy was enraged on his behalf, but the strike spirit had been agitated, in any case, had needed to circulate, to fight against another last strike crisis. "Just give me a doll or something on the roof," he said. "Just something."

"We need to find Grisamentum," Billy had said. "He's got to be—"

And Wati had said, "I'll do what I can, Billy. I'll do what I can. There's things I have to . . ."

Where could Grisamentum be? Much of the city was still in denial about the fact that he was anywhere at all other than heaven or hell,

but there was no way the monsterherds and Byrne's strange intercession, that terrible knacked gang fight, could be finessed out of factic-
ity. London knew who was back. It just didn't know where, why or
how, and no amount of cajoling of even the most eagerly treacherous
or venal set of the city's streets, grifters or apocalypse chancers would
reveal anything.

"What would you rather we'd done?" Dane said to Saira.

"We don't have much time," Billy said.

"It's coming," Fitch said. "It's suddenly closer. Much more certain.
Something happened to make it . . . more near."

"We've got the *Tattoo*," Billy said. "Do you not get that?"

"We needed to get this poor sod off the streets as quick as," Dane
said. Paul sat still, looked at them all. He stared at the kraken in its
stinking liquid, through its glass.

"Don't show *him* that," Paul whispered. They looked at him. He
wiggled his shoulders to indicate who he meant.

"No one's going to show him anything," Billy said carefully.
"Promise."

"We've interrupted him," Dane muttered to Saira and Fitch. "We
can find out what his plans are."

"His *plans*?" said Saira.

"He's been trying to get hold of the kraken," Billy said. He tapped
Paul gently on the back.

"Oh, but it's . . . look," Saira said. "Whatever it is . . . it's already
happening," she said. She actually mopped her forehead with whatever expensive scarf it was she was wearing. "The burning's started."
In the last two days, two smallholdings had gone. Been burned, acts
of strange arson. Self-cancelling. The memories of the destroyed
buildings went almost, not quite but almost, as totally as the buildings themselves.

One had been part of the Tattoo's empire, a kebab shop in Balham
that doubled as a lucrative source of drug money, distilling down the
third eyes extracted from and sold by the desperate. The other, a
medium-scale jeweller in Bloomsbury, had historically had an asso-
ciation with Grisamentum. Both had gone, and according to most
attempted recall, Saira said, there had never been either such place.

"You remember them, Dane?" Saira said.

"No."

"Yeah." She crossed her arms. "You don't." The lorry lurched and she adjusted while Fitch staggered, his beard and hair wild. "You and everyone else."

"So how do *you* know there was ever anything there?" Billy said. She stared at him.

"Hello," she said. "Perhaps we haven't met. Hi. My name's Saira Mukhopadhyay, I'm a Londonmancer. London's my job."

"You remember them?" Billy said.

"I don't, but the city does. A bit. It knows something's up. The burn's not perfect. The . . . skin's puckered, sort of. I remember remembering one of them. But they were never here. We've checked records. Never there. There was a fire-engine farting around the day Grisamentum's must have gone up. The firemen were just driving around, didn't know why they were supposed to be there."

"It's Cole's thing, it's got to be," Dane said slowly. "Who is it getting him to . . . Where's that paper? The one that was in the book?" Billy gave it. "Here. 'Katachronophlogiston.' Look."

"Burning stuff right out of time," Billy said. "Yeah. So, who and why?"

"*He* might know," Saira said. "He knows more than us." She stared at Paul. Indicated his back. A long, unhappy pause. "He might know stuff about Cole. Might not even know he does." They waited, they hesitated. They tried to think of interrogator's tricks.

Paul spoke. "Don't," he said. "He won't . . . I can tell you." He was so quiet they thought they had misheard, until he said it again. "I can tell you. Why he wants it. What he wants it for. I can tell you everything."

"It was a tattooist in Brixton," he said. "I came in to have a big, you know, Celtic cross on my back, but not only black and white—I wanted greens and stuff too, you know, and it was going to take hours. I always rather do that in one go—I can't get my head around loads of sessions, you know, it's all or nothing for me; it was always that way." No one interrupted him. Someone brought him a drink that he drank without looking anywhere other than the nowhere at which he was staring.

"I knew it was going to hurt, but I'd got drunk even though you ain't supposed to. I been to that tattooist before. We'd talked, so he knew a bit about me. About the people I knew, about what I did, that sort of thing, you know? I think he was saying what he'd been told, because I think he was like searching for candidates.

"He asked if I minded him having this other bloke there, who was like another tattooist, he said, and they were comparing designs, and I said no, I didn't care. He wasn't much like a tattooist, I thought. I don't know what I meant. I was too drunk, though, to care.

"He watched while the guy did me, and he was like giving him advice. He kept going into a back room. I think we know what was in there? *Who* I mean I should say." He gave a horrible sad little pretend laugh. This was not the story they had hoped for, but who could interrupt him?

"They kept showing me my back in the mirror. The tattooist was giggling every time he did, but the other bloke wasn't—he was all quiet about it. They must've done something to the mirror. Because when I looked in it, it was a cross. It looked fine. I don't know how they did that.

"The second day I unwrap the bandages to show a friend, and she's like, "I thought you was going to get a cross." I thought she meant it was too finickety. I didn't even look at it. It was a little while after that, when the scabs came off, that it woke up."

It had been Grisamentum overseeing the design. And there in that back room, imprisoned and diminished over the hours, the man who then became the Tattoo. What an arcane gang hit. Not a murder—these men were too baroquely cruel for that—but a banishing, an imprisonment. Perhaps it had been blood colouring the ink. Certainly some essence, call it soul, drained from the man and left a man-shaped meat husk behind.

PAUL HAD WOKEN TO THE MUTTERINGS FROM HIS SKIN. THERE WAS no one in his bed but him. The voice was muffled.

"What did they do? What did they do?" That was what Paul first heard. "What did those fuckers do to me?"

When at very last he unwound his bandages the glam had faded and Paul saw the real tattoo. Two shocks in immediate succession:

that what he wore was a face; and much worse—much much worse, much greater, quite shattering—that it was moving.

The face was shocked too. It took minutes for it to understand what had happened to it. It terrorised Paul. It began to tell him what to do.

He had not eaten. "I need you healthy," said the tattoo on his back. "Eat, eat, eat," until Paul ate. It had him test his strength. It appraised him like a trainer. He told it to leave him alone, that it did not exist. Of course he went to a doctor and demanded to know how it might be removed. The Tattoo stayed motionless, so the doctor assumed Paul was merely an agitated drunk who had taken against his hideous design. There would be a very long waiting list, she told him. For cosmetics.

Paul attempted home-grown removals with sandpaper, but each time he, screaming, failed, the Tattoo screaming with him. It had him return to the tattooist's shop, but the proprietor was long gone.

He covered it, but such muffling would never last. When the gags fell the Tattoo would shout when he was out in the street, curse him and mock him. It shouted filthy slurs, swear words and racist names, trying, with success sometimes, to have Paul beaten up. "Hush now," it would whisper to him afterward. "Hush. Just do what I say, never need happen again."

It sent him to mages' speakeasies. It made him connections, whispering to him the code words necessary to get in, had him sotto voce describe the clientele, or turn and let the Tattoo glance through his thin shirt, so the Tattoo would know who was where and direct Paul to those he knew.

"Borch," it would say, when Paul sat down backward at the tables across from startled operators. "Ken." "Daria." "Goss." "It's me. Look. It's *me*."

Grisamentum's intent must have been to exile him into that mobile skin prison where he would be powerless, carried by a host who hated him, tormented with bodilessness until his weak bearer died. But the Tattoo sent Paul to find his associates. He drew them back into his orbit. He sent Paul to secret stashes of money, used them to buy the services of magicians and underworld knowers-how. The Tattoo had only his voice and mind, but it was enough to grow his empire again.

Among the first jobs he carried out while on Paul's body was to track down and execute the tattooist who had trapped him. Paul did not see it—he had his back to the butchery, of course—but he could hear it. It was not quick nor quiet. He shook as blood spattered the back of his legs, held in place by the first of his followers the Tattoo had had made into fistmen.

The Tattoo wanted to ignore Paul. It would let him eat what he wanted, read, watch DVDs with headphones on while the Tattoo did business. Paul might have been granted evenings out, trips to the cinema, sex. But after his first escape attempt the relationship hardened. After his second, the Tattoo had warned that one more would result in his legs being amputated, with anaesthetic an open question.

The Tattoo was plotting his revenge. But as he auditioned assassins, he heard the stories: Grisamentum had been dying anyway.

"WHY DOES THE TATTOO WANT THE KRAKEN?" FITCH SAID. PAUL stared at the bottled god.

"He doesn't know," he said. "He just clocked that someone else wanted it. So he wants it first." Paul shrugged. "That's all. That's his plan. 'Don't let anyone else get it.' He might as well burn it . . ." Paul did not acknowledge the looks that occasioned. "I know who you are," he said to Billy and Dane. "I heard everything he was saying."

"Look," said Billy to Fitch. "We're here. We've got it. We're protecting it. We're not going to let it burn, and that's what kicks it off. Now we've got one of the big players. The whole . . . burning should be getting a lot less probable, right?" The Londonmancers had been future-hunting frantically. Fitch grinding pavements at every snatched stop; rushed ambulomantic walks to see what the twists of city nudge-nudged; ailuromancy over light-footed cats; the readings of dust and chance London objects. "This must've all helped, right?"

"No," said Fitch. He opened and closed his mouth and tried again. "It closes harder than ever. Soon. I don't know how, but we've achieved nothing."

No redemption, no remission, no reversion. Still just that oncoming.

Chapter Sixty-Four

COLE WORKED LATE. THE DEBRIS FROM THE FIGHT HAD BEEN cleared. He shook his head and sifted through the papers that remained on the desk, listing what was there and working out what must therefore have been taken. He ignored a knock, but his door opened. A man peered in.

"Knock knock?" he said. "Professor Cole?"

"Who are you?" The man shut the door behind him.

"My name is Vardy, Professor. Professor Vardy, in fact." He smiled, not very well. "I work with the police." Cole rubbed his eyes.

"Look, Mister, Professor, Doctor, whatever, Vardy, I've already . . ." He looked through his fingers and paused. "The police? I've had two visits from the police, and I've told them everything. It was a stupid prank, it's all finished. Which police do you work with?"

"You're wondering whether I'm part of the conventional crime squad come to do a bit more dusting, or whether I'm with the—what do my colleagues call us? special unit?—and whether I know about all your other less conventional interests. Did they buy it? The regulars? That this was just a 'prank'? Two men too old to be students breaking in and beating you up?"

"They believed what I told them," Cole said.

"I'm sure they did. They've every reason not to want to get too involved. What with everything else going on. The sky, the city . . . Well, you can feel it all."

Cole shrugged. "It doesn't make much difference."

"That's an odd thing to say."

"Look . . ." said Cole.

"Professor Cole, listen. I know you were part of Grisamentum's team."

"Just because I did some work for him . . ."

"Please. Every knacker in London did some work for him at some point or other. And it was you behind that spectacular send-off. The funeral. Great fire. The *cremation*." Cole watched him. "You must know you're not talking to a moron. Word's getting out anyway. Did you hear about the rumble last night? Everyone's saying Grisamentum was there. It's not just me who knows he never died."

"I swear to you," Cole said, "I'm not in touch with him. I don't know what he's doing, and whatever his plans are, I've got *nothing* to do with them."

"Professor Cole, you're probably one of the few people who knows that things have been burning and disappearing, and might even have a chance of explaining how."

"That's way beyond me! The principle's the same as some of the stuff I've done, but that's out of my league."

"Oh, I do know that."

"You know?"

"It's my job to have a pretty clear sense of what you can do and what you can't do. So I know you couldn't have burnt all that stuff out of time. But I also know that you did have something to do with it. You've been delivering information and charges, haven't you? According to demands?"

". . . I . . ."

"And no, I don't think you're in cahoots with Grisamentum. And I know why you're doing this. Family. Professor, I know your daughter's disappeared." Cole's face collapsed. Agony, relief, agony.

"Oh, *God* . . ."

"I know your wife's no longer with us," Cole said. "From what I gather—she's at a C of E school, isn't she?—your daughter probably

takes more after you than her mother. But she's mixed-race and she'll
have certain abilities. Combine that with whatever you've been handing over, in the right hands . . ."

"You think she's being *used*? You think they're making her do this
stuff?"

"Could be. But if so, well. We can use right back. We can use *you* to
track down whoever's doing this. I'm asking you to work with me. To
trust me."

HE MUST BE A PIG IN SHIT RIGHT NOW, GRISAMENTUM, BILLY
thought. His worst enemy down, captive. Without their Svengali,
enforcers like the Tattoo's fistmen would fall back unhappily on a
loose network of contacts and half-trusted lieutenants, trying to
decide what to do. Subby and Goss were the most important of these,
and they were many things—including back from wherever they'd
been, apparently—but not leaders.

"Goss and Subby went to get something," Paul told Dane, Billy and
the innermost Londonmancers. "They went hunting for something.
I don't know more."

Baron and his crew must be highly in demand now, Billy
thought, as local forces struggled with irrupting violence nightmar-
ing their usual run. What would be turning up in these last days
was not stabbed dealers of disallowed drugs and smashed shop
windows, but strangely dead new figures with blood that did
not run as blood should. Terrorised pushers of building-site dust.
The Tattoo was gone, the dead Grisamentum was back, the balance of power was fucked, and the boroughs of London were
Peloponnesea—as the world got ready to end, this was their great
multivalent war.

"I need to . . ." Billy said, but what? He needed to what? He and
Dane looked at each other.

Freelancers were rampaging. Puffed-up thugs with imperfectly
learned knacks; consciousnesses born in vats, escapees from experiments; seconds-in-command of all kinds of minor ganglets decided
that *this was it!*—their chance. The city was full of mercenaries

carrying out long-delayed vendettas as the strike fell and the familiars came back to work, bit by defeated bit, on terrible, punitive terms.

Never mind, some thought, those in the worst circumstances. *Only a few more days and we'll all be gone forever.*

Chapter Sixty-Five

ABSOLUTELY SOD-ALL WAS WHAT THEY HAD TO SHOW FOR THAT, Collingswood thought. Absolutely cack. It was obvious *something* big had happened. Not that she knew what it was yet: she'd pitched up at the site of some shitstorm or other, tasting familiar people in the air, tasting the very Billy and Dane they'd been there hoping to snatch, the knacks she threw out unpleasantly degrading in that atmosphere, slugs in salt. There was a shift, alright. Something had seesawed, and it was maddening and ridiculous how hard it was to work out what. And Baron and Vardy didn't help.

That's fucking it. Collingswood cooked up everything she had. Rang around and called in favours, sent out eager Perky on sniffing errands, stressed as shit by hurry, by whatever it was impending. Took, though she assiduously avoided reflecting on the fact, charge of the investigation. Seemed as if figures she'd never expected to hear from again, that she'd never faced herself but that were well known in the specialist police milieu, were back, or back again, or not dead, or pushing for the end of the world, or coming to get you.

This time it was her ignoring Baron's calls for a bit. Working from home, from ley line—squatting cafés, with a laptop. Some stop-offs with contacts. "What are you hearing? Don't give me that *no one knows* bollocks, there ain't nothing no one knows nothing about."

Because the one line of stories that kept coming, the one connection that made her think she still had it, in these winding-down times, concerned the gunfarmers. Whom she had officially mentally upgraded from rumour. Which she had done, she reminded herself later, scrabbling for pride in that wrecked time, *before* all those gathered hints reached her and critical massed into intuition, and she suddenly knew not only that the gunfarmers were about to attack, but where.

Holy shit. *What? Why?* That would have to wait. But still, Collingswood couldn't stop herself thinking, *If they're being targeted they must've took it.* Which meant the FSRC had even less of a clue than they thought they did.

"Boss. *Boss*. Shut up and listen."

"Where are you, Collingswood? Where've you been? We need to talk about—"

"Boss, shut up. You have to meet me."

She was shaking her head. The lurchingly sudden clarity of the intercepted intent staggered her. She knew she was good, but for her to get this kind of knowledge? *They've given up hiding, they don't care anymore.*

"Meet you where? Why?"

"Because there's about to be a big-ass attack, so bring backup. Bring guns."

WOULD IT ESCAPE THE ATTENTION OF OCCULT LONDON THAT ON that night when small-scale apocalypse competition had been a wedge to crack the city open, Fitch and his Londonmancer cadre had been missing from the proximity of the London Stone? Could that be ignored?

"We're on borrowed time," Saira said. None of this could last. Those among the Londonmancer cadre who could obsessively parse the future—or, they reminded themselves to say, possible futures—from the safety of the trailer. Their job had become simple and minimal: keep the kraken out of the trouble until, up through and after the closing-in last day. To stop it being that day. That was all they could see to do. A new sacred duty.

"There was another one." "Another two." The Londonmancers, by agonising dream and memory interpretations interpreted the city's history and burnlike blebs in its timeline, collected these new strange outriders, these architectural, temporal arson victims. "You remember that garage out by the gasworks? The really cool old Deco one?" "No." "Well, that's the point, it was never there anymore. But look." A preserved postcard of the building, soot-stained and unstable-looking as it struggled gamely to exist, not to be snuffed in the burn-damaged timeline.

Wati went for hours, then a day. He would not respond to any whispers to figurines held out of the vehicle. Was it a retreat, a surrender he was negotiating?

They kept Paul comfortable. They had no trouble with food. Stop for a moment and Saira would dig her hands into the brickwork of an alley corner, knead like clay, and the bricks might go from being a buckle of scaffolding to a key ring and keys to at last a bag of takeaway.

Twice they unwound the tape from the Tattoo's mouth, in reasonless hope that he would say something incriminating or helpful or illuminating. Everything should be falling into place now, in the presence of this malevolent player, and it was not. The Tattoo remained silent. It was wildly unlike him. But for a certain moue of ink face lines, you might have thought him uncharmed.

"He's still got troops out there," Paul said. Desperate little rear-guard actions. Knuckleheads in half-assaults/half-defences, against traditional enemies, forced to take their own initiatives, the very thing they had strived so hard to avoid. People mindlessly showing secrets, knuckleheads fighting for them, winning some and dying, falling, their leather armours ripped, their helmets shattered, little dwarf-hand replacing their cocks and balls suddenly visible, meat-echoes of their head-hands. "Maybe Goss and Subby are back."

Fitch screamed. The lorry lurched. Not in response to the sound of him—the Londonmancer driving could not have heard him—but because of something striking at the driver as it struck at Fitch, in that same instant. Fitch screamed.

"We have to go back," he said, again and again. Everyone was up. Even Paul had jumped up, ready for whatever this was. "Back, back,

back at the heart," Fitch said. "I heard a . . ." In the twanging of aerials, in the cry from the city. "Someone's come for them."

They had to take the lorry out of its avoidance circle along streets it barely fit through, so tight Billy could tell the driver knacked to keep them from crashing. They passed violence everywhere, occult and everyday. Police and ambulances and aimlessly meandering fire engines, the buildings that had gone up and the callouts themselves charring out of memory, so midway en route no firefighter could remember what they were out for. The lorry came as close as it could go to the tumbledown sports shop where the London Stone was homed. They heard more sirens and they heard shots.

There were a few pedestrians on the street, but far too few for what was still not yet night. Those out moved like what they were—people in a regime at war. There was police tape around the building. Armed officers waving them back, cauterising the area.

"We can't get through," Billy said. But he was with the London-mancers. As if these alleys they ducked into would deny them, as if the alleys wouldn't switch back and kink obligingly for Fitch and Saira and their comrades now they weren't hiding and didn't care if the city noticed. So they led Dane and Billy running like scarpering schoolkids down some bricky cul-de-sac that tipped them with architectural abruptness into a corridor within that ugly place, near the London heart, where there was battle, still.

The police would not enter a free-fire zone. From the London-mancers' lair in the corridor of shop fronts, two dark-dressed figures emerged. They held pistols, and were shooting behind them as they came. Dane kicked in the door of an empty shop, and Billy dragged Saira and the others inside out of their range. Fitch sat heavily and wheezed.

"Get off me," Saira said. She was straining to make the plastic stuff of London into something deadly, pressing her fingers on what had been a bit of wall and was becoming that other part of London, a pistol. She was shaking, brave and terrified. The men fired, and two Londonmancers still in the hallway flew backward.

The men wore dark suits, hats, long coats—assassin-wear. Billy fired and missed, and the blast from his phaser was crackling and unconvincing. It was winding down. A blast from Dane's gun hit one man but did not kill him and set him snarling.

Clattering shapes came out of the store doorway behind them. There were composite things, made of city. Paper, brick, slate, tar, road sign and smell. One's motion was almost arthropod, one more bird, but neither was *like* anything. Legs of scaffold tubes or girder, wood-splinter arms; one had a dorsal fin of broken glass in cement, cheval-de-frise. Billy cried out at the mongrel urban things. One took hold with autumn-gutter fingers of the closest attacker and bit exactly as a rooftop bites. He screamed, but it sucked him, so he kicked as he was emptied. His colleague ran. Somewhere.

Both the shot Londonmancers were dead. Saira clenched her teeth. The predator city bits came toward her. "Quick," Billy shouted, but she clicked her fingers as if at dogs.

"It's alright," she said. "They're London's antibodies. They know me."

The immune system trilled and clattered. Another young Londonmancer joined Saira, and she did not look up. When Dane and Billy approached, the defence-things reared in complex ways, displayed cityness in weapons. Saira clucked and they calmed.

Inside the sports shop was a rubble of smashed fittings and bodies. Not all the Londonmancers left were quite dead. Most were, with bullet wounds in their heads and chests. Saira went from survivor to survivor.

"Ben," she said. "What happened?"

"Men," he said. His teeth chattered. He stared at his blood-sodden thigh.

The dark-suited men had entered. They had shot anyone who opposed them, with ferocious, astonishing guns. Of those left alive they had demanded, repeatedly, "Where's the kraken?" They had heard the police come, but the police, following no-entry protocol, had sealed the attackers and attacked in together.

"We have to hurry," Billy said to Dane. He waited, bided, as best he could, but he had to tell Saira to hurry too. She stared at him expressionless.

The attackers knew the secret Fitch and Saira and their treacherous comrades kept. But the rest of the Londonmancers they had come to butcher did not, had been the out-of-the-loop, the hard core of excluded, an unwitting camouflage left in place to pretend all was as it should be. Some were aware that they were being kept in a cloud of unknowing, but they had no knowledge of what that secret knowledge was. They did not understand the gunfarmers' question. Which surely must be provoking to a killer. Some frantic seers had managed to provoke the antibodies into appearance, a little late.

"We were trying to keep them safe," Saira said. "That's why we didn't tell them anything." With a clatter of wood-bits and kicked-away plaster, Fitch arrived at the threshold. He looked in and simply wailed. He gripped the entrance.

"We have to go," Billy said. "Saira, I'm sorry. The cops'll come in any minute. And the bastards who did this know we've got the kraken."

Dane put Billy's hand to a dead woman's wound. In the London-mancer's cooling flesh was a warmth. "Incubation," Dane said. "Gunfarmers." In the dead the bullets were eggs. Guns would grow and hatch, and perhaps one or two little pistols might muster the strength to emerge, call for their parents.

"We can't take them," Billy whispered.

"We can't take them," Saira said, dead-voiced, seeing Dane's action.

The last of the Londonmancers and the London antibodies went with their leader, if that's what Fitch still was, down those attention-drawing urban kinkways back to their lorry. "We're the London-mancers," Fitch kept saying, and moaning. "Who would *do* this?" *You broke neutrality first*, Billy did not say.

"It's new rules," Dane said. "Everything's up for grabs. This is just nuts. They didn't care they'd be seen." Like they wanted it. That's how terror works. They stared at Paul.

"Not this one," he said. Jerked his head at his own back. "Nazis and fists and Boba Fetts, but not gunfarmers."

Blood puddled. Those Londonmancers who had survived stared at the kraken sloshing in its tank. "But why is it . . . ?" they said. "What's it doing *here*? What's going on?" Fitch did not answer. Saira looked away. Paul watched them all. Billy felt as if the kraken were staring at him with its missing eyes.

Chapter Sixty-Six

"MARGE AIN'T HOME. AND SHE AIN'T PICKING UP HER MESSAGES. And I don't know what she was doing there at the double-team. So what do you want us to do?" Collingswood reeled from a wave of the balefulness she had once called Panda. The nickname did not hold in her head, these worse days. "Was all a bit of a fucking balls-up, eh, boss? What now?"

Containment was all they could hope for on a night like this, with so many little wars under way. They could only intervene where possible, stand in the way of some carnages, patch up whatever aftermaths. The madness of, what—some kraken's pain, perhaps?—seemed to have infected everything. The city was hacking itself.

So Collingswood asked the question not for elucidation—stepping into the ruins of the housing of the London Stone, the obvious signs that there had been murder there, though all they could do was log it and move on—but to make it clear that Baron had no answer. He was on the doorstep, looking in and shaking his head with the studied mildness that Collingswood had grown into her job witnessing. Around the room constables brushed things and pretended they were looking for fingerprints—conventional protocols increasingly ridiculous. They glanced at Baron to see if he would tell them what to do.

"Bloody hell," he said, and raised his eyebrows at her. "This is all a bit much."

Fucking no, she thought. She crossed her arms and waited for him to say something else. *Not this time.* She was so used to reading his nonchalance, his asides, his patient waiting for suggestions as if ped-agogically, as signs that there was nothing that could faze him, as symptomatic of absolute police-officerly control, that it was not only with surprise but rage that she realised he had no idea what to do.

When was the last fucking time you came up with shit? she thought. *When did you tell us what to do?* She shamed him into meeting her eye, and what she saw in the deeps of his, like a lighthouse a long way away, was fear.

kollywood? She brushed the tiny voice out of the way as if her hair had irritated her. She did not need Baron knowing that Perky, her little pig-spirit friend, was with her.

"So," he said at last. If you hadn't known him a long time you might buy it. You might think he was calm. "Still no word from Vardy?"

"You already asked me. I told you. No." Vardy had gone to speak to Cole, he'd said, to sound him out. That was the last anyone had heard. They could not track him down, nor could they Cole. Baron nodded. Looked away and back again. "It was his sodding idea that we decoy the end of the world; it was him who pulled whatever he does and tweaked the dates," Baron said.

"Exfuckingscuse me, you reckon it was him spent a day with his head in the fucking astral persuading constellations to fart around a bit quicker?" she said. "Fuck off it was him, he had me do it."

"Alright, well. I thought the whole idea was to flush everyone out and that it certainly did."

"I think I was never a hundred percent sure what exactly the sod-ding idea was, boss."

"Perhaps he'll be good enough to join us," Baron said.

"I'm going," Collingswood said.

"What's that?"

"Can't help the London-tossers now. I'm *going*. I'm going *out*." She pointed, in any direction. They could hear the rumpus of the night. "I been thinking. I know what I'm good at and I know what I can get. This information about this right here? That ain't it. They got me here too early. I was *supposed* to hear about this. This was a fucking fake duck noise." She blew a raspberry. "I'm police," she said. "I'm going policing. You." With three points she commandeered three officers. All obeyed her summons immediately. Baron opened his mouth as if he would call her back, then hesitated.

"I think I'll come with," he said.

"No," she said. She left with her little crew following.

She trod over the smashed-up entrance into the night street. "Where to, guv?" one of the officers asked her.

where we goin kollywood? Perky said.

She had been trying to gather friends; given her druthers Collingswood would have been completely enveloped in amiable presences. But it was hard to get their attention, now. As time stretched toward whatever was at its end, the minds, wills, spirits, quasi-ghosts and animal intents she might have had flit around her in better times were skittish, and too nervy to be much help. She had Perky, with its uncanny porcine affection, and a very few diffuse policely functions too vague to do more than emit words so drawled in her hidden hearing that she could not tell if they were words or imitation of a siren, whispered *now-then-now-then* or *nee-naw-nee-naw* incessantly. Just her, three men, a fidgety pig and lawful intent.

"Perky," she said. The officers looked at her, but they had learned on recent FSRC-seconded business not to ask questions like *Who are you talking to?* or *What the fuck is that thing?* "Perky, scoot off a bit, tell me where there's fighting. Let's see what we can do."

kay kollywood sminit

Collingswood thought of Vardy, and what came to her mind was a tug of anger and concern comingled. *You better be okay*, she thought. *And if you are, I'm fucking livid with you. Where the fuck are you? I need to know what this is.*

Although—did she? Not really. It would not have made a great deal of difference.

She had spent some hours watching CCTV footage. Like radiographers, the FSRC knew what to look at, how to make sense of what shadows, which filters to switch on to bring which whats to the fore. What was artefact on the electric image and what a witch really breaking the world.

Rumours and scabby video came through of two figures who did not attempt to stay hidden. Goss and Subby. Goss *completely unperturbed* by all the salvos against him, unfussed by damage, killing offhandedly. "Where's my boss?" he demanded of those he crippled, the few not murdered attested. "I've counted to a hundred over by the wall and it's time to go in for tea and he's still in the garden somewhere, Aunty's getting tetchy," and so on. After a strange and blessed absence, he was manifesting with his mute boy all over the place.

Did Collingswood's less specialist colleagues think it was an endless day and night of causeless burglary, ferocious muggings and dangerous driving? Perhaps they might allow themselves to think here and there in terms of *gang fights*, muttered about Yardies or Kosovans or whatever, even with the reports of what she knew must be refugees from the Tattoo's workshop—women and men shambling nude and altered, with lightbulbs, diodes, speakers and oscilloscope screens in them—horrifying everyday citizens who could only tell themselves for so long that they witnessed an art event.

Collingswood leaned on the wall and smoked while her companion zipped through the city looking for trouble like a pig for truffles, so that she could do something to look after London. It was better than nothing, she thought. *Really?* she asked herself, and, *Yeah, really*, she answered back.

THE WORLD LURCHED AGAIN. REELED, IN THE WAS *PUNCHED* SENSE, rather than the *dancing*. Marge felt it. She had not gone home since the foiled Armaggedons. There were places to stay if you didn't much care. She did not know if she had a home left, and if she did she assumed it was not safe anymore, that she had been brought back into the attention of the dying city.

You say it best, hmm hmm it best. Boyzone was not one of her iPod-devil's favourites, but it was muttering its version into her ears gamely enough. This was the track that had kept her safe in the brief moment when she had felt a hungry mammal consciousness of one of the gods notice her.

She was in an arriviste corner of Battersea, where late bars stayed open and proudly displayed doctored B-movie posters, and she could feel the *bang bang* of dance bass through doors, through the pavement and her feet. There were lights in the windows of offices, people working late as if in a month's time they would still have a job and the world would still revolve. Gangs outside fast-food restaurants and cafés that pottered along as if it were not after midnight, their premises abutting the alleys that were the conduits to the other city that, over the incompetent supernatural impersonation of Ronan Keating, Marge could hear.

The littler streets were as lit as the main ones, but they were furtive. A landscape of degenerating knackery, violence and eschatological terror. Marge would swear she could hear shots, metres, only metres from where laughing hipsters drank.

She was beyond fear, really. She just drifted, she just went. Trying to ride out the night, which felt to her like a last night.

Chapter Sixty-Seven

Some hospitals were known to be friendly, to ask no questions about odd wounds and sicknesses. There were quiet wings, where you could get treatment for lukundoo, for jigsaw disease, where no one would be put out if a patient spasmed out of phase with the world. The worst wounded of the Londonmancers were delivered, with whispered warnings that the bullets inside them might hatch.

Dane was lashed in place on the lorry roof like some Odysseus. He was pushed, lit up and darkened by the lorry's passage. Dane held his Kirk and waved it, called Wati's name. He made it an aerial. It was a long time until Wati found it.

"Oh God, Dane," the figurine suddenly said.

"Wati, where've you *been?*" Dane hammered on the hatch. Billy looked through. The wind made him blink. Around him the city, like something fat, staggered toward a heart attack. The statuette coughed as if it had something caught in its nonexistent throat, as if its non-existent lungs were bruised. "You heard about the Londonmancers?"

"Oh man," Wati said. "I been, oh, God. They beat us, Dane. They brought in scabs. Goss and Subby are back."

"They're fighting you?" Billy said. "Even without the Tattoo around?"

"Most of the Tattoo's guys must be screwed," Dane said. "But if Goss and Subby're still at it . . ."

"Griz's got gunfarmers working for him."

"It *is*," Dane said. "It *is* him bringing the war. *Grisamentum* . . . *Why* the Londonmancers?"

"*Wait*," Wati said. "Wait." Coughing again. "I can't move like I should. That's why it took me so long to find you."

"Take it easy," said Dane.

"*No*, listen," Wati said. "Oh God, Dane, no one's told you, have they? It ain't just the strike or the London Stone. There's *no* neutrals now."

"What do you mean?"

"It weren't just the Londonmancers. They went for your people too."

"What?" said Dane.

"What?" said Billy. *That ostentatious assault of Fitch's comrades, as if it were meant to be seen.* "Who? Goss and Subby? Who've they——?"

"No. Gunfarmers. For the Krakenists. They attacked your church."

DANE STOLE A CAR. HE WOULD NOT LET ANYONE BUT BILLY COME with him.

"They didn't even have anyone *out* there," Dane kept saying, slamming his hands on the dash. "They kept their heads down. How could anyone . . . ? Why?"

"I don't know."

"I was the only one, and I'm not . . ."

"I don't know."

A little crowd was outside the community church. Tutted at the smouldering from the windows, the broken glass, the obscene graffiti that now covered it.

"Hooligans." "Awful." Dane shoved through them and inside. The hall was smashed up. It was very much as it would be had the perpetrators been a rampaging group of fools. Dane went through the junk room and pulled the hatch open. Billy could hear how he was breathing. There was blood in the corridors below.

There, in that buried complex, were the ruins left by the real attack. Very different from the foolish display above.

Throughout the halls were bodies. They were punctured and

blood-sodden, hosts for grubbing little bullets. There were those who looked killed in other ways—by bludgeons, suffocation, wetness and magic. Billy walked as if in a slowed-down film, through carnage. The ruined bodies of Dane's erstwhile congregation lay like litter.

Dane stopped to feel pulses, but without urgency. The situation was clear. There were no sounds but their footsteps.

Desks had been ransacked. As well as mud, in a few places on the floor were trampled origami planes, like the one that had alerted Dane to Grisamentum's attention. Billy picked up two or three of the cleanest. On each folded dart was the remain or smudge of a design in grey ink—a random word, a symbol, two sketched eyes.

"Grisamentum," he said. "It's him. He sent them." Dane looked at him without any sign of emotion.

In the church, before the altar, was the bullet-ruined body of the Teuthex. Dane made no sound. The Teuthex lay behind the altar, reaching for it with his right hand. Dane gently held the dead man. Billy left him alone.

Like arrows drawn on the floor, more fallen planes pointed in higgledy-piggledy direction to the library. Billy followed them. When he pushed open the library door, he stopped, at the top of the shaft of shelves, and stared.

He walked back to where Dane mourned. He waited as long as he could bear. "Dane," he said. "I need you to see this."

The books were gone. Every single book was gone.

"THIS MUST BE WHAT THEY CAME FOR," DANE SAID. THEY STARED into the empty word-pit. "He wanted the library."

"He's—Grisamentum must be researching the kraken," Billy said.

Dane nodded. "That must be why . . . Remember when he wanted us to join him? That's why. Because of what I know. And you. Whether you know it or not."

"He's taken it all." Centuries of dissident cephalopod gnosis.

"Grisamentum," Dane whispered.

"It is him," Billy said. "Whatever it is, it is his plan. He's the one who wants the kraken, and he wants to know everything about it."

"But he doesn't *have* it," Dane said. "So what's he going to do?"

Billy descended the ladder. There was blood from something on his glasses. He shook his head. "He can't read even a *fraction* of these. It would take centuries."

"I don't know where he is." Dane made fists and raised them and could only lower them again. "The last time I even saw him was . . ." Dane did not smile. "Just before his funeral."

"Why is it we don't see him?" Billy said. "Only Byrne."

"He's hiding."

"Yeah but even when there was . . . like when they fought the Tattoo. Tattoo was there. You'd think for a night like that Grisamentum would show in person. We know he must be desperate to get his hands on the kraken."

"I don't know," Dane said. He ran his hand along the shelves. Billy was reading the strange words and examining the odd figures on the paper planes he had picked up. Dane descended, picking up dust on his trailing fingers. He turned and looked at Billy, who was still, and staring at the planes.

"Remember what you were saying about when Grisamentum died?" Billy said. "About when he was cremated?"

"No."

"I just . . ." Billy stared into an ink blot. He moved it and kept staring at it. "This ink," he said. "It's greyer than you'd think," he said. "It's . . ." He looked up into Dane's eyes.

"It was Cole did his cremation," Dane said at last. He ascended.

"It was," Billy said, staring at him. "Remember the kind of fires he deals in?" They stared at the paper. It riffled as if in a little wind. There was no little wind.

"Kraken," whispered Dane, and Billy said, "Oh my Christ."

WHEN GRISAMENTUM DISCOVERED HE WAS DYING IT WOULD HAVE offended him. There were no techniques to prevail against his own injurious blood. He was uninterested in an heir: his desire was never dynastic but to rule.

History was punctuated with women and men who had by grit forced their ghost-selves back to continue their business, who had wedged their minds out into host after host, who had by simple doggedness failed to die. But these were not Grisamentum's knacks. Byrne was good, her expertise indispensable, her commitment to the project swiftly personal, but she could not unwind death itself. Only filigree it, in certain ways.

"Christ, he must have made . . . other arrangements," Billy said.

He planned his funeral, his oration, the invitations, the snubs, but that, death itself, was always plan B. How, he would have said to his specialists, might we bypass this unpleasantness?

Was it when he decided on the spectacle of cremation that something had occurred? Perhaps he was writing the order of the service. Perhaps scribbling instructions to Byrne he began to stare at the pen he held, the paper, the black ink.

"Pyros, he was talking to," Billy said. "And necros. What if Byrne wasn't remote-talking to him at all, when we saw her? Remember how she wrote?" He unfolded the little eyes. "Why are there paper planes here? Remember how he found us in the first place? Why's this ink *grey*?"

Grisamentum had burnt *alive*, in that temporally and psychically knacked variant of memory fire, that mongrel of expertise, the pyros' and Byrne's, her deadist insights. But he had not quite died. He had never died. That was the point.

After hours of it, after the mourners had left, he would have been collected. He was ash. But he never quite died. He was safe from his illness—he had no veins for it to poison, no organs for it to ruin. Byrne (her name a sudden joke) must have taken him, charcoal-coloured in his urn, ground any last black bone shards and carbon into powder. Mixed him into the base he had had prepared: gum, spirit, water, and rich knack.

Then she must have dipped her pen into him, closed her eyes, dragged the point across her paper. To see the thin line jag into scrappy calligraphy, a substance learning itself, she gasping in loyalty and delight as the ink self-wrote: *hello again.*

"Why's he done all this?" Dane said. He stared at the paper. It stared inkly back. "Why does he want the world to burn? Because he did? Revenge on it all?"

"I don't know." Billy was gathering the paper planes. He held one up. The word on it was *Poplar*. On another *Binding*. Another said *Telephone*. In super-thin writing. All incorporating two little scribbled eyes. This was the remnant of honour, nostalgic for spurious legendary times.

Was it always a lie, Billy thought? Had this neutrality-breaching killer always been so savage? Had something happened to make him the purveyor of this? The vastness of this murder.

Dane went from room to ruined room and gathered bits of Krakenist culture, accoutrements here and there, weapons. There must have been some of the Krakenist congregation out, on errands, having their lives, who would find out soon what had happened to their religion. Like the last of the Londonmancers they were now an exiled people. Their pope murdered before his altar. But in that burrow at that moment, sifting through the rubbish of the dead, Dane was the last man on earth.

Where was the light coming from? There were some bulbs not smashed, but the grey illumination in the corridors seemed greater than those little sepia efforts. The blood everywhere looked black. Billy had heard moonlight made blood look black. He met the eyes of one of the paper planes. It regarded him. Its paper fluttered again, unblown.

"It's trying to get away," he said. "Why would they . . . he . . . why would he actually come here, not just issue orders? He's watching. See how thin this pen is? Remember how careful Byrne was with the papers she wrote on? How she swapped pens? So she could scrape the ink off again. There can only be so much of him."

"Why would he *do* this?" Dane shouted. Billy still looked at the fallen paper's eyes.

"I don't know. That's what we have to find out. So my question is, how do we interrogate ink?"

Chapter Sixty-Eight

THEY WORKED IN THE LORRY. SAFER THAN IN WHAT WAS SUD-
denly a sepulchre. Billy had all the planes he could find, all with
blood and mud torn off, so it was only ink that stained them.

The kraken overlooked them. Dane prayed to it. While the Londonmancers muttered and looked at Dane, suddenly bereft like
them, Billy soaked the paper in distilled water, pulped it and
squeezed it out. Paul watched him, his back, his tattoo, to the wall.
Billy extracted the weak-tea-coloured water and boiled off a little
excess. The liquid rilled away from him in a way not right.

"Be careful," said Saira. If the ink was Grisamentum, perhaps each
drop of him was him. Perhaps each had all his senses and his
thoughts and a little portion of his power.

"She scraped him off each time she got him back and remixed
him," Billy said. Each separate pipette full added back to Grisamentum's bottled consciousness. Why else would there be these eyes? The
ink must know what all those rejoined drips of him had known. "I
guess they've got to husband him." He was finite. Every order he
wrote, every spell he became, his communications *were* him, and
eroded him. If he was all written up, there would be only ten thousand little Grisamenta on scraps, each enough to be perhaps a magic
postcard in some pathetic way.

When Billy was done there was a thimbleful, more than a drop but not much more. He dipped a needle into it. Dane stood, made a devotional sign, joined them. He glanced up. Wati hibernated through the union's defeat in a doll strapped on the vehicle's roof. Billy rifled through the papers he was using, scraps from his bag, all manner of odds and ends.

"Is this going to work?" Saira said.

"Works for Byrne," Billy said. "Let's see."

"Are we actually finally going to find out what his plans are?"

Billy kept his eyes on Dane's. He put the needle to the paper and dragged his hand, without looking, across the page. He drew a line, only a line.

"Oy," Billy said. "Grisamentum. Pay attention."

He drew another line, and a third, and this last time suddenly it spasmed like a cardiogram, and there was writing. UP YOURS, the writing wrote. Tiny scratchy font. Billy redipped the needle.

"Let me," Dane whispered, and Billy waved him back.

"You aren't thinking straight," Billy whispered to the little residue at the bottom of the container. "You're probably a bit foggy. You must be a bit dilute, a bit mucky. Your little brain must be . . . little." He held a pipette over the ink.

"We can dilute you a bit more. Does alcohol sting? We've got some lemon juice. We've got some acid." Billy would swear the tiny pool flinched at that. The pigment that was Grisamentum swilled in the cup.

"What are you doing?" Billy said to the ink.

"My people . . ." Dane said.

Billy dipped, scratched, wrote. FUCK YOU.

"Right," said Billy. He dipped the needle in bleach, and then into the ink. A tiny amount: this had to be a delicate kind of attack. The colour twitched, left a little fade. Billy mixed it, dragged the needle again.

BASTARDS, Grisamentum wrote in itself.

"What are you doing?" Billy said.

FUCK YOU.

"Where's the rest of you?" Billy said.

FUCK U.

Billy dripped in more bleach and the ink rolled. "We're not going to pour you down the sink. You don't get to dissipate painlessly with rats and turds." He held the pipette over the glass. "I will piss in you and then bleach you so you dissolve. *Where* is the rest of you?"

He wrote. The penmanship was ragged. FUCKERS.

"Alright," said Dane. "Bleach that murdering bastard."

WAIT. Billy scratched. INK FACTRY. CLOSED.

Billy looked at Saira. Dane whispered to the toy he carried, though Wati was not in it. "Why take all the books?" He dipped more bleach again.

RESERCH.

"How can he read them all?" said Dane. "*Research*? Why does he care anyway? What in the name of God has all this been about?"

It was Grisamentum's plan that started the countdown to the fire to come. Kicked everything into motion. Only by the superstition of Adler, one of the few who knew his boss still lived in that intermediate ashy way, had the Londonmancers found out about the scheme. Grisamentum's intended theft had made them intervene, against their own oaths, because they could not have that burning.

"*Why*," whispered Billy, "do you want to *burn* it?"

DONT CRAZY WHY?

"So what is it?" Billy said.

"What's he doing?" Fitch said. "Why did he even want the kraken?"

CANT U GUESS?

The ink wrote that, forcing the needle unexpectedly to the paper and scribbling with Billy's hand. Billy redipped.

MAGIC.

ONLY I CAN BE.

"Okay," said Billy after seconds of silence. "Does anyone understand this?"

"Why's he saying this?" Dane said. "You're not even bleaching him."

"He's crowing," said Paul, suddenly. Billy nodded.

"Bleach the motherfucker," said Dane. "Just on *principle*." Billy dipped the bleach-tipped needle and the ink swilled to get away.

NO NO BE ITS MAGC ONLY I CAN. NO 1 ELS IN LONDONN CN BE.

"He's losing it," Saira said.

"Ink," Billy said.

• • •

Tʜᴇʏ sᴛᴀʀᴇᴅ ᴀᴛ ʜɪᴍ.

"That's what he means," Billy said. "That's what no one else in London can be. The kraken's *ink*. Anyone else might be able to *use* it, but Grisamentum can *be* it."

Such a magic beast. Alien hunter god in its squiddity. Englassed. Knowing how this stuff worked, Billy thought. It had the biggest eyes—so *all-seeing*. Bastard of myth and science, specimen-magic. *And what other entity, possessing those characteristics, being that thing, had the means to write it all down?*

"Jesus," Billy said. "This has always been about *writing*. What do you mean?" he said to the ink. "How does it work?"

CAN B IT CAN WILL BE INNNK

It was too gone, too bleached and limited, that little drip of Grisamentum, to answer. Alright. Analogies, metaphors, persuasion—this, Billy knew, was how London did it. He remembered watching Vardy gnosis up, from will, and Billy decluttered his mind and tried to mimic him. So.

With script, a new kind of memory, grimoires and accounts. Traditions could be created, lies made more tenacious. History written down sped up, travelled at the speed of ink. And all the tedious antique centuries before we were ready, the pigment was stored for us in the cephalopod containers—motile ink, ink we caught and ate and let run down and stain our chins.

Oh, what, he thought, it was *camouflage*? Please. *Architeuthis* lives in the aphotic zone: what purpose would the spray of dark sepia serve in a world without light? It was there for other reasons. We just *would not get the hint*, not for millennia. We didn't invent ink: ink was waiting for us, aeons before writing. In the sacs of the deepwater god.

"What could you do with kraken ink?" Dane said. Not scornful—breathless.

"What can you *be* with it?" Billy corrected.

The very writing on the wall. The logbook, the instructions by which the world worked. Commandments.

"But it's dead," Billy said.

"Come on, look at Byrne, he's worked with thanatechs before," Dane said. "All he needs is to wake its body up, just a little bit. For a little bit of ink. All he has to do is milk it."

It would not take so much to bring that preserved kraken an inter-zone closer to life. Thanks to Billy and his colleagues there was no corruption, after all, no rot to cajole backward, which was always the hardest battle for necrosmiths. A threshold-life would be enough to stimulate the ink sacs.

"But why would he burn it?" Saira said. "Why the burning?"

"His plan sets it in motion," said Fitch at last. "That's all we know."

"Maybe it's to do with his crew," Billy said. "It must be him has Cole's daughter. Maybe it's out of his control. What are you doing with the girl?" He said the last sentence loudly to the ink spot. "What are you doing with Cole's daughter?" He shook it to wake it.

WAT? ? ALK? NO GIRLL INK

"Bleach it away," said Saira. Billy wrote an alarming jagged line, and the words IS TATOO IS U? An arrow. Pointing at Paul. Paul stood.

"Hey," said Billy. "Why do you have the girl?" He wrote in tiny print again. TA2 NO CATCH YOU YES. HELO

"That's enough," Billy said. A couple more meaningless scrawls, the words came again, and this time fast.

WHAT WILL THEY DO 2 U?

"What? Do what?" Billy wrote, looking away. "What's he talking about?"

"Wait wait," shouted Fitch, and Billy pulled the nib up and looked at what he had written.

THEY HAVE U & TA2. WONT LET YOU LIV I PRTECT U QIK

"What . . . ?" "Wait . . ." "Is that . . . ?" Everyone was sounding it out.

They have you. Paul was standing. And Tattoo. Dane was beside him. They won't let you live.

Billy stared at Saira and Fitch. I protect you, Grisamentum was telling Paul. Quick.

"Hold on, now," Fitch said.

"What?" said Billy.

"Wait," Dane said. "He's messing with you." He looked at Fitch. Paul moved faster than Billy would have thought he could. Paul snatched the container of ink and the papers on which Grisamentum had written from Billy's hand. Grabbed scissors from a table. He backed to the lorry door.

Billy looked at Fitch's face, and did not try hard to stop Paul.

"Look," Fitch said. "See? It's stirring between us all."

"Alright," said Dane. He stood between Paul and the London-mancers. "Let's calm down . . ."

Billy lowered the needle and wrote with the last of what was on the needle. "Don't," said Fitch, but Billy ignored him and read out loud.

" 'Why would they let you live?' "

Billy caught Dane's eye. A recognition sparked between them that the tiny fuggy-minded drop of Grisamentum had a point.

BILLY SWUNG HIS PHASER AT THE LONDONMANCERS. THEY DID NOT know it was empty, or almost. He doubted it would fire. "Look," said Saira. She stood in a pugilist's pose, but glanced at Fitch. "This is bull-shit."

"Don't be foolish," Fitch said. He stammered, "No one intends any, no one has any . . . why would we . . . ?"

"You . . ." whispered Paul. "He's right." He moved back against the door.

"Wait," shouted Fitch, but even as his last able-bodied London-mancers stepped forward, Dane came to meet them.

"Back," said Billy, standing by Dane, now. Protecting Paul. "What the hell are you planning?" he said.

The lorry reached a stop sign, or a red light, or a hazard, or just stopped, and Paul did not hesitate. He opened the back so there was a glow of headlights in from behind them lurching side to side, as perhaps some glimpse of kraken was granted a startled motorist. Too fast to be stopped, Paul was down, gone, out of the lorry, ink and papers in his hand, slamming the door closed.

"Shit!" said Dane. He fumbled, but the lorry, its driver unaware, was speeding up. When Dane at last got the door open again, it had moved some way off and Paul was gone.

"We have to find him," Billy said. "We have to . . ." To bring him back to the Londonmancers, to Fitch, who had not made a full denial of the ink's allegation. Billy hesitated. Dane had taken a right old time opening that door.

Chapter Sixty-Nine

"YOU LET HIM GO," FITCH SAID. "WE HAD THE TATTOO AND YOU LET him *go*."

"Do *not* give me this shit," Billy said. "You shut your face. Paul is not the Tattoo."

"We weren't going to let you kill him, Fitch," Dane said.

"We weren't going to kill him."

"We saw you," Billy said. "Couldn't even meet his eye. Don't come the innocent, we know what you did to Adler."

"Anyone could get hold of Paul and then we're all in trouble," Fitch said. "I have no intention of hurting him, but I make no apology for keeping all options open."

"*All options open?*" Billy more or less screamed.

"What?" Saira said to Fitch.

"We had one of the two kings of London right here," Fitch said. He trembled. "Responsible for God knows how much. We had to be ready to secure the situation. What could we do?"

"I can't believe I'm hearing this," Saira said. "We're not *murderers*."

"Such drama." Fitch tried to look unrepentant.

"You weren't going to let him go," said Billy. "Don't you think he'd had enough of being someone else's property?"

"There was a debate to be had," Fitch said.

"I imagine," Billy said, "Paul would have disagreed strongly with those who proposed the motion that his incarceration or death were the least bad option. I bet he'd have *strongly seconded* those who leaned toward not that."

"Now would you all listen?" Fitch said. "Paul knows where we are."

"What are you talking about?" Billy said. He gestured beyond the trailer. "I don't know where we are and I'm there."

"He knows how we travel; he's seen the vehicle. If the Tattoo gets the better of him again, and *it did it before*, then it'll gather its strength and forces and then we are in serious trouble. We have to assume we're compromised."

I T COULD HAVE GONE NIGHT TO NIGHT, SKIPPING DAY ALTOGETHER, was how long it seemed to have been dark. Paul did not mind. He liked it that way. He manoeuvred away from sounds, breathed deep and tracked whatever London silence he could find. He was panicked, exhilarated. It was the first time for many years that he had walked without chaperone and threat, that he decided which way he was going.

So which way *was* he going? He kept running for a long time. There were many people running that night, he learnt. He glimpsed them at junctions, at roundabouts, escaping whatever sort of catastrophes chased them.

Despite years of effort to numb himself from the acts ordered and committed by the ink on his back (memories of murders committed behind him, the screams of those close by he did not see die), Paul had picked up various criminal tips. How could he not? He knew that most escapees were recaptured because they underestimated how far they needed to get away before they slowed, so he just kept running.

He held his hand closing the ink's container. He felt the liquid bite his thumb when it splashed it. It was too weak for anything else. He knew he would be sought not only by the Londonmancers, but by the Tattoo's old employees, missing their boss. He knew he would be found.

Goss and Subby would be hunting. Buy them and you bought them. They would be *raging* to get back into the service of the illustration he wore.

Paul would be crippled, this time. He knew he would be blinded, boxed without limbs, forced to swallow vitamined gruel without the tongue that would not be left him.

He slowed at very last. He did not feel tired. He looked carefully around him.

"Is it driving you crazy?" he whispered, so only his own skin could hear. "Not knowing what's going on?" Blind and mute. "You must be able to feel I'm running."

He heard breaking glass. He felt knacked percussions that the news would probably nervously report as Molotov cocktails. Paul vaulted iron railings into a scrub-filled corner between streets, a green oversight too small to be a park. Huddled runaway animal out of sight of the estates, he lay in shrubbery and thought.

The Tattoo stayed quiet. At last Paul stood. It really did: the Tattoo was still. He put the tiny container he had grabbed in front of him. He stared at it as if he might throw in his lot with this adversary of his tormenting skin, as if he might collaborate with Grisamentum. He watched the ink watch him.

He whispered to it. "Thanks for the offer," he said. "Thanks. For, you know. Warning me. And saying that you'd take care of me. Thanks. Do you think I'm going to let *you* run me instead?"

He stood. He unzipped his fly and urinated messily into the tiny pot, dissipating and spattering the tiny self of the ash king of London, pissing him away. "Fuck you," he whispered. "Fuck you too. Fuck you as much as him."

When he was done there was only his urine in the bottle. He took out the paper on which Billy's hand had let Grisamentum write himself. Helpful wind moved the last clinging leaves so a streetlamp could shine on it directly. Paul looked through every piece he had. He put together bits of information about Billy from these remnants from Billy's bag. Patchwork detecting. He worked things out.

One sheet he kept hold of. He sat, his back to the railings, and read and reread it many times. He folded it and put it to his head and thought and thought.

At last, treading the streets again in his shabby Converse he found a phone box. He went through a thicket of front organisations reversing charges and taking their cuts, even then, that night, before connecting to the number on the paper. It was voice mail.

"I have the leaflet you put out here," he said. He cleared his throat. "Is that Marge? I have your leaflet. I know where Billy is. Do you want to meet? I know it's all going weird tonight, but it's now or it's not going to happen. I'll wait here. Here's the number. Call me when you get this." He gave it. "I need you to pick me up, and I need you to come now. I'll tell you everything."

Finally, but hesitantly, the Tattoo twitched. The movement was, by chance or not, in time with a horrible twitch in history. Everyone felt that. A heating up, a smoulder and disappearance. History was scorching.

"DID YOU FEEL THAT?" FITCH SAID.

If Paul surrendered to what he wore and the Tattoo regrouped and came back for them, they were done. The Londonmancers agreed. Or perhaps Paul might even collaborate with Grisamentum, the little drips he carried, take them back to the rest of the liquid criminal, in which case it was all finished, too.

"What kind of team-up would that be?" Billy said.

No one heard him over the overlapping arguments. Fitch shouting at Dane and Billy for letting Paul go, then lapsing into muttering. Dane growling back in a truly scary way, then giving up suddenly and sticking his head out of the trapdoor or window and whispering to Wati, who if he woke in the doll said nothing anyone else could hear. Londonmancers shouting at Fitch, despite who he was, at the plan they could still hardly believe he might have countenanced. Saira saying nothing.

"There's just too many dangers," Fitch said. "He's not stable. The Tattoo's back out there, now. First thing it can, it's going to be making for *Goss and Subby.* You understand? Then they'll come for us . . . and it's not just us who'll die."

They could not let it happen. They had to keep the kraken safe from the burning approach.

"What did we say in front of him?" someone said.

"I don't know," Fitch said. "We have to take the kraken somewhere safe."

"Where do you fucking propose?" Dane said. "It's starting."

"Don't you understand?" Saira said. "We could only keep this safe so long as no one knew it was us, and no one knew where we were. Well, the worst two people in the world know, now."

Chapter Seventy

Paul and Marginalia sat opposite each other. *Where the fuck to begin?*

She would not risk answering any of her phones anymore, but she checked her messages, and she had arrived after many hours in her cheap car. She had sneaked back to her flat for it and come for him. Paul had watched it arrive, pulling slowly like some sea-carriage through sunken streets. It was quiet in the London corner he had found.

She had parked metres away from him under a different lamp. She had waited and waited and when he did not run for her or do anything other than wait, too, she had beckoned. Marge wore headphones. Paul could hear a tiny tinny yattering voice from them, but she seemed to be able to hear him reasonably over it. "Drive," he had said. "I'll keep you out of sight."

They had driven around and around the night. She followed his directions. He'd listened to his ink parasite; he knew how to have her drive a sigil. "Here," he said. "Turn."

"Where are we going?"

"There's places it's hard to find us."

He directed her a long way through London, sticking to rear alleys, intricate convolutes. "Where was it?" he muttered, nodding at memories. At last to an underground carpark at the entrance to some swanky flats. Between pillars in the dark they stared at each other.

Paul looked at her. Marge looked at the ruin-faced man. He was agitated. He was a man, she thought, with plans.

"Where are we?"

"Hoxton."

"I don't even know what to ask you . . ." she said. "I don't know what to—"

"Me too."

"Who are you? What's your story?"

"I got away."

Silence. Marge kept her grip on the stun-gun Taser thing she had got hold of. You could get anything. He looked at it.

"Why you talking to me?" she said. "Where are you in all this?"

"I know a friend of yours, I think . . ."

"Leon?" The hope was ebbing from her voice before the end of the word. "Not Leon . . ."

"I don't know who that is," he said gently.

"Billy?"

"Billy. He's with the Londonmancers. He's with the squid."

"Did he send you?"

"Not exactly. It's complicated." He spoke as if unpracticed at it.

"Tell me."

"Let's both."

Over hours she gave him what small details she had, descriptions of her altercations with Goss and Subby, which made him wince and nod. He said he would tell her his story, and said that he was doing so, but what came out was a soup of specifics, names, images that made little sense. She listened, though she never removed her earphones, and did not learn anything she could make sense of. At the end of it, she understood only that Billy was way deep in something, and that the sense of something ending was not a paranoia of hers.

"Why did you find me?"

"I think we can help each other," Paul said. "See, I want to get a message back to the Londonmancers, and to Dane and Billy, but I've got good reason not to think they'll play straight. Not with me. Dane and Billy I don't know. I don't know about them. But I need them to listen to me too because I got plans. When I saw your paper, I thought, *Oh, she knows Billy.* I remembered I heard about you. *He'll play straight with her,* I thought."

"You want me to be a go-between?"

"Yeah. I got access to . . . It's difficult to explain, but I've got access to some . . . *powers* that they want. But I need protection. From *them.* And other stuff too. I can make them a deal. But they might think they've got reason not to trust me. I've not been myself. I'm being chased."

"You're the one that knows where they are, I don't have any idea, I told you, they haven't contacted me, even though they've got my number . . ."

"Billy was trying to protect you. Don't think too hard of him. But *you* can still get a message to *him.* Like I say he'll trust you." He met her eye, looked around.

"How? Got a number?"

"Hardly. I mean through the city. The Londonmancers'll get that."

". . . I got a message through the city myself, once." He looked closely at her when she said that. "From Billy."

"Is it?" he said quietly. "Did you? Noise? Light? Brick Braille?"

"Light." He smiled quickly and rather beautifully at that.

"Light? Did he? Yeah. Perfect, then, light." He stepped out of the car and Marge followed. "Already a little connection then, between you. Makes this easier." He peered toward the bins, toward the shadows, then pointed—"Look"—at a fluttering bulb in the concrete roof, one among several, but one about to fail. "Give you an idea the way it comes on and off?"

"Oh," Marge said. She almost whispered. "That's how this all started."

He smiled tightly again. "Don't need to know where Billy is. By now, I got no idea. But the Londonmancers always listen to it. The city'll pass a message to them. Yeah, I know Morse Code. I learned *all kinds of things* these past few years. All kinds of useful things. Do you trust me?" He stood in full view, put his arms a tiny bit out, to show her he held nothing. "I can do him a deal. We can help each other. And he wants to see you. You can ask him to come to you."

∙ ∙ ∙

Billy, she wrote, *it's marge meet me.*

"He'll think it's a trap," she said. Paul shook his head.

"Maybe. He might have a pootle around to check if it's you." A momentarily humorous saint. "Maybe he'll just come. He's worried about you." *Is he?* she thought. "Tell him something secret if you want. So he knows it's you." She wrote Leon's middle name. She wrote the address of the carpark where they were. Paul translated it into the longs and shorts of Morse and transcribed dots and dashes under the letters. She was the one getting Billy a message, he told her. It was *her* message, he told her, to *her* friend, her way.

If Paul was out to kill her, she thought, this was the longest way around to do it. She stood on her bonnet as her companion crooned, *done have to be rich la la to be my girl.* She untwisted the fluorescent bulb enough to break the connection.

Paul said, "Dash dot dot dot," and so on. Screwing and unscrewing the bulb, she shed its light and darkness in a not-very-expert, she hoped legible, coded message, for the city to pass on, tap-tapping London, entrusting the metropolis with her information like a vast concrete-and-brick telegraph machine.

You never know, she thought. *Worked before.*

Dane would not let Londonmancers reenter the ruined rooms of the kraken church to which he returned. They were not sure of their relationship to him nor he of his to them anymore— were they allies, still? Wati, traumatised and almost unconscious, could not breach the still-extant barriers. Only Billy came with Dane. When they descended, there were others there, though. The last scattered Krakenists, come home, in mourning.

Around the same number as there had been for the service that Billy had witnessed, but that had been just a regular Sabbath, a sermon: this was the last gathering in the world. Those lapsed, busy, usually too tainted by secularism and the exhaustions of everyday life to attend with the regularity the faith they professed would prefer were all here.

A couple of those muscular young men, though most of the

enforcers of devotion had been guards, and guarding, and were gone. Mostly these were unremarkable men and women of all types. The end of a church.

They did not look hard at Billy. They did not care anymore if he was a feral prophet, some pointless urban Saint Anthony. They were uninterested in anything but grief. They treated Dane as if he were the Teuthex. Though his role had always been that of licenced outsider, then renegade, he was as close as they came, now, to authority. None of them even shouted blame, called him apostate. He all but glowed with their piety.

"Grisamentum's going to come for us, you know," Billy said.

"Yes."

"For the kraken."

"Yes."

"He'll find it."

"Yes."

They sat. This was a time for valedictories.

"Dane. You can feel it. It's now, it's got to be tonight, or tomorrow night, or just maybe the night after. All we have to do's keep the kraken out of danger till then, and we'll have beat that prophecy."

"I don't care. And you don't believe that anyway."

"You don't mean that."

"Which?" Dane said.

"Neither," said Billy. "Either."

"No, I do. Both." Dane dialled a number on the desktop phone, still unsmashed, handed it to Billy. "It's a voice-mail box," he said. "Mine."

"*You have seventeen messages,*" Billy heard. "*First message.*" A click, and the voice was the Teuthex's. "*Alright. I want to know what exactly you think you're bloody doing? I read your note. You have a certain bloody leeway, but stealing a prophet is pushing your luck.*"

Billy looked at Dane. Dane took the phone, pressed buttons to scroll on many days. To quite a recent moment.

"Yeah," Dane said. "*What you are doing now,*" Billy heard, the Teuthex again, voice terse, "*is blasphemy. I have given you a direct order. I've told you. Bring it in. Now is not the time to be having crises of faith. We can end this bloody abomination.*"

"What's this?" Billy said. He held the receiver up.

"I'm an operative," Dane said.

"You were excommunicated . . ."

"Come on now. Please."

Who would ever have trusted a representative of the cephalopod fundamentalists to deal with the issue of the kraken? A rogue, on the other hand . . . Who could be more trustworthy?

Billy shook his head. "Jesus Christ," he said. "It was all an act. You were under the Teuthex's orders all along."

"It wasn't an *act*. It was a *mission*." That ostentatious renegacy. "People are more likely to help if you're exile."

"Who knew?"

"Only the Teuthex."

"So the rest of the church thought you really *were* . . . ," Billy said, and stopped. If your whole congregation thinks you outcast, are you not?

"They don't care now," Dane said.

"But you took me with you. Were you . . . you weren't supposed to?"

"I needed all the edge I could get. You knew things. Still do. You bottled it, Billy. You never thought you was, Billy, but you *are* a prophet. Sorry, mate."

"So the Teuthex telling everyone at that meeting that he wasn't going to hunt for it . . ." The stance, that benthic remove, had been a lie, of which, in their loyalty to their pope, the church had been persuaded. Only the Teuthex and his faux-exile operative knowing the squiddish truth, and hunting for the body of god.

"But . . ." Billy said slowly, "you disobeyed orders."

"Yeah. I brought you with me and wouldn't bring you back. And when we found it I didn't bring it back to them."

"*Why*?"

"Because they were going to get rid of it, Billy, as they should. And they were right, but you know how you'd get rid of it? Everyone's said. It's true. They would've burnt it. That's the holy way. Having that kraken out there in that tank like that . . . it's a blasphemy. So I was to bring it back. But the Teuthex was going to *burn* it."

"And then you saw the prophecy."

"The Teuthex was going to *burn the squid*. And that's what they said started . . . this. This whole thing. What if it *was* us?" Dane said. He sounded very tired. "What if it *was* my church, doing the right thing, releasing it like that, but bringing on . . . whatever it is that's coming?"

It would not have been Dane's church's planned end, their infolding of convolutes into the glint on a giant eye, when roaring perhaps at the surface the elder kraken might rise like belligerent continents and die, and spurt out like ink a new time. This would not have been *that* hallelujah-worthy end, but an antiapocalypse, a numinousless revelation, time-eating fire. An accident.

What terrible anxiety. Dane's horror had been that his church would be the butt of a cosmic banana-skin-slip. It's no one's fault, but we set fire to the future. God, how embarrassed are *we*?

"But look," Dane said. He indicated around him. "There's no one left to burn it now, and that ending still hasn't gone. So that's not what's going to cause it. I was wrong. Maybe if I'd done what I was told to do, we would have saved everything." He swallowed.

"This isn't your fault."

"Reckon?" Dane said, and Billy had no idea. Should have would have could have. They sat in the office of the dead Teuthex and looked at broken pictures.

"Where are the Londonmancers?"

"Panicking," said Billy. "Grisamentum must be coming, and it isn't going to be long before he finds us. All we need to do, what they think, is just keep the kraken safe till that night's over. That's the plan."

"That's a bullshit plan."

"I know," Billy said.

"It is," Dane said. "How many times they going to say the night's about to come? If Paul hasn't given in to the Tattoo it won't be long before he does. Or Goss and Subby'll find him. Or Griz'll burn the world down first." Something somewhere was dripping. Dane spoke to its rhythm.

"So," said Billy.

"So we *make* it the night," Dane said. "Don't run. Take it to Grisamentum. It's his plan that gets everything burning, for whatever reason, whether that's what he has in mind or not. So we get rid of *him*, when he's gone . . ." He brushed imaginary dust from his hands. "Problem solved."

Billy had to smile a bit. "We don't even know where he is. He's got gunfarmers, he's got monsterherds, he's got who-knows-what paper-and-ink magic—what do we have?" Billy said. He barely even heard the absurdity of words like that in his mouth anymore. "Don't get me wrong, I'd love to—"

"Remember how we found the Teuthex?" Dane said. "Why d'you think he was reaching for the altar?"

IN THE CHURCH ROOM THE LAST TWENTY OR SO KRAKENISTS WERE gathered. Old women and men and young, in all manner of clothes. A slice of London, weak with grief. New unwilling recruits to a tiny historical crew, who had outlived their own religion.

"Brothers and sisters," Dane muttered.

"This is the last Krakenist brigade," he said to Billy. "Any others out there ain't coming back."

The altar, of course, was a mass of carved suckers and interwoven arms. Dane pressed certain of the pads in a certain order. "This is what the Teuthex was going for," he said.

It had not been some mere valedictory nearer-my-god gesture, the Teuthex's reach. An inset section of the altar uncoiled. Dane slowly swung the metal front of the altar down.

Behind it was glass. Behind the glass, things preserved. Relics of kraken. Billy gasped as the scale of what he saw made sense to him. The altar was as high as his chest. Filling it almost completely was a beak.

He had seen its shape many times before. Vaguely parrot, extravagantly wicked in its curve. But the largest he had ever seen would have fit his hand, and that would have belonged to an *Architeuthis* close to ten metres long. This mouthpiece reached from the floor to his sternum. It would gape large enough to swallow him. When those chitin edges met they might shear trees.

"It's going to bite me," Dane said. He spoke dreamily. "Just a nip. Just to draw blood."

"What? What, Dane? *Why?*"

"All this lot left. We're the end crew."

"But why?"

"So we can attack."

"What?" said Billy. Dane told him.

Last-ditch defenders were not new. There were always kings under the hill. The golem of Prague—though that was a bad example, had missed its call, a dreadful oversleeping. Each of the cults of London had hopes in its own constructs, its own secret spirits, its own sleeping paladins, to intervene when the minute hand went vertical. The Krakenists had had their berserkers. But the fighters who had volunteered and been chosen for that sacred final duty were all dead, before the Teuthex could effect their becomings. So the last Krakencorps had to be from the ranks of the church's clerks, functionaries, cleaners and everyday faithful.

What was squiddity but otherness, incomprehensibility. Why would such a deity understand those bent on its glory? Why should it offer anything? Anything at all?

The krakens' lack of desire for recompense was part of what, their faithful said, distinguished them from the avaricious Abrahamic triad and their quids pro quo, *I'll take you to heaven if you worship me.* But even the kraken would give them *this* transmutation, this squid pro quo, by the contingencies of worship, toxin and faith.

"Twenty krakenbit is not nothing. It's down to us, now. We have to bring the night," Dane said. "Bring it on and rule it. And it ain't just us, is it? There's the Londonmancers and the London antibodies. They'll piss and moan, but. Well, we're going in, so they've got two choices. Be part of that, or try to disappear. Good luck with that. Fuck Fitch, talk to Saira. She'll do it."

"Why are you telling *me* to—" Billy stopped. "You really think you can take on Grisamentum?"

"Let's have a little last crusade, eh?"

"You think this'll win it for us? You think you can take him?"

"Come on," Dane said.

Billy had learnt about the rules of this sort of landscape. He hesitated, but there was no getting away from what he thought he knew.

"This . . ." he said. "It'll kill you, won't it?" He said it quietly. He pointed at the beak.

Dane shrugged. Neither of them spoke for seconds.

"It'll change us," Dane said at last. "I don't know. We weren't meant to be vessels for that kind of power. It's a glorious way to go, but."

Billy tried to work out what to say. "Dane," he said. He stared at those impossibly huge bite-parts. "I'm begging you not to do this."

"Billy."

"Seriously, you can't . . . You have to . . ." There was so little crazy fervour to Dane. Okay, not counting those incredible facts of what he *did*, and why he did it, his demeanour was everyday. A very English faith. And it was as shocking to discover about him as it would have been about the polite and subdued-dressed congregation of any country church, that he, and they, would die for their belief.

"Wait," said Billy. "What if you fail? If you fail, that's our last line down."

"Billy, Billy, Billy." Dane did not care if the world survived.

"Tomorrow night, Billy," Dane said. "I know where Grisamentum is."

"How?"

"There aren't that many old ink plants in the city, mate. I sent Wati around when he was last awake. There's statues most places."

"They can't have been so stupid, can they, to leave them there . . . ?"

"No, but they're pretty much everywhere, so where there's *none* in a place, nowhere for Wati to go, that kind of gap is information. Tells him something. Someone's making an effort to keep him out. I know where Grisamentum is, and he won't be expecting dick. Tomorrow, Billy."

When they emerged Saira was waiting for them aboveground. "At last," she said. She was antsy, looking around and swallowing. A young Londonmancer was with her. The police would come sometime, though there were other things taking their time, and a vandalised community church was a very low priority right then. "Billy, you got a message."

"What did you say?"

"It came through the city. Bax heard it. It's from your friend. Marge."

"Marge? What are you talking about? Marge?"

"She got back to us," Saira said. "She answered. The same way you got a message to her. Through the city."

That pitched Billy back to that odd little Londonmancer intercession, his message to Marge whispered into the darkness of the post. That he'd hardly thought of since. It abruptly shamed him that he had thought it some therapeutic performance to make him feel better. Perhaps it had been that as well, but could he have been so trite and unliteral as to doubt that it was, as described, a message? And if she got it, why would he think Marge would, as he had adjured, stay away?

With something like vertigo, he thought of all she must have been doing, how many things she must have gone through and seen, to get her to this point, where she was able to send him this word, this way. Without, he thought, a Dane to lead her. And with her partner dead. The hunt for the facts of which must surely have been what got her here. His message must have started that journey. He closed his eyes.

"I wanted to keep her out of it," he said, a last disingenuousness. He apologised to her, silently. She was in it, and more power to her. "Christ, what's been happening? What did she say?"

"She told you to meet her," the man Bax said. "She's in a carpark, in Hoxton. She's with Tattoo."

"*What?*" Billy said. Dane stuttered to a stop.

"Actually that is not quite what she said," Saira said. "What she said was that she was with *Paul*. She said he had a proposition." Billy and Dane looked at each other.

"What the hell's she been doing?" Billy said. "How's she mixed up with *him*?"

"You sure she wasn't witch to start with?" Dane said.

"I'm not sure of anything," Billy said. "But I don't . . . I don't see how, I don't think she . . ."

"Then she's going to get killed," Dane said.

"She's . . . Shit," said Billy.

"If it's really her," Dane said.

"She said to tell you 'Gideon'," Saira said.

"It's her," he said. He shook his head and shut his eyes. "But why would she be with him? Where's Wati?"

"Here, Billy." Wati sounded exhausted. He was in a little fisherman figure made by one of the children of the churchgoers, lying on a windowsill. A man made of toilet rolls and cotton wool. He looked at Billy out of penny eyes.

"Wati, did you hear that? Can you get there?" Billy said. He tried to speak gently, but he was urgent. "We need to see if this is real. If it's her. She might not have any idea what she's getting into, and that name means it either is her or it's someone who got it from her."

"What's he doing?" Dane said. "Why's Paul—or the Tattoo—drawing attention to himself? He must know everyone from Griz to Goss and Subby are after him."

"He wants something. She even said so. We get there he might have a knife to her throat," Billy said. "He's not going to negotiate toothless. Maybe he's holding her hostage. Maybe he's holding her hostage and she doesn't even know." Billy and Dane looked at each other.

"Paul didn't look in shape to do much when he left," Saira said.

"Wati, can you get to her?" Billy said.

"There may not even be any bodies there for me," Wati said.

"There's a doll in her car. And she wears a crucifix," Billy said. There was a silence.

"Wati," Dane said. "Listen to yourself. You sound rough."

"I'll see," Wati said. He was gone. Limping from figure to figure across London.

Fitch said they should hide. One Londonmancer, giddy at his own heresy, suggested they *leave the city.*

"Let's just drive!" he said. "Up! To Scotland or whatever!" But there was no certainty that Fitch, for example, so much a function of the city, could even live for very long beyond its limits. Billy imagined himself on the motorways, becoming expert at the ungainly swing of the trailer, pulling the preserved squid through the damp English countryside and on into Scottish hills.

"Griz'd find us in ten seconds." He would. There was something about the surrounds of slate, the angles of the turns that kept them hidden, even if it was a trap too. The city bent just enough that the Londonmancers stayed out of sight. An organic reflex.

If they left they would be nude. A giant squid in a lorry, heading north between hedgerows. Fuck's sake, everything sensitive within ten miles would start to bleed.

"We're going to do it this way," Billy said. "Dane's way." He did not look at him. "Because he isn't going to change his mind, and this way we can stop guessing whether it's the last night, because we'll *know* it is. And Dane's going to do it, whatever the rest of us do."

Saira was of his party—the warmakers. He could tell she was afraid, but still, that was her vote. Crisis forced the Londonmancers into democracy. Billy smiled at Saira, and she swallowed and smiled back.

Chapter Seventy-One

Wrappers surrounding them, Marge and Paul shifted in their seats. They had been sat for very many hours in the car. Marge recharged the iPod and tried to remain stoic about the increasingly grating warble of her protector.

"What are you listening to?" Paul asked her, finally. It had taken him long enough. She ignored his question. They ate trash calories, ducking below window-level on the few occasions they thought they heard someone approaching. Paul ground his back against the seat as if an insect bit him.

"What's your story?" Marge said. Maybe calmed down he might be more comprehensible.

"I got tangled up with all this stuff years ago." That was all he would say.

More hours. Right then, that carpark was where Marge had lived forever. Emotions and surprise had a hard time getting in to that carpark. So she could merely sit.

It was not silent. All buildings whisper. This one did it with drips, with the scuff of rubbish crawling in breezes, with the exhalations of concrete. Long into dead time, there was another breath at last, a tiny breath. From the kewpie figure dangling above Marge's dash. She turned her iPod down.

"Paul," the little figure said, in a man's tiny voice. "And you must be Marge."

"Wati," said Paul. "Marge," Paul said, "this is Wati." He spoke carefully. It had been a long time since he had said anything. Marge said nothing. She looked at the doll and waited. "Where's everyone else?" Paul said.

"What are you offering, Paul?" the doll said. "What's going on? Will you come back?"

"Wait," Marge said. To the figurine. "Are you . . . Are you with Billy? Where is he?"

"Billy can't come," it said. "There's a spot of bother going on." What a sad laugh it gave. "He says hi, by the way. He's very worried about you. Didn't expect to hear from you. He's sort of concerned about . . . your man here. I don't think you know everything about him that might be helpful. Paul, what is it you want to say to us?"

"Oh, you know, you know, Wati, now you're here I don't even know what to say," Paul said. "I have so much to say, I don't even— I've been having plans, you see." He spoke fast, a wordspill. Marge stared at him. He was quite suddenly like this. "What do I want? Wati, I want you to split, I think, and bring, bring Billy. I want you to . . ." He paused. "You know what happened, Wati. What the Londonmancers had planned? They were ready to *kill* me. You know that? You think that's okay?"

"We don't know for sure they planned anything, Paul. But where do we go now? What do you want?"

"They *were* . . ."

"Where's the little bits of Grisamentum?" Wati said. "It was in a bottle, weren't it?" Paul made a face and waved his hand: *It's nowhere, it's nothing.* "Where do we go now?"

"I don't go anywhere, Wati, but you should," Paul said, urgently. "You should go. Get Billy and Dane and the Londonmancers."

"I'm here to hear you out," Wati said.

It was only now, hearing this strange discussion over the muttering awful music in her ears, that Marge's chest felt suddenly tight as she had the thought, the wonder, if what she heard was a hostage negotiation, about her.

"You go, Wati," Paul said. "Go on now."

"No don't," said a new voice. "Not now, really don't." It was a voice Marge knew. Two people were approaching, in and out of the light pools by the cars. A man and a boy. "Now's we're all together it's time for us to really fix those threads once and for all. The party's tonight, after all, and everybody's coming."

GOSS AND SUBBY.

Oh my dear sweet Lord.

The leerer and his empty-faced boy. They came out of blackness. Trench coats spattered with gore and dirt, swaggering in shadow. Every few breaths, cigaretteless Goss breathed out smoke.

Marge made a mewling noise. She reached for them, but her car keys were gone. She whimpered. She could not breathe. She turned up the iPod violently, so her ears were full of a stupid crooning rendition of TLC's "No Scrubs" so loud it hurt her. One earpiece fell out. She clawed around the floor for the keys.

"Run," Wati whispered from the tiny cutesy figure. "I'll get help." And he was gone—Marge felt him go.

But though Wati had spoken quietly, she heard Goss say as he walked stiff and twitchy out of nowhere into that place, "Will you though, my best fellow? Will you really?"

She saw Goss hold up what looked like a handle of stone. A figure in clay, degraded by millennia. "Hello, boss-carrier," he said to Paul. "You've got something of mine on your person. I suppose what we should say is you've got something of which I'm its. Looking for help, are you? Waiting on the bluff for the cavalry? Round you go, Subby, Son."

Marge scrabbled to get away, but here was the boy Subby staring right in at her as *I dun wun no scrubs no scrubs no scrubs* warbled in one ear. She cried out and jerked away from him. Goss stood by the other door.

"Hello, boss!" he shouted. He reached over Paul and yanked the iPod from Marge's lap, and she moaned and her hands twitched and clutched as nothing stopped him, as there was no skip of escape, no hesitation, as the trembling voice continued from the receding headphones, and Goss without looking hurled it away from him and it shot too fast an impossible distance away across the concrete cavern and shattered out of sight.

"How you doing under there, boss?" Goss shouted at Paul. "What d'you reckon? Has old Wati had his minute?" He looked at his wrist, as if he wore a watch, and stretched out the hand that held that ruined figure.

(Wati was flickering fast, his manifestation a little discorporeally crippled, limping, like some fast-running three-legged dog. Quick quick! In ceramic bust, general on a horse, plastic pilot in a travel agent doll doll gargoyle puppet across miles back to where the Krakenist remnants and the Londonmancers waited, hauling his exhausted self into the doll one of them carried, shouting breathlessly, "Goss and Subby! They're there, they've ambushed Paul and Marge, they're going to—" And then as his companions looked appalled at the little plastic man Wati suddenly and violently receded from them, hauled back hard as) Goss yanked the old shape as if angling or starting a motor or pulling muck from a drain. There was an inrush, a gasp, the slap of a soul hitting stone, and Wati came slamming back into the thing Goss held.

"Blimey! Nearly brought your dolly back with you with that one!" Goss said. "Recall this old thing?" He wagged the statue. Camouflaged by collapse, but there were shoulders, a head of some remnant stump kind. The clay memory of a mouth, from which Wati wordlessly shouted. "Recall this old thing, Wati my boy?" Goss said. "Do you know, do you effing know how many bleeding *ages* it took us to track this little gewgaw down, all the way over in the sands? How do you like my tan?"

The shabti. Of course. The first body, from which Wati was born. Swiped from a museum or from its interment in a tomb. Wati screamed, pulled and pulled to rip himself from the threads that kept his soul in that slave body, but it snagged him. Maybe reoriented, with a few minutes to gather himself and focus his class-rage into more rebel-magic, he might have wriggled free.

"Events have rather done a runner on us, Wati, old pal," Goss said, as Wati bellowed in his tiny pebble voice. Goss held him head down. "You were quite a little scamp. Let's wrap you up tight. Time for bed."

He dropped to his knees. Wati screamed. Goss raised the shabti above the concrete and stabbed it down, and shattered it into grit and dust.

Wati's voice went out.

There was one less presence in the chamber. All around London, members of the defeated Union of Magicked Assistants stopped what they were doing and gasped and looked up and howled.

Goss kicked the shabti powder. He winked at Subby.

"Thing is, Paul," Goss said, and crouched by the passenger door. "Hallo, girlie! Long time. We been here a long time, waiting, to see who you'd get to turn up. Because. Thing is. Do you think we don't hear the messages that get sent through London? Do you think you can try to talk to your friends and we won't hear? Chat chat chat through the lights." He shook his head.

"Now, young squire, what I'm keen to do, very keen, is have a little chinwag with my boss man. So. Get out of the car. Take off your jacket and your shirt. Unwind whatever the tish it is you got keeping his nibs shtum. And let me have a word. Alright? Because it's all going a bit fiddly out here."

With little fear noises Marge gritted her teeth and tried to shove out and through Subby, but he pushed back much stronger than he looked. Paul opened his own door and stepped out. Marge tried to tell him *no*. She grabbed for him and tried to pull the door closed.

"Back off a second, Goss," Paul said. His voice was perfectly steady. Goss obeyed him. Paul took off his jacket. "Let me ask you something, Goss," Paul said. "Watch her, Subby! Keep her in the car." He was taking off his shirt. "Think about it," Paul said. "Do you think I could live with your boss for however many years it is, and not know where you could listen in? Not know that if I send a Londonmancer a message via Southwark, it'll get there, but that Hoxton's always been a traitor? Why d'you think I sent them word from here? I *knew* you'd get it."

Shirtless in the cold, his skin was all-over goose bumps. Wound around him like a shit-coloured girdle was parcel tape. A little sound came from behind him. Paul took Marge's car keys from his pocket and threw them into the dark. He glanced at Goss and then at Subby. "I wanted you to get the message so I could deliver her to you."

Marge's insides went quite hollow. She folded away from him.

"I was kind of hoping I could deliver the others too. And they might still come, especially if Wati got word to them before you . . ." He made reeling motions. "And then they're yours."

Marge crawled across the gear stick, through the open passenger door. The two men and the boy watched her with what looked like mild interest. She crept and stumbled away.

"What's all this about, Paul?" Goss said. He sounded genuinely intrigued. "When am I going to talk to the boss? Do let's undo you."

"Yeah. In a second. But I wanted you to hear this, and I wanted *him* to hear. From me. You listening?" he shouted to his own skin. "I want you, and him, to know that I'm offering you a deal. I'm not stupid— I knew you'd find me. So. No more locking me up like a, a zoo thing. We work together. That's the deal now. And this is a goodwill offering." He pointed at Marge. "I know you want Billy. Well, there's Billy-bait."

Air felt like it was clotting in Marge's windpipe as she crawled.

"I'm sorry," Paul said to her. "But you don't know what it's been like. There was no way I was going to get away."

He took scissors from his pocket and tore the plastic-and-glue carapace from himself. His skin was red beneath it. "Did you get all that, you?" he said. "You've still got time to fix this situation. Grisamentum's gone to war—he's got some mad plan—but I can tell you where the squid is. Do we have a deal?"

Paul turned, so that his back faced Marge. In her already-horror she was not even surprised to see the malevolent tattoo on his back raise its eyebrows at her.

"Maybe," it said.

Paul turned to her again. Goss and Subby stared at him. Goss was admiring. Marge was on her hands and knees on the carpark floor, in Wati's dust, and moving as fast as she could when she could not breathe and her heart shook her.

"Oy, turn back, I want to see," the voice of the Tattoo said.

"Don't talk to me like that," Paul said. "We're partners now. Look." He waited another second. "She's getting away." He pointed, and glanced at Goss, who clicked his tongue, and strode round the car after Marge.

"Where are you off to, you little bantam?" He chuckled. She managed to stand, and ran, but within a few metres he was with her. He grabbed her by the hair. She let out a sound like nothing she could have imagined. He hauled her.

On the other side of the car Paul and Subby watched him. "What's going on? Turn around," the voice from Paul's back bleated.

"Hey, there's one other thing I worked out in my time, Goss," Paul called to him, and held up the scissors. "I worked out what this thing is." He patted Subby. "I worked out where you keep your heart."

A moment cracked. Marge saw Goss way in front of her before she even realised he had let go. She saw him running. She glimpsed a look on his face so aghast it almost made you wince to see it, almost you could sob for it if you weren't held in still-split time. But no matter how fast he moved Goss was too far away, even with the moments Paul had wasted with that taunt, to get between the scissors and Subby.

Paul brought the blades double-dagger into Subby's neck. Quick repeated punches. Blood, and the boy's mindless face did not move except that his eyes widened. Paul stabbed hard. The blood that spattered him was very dark.

Subby dropped to his knees, looking quizzical. "What? What? What's happening?" the Tattoo foolishly demanded, just like a child.

Goss screeched and screamed and howled. He collapsed midleap. The scissors quivered, embedded in Subby's neck. Paul shuddered. Goss sprawled across the car bonnet, puking up his own much brighter blood.

"No no *no* no *no* no." He whined and drummed his heels and stared in outrage at the dying boy-thing.

"Do you think," Paul said—while "what? what's happening? what?" the Tattoo kept saying—"that I would work with you?" Paul pulled the scissors from Subby's neck, pushed them back again. Subby looked from side to side and closed his eyes. Goss screamed and bubbled and kicked and drooled sudden smoke and could not stand. *Screamed.*

"Do you think I would let you come anywhere near me?" Paul said to him. "Did you think I'd collaborate with you? Do you think I'd let you be the muscle for this purebred scum evil motherfucker on my back? Did you *think* I wouldn't *kill* you?" Paul spat at the dying Goss. Spat at the ground in front of him. "You've got this flesh basket to hold what makes you tick, and you think that'll stop me? Goss, stop up your noise. It is time for you to go to hell and take your poor fucking empty little life-carrier with you."

Subby was immobile. The blood was coming out of him slower. Goss wheezed and gurgled and looked as if he was trying to level some good-bye curse, but as Subby died with closing eyes, he died too. His last breath went without smoke.

And whatever else was happening—
in times and places all over—
unmentionably many—
that going out—
that finishedness—
rippled—
was very felt—
and every one of London's bullied and terrified were for a metamoment, from 1065 to 2006, all in their own instants and entangled for a blink, in every awful situation, every little room where they were head-flushed, thumbscrewed, decried, name-debased, taunted, punched, sneered at, the foil of brutality, for a moment just then, for one instant, which might not save them but which would at the very least be a tiny comfort, for always, felt better—
felt joy.

PAUL WATCHED GOSS GO.

"What's happening? What's happening? What? What?" the Tattoo said. Paul ignored it. Marge ignored it.

She watched without motion, holding her head where Goss had hurt her. When Subby died—as if he was a "he," as if it were more than a box with a face—he mouldered away. He crumbled into a disgustingness, and then that crumbled too, into nothing, leaving only a heart, a man's unbeating heart too big for Subby's chest.

Goss did not crumble. Goss lay there like the dead man he was.

"I'm sorry," Paul said to her, at last.

"I needed him to trust me," Paul said. "He never would have left Subby alone otherwise." They stared at each other. The Tattoo screamed, forced to stare into the parking lot darkness where nothing was happening.

"What did you *do*?" the Tattoo said.

"I knew they'd find me," Paul said. "And I could never take him. This was all I could think to do. I knew they'd hear what we said if we sent it from here, and I *needed* them to listen in and come. Can you help me cover him? Him." He raised his arms. "The Tattoo."

He said, "I didn't mean that to happen to Wati. I'm sorry. I thought Goss and Subby would get here first. Well, they did, but I didn't think they'd hide and wait. I tried to persuade him to leave."

"I don't understand," she said. "Anything."

"Yeah. I'm sorry. Let me tell you what I can."

Chapter Seventy-Two

THEY KNEW—PAUL EXPLICITLY, MARGE BY THE INSTINCTS SHE was accruing—that that was hardly the end of it as far as London went. For them, though, it had been an epoch-ending execution. They sat where they had fallen, talking a little, but often just sitting and breathing in Goss-and-Subbyless air. Paul kicked Goss's heart across the concrete.

When Goss died, the lights in the garage had dimmed twice and gone up again in a hip-hip-hooray, in object joy. Colours changed and shadows moved as emissaries from various courts—seelie, unseelie, abseelie, paraseelie—passed through to check out the spreading rumour. A few ghosts that Marge did not see but felt as movements of sad warmth. With a *squee*, a pigness passed her. It was not long after that that they heard a car.

Without a siren but with lights whirling a police car bumped down the ramp and to them. Three officers emerged, their batons out, pepper spray and Tasers out, their hands overfull of weapons. Their terror was quite obvious. After a pause, out of the car in a smart sweep, her clothes and hair jouncing, leaking smoke from one corner of her mouth, a cigarette bobbing from the other, her eyes narrow and turning her head a little, splendid as Boudicca, was Collingswood.

She stared at Paul, put one hand out, took her Taser from her belt.

She looked at Marge, raised an eyebrow and nodded in recognition. She chirruped and whistled, and stroked the air as if it were a piglet's head.

Collingswood smacked her lips. "Fucking fucking fuck me," she whispered. She smiled an utterly beautiful smile. "It's true. You really did. Fuck me. Finally. Oh . . . my . . . gosh. We could do with a bit of good news tonight."

"I told you there was stuff going on with me," Marge said.

"And look," said Collingswood. "Slap my naughty knuckles for making the wrong call. And it's you." She said that to Paul. "Well, I mean not *you* but *you*. Fucked if I know what's the point tonight, but you got to do what you can, right? Come on then." She motioned the two of them up. They obeyed.

"What is this?" Marge said. She sounded mild, not outraged— curious.

"Give me a minute I'll come up with a bunch of stuff to charge you with," Collingswood said. "Basically, the gist of it is, you're coming with me. Might as well salvage something. You too." She looked at Paul. He stood meekly enough. He looked side to side as something invisible circled him. "I don't want any trouble. From you *or* from, y'know. Your passenger. For fuck's sake, don't you want to get out of all this?" she said.

Yes, thought Marge. *Really*. Collingswood nodded at her. The officer did not need her sensitivities to read that answer. "Come on then," she said. "Bloody star, you."

Paul slumped, walked toward the car too, then abruptly raced past Collingswood and her fumbling officers, toward the exit. He knocked her as he went, so she staggered and dropped her cigarette.

"Naughty fucking naughty," she shouted. "Tase the bastard." One of the officers missed, but another got Paul in the back, in his unseen Tattoo, with the electricity-spitting wires. Paul shrieked and fell, spasming.

"Stop, stop!" shouted Marge. "Don't you know who he is, don't you know what he's . . . ? He can't face being locked up anymore, that's why—"

"Boohoo," said Collingswood. "Do I look like I give a shit?" She stood over Paul as he strained to breathe. In truth she did look like she gave a little of a shit. She wore an expression not of regret, exactly, but of troubled irritation, as if the paper in the photocopier had run out.

"No one's out to fuck you up," she said to him. "Will you stop it?" A swiney scream screamed in dimensions close enough for Marge to hear it, and receded. "Now you scared off Perky," Collingswood said. "Get him in the car," she shouted at her men. "If there's still London in the morning, we'll see what we do."

All the cops were as ineffective as keystones, hauling the moaning Paul toward the car. The thought came to Marge that she could run. It was followed by the knowledge that she would not. She walked after them, as she had been told.

The arrest, the invitation, was enticing. After all that work she had done, everything she had faced, police tea, a holding room, someone else making the running. *I*, Marge thought as she settled into the back, offered her shoulder as a pillow for Paul's still lolling head, *am bloody tired.*

"You two are walking home," Collingswood was saying to her officers. "Only room for one more. I wasn't expecting arrests. But seeing as Baz took the shot, he gets the gig." The other two grumbled. "Fuck, you are a wet pair. Look on the bright side: you'll both be burned out of history by morning, so never mind, eh?" She got in. "Baz. Station. Let's ensconce our little charges, then see what else is going on."

I really am, thought Marge, *extremely tired.* Paul raised his head and opened his mouth, but Collingswood switched her finger at him in the mirror, and nothing came out. Marge wished he had got away.

"WHERE'S WATI?" DANE SHOUTED. "WHAT'S *HAPPENED* TO HIM?"

"Marge was . . ." Billy said. "You heard what Wati said just before . . ." His words ebbed out, and he shook his head and covered his eyes. Dead, or hostage at very least.

"Wati!" Dane shouted and raged. "Again! Another! Kraken!"

They had, contemptuous almost, evaded the police tape without breaking stride, and were back in the kraken church. The last Krakenists queued like obedient children by the huge beak in the temple.

The Londonmancers were in the lorry, winding through suburbs nearby. Fitch and some of his last followers were in a strange situation. Disapproving this strategy of war, they were nonetheless tied to it, dependent on its success now that it would happen. So having lost the argument they could only aid those who had won. An extreme cabinet responsibility. They would deliver Londonmancers willing to fight to the battleground.

The Krakenists had only legends to go on, as to what would happen to them when they went to this war, altar-altered, newly dragooned into an army. A dreg regiment. Cars were ready for the afflicted blessed, those about to be bitten. The Krakenists were wishing each other good-bye. After these embraces, they would drive across London to an old ink factory—in awkward silence? Listening to the radio?

Strong kraken-cultists held the mouthpart, bracing themselves to each side. They were audibly praying.

"Is that all of them?" Billy said.

Dane nodded. Few of the last of the church had taken much persuasion. Billy looked at Dane.

"You are going too," Billy said.

"Yeah."

"Dane . . ." Billy shook his head and closed his eyes. "Please . . . Can I persuade you not to?"

"No. Is everything ready?" Dane said. A worshipper. "Then let's do this."

Chapter Seventy-Three

Billy watched the last-ever kraken mass. He sat at the back of the church. He watched tears and heard benedictions. Dane was faltering, but with grace, repeating the liturgies he had not been part of for a long time. The shepherdless flock herded themselves. Billy shifted in his seat and fiddled with the phaser in his pocket.

The congregation sang hymns to torpedo-shaped, many-armed gods. At last Dane said, "Right then."

Some of the volunteers tried to smile as they made a line. One by one they placed their hand at the point of the kraken jaw. The hinge-men would very carefully scissor the great bite together on their skin. Twice the hook of the jaw tore worse wounds than intended and made the faithful cry out. Mostly the snips were precise—the skin broke, there was a little blood.

Billy waited for drama. The bitten seemed clumsy and large, seemed to cram the cavelike hall. They embraced each other and held their bleeding hands. Dane, the last one, put his own hand in the jaws and had his congregation bite them down. Billy made no reaction at all.

The plan was simple or stupid. They did not have the time, numbers or expertise for sophistication. They had one advantage and only one, which was that Grisamentum did not know they knew where he was, or that they were coming. All they had was that surprise. A one-two, misdirect and real attack. Anyone who thought for more than one second must realise that what came first was a diversion. So they would not give them that second.

They had a few pistols, swords, knacked things of various designs. They did not know what Grisamentum was, now. En-inked on paper, in liquid? He'd avoided death once already. Fire might dry him out, but it would leave his pigment behind. Bleach, then. He had seemed scared of it. They carried bottles. Their most important weapon a household cleanser. Some wore plant sprayers filled with it like bulky pistols on their belts.

"Come on then," Billy said at last to Dane. He led him to the car. It was he who drove, now. Didn't even need directions, and drove like a man who knew what he was doing. Billy looked out of the window. He did not look at Dane: he did not want to see changes. He glanced into all the dark streets they passed; he kept hoping that the angel of memory would come, but there was no glass-and-bone figure under the swaying, leafless trees, the canopies of London's buildings, no skull and jar rolling among the small night crowd. There were running people, small fires.

"Christ," Billy said. He wished that Wati raced ahead from figure to figure, returned to the hula girl on the car dashboard.

He parked near the factory compound Dane had shown him on the map, by metal gates black with rust. Others of the attacking party parked elsewhere, in studiedly random patterns, sauntered into position. Billy put his finger to his lips and looked at Dane in warning. Sirens were audible, but not as many as the signs of fires and the sounds of violence would suggest were necessary. The parents of London would have their children at home that night, be lyingly whispering to them that everything would be alright.

"Where do you reckon the Tattoo's most loyal troops are now?" Dane said. "The fist-heads and the, the people from the workshops?" He was sweating. His eyes were wide.

"Fighting," Billy said.

Out into the strange warm night. Some of the fitter London-mancers followed. Saira's war party. Out of sight they climbed the layered walls of the building and sidled along the architecture. They watched the factory as if it might do something.

Behind the wall was a forecourt where a derelict car lorded over weeds. The factory sat surrounded by that emptiness. Nothing moved that they could see. There was perhaps a slight diminution of the darkness in one of the big windows overlooking nothing. The wall they were on led like a spine to the building itself: they need not touch the ground. Billy pointed at a few of the following fighters, pointed where he wanted them to go.

Even if Wati had been there he could not have spied for them: the clay figures on the roof, Billy saw, were smashed up. Grisamentum's court had blinded their architecture. Billy took the little Kirk figure from his pocket. He held it up as he had done many times since the shabti's awful lurching recall and whispered Wati's name. Again, nothing.

Billy pointed. Dane sighted along a rifle he had taken from the kraken armoury, at tiny motion on the building's roof. A man, putting his hands on railings and leaning out toward him.

"He's seen us," Billy said.

"He's not sure yet," Dane whispered. His weapon bucked. The man dropped, silently.

"Wow," Billy said.

"Shit," said Dane. He was trembling.

"We don't have long now," Billy said.

The krakenbit were emerging from their cars, moving with strange ungainliness. As they came forward, their diversion arrived.

THE LONDONMANCER ATTACKERS CAME AS AGREED, WITH DRAMA. An army of masonry. Those few left whose knack was to wake the city's defences had done what they could do. They had sent their alarums in parachemicals, waves of pathogen anxiety. They stimulated immune response in the factory grounds. Birthing of brick angles; emerging from hollows in boscage; unwinding from the ruined car; London's leucocytes came on in attack.

One was ambulant architecture; another a trash marionette; another a window onto another part of the city, a monster-shaped hole. They moved across urban matter, niche-filling and/or huge. Their footsteps made the sounds of barking dogs and braking cars.

One threw back its head-analogue and shouting a war shout that was the puttering-engine call of a bus.

It threw open the compound doors. The bravest Londonmancers ran in. They raised weapons, or goads with which to direct their giant cellular charges. There was movement behind the factory windows.

Emerging from side doors and from behind dustbins came gun-farmers, murmuring fertility prayers as they shot. A canine shape of discarded paper leapt from a window. For seconds Billy thought it was blown by monsterherds, but there was no one to gust it. Each shred of paper in that wolf totality was ink-stained.

"Jesus," Billy said. "Dane. That's him. He's all over them." Enough of Grisamentum's ink presence was on each piece to knack his motion. He was profligate now, impatient at the edge of his intended apotheosis. The ink-paper wolf jumped onto a screaming London-mancer, and the paper teeth tore her as if they were bone.

"Oh Christ," Billy said. "Time to move." He aimed his phaser and crawled.

Below him in the wall a stretch of crumbled brick changed, was pressed into new shape, become an ancient door with a long-broken lock so it could be pushed open. Saira came in and bit her lip and stood aside, and the krakenbit came in behind her. Billy saw those nipped by the squid god.

They were stronger than they had any right to be. They picked up masonry and hurled it. They were misshapen and changing. Tides moved on them; their muscles fluttered in directions they had not been made to take. "Christ," he whispered. He fired a weak whining jolt at the building, a wild distraction as he stared.

One man was growing *Architeuthis* eyes, fierce black circles taking up each side of his head, squeezing his features between them. A woman bulged, her body become a muscular tube from which her limbs poked, absurd but strong. A woman streaked across the dis-tance, jetted by her new siphon, moving through air as if it were water, her hair billowed by currents in the sea miles off. There was a man with arms raised to display blisters bursting and making them-selves squid suckers, another with a wicked beak where he had had a mouth.

They tore at the gunfarmers and through the swirl of inked paper.

Bullets ripped them, and they roared and bit and smashed back. The suckered man looked hopefully at the inside of his arms. The marks were blebbing into little vacuums, but arms his arms remained. Billy watched him. It was awesome, yes, but.

But was it a godly tease that none of the krakenbit had tentacles?

Dane was not newly shaped. Only, he looked back at Billy and his eyes were all pupil now, all dark. He had no hunting arms.

"Billy." A tiny voice from Billy's plastic man.

"Wati!" Billy snapped to draw Dane's attention. He waved the figure. "Wati."

". . . Found you," the voice said, and coughed again. Faded out.

"Wati . . ."

After seconds of silence, Wati said, "First thing I did ever that was mine was un-be that body that got made. Could do it again. They caught me off guard, is all. I just got to . . ." The rude reanchoring in that doll of exploitation had hurt him terribly. "This was the only place I could find. Been in it so much." He was half-awake, at best, from the no-soul's-land between statues where he had been in coma. He drifted back into silence.

"Damn it," Billy said. "Wati." There was nothing more, and their time was up. Billy beckoned and crept forward, and Dane crouched with him on the balcony below the factory's high window, looking down within at the last preparations of Grisamentum.

Chapter Seventy-Four

THE CHAMBER SWARMED WITH PAPER. IN PLANES AND SHREDS, torn-up pieces, flitting with purpose, all smeared with ink. Below them the room was scattered with old machinery, the remains of printing presses and cutters. Walkways circled at several levels. Billy sighted the core of gunfarmers remaining.

There was Byrne, scribbling notes, looking down and arguing, writing Grisamentum's response to her in himself. By a huge pile of torn-off hardcovers, technicians fiddled with gears, ignoring the chaos, pressing soaked paper pulp in a hydraulic machine and collecting the dirt-coloured off-run.

"It's the library," Billy said. The soaked, shredded kraken library, rendered to its ink. He pointed through the glass.

All that antique knowledge poured over with solvent, the inks seeped out of the pages where they had been words. Some pigment must be the remains of coffee, the dark of age, the chitin of crushed beetles. Even so, the juice they were collecting was the distillate of all kraken knowledge. And Billy saw, there, presiding over the rendering, on a raised dais, in a great big plain pail, the bulk of Grisamentum. His sloshing liquid body.

Dane shoved into the glass and made some enraged noise. He was radiating cold.

"He's going to add it to himself," Billy said. "Or himself to it." It would be rich, that liquid print. A liquid darkness that had been all the *Architeuthis* secrets, homeopathically recalling the shapes it had once taken, the writing, the secrets it had been. Metabolise that, and Grisamentum would know more about the kraken than any Teuthex ever had.

"Speed this up!" They could hear Byrne through the glass. Like the glass was thinning to help them. "There's time to finish this. We can track down the animal, but we've got to get the last of the knowledge down. Quick." The paper stormed as if a whirlwind filled the room.

A high-flying scrap at the top of the rustling column flattened itself against the glass beside Billy and Dane. The ink on it regarded them. A still second. It plummeted back through the paper vortex. The rest followed, the swirl falling through its own centre.

"Come *on!*" shouted Billy. He kicked the glass into the room and fired through the paperstrom, but no beam came out. He threw the dead phaser at the giant inkwell full of Grisamentum.

There were shots, and one, two of the Krakenists who had fought their way in fell. Dane did not move. Billy heard a percussion and a damp smacking into Dane's body. A new wound in Dane's side oozed black blood. Dane looked at Billy with abyssal eyes. He smiled not very human. He made himself bigger.

Billy grabbed for the pistol in Dane's belt, and the papers bombed him. Some came at him as a biting skull. He swung the bleach bottle he carried and sent a spray of the stuff in a curve like a spreading-out sabre. It depigmented where it landed. He could smell bleach amid the gun smell, the same ammoniac scent as that of *Architeuthis*.

Screams. A Krakenist was being devoured by a flock of Grisamentum stains shaped playfully murderous into a paper tiger. Billy caught Dane's eye. They looked something at each other. Dane vaulted the fence, his wound not slowing him at all. He fell fast, but not at gravity's idiot control. The paper tried to disrupt him, but he twisted as he fell. He fired and killed an engineer. He sprayed bleach on his way down, streaming it through papers that instinctively flinched away, at Grisamentum.

His aim was predator perfect. But Byrne stepped into the way. She took the liquid across her front. It cut colour like an invert Pollock assault, her clothes fading under the spattered line. She shoved an old-fashioned perfume nebuliser into Dane's face and squeezed the bulb.

Billy clenched. He closed his fist, tightened his stomach, tensed everything he knew how to tense. Nothing happened. Time did not pause. Byrne sprayed dark vapour into Dane's face.

Dane staggered. His face was wet with dark grey. A billow of Grisamentum into him. Dane could not help breathing him in.

He retched, tried to puke Grisamentum out. Billy aimed at Byrne with Dane's pistol, which he had no idea how to use, but in any case she dipped her fingers right into Grisamentum and shook them in front of her. The air around her *closed*, and when he fired his bullet ricocheted off nothing.

Dane was down. His body rilled. Grisamentum filled him, shaped himself on the Dane's alveoli. Wrote bad spells on the inside of Dane's lungs. Billy watched Dane die.

THE PAPERS ENCASED BYRNE IN AN ARGUMENTATIVE FLURRY, LIKE feeding birds.

"You're sure?" Billy heard her say.

She poured the last of the dark liquid pulped from the Krakenist library into Grisamentum. He swirled. It must be giving him psychic indigestion to do this so fast, but he needed the final teuthic wisdom. He had to understand his quarry. Byrne stirred him and flicked the dipstick all around her. The papers eddied faster as the pigment splashed them. Older dried-up blots of Grisamentum were overlaid with less ignorant stains.

"It has to be close," Byrne shouted. "Find it and send some of you back here to tell me where. I'll bring the rest of you. Go!"

Dane had thank God stopped moving. Billy wanted to rally the last of the krakenbit, to destroy the gunfarmers and paper-swirl monsters. But he saw the chaos, his side's rout, in the chamber. He climbed back out of the window.

Outside, Londonmancers and antibodies stood off against gunfarmers and a devil of inky paper. Littering the ground were bodies, and spots of troubled perspective where London functions had fallen. Krakenbit wheezed like fish in air, or lay still, brine dripping

from their bodies. Billy saw one still fighting, with, at last, his left
hand replaced with a twenty-foot hunting limb, which he dragged
and flailed.

"Saira!"

She smiled to see him, even as she shook with war. She tugged a bit
of London claylike into a police riot shield, crouched behind it,
crossed the combat to him.

"Billy." She even hugged him. "What's happening?" He shook his
head. "Dane?" she said. He shook his head. Her eyes went very wide.
Billy began to shake.

"Disaster," he said at last. "We couldn't get close. He's just, he's
doing the last of the knowledging now. Where's my guardian angel,
eh?" He was striving to speak to his headache again, as he had the last
time the angel was near, but this time it was only pain.

"Billy . . ." It was Wati, groping to vague consciousness in his
pocket. Billy said his name.

"He's alive?" Saira said. There was a massive sound. From the
building's roof, a flock of black-stained papers streamed batlike out.
They rampaged across the sky.

"He's going," Wati said. "He's . . ."

"They're covered in him; he can knack them more," Billy said. "He
doesn't care. We forced his hand. He's going all out. He's looking for
the kraken, and when he's found it, Byrne's going to milk it, and . . ."
They looked at each other. "Can you find them? Get a message to the
lorry?"

"They're Londonmancers." Saira nodded. "And so am I."

"Tell them to get out of here. Tell them to go . . . *Wait.*" Billy held
out the Kirk figure, its little plastic eyes watching him. Billy thought
and thought, as fast as he could. "Wati."

"Yeah," the Kirk said.

"We've got as long as it takes for Grisamentum to find the lorry,"
Billy said. "And you saw how many of him there are. Wati, I know
you're hurt, but can you wake up? Can you hear me?" No answer. "If
he doesn't wake up," he said to Saira, "we'll have to try to go ourselves,
but—"

"Where?" Wati said. "Go where?"

"How are you?"

"Hurt."

"Can you . . . can you travel?"

"Don't know."

"You got here."

"This doll . . . used it so much it's like a chair shaped to my bum."

"Wati, what happened?"

There was silence. "I thought I was dead. I thought your friend Marge was . . . It was Goss and Subby." Billy waited. "I can *feel* her. Still. Now. I can feel her because she's got the dust of my old body all over her hands. I can sniff that."

"She was in Hoxton."

". . . She must have . . . she got away from Goss and Subby." Even exhausted, Wati's voice was awed.

"Can you get to her?"

"That body's gone."

"She wears one." Billy grabbed the front of his shirt where a pendant would be. "Can you use the dust to find her? Can you try?"

"Where's Dane?"

The fighting continued, the noise of arcane murder. "They killed him, Wati," Billy said.

At last, Wati said, "What's the message?"

Saira whispered things into London's ears, cajoled and begged it, even aghast as it must be that night, to pass a message to her onetime teacher in the lorry. "All we've got is speed," Billy said to her, and told her where to send them. She moulded the wall and made a patch of it an urban hedge, through which she pushed, out into the street.

Billy took some seconds of solitude, as alone as he could be in the dregs of that fighting and that noise. He stared back at the building where his friend had died. Billy wished he knew how to make whatever tentacle-imitating sign wished a killed soldier of the krakens peace. Billy shut his eyes tight and swallowed and said Dane's name and kept his eyes closed. That was the ceremony he invented.

Chapter Seventy-Five

How could you keep something the size of a lorry hidden from the skies? Fitch's indecision protected him awhile: unable either to commit to his fighting sisters and brothers or to desert them, he had stayed less than a mile away and ordered the vehicle into a tunnel, and there in the orange striplight under the pavement had put on the hazard lights as if stalled. And waited, while refugees from that night surged past in their cars. When Saira sent her message, it, London, did not have far to go to pass it on.

While over their head scudded the inked scout selves of Grisamentum, she and Billy ran toward the vehicle's hide, past birdlime streaks and posters for albums and exhibitions. *Come meet us,* she had said. *We need you.* Shamed, Fitch had the engine gun and the lorry lurch out of its burrow into the surveilled streets.

The paper helixed plughole out of the dark sky and mobbed the lorry. It pushed through them. They were sentient, but the papers had the feeding-frenzy throng of multitude predators, mothlike butting themselves against the windscreen. When it met Saira, Billy and the few Londonmancers and squidly loping krakenbit who had been able to run, the vehicle was thronged with excited paper.

Dear God, Billy thought, at the thought of what the appalled locals must think they saw from behind their curtains. Close to him were two Londonmancers and two krakenbit still morphing into teuthic midway forms. They whipped their limbs and sprayed the last of their bleach. Fitch threw open the back and yelled at them to enter. With the unity of a school of fish, the papers gusted back toward the factory.

"They're going to get Byrne and the rest of himself," Billy said. "They're going to come for us now they know where we are. We have to go."

"But where?" Fitch said.

"Drive," said Billy. "We're meeting someone."

"So what do you reckon?" Collingswood said to her commandeered assistant.

"About what?" he said. They were the same rank. He did not call her *ma'am*. But he went where she told him to and did as she said.

"What now? Got any burglaries?" She laughed. They drove through a little rain, through sliding, dark and lit-up streets where people still lounged by twenty-four-hour shops while others ran from unholy gang fights.

"Don't know," he said.

"Let's just get back to the bloody office."

Marge felt safe in the car. She watched Paul. His face was anguished but resigned. He did not speak. His tattoo spoke. Marge could hear its smothered rage, its terror, in wordless growling from under his shirt.

"It'll be alright," she said to him foolishly.

She heard another tiny mumbling. She looked about. The words came from her neck.

Marge blinked. She looked at Collingswood, who continued to tease her colleague. Marge touched her little crucifix. At the contact of her dirty fingers the voice came again, a little stronger. "Hey," it said.

The silver Jesus whispered. Marge looked away into the violent night streets, into what she had gathered might be the end of the world. And here came this messenger.

"Hey," she whispered herself, and raised the crucifix. Paul watched her. She focused on the tiny bearded face.

"Hey," it said again.

"So," she said. "What's the word from heaven?"

"Wha?" the metal Christ said. "Oh right. Funny." It coughed. "Put me to your ear," it said. "Can't talk loud."

"Who are you?" she said. Collingswood was watching her in the mirror, now.

"It's Wati again," he said. "I got a message, so listen."

"I thought you were dead."

"So did I. Don't wash your hands. Billy needs you to do something."

"What's up back there?" Collingswood said. "Who you chatting to?"

Marge held up her finger so peremptorily Collingswood actually obeyed. The tiny chained Messiah whispered to her, for a long time. Marge nodded, nodded, swallowed, said "yeah" as if at a telephone call. "Tell him yeah." Finally she let the crucifix dangle back below her neck.

She sighed and closed her eyes, then looked at Collingswood. "We have to go somewhere. We have to pick someone up." Paul sat up. The other officer looked backward nervously.

"Yeah . . ." Collingswood said thoughtfully. "Not very clear on the whole *police prisoner* thing, are you?"

"Listen," Marge said slowly. "You want to take us in? Take us in. But look around and listen to me." There was a helpful scream of fighting from some nearby street. Marge gave it a moment. "I've just been given a job to do, by Billy. You know Billy? And by this little guy on my necklace who I just saw killed by the most evil, terrifying bastard. Who was out for *me*.

"Now, I've been given this job on the grounds that it might be the one thing that stops the *end of the world. So.* Do you think your arrest report can wait a couple of hours? Where do you want to go on this?"

Collingswood kept staring at her. "Goss and Subby," Collingswood said.

"You know them, then."

"I've had my tangles," Collingswood said.

"There you go then."

"Wati just had his own little barney with them?"

"He's told me where to go, and what to do."

"How about you tell me what he said, and we can have a chat about it?" Collingswood said.

"How about you fuck off?" Marge said without rancour. She sounded as tired as she was. "Look around and tell me if you think we've got time to waste. How about—look, I'm just throwing this out there. How about we save the world first, and *then* you arrest us?"

There was silence within the car. Above them was the excited mourning of the siren. "I tell you what, boss," the other officer, the young man driving, said suddenly. "I like *her* plan. I'm for that."

Collingswood laughed. Looked away and up into the sky over London where clouds wriggled. "Yeah," Collingswood said. "Might be nice to see tomorrow. You never know. But *then*," she said, and wagged her finger at Marge and Paul, "we are *definitely* taking you in. So what's the plan?"

"WHO THE HELL ARE YOU?" SAID MO OUTSIDE HER HOUSE, HER broom held up like a weapon. Trees shuddered. Marge held the crucifix out at her. "I'm not a vampire," the woman said.

"No, for God's sake," Marge said. "You know Wati? We're Dane's friends."

"Jesus bollocks," said Collingswood to Mo. "Am I going to have to police brutality you? Let us in and listen."

"We're here for Simon," Marge said in the hallway.

"That's a bad idea. Simon's still haunted."

"Tough," said Collingswood.

"We're down to the last one." One tenacious dead self. Mo hesitated. "He needs rest."

"Yeah," said Marge. "I need a holiday in the Maldives. And needs must."

"She ain't wrong," Collingswood said. "I'm with the prisoner here on this."

Simon looked up at their entry. He was in a dressing gown and pyjamas. He held a ball of squeaking fur.

"We're friends of Billy and Dane," Marge said.

Simon nodded. From the air came a faint wrathful ghostly melisma. He shook his head. "Sorry about that," he said.

"Message," Marge said. "We need you to move something. For Billy. Don't look at me like that . . ."

"But . . . I can't. That's why I'm *here*. This . . . it's like an addiction," Simon said. "The knack's like a drug. I can't go down that road again, I . . ."

"Bullshit," said Wati, faint but audible.

"Let me lay it out for you." Paul spoke, for the first time. He coughed. There was a groaning from his back, and Simon's ghost responded in moaning kind. Paul scratched himself hard against the doorframe until his back was silent.

"I just done in the most dangerous piece of shit you can imagine by the most horrible method I ever had to use to do anything," he said. "Wati said you got into this because you was paid to and you might've saved the world. If Griz'd got what he wanted earlier . . . So thank you. For that. But you *are* going to help. Knacking *ain't* a drug. What did for you was dying and not noticing you'd died, again and again.

"Tomorrow you can do whatever you want. But London owns you now. Understand? One more thing needs porting. You don't even have to beam yourself, no more snuffing it. You are going to do this. I'm not even saying please."

Chapter Seventy-Six

THE LORRY ROARED ON, IN PLAIN SIGHT, HARASSED BY A HARD core of inked papers that stayed in its slipstream to track its breakneck journey.

"We're not going to lose them," Saira said. She was driving now. "Just got to get there fast and do the job. They can't take us, not this few. It's when the rest of Grisamentum arrives we're in trouble."

Finally they reached the street Billy remembered. It was still all quiet, as if there were no war. People looked from houses at them and hurriedly away. Saira braked by the last, dim house.

"Are we here?" Fitch said. The trailer was stinking and crowded. The last Londonmancers waited by the dead kraken. "Why are we here? What's the *sea* going to do?"

The papers rose, a malevolent little covey, circled. *Fuck you*, Billy mouthed, as they gusted over the roofs and away. "They're fetching the rest of him," he said. "Come on, come on." He froze at approaching blue lights. A police car tore toward them and rubber-burned to a stop. Collingswood emerged, and Billy opened his mouth to yell at Saira to drive, but he heard Marge's voice.

"Billy!" she almost screamed. She got out and stared at him. "Billy." He ran for her, and they held on to each other a long time.

"Look," said Collingswood. "It's beautiful, innit?"

"I'm so sorry," Billy said to Marge. "Leon . . ."

"I know," she said. "I know. I got your message. And I got your other message. Look, I brought him." Sitting in the car by Paul was Simon Shaw.

WHEN FITCH SAW PAUL, HE STARTED, AND OPENED HIS MOUTH BUT obviously did not know what to say. The other Londonmancers looked uneasily between the two. Fitch tried again to speak, and Paul just shook his finger no. "We got nothing to talk about," Paul said. "Not while he's on his way." He pointed. Circling like a blown leaf was a single scrap of Grisamentum. "He's coming, so let's get this done."

There would almost be a showdown between Grisamentum and the Tattoo, Billy thought, at last. But it would, rather, be between Grisamentum and Paul. Whatever Fitch's plans had been or now were, Billy realised, Paul was not afraid of him anymore.

"Billy," Collingswood said. "*Mate.* What the shit have you been up to?" She winked at him. "If you didn't want the job you should've just said no, fuck's sake."

"Officer Collingswood," he said. Found himself grinning at her for a second. She pursed her lips.

"What's the plan then, geezer?"

"Come on," Billy said. "Let's move. You ready?" Simon looked terrified but nodded. They opened the lorry so he could stare at the kraken's tank. Metabolise its position in his head. "Good man," Billy said. "You know what's going to happen?"

Billy had prepared his case in writing. It was a long and detailed message, which he had sealed in a glass bottle. "Shall we?" he said to Saira and Simon. "We need its permission."

"And bearings," Simon said. "I told you, I can't do it without pretty precise bearings."

Billy tapped the bottle. "I said all that. It's in there. Don't panic."

The message in the bottle begged.

YOU SAID THE KRAKEN WAS NO LONGER YOURS. PLEASE, YOU HAVE TO *help us. Even if it's not one of yours, for the sake of the city where you've been for however long, please, we are asking you to use your neutrality and your power like when you helped against the Nazis. We need a safe place. We all heard about how the Tattoo wouldn't face you that time, and we need that sort of clout again.*

Everything is at stake, Billy had written. *We just need to get past this night. And protect it. We are desperate.* He pushed the message into the letter box.

They stood quietly in the dark. A man rode by them on a bike, with squeaking pedal-strokes. Fitch and the Londonmancers waited. The last krakenbit hid their teuthic tumourous amendations in the lorry. The sea inside the house did not answer the bottle for a long time.

"What's happening?" Simon whispered.

"We can't stick around forever," Saira whispered.

Billy raised his hand, to rap the window, with a sense of blasphemy, when he was preempted. Something knocked instead from the inside. A slow beat through the curtain. A lower corner of the cloth moved. It was pulled slowly back.

"It's showing us," Billy said. "So you can see for coordinates, Simon. Do what you need to do."

"Bloody hell," said Saira. "I guess that's permission."

The curtain retreated from a corner of darkness. There was nothing visible behind it, until from deep within that dark came motions—insinuations in the pitch. They came closer, halting inches behind the glass. Staring out from the dim light that streetlamps shone into the room were tiny translucent fish.

Their ventral fins thrummed. They regarded Billy with see-through eyes. A suddenness came, a quick thing, viper-mouth agape, and the little fish were gone. The curtains gently eddied.

Lights came on in the dark room. The lights were moving. They came up on a grotto. A room full of sea. A living room, sofa, chairs, pictures on the walls, a television, lamps and tables, sunk in deep green water, investigated by fish and weeds. Those lights were the pearl tint of bioluminescent animals.

A living room, furnishings interrupted with coral, grazed on by sea cucumbers. The tassels of a lampshade moved with current, and an anemone waved its feathery stingers in filigree echo. Fish moved throughout, ghost-lit by themselves and their neighbours.

Fingernail-sized things, arm-thick eels. By a sunken hi-fi riveted with barnacles, a fist-sized light moved like a long-armed metronome. The tick-tock light made Billy stare.

"Have you got it?" he said to Simon, with effort. "What you need?"

"I'll have to move the water out, just before, in the right shape," Simon murmured. He stared and itemised to himself according to the strange techniques he had perfected.

"Done," he said. A moray glided from some dark, coiled around the sofa leg, tugged it into a new position, to make space for what was coming. "Okay," Simon said. He closed his eyes, and Billy heard in the air around them the muttering of Simon's last imbecilic vengeful ghost.

"He knows what I'm doing," Simon said. "He thinks I'm going myself. He's trying to stop me murdering me again." He even smiled.

Chapter Seventy-Seven

There was the noise of paper. "They're here!" Fitch leaned
from the lorry. "Grisamentum! He's coming!"

"Are you ready?" Billy said.

"They're *coming*," shouted Fitch. The air of the street was filling
with papers. They investigated front gardens. They came at the lorry,
staring with ink-blot eyes.

"Whatever the bloody hell you are going to do I suggest you do it,"
Collingswood said.

Simon went to the kraken's tank and put his hands on it. He closed
his eyes. Headlights moved across the face of houses. There was the
familiar prickling sound, the sequin glimmer. It faded up and down,
and the tank was no longer there.

There was a rumbling from the house. A burp of water spilled
from the letter slot. With no tank to brace him, Simon fell to his
knees.

"Big," he muttered. He looked up and smiled. His ghost howled.

The kraken was in the embassy of the sea. Billy and Simon and
Saira stared at each other.

"Did we . . . ?" said Saira.

"It's done," said Billy.

"Congratufuckinglations," Collingswood said. "Now will you please get in sodding prison?"

"It's safe," Billy said. The paper raged and raged around them. Cars came closer and stopped. Papers began to batter them angrily, pelleting into missiles. Paul shifted his chest out, as if he, not the picture he bore, were the ink's enemy. Billy heard a voice he recognised. Byrne shouting "God*dam*mit!" from somewhere, as she approached and saw the empty lorry. "Time to go," he said.

Collingswood saw the motorcade of Grisamentum's last troops. She appeared to consider her options. The other officer ran. "You cheeky little fucker," she shouted at his back as he went. She jabbed the air in his direction, and his legs tangled and he went down hard enough to break his nose, but she turned away as he scrambled back to his feet and continued running. She let him go.

"You're welcome to try to arrest Griz if you want, Collingswood," Billy said. "Fancy that?"

"I do fancy that yeah, actually, blood." Not that she was moving.

Saira hesitated. Simon was helping Fitch into the lorry. "Let's get out of here," Billy said. Marge and Paul scrambled in too, the vanguard of the papers harassing Paul in confused habitual animosity, thinking he was his adornment. Billy, Saira and even Collingswood wordlessly moved toward the lorry, but they had left it too late. Byrne was close, and she was directing two cars of gunfarmers toward the big vehicle.

"*Shit*," said Saira, judging the distance. She caught Billy's eye a moment. He nodded minutely and she indicated the lorry to go. It lurched from the kerb, its rear door flapping, a bewildered Londonmancer and Marge still leaning from its back, Marge shouting in protest as they left the others behind. But they were gone, around a corner, gone. Simon wailed, held out his hands like a baby. Billy grabbed him and hauled him away.

Saira kneaded the wall beside them and gave it a mossy weathered gateway. They got in out of sight. They hunkered by the wall of the sea-house and crept as Byrne and Grisamentum's crew came near, ready to scatter into the streets the moment angry papers careened around them.

"They must be going spare," Billy said.

"Fine bunch of mates you have," Collingswood said.

"They left with*out* us," Simon said, loudly enough that Billy pinched his mouth shut.

"They didn't have any choice," Saira said. "I told them to. I'll find them . . ."

They heard a loud slam. The wall faintly shook.

"What the hell?" Saira said. She and Billy stared at each other. The noise came again. "Oh my God," Saira said. "He couldn't be so stupid . . . The sea?"

Would he? They crept to the corner and looked.

The land could never defeat the sea. As Canute had illustrated for his fawning courtiers, tides are implacable. Even Tattoo, bluster notwithstanding, had known to duck that confrontation. It was just an inevitable rule.

But rules were what Grisamentum wanted to rewrite.

Scratch out the writing on the wall, rewrite the rules, rework the blueprint, using the inks stored in the ocean itself. Would he stop this now? All he needed was tonight.

This was why when Billy peered around the edge of brick, he saw the papers corkscrewing in impatience, he saw Byrne carrying a big bottle of her boss protectively, he saw gunfarmers on guard, and he saw their colleagues kicking and kicking like thugs and police at the front door.

The redoubt of the ocean in residence in London, this house was encircled in thalassic knacks. But part of its defence was the certainty that it would never be needed, and now the attack was backed by the unremitting focused hex attention of Grisamentum. Byrne squirted him with a turkey baster into the lock mechanism, onto the hinges. This close to his becoming, he was cavalier with the stuff of his substance. He wrote weakening spells on the innards of the keyhole. One more onslaught of boots.

"No no," said Billy, trying very much to think of something, to gather a plan, but a gunfarmer stepped up and slammed his boot at the door, and it *flew* open. It flew open and threw the man aside, and with it came an onrush piston of water, a giant brine fist.

• • •

Seawater exploded into the scrubby front garden, skittling gathered attackers. From the top of the house down, the windows imploded. Sea slicked into the road, bringing its inhabitants. Weeds piled. Fauna was dragged into the street, coming dying to rest. Jellies, hagfish, fat deepwater creatures twitching and doleful between the bare trees. A person-sized blind shark gaped pale jaws, hopelessly biting at a car. In other houses, people began to scream.

Gunfarmers picked themselves up. They kicked fish from their feet, pulled wracks and weeds from their sodden suits. Byrne and the ink went in.

"What do we do? What do we do?" Simon said. "What do we do?" He was collapsed onto his knees.

"Get it out of there," Billy said. "Send it anywhere." Simon closed his eyes.

"I can't, I . . . They've moved it. My bearings are screwed, I can't get a lock on."

"Your lot'll be here soon, won't they?" Saira said to Collingswood.

"And what the fuck are they supposed to do?" Collingswood said urgently.

"What do we do?" Saira said.

With the library he had imbibed, Grisamentum knew kraken physiology. He could have Byrne undeath-magic it just back enough to life to coax its flesh into a fear reaction, for its sepia cloud. That was all, Billy thought, he needed to do.

"Saira," Billy said, calm. "Come with me."

"Baron," Collingswood was saying into her phone. "Baron, bring everyone." She gesticulated angrily—*wait a minute*—but did nothing to stop Billy as he climbed the rear of the house, helping Saira after him. Billy looked down into the garden littered with building rubble and rubbish.

"Get us in," he said to Saira.

She pushed at the rear wall, moulding the bricks, pressing them into flatness and transparency, making a window. Faded to glass clarity they could see through a film of undersea slime into a small bathroom. Saira opened the window she had made. She shivered with more than cold; she was shaking violently. She made as if she would crawl in and hesitated.

"Fuck's *sake*," said Collingswood below them, and snapped her phone shut. She shook her head as if at a friend's unfunny joke. She pushed her hands apart and rose, not in a leap but an abrupt dainty dangling, up through the impossible twelve feet or more to land on the ledge by Saira and Billy.

Billy and Saira stared at her. "You," she said to Saira, "wuss-girl, get down there and hold wuss-boy's hand. You," she said to Billy, "get in there and tell me what's what."

It was freezing within. The stink was astonishing, fish and rot.

They stood in a typical London-house bathroom: stubby bath with shower, sink and toilet, a tiny cupboard. The surfaces were white tiled under layers of grey silt, green growth, sponges and anemones reduced to lumps in the sudden air. The floor was inch-deep in water full of organisms, some still slightly alive. By the door was a half-grown sunfish—a huge, ridiculous thing—dead and sad. The bathtub brimmed with a panicking crowd of fish. Something splashed in the toilet bowl. The infiltrators held their hands to their faces.

Outside in the corridor furniture was tugged skew-whiff by a rubble of piscine bodies. The vivid colours of pelagic dwellers, the drabs and see-through oddities of deep water in hecatomb heaps. Creatures from the top floors where the pressure was gentle and skylights illuminated the water.

Shouted orders were audible. Billy set out through the flopping drowning. He steadied himself on banisters interwoven with kelp.

In the kitchen there was a sea-softened door into the living room. The floor was littered with broken crockery. In the sink an octopus floundered. Billy watched it but felt no kinship. He could hear muffled noises from the next room.

"There's quite a bloody few of them," Collingswood said.

"We have to get in there," Billy whispered. They stared at each other. "We have to." She kissed her teeth.

"Give me a second, Billy," she said. "Alright? You understand?"

"What are you . . . ?" He started to say. She raised an eyebrow. He nodded, readied the pistol he had taken from Dane.

"If I've got all this right . . . Spill him," she said. "Alright, Billy? Don't be a loser all your life." She pursed her lip and threw a sign with her fingers, something from a music video. "East side," she said.

She stepped back into the corridor toward the living room's main door. He heard her do something, some knack, some noise, some unnatural percussion. He heard the door open, a commotion, "*Keep them out!*" in Byrne's voice, the stamp of footsteps toward her ingress and out of the door. Billy kicked open the other rotting entrance, his weapon raised.

Chapter Seventy-Eight

Into the grotto, the sea's front room. Billy was absolutely calm.

He emerged with a burst of wall-stuff. There were the coralline constructions, the brine-stained everything, big fish lying still. In a corner was a huge sagging body, something he could not work out, though he saw eyes see him from a meat heap. The gunfarmers had left the room to hunt Saira.

There was the kraken in its tank, now emptied of all but a thin layer of preserver. There was Byrne, some bad-magic book under her arm, the bottle of Grisamentum in her hand. A huge syringe jutted from the kraken's skin. Byrne was tickling, stimulating the dead animal in some obscene-looking way.

The kraken was *moving*.

Its empty eye-holes twitched. The last, brine-dilute Formalin swilled as the animal turned. Its limbs stretched and untwined, too weak still to thrash, its skin still scabrous and unrejuvenated, but the kraken was alive, or not-dead. It was zombie. Undead.

In panic at the sudden end of its death, it was spurting dark black-brown-grey ink. It spattered against the inside of its tank, and pooled in that last liquid in which the kraken lay.

Billy saw Byrne go for the syringe. He saw her move. He fired. The container of Grisamentum exploded.

• • •

Byrne screamed as glass, ink and blood from her lacerated hand erupted across her front, fell through her fingers. Ink spattered across the floor, dissipated in the currents of the emptying house. A gunfarmer reentered and stared at Byrne and the ink-slick down her front. Billy roared a triumphant *haaa!* and stepped back through into the kitchen.

"Collingswood!" he shouted.

"What?" he heard. Billy glanced through the doorway and saw the kraken move.

"You got him?" Collingswood shouted.

"I *did*," Billy gasped in delight. "I spilt him, he's—"

Byrne was whispering into the tank. She was dripping, squeezing the ink that drenched her top into the kraken's ink.

"Shit," said Billy. He stared. "How much . . ."

The world answered him.

How much of Grisamentum does he need to merge with the kraken ink? To take it into him?

The world showed him: *not much.*

Plenty of Grisamentum was raging in wordless liquidity as the slosh of footprints dispersed him. But wrung out by his vizier was a small glassful of him, bloated with Krakenist knowledge from his hungry learning, squeezed into the tank. He swilled and bonded. He mixed with the kraken's ink, ink also, the two inks one new ink, and changed.

The liquid in the tank began to bubble. The zombie squid flopped and wriggled and butted up against the Perspex. Its ink effervesced.

Billy fired at the tank, urgently. He punctured it right through, breaking off sections, and his bullets hit the dense body of the kraken. The liquid within did not flow from the holes. It held its tank-shape against gravity. A presence gathered into swirl-self out of the conjoined inks, burned man and kraken-writ. A voice made of bubbling laughed.

The dark liquid rose. A pillar, a man-shape that laughed and pointed. That raised both arms.

And started to rewrite rules.

So the wall that hid Billy disappeared. It did not fall down, did not evaporate, did not crumble but instead simply had not been there, was un. The kitchen was all part of the living room now, sinkless and cutleryless, full of lounges and bookshelves, wet with remnant sea.

The pistol in Billy's hand was gone. Because Grisamentum wrote that there were no guns in that room. "Oh Jesus," Billy managed to say, and the ink of Grisamentum wrote *no* across his consciousness. Not even God: he was the very rules God wrote. The gunfarmers stumbled. Byrne was laughing, was rising into the air, tugged by the boss she loved.

Billy felt something very dangerous and forlorn settle, the closing of something open across everything, as history began to flex at someone else's will. He felt something get ready to rewrite the sky.

The ink gathered into a globe, hovering above the tank. Threads from it took word-shape and changed things. Writs in the air.

The kraken looked at Billy with its missing eyes. It moved. Spasmed. Not afraid, he saw, not in pain. Bottling it up. Bottling it up. Where was his angel? Where his glass-container hero?

This is a fiasco. He might almost have laughed at that strange formulation. It was the catastrophe, the disaster, the, the word was weirdly tenacious in his head, *fiasco.*

He opened his eyes. That word meant bottle.

It's all metaphor, Billy remembered. *It's persuasion.*

"It's not a kraken," he said. The ink-god did not hear him until he said it again, and all the attention in the world was, amused, upon him. "It's not a kraken and it's not a squid," Billy said. The eyeless thing in the tank held his gaze.

"Kraken's a kraken," Billy said. "Nothing to do with us. *That*? That's a *specimen.* I know. I made it. That's ours."

A troubled look went across Byrne's face as she spun on her axis. *Bottle magic,* Billy thought. The ink shuddered.

"Thing is," Billy said, in abrupt adrenalized bursts, "thing is the Krakenists thought I was a prophet of krakens because of what I'd done—but I never was. What I am—" Even if by mistake; even if a misunderstanding, a joke gone wrong; even if a will-this-do; how are any messiahs chosen? "What I am is a *bottle* prophet." An accidental power of glass and memory. "So I know what that is."

There was a sink by Billy again, and the wall was coming back, a few inches of it. The bottled kraken wheezed from its siphon. The wall grew.

"It's not an animal or a god," Billy said. "It didn't exist until I curated it. That's my specimen."

The new rules were being crossed out. Billy could feel the fight. He saw the wall shrink and grow, be there and un-be and have been and not have been; he felt able to stand and not; he felt the fucking *sky* reshape and rework as with instructions written and put under erasure in penmanship-duel the consciousness of Grisamentum—full of new krakeny power, ink-magic—battled with the tentacled thing that *was not kraken at all.*

The specimen pressed its arms against its tank. Suckers pressed vacuum-flush against the plastic, pulling the great body into position. It was not trying to get out—*that was where it belonged.*

Billy was standing.

He had birthed it into consciousness. It was *Architeuthis dux.* Specimen, pining for preservative. Squid-shaped paradox but not the animal of the ocean. *Architeuthis*, Billy understood for the first time, was not that undefined thing in deep water, which was only ever itself. *Architeuthis* was a human term.

"It's ours," he said.

Its ink was vast magic: Grisamentum had been right about that. But the universe had heard Billy, and he had been persuasive.

Maybe if Grisamentum had harvested ink direct from those trench dwellers, not from a jarred, cured, curated thing, the power would have been as protean as he had intended. But this was *Architeuthis* ink, and it was disinclined to be his whim. "It's a specimen and it's in the books," Billy said. "We've written it up."

The comixed inks raged against each other. The universe flexed as they fought. But as Grisamentum mixed with the ink it mixed with him; as he took its power it took his. And much of Grisamentum had been spilt: there was more of it than of him. It was specimen ink, curated by a citizen of London, by Billy, and bit by bit it metabolised the ink-man. The wall was rising again, and Byrne was falling to the ground.

Grisamentum sent out anguish that made the house quake. He slipped out of selfness like all the rest of him, in the tide, in the drains. He was overwritten. He was effaced by ink that, as it won, in an instant's satisfaction returned to its unthinking form and fell out of the air like dark rain.

THE WALL WAS BACK. THE KITCHEN WAS BACK. THE WET HOUSE WAS full again of dead fish.

"What did you do?" Byrne screamed at Billy. "What did you do?"

The sense, all sense, of Grisamentum, was gone. There was only the undead *Architeuthis*, still moving, stinking, chemical in its tank, poor skin flaking, poor tentacles palsied, drenched in ink that was nothing, now, but dark grey-brown liquid.

Chapter Seventy-Nine

THE GUNFARMERS RAN. WHY WOULD THEY STAY? BYRNE STAYED.
Why, and where, would she go? She let Billy disarm her. She ran her
fingers through the water on the floor.

"Nice one, rudeboy," Collingswood said to Billy.

He sat with his back to the streaming walls. London was safe, Billy
kept thinking, not subject to that cosmic scriptic totalitarianism. He
heard Saira and Simon coming, having seen their enemies run.
Collingswood turned as they entered.

"Alright, nobody move," she said. "This is the police." They stared
at her. "Nah, I'm just fucking with you," she said. "What happened,
Billy? Jesus, look at that thing. And it's fucking *moving*." *Architeuthis*
wriggled sluggishly.

Collingswood took half-hold of Byrne, who slumped and did not
try to fight.

"Where's your ghost?" Billy said to Simon.

". . . I think it's gone." They heard sirens, the swish of wheels on the
sea-wet street. Police came to the house, in not a very long time.

"Hi Baron," Billy said, as Baron came blinking in, pistol outstretched, blinking at the sea ruin. Baron and his officers stared at the
twitching squid, the exhausted fighters.

"Billy," Baron said. "Billy bloody Harrow, as I live and breathe . . ."

"Boss," said Collingswood, and turned her back. "See you made it." She lit a cigarette.

"What the bloody hell have you lot been up to?" Baron said.

"Want me to fill you in?" Collingswood said.

"No Vardy?" Billy said.

Baron shrugged. "You're coming with me, Billy."

"Ataboy boss," said Collingswood. "That's sorted them."

"Enough of your shit, Kath," he said.

"I'll come with you." Billy nodded. "As long as I can sleep."

"What are the plods going to make of this?" Baron said.

"Collingswood'll do you a report," Billy said.

"Doubt it," she said. She was looking around the room, squinting, sniffing, knacking. "Hang on."

Billy approached the *Architeuthis*. Baron watched and let him go. He whispered to it as if it were a skittish dog. "Hello," he said to the preserved eight-metre many-armed newborn thing, moving in the dregs of its preserver, slathering itself with its prehensile undead arms, pining for the ullage.

"It ain't finished," Collingswood said, in a dead voice.

"Look," Billy said to the *Architeuthis*. It wriggled its wrist-thick arms. "You sorted it. Made us safe."

A squelch answered him. Collingswood was breathing deep and looking at him with some kind of ragged expression. Saira was frowning. Billy heard the wet sound again.

It was the fattest pile of fish-flesh he had noticed. He saw its glowering eyes. Something switched one side to the other. It was a ceratioid enormity, a huge anglerfish beached and collapsing under its own weight. It struggled to open the snaggled split of its mouth. It watched him come and swung again the organic spit before it—its lure, a still-glowing snare on a limb-long spur from its forehead. It wagged it side to side. Was it trying to fool him into its mouth, even now as it drowned in air?

No. The motion of its bait-flesh had none of the fitful jerk of little swimming life that it would mimic to hunt. It tick-tocked the lure in what was not a fish motion at all, but a human one. Speaking his language. The motion of its lure was the wag of a correcting finger. He had said to the *Architeuthis* specimen, *You made us safe*, and the sea said no, no, no, no, no.

"What the hell?" Billy whispered.

"What does it mean?" Saira said. "What's happening?"

"It is *not* finished," Collingswood said. "Oh shitting fuck." She was bleeding. Her eyes, her nose, her lips. She spat the cigarette and blood away. "It just got a bloodyfuck sight closer."

Billy closed his eyes. He was trembling, a preemptive allergy to whatever was to happen.

"It's still . . ." he said. To his shock, he felt his hands yanked behind him. Baron had cuffed him. "Are you out of your *mind*?" he said. "It's all about to *burn*."

"Shut your cakehole, you," Baron said. He indicated one of his men to cuff Saira too.

"Oh, something's very fucking up," Collingswood said. "Boss, don't be a prick." Sensitives all across the heresiopolis must be praying to be wrong, for something other than the burnt nothing they felt fast coming.

"Let me go," Billy said.

"Baron, wait," Collingswood said.

"It *never* made any sense," Saira said to Billy. They stared at each other. "No matter how powerful kraken ink is, there was no way it could have . . . let him end *everything*. In fire. Even if he wanted to, which why . . . ?"

"*Boss*," said Collingswood. "Give them a *second*."

"What makes everything stop?" Saira said. "Fire, the squid, the . . ."

Billy stared, and thought, and remembered. Things he had heard and seen, moments, from weeks and weeks before.

"You end to start again," he said. "From the beginning. So you burn backward. This isn't an end . . . This is a rebooting."

"Get out," Baron said. "Shift, Harrow."

"How?" said Saira to Billy.

"Burn out whatever set us in the wrong direction. If you want to run a different program. Oh my God, this was never about the poor squid . . . it was a *bystander*. We started this. You did. Fitch kept saying it got closer, the harder you lot tried to protect it. You brought it to attention." There was a straining sound. Everyone looked up. That was the sky stretching, ready to break into flames.

"How far to the Darwin Centre?" Billy said. "*How far to the museum?*"

"Four, five miles," Collingswood said.

"Get out," Baron, uselessly, said.

"It's too far . . . Baron, can you send a message to . . . You need to get someone . . ."

"Shut up or I will pepper-spray you," Baron said. "I'm sick of this."

"Boss, shut *up*," Collingswood said. She shook her head. Pointed, and Baron blinked in outrage, suddenly unable to speak. "What you saying, Harrow?"

Something new had walked when the Londonmancers had learnt of Grisamentum's plan, when Al Adler had indulged the traditions and respect his boss had taught him and gone for a supposedly useless reading. The new thing had grown stronger into itself when the kraken was taken and the alternatives narrowed. But it was *after* that that the memory angels had gone for it, that its sentience, its meta-selfhood, had become great enough.

"Why's the angel of memory not here?" Billy said. "It's supposed to be my guardian angel, right? It wants to protect me, right, and to beat this bloody prophecy, right? So *why isn't it here?* What's it got to do that's more important?"

Billy knew exactly where he had been when that last phase had begun, and what he had been showing to whom. He knew what was the concatenate development that had made the sea, that soup of life, what it was, and why it had sensed it was under threat. He knew what was happening, and why, and at whose hand, and he could not get anyone else where they needed to be, and he could not explain fast enough.

He needed to be at the Darwin Centre, now. "Oh, *God*," he breathed, and slumped, then stood up straight. The anglerfish had stopped moving. Billy silently said good-bye to everything.

"Simon," he said. "Simon," he ordered. "You know the bearings of the Darwin Centre. The heart of it. Get me there, now. Now."

Simon hesitated. Baron strained and failed to speak. "But you know what that means. That's how I . . ."

"*Put. Me. There.*" Simon would not disobey that voice. Billy tried quickly to catch everyone's eye. Saira half understanding, stricken. Simon, miserable at committing murder again. Baron actually shouting, quite unheard. Collingswood nodded at him, like a soldier saying good-bye.

There was the shimmered static sound, a muffled cry as Billy made a noise, the last thing he would ever do, as light enveloped him from the inside, faded out and he was gone, and Baron was tugging at nothing.

Chapter Eighty

AND THE SMELL OF THE SEA (SEEMED TO) EBB, SUDDENLY replaced with chemical. Light shimmied in front of Billy's eyes, different from how it had (not) been in his eyes a moment before. He knew he remembered nothing, that these were rather images he was born with. But he would not think about that now.

He was inside of the tank room, in the Darwin Centre. Across from him, beyond two rows of steel tanks, was Vardy. Who turned.

Billy had time to see that the work surface in front of Vardy was littered with vials, tubes and beakers, liquids bubbling, electric cells. He had time to see that Vardy was aiming a pistol at him, and he dropped. The bullet went above him, bursting a thigh-high bottle of long-preserved monkeys. They slumped as reeking preservative sprayed. Billy strained against the handcuffs that still (so to speak) constrained him. He stayed below the level of the steel and crawled. Another shot. Glass and Formalin littered the floor ahead of him, and an eviscerated dolphin baby flopped in his path.

"Billy," said Vardy, his voice grim, terse, as ever, just the same. It could be a statement, a greeting, a curse. When Billy tried to creep closer another bullet ruined another specimen. "I'll kill you," said Vardy. "The angel of memory couldn't stop me, you're certainly not going to."

There was a jabbering, a tiny high-pitched mouthing-off. Through cracks between furniture, Billy saw on the side a tiny raging figure. It was the mnemophylax—a bottle-of-Formalin body, bone arms and claws, a skull head, snapping like a guard dog. It was under a bell jar. Vardy had not even bothered to kill it. It had come and gone so many times, had emerged and been dissipated so often, it was tiny. A finger-sized glass tube that might have been used to contain one insect, and its limbs must have been, what, mouse legs? The skull that topped it was from some pygmy marmoset or something. It was a joke, a little animate failure like a cartoon.

"What did you do with the pyro?" Billy called.

Vardy said. "Cole's right as rain. Did exactly as I asked—wouldn't you, if you had it patiently explained that your daughter was in my protective custody?"

"So you got what you needed. Time-fire."

"Between the two of them, I did." Vardy fired again and ruined an eighty-year-old dwarf crocodile. "Been trying versions out and I think we're good. Stay where you are, Billy, I can hear every move you make."

"Kata . . ."

"Katachronophlogiston. Shut up, Billy. It'll be finished soon."

Billy huddled. It was him who had given Vardy the idea. The prophecy had given rise to itself. It had snared him and Dane and his friends because they had paid it attention like it was a disease, a pathological machine. He cursed it without sound. That was what the angel of memory had been fighting, that certitude, struggling for the fact of itself. So long as it fated, fate didn't care what it fated. There was a clink as the phylax jumped up and down and banged its tiny skull head on the underside of the jar that jailed it.

The noise of porting came again. The shadows and reflections shifted. The *Architeuthis* in its tank had returned to the place from where it had been stolen. Billy stared at it. Again, the eyeless thing seemed to try to look at him. It wriggled its coiling zombie arms. *What the fuck?* Billy thought.

"You brought it to life?" Vardy said. "Whatever for?"

"Vardy, please don't," Billy said. "This won't work, this'll never work. It's over, Vardy, and your old god lost."

"It may not," Vardy said. There was the noise of combustion from his workstation. "Work. It may not. But it may. You're right—he did lose, my god, and I cannot forgive the cowardly bastard for that. Nothing bloody ventured, say I."

"You really think they're that powerful? That symbolic?" Billy crept on.

"It's all a matter of persuasion, as perhaps by now you know. It's *all* a matter of making an argument. That's why I wasn't too bothered by Griz. Is that where you've been, with him? With a category error like that in his plan . . ." He shook his head. Billy wondered how long ago Vardy had insighted what Grisamentum had in mind, and how. "Now, *these* things were the start of it. They're where the argument started."

Billy crept close to the real targets of the time-fire, the real subject of the predatory prophecy. Not and never the squid, which had only ever been a bystander, caught up by proximity. Those other occupants of the room, in their nondescript cabinet, like any other specimen, exemplary and paradigmatic. The preserved little animals of Darwin's *Beagle* voyage.

THIS WAS A FIERY REBOOTING. UPLOADING NEW WORLDWARE.

He had remembered Vardy's melancholy, the *rage* in him, and what Collingswood had once said. She was right. Vardy's tragedy was that his faith had been defeated by the evidence, and he could not stop missing that faith. He was not a creationist, not any longer, not for years. And that was unbearable to him. He could only wish that his erstwhile wrongness had been right.

Vardy did not want to eradicate the idea of evolution: he wanted to rewind the fact of it. And with evolution—that key, that wedge, that wellspring—would all those other things follow, the drably vulgar contingent weak godlessness that had absolutely nothing going for it at all except, infuriatingly, its truth.

And he was persuaded, and was trying to persuade the city and history, that it was in these contemplated specimens, these fading animals in their antique preserve, that evolution had come to be. What would evolution be if humans had not noticed it? Nothing. Not even a detail. In seeing it, Darwin had made it be, and always have been. These *Beagle* things were bloated.

Vardy would burn them into un-having-been-ness, unwind the threads that Darwin had woven, eradicate the facts. This was Vardy's strategy to help his own unborn god, the stern and loving literalist god he had read in texts. He could not make it win—the battle was lost—but he might make it *have won*. Burn evolution until it never was and the rebooted universe and the people in it might be, instead, created, as it and they should have been.

It only happened that night because Billy and his comrades had made it that night, had provoked the end-war, and this chaos and crisis. So Vardy had known when he had to act.

"It won't work," Billy said again, but he could feel the strain in time and the sky, and it seemed very much as if it would work. The bloody universe was plastic. Vardy held a Molotov cocktail.

"Look," said Vardy. "Bottle magic." Filled with the phlogiston he had coerced Cole to make, with his daughter's untutored help, at threat of his daughter's life. A combusting tachyon flame. It roared with inrushing sound, illumined Vardy's face.

He brought it closer, and its glow lit the pickled frogs within a jar. They shifted. They shrank in the time-blistering warmth, tugged their limbs into their trunks. They became more paltry, ungainly long-tailed legless tadpoles. He held the flame so it licked the glass of their jar, and after a second of warming it burst into sand and sent the tadpoles spraying. They reversed and undid their having been and shrank as they fell, and never were, and nothing hit the floor.

Vardy turned to the shelf of Darwin's specimens and raised his arm.

Billy struggled to his feet. He could think only, *Not like this*. He would try to spill the fire. Perhaps it would reverse the life cycle of the heavy-duty floor, rubbers separating, the chemicals racing back to elemental forms. But his hands were behind him and he was far too far away.

"No!" Billy wheezed, bleeding.

The shadows shed by fire danced over labels handwritten by Charles Darwin. Billy sprawled flat like a mudfish. With a bark of religious joy, Vardy threw the time-flaming missile.

• • •

IT FLEW AND TURNED AS IT FLEW. BILLY'S ARMS WERE TRAPPED. But there were other arms aplenty in that room.

The undead specimen *Architeuthis* shot out its long hunting limbs all the way across the room, from far away. A last predation. It caught the bottle. Took it from the air.

Vardy stared. Vardy screamed in rage.

The time-fire was touching the *Architeuthis*'s skin, and was burning. The zombie squid's second hunting arm whipped Formalin-heavy up, around Vardy's waist with a *thwack*. It coiled him in. It whipped the bottle toward its mouth. Vardy howled as its shorter arms spread to receive him.

Vardy screamed. The time-fire was roaring, and spreading. The squid was shrinking. Vardy's arms and legs were shortening.

The squid looked at Billy. He could never put into precise words what it was in that gaze, those sudden eyes, what the bottled specimen communicated to him, but it was a fellowship. Not servility. It did not *obey*. But it did what it did deliberately, offered it up and looked at him in good-bye.

The time-fire shrank it further, cleared the deadness from its skin, made it smooth. A selfless selfishness. Without evolution, what would it and its siblings be? The deep gods were not this thing's siblings: it let itself be taken for the sake not of kraken but of the *exemplae*, all these specimens around them, of all shapes, these bottled science gods.

The tank was roaring with fire. The flesh was burning younger. There was a last flurry of combat. Silhouetted in the glow, Billy saw a baby screaming adult fury at the little arm-length squid that encoiled it. Both were on fire. Then both, still wrestling, were hot embryos, that intertwined and stilled in grotesque protoplasmic détente, and were burning gone.

The sides of the tank fell in, into smouldering crystals of ore and chemical and then atoms before they could even shatter.

Chapter Eighty-One

Tʜᴇ ʟᴀsᴛ ᴏғ ᴛʜᴇ ʙᴜʀɴɪɴɢ ᴇʙʙᴇᴅ ᴀᴡᴀʏ. Tʜᴇ ʟɪɢʜᴛ ᴏғ ғɪʀᴇ ᴡᴀs
gone. Only the glow of fluorescent bulbs.

Something a little rucked

singed and melted

and

There was an inrush growth rejig. An imperfect healing but healing. A huge, epochal sealing. London reskinned. Fire scorched and
then went out.

And there was Billy in the new skin, there in time. There was a
Billy. Billy breathing out from something, and he breathed in, shook
with release. He was in a room.

Dᴀʀᴡɪɴ's sᴘᴇᴄɪᴍᴇɴs ᴡᴇʀᴇ sᴀғᴇ. Bɪʟʟʏ ᴛᴏᴜᴄʜᴇᴅ ᴛʜᴇᴍ, ᴏɴᴇ ʙʏ
one, stretching out his tethered hands behind him. He ran his fingers
along the steel surface where no *Architeuthis* had ever been. The tiny
mnemophylax watched from under its bell jar. Its bone head tracked
his movements.

Nothing had gone. Billy thought that very exactly.

Billy knew with a strange precision that in all his recent adventures, the specificities of which were slightly vague, no giant cryptid
animal had ever been here in this room. The angel of memory rolled

on its tiny base and shook its skull head. Billy laughed and was not sure why. There was a pyromancer who was alive and waiting for his daughter, because there was no one nor had there ever been who could have blackmailed him with her. Time felt a little raw. The threat that Billy had defeated in this room, and it had been baleful, had neither involved anyone, nor existed. He laughed.

The sky was different. Billy could feel it beyond the roof. Different from how it had not been. The strain was gone. The end of the world, a true finish, was only one very unlikely possibility among many.

There were details missing. Billy was canny enough by now, after everything, to know what that might mean. There was a burn scar in history. There was still a smell of burning. Billy was definitely descended from simians and ultimately from fish in the sea.

He met the gaze of the mnemophylax across the room, eye socket to eye. Though it had no face to crease he would have said it smiled back. It wriggled and wrote with its tiny fingers on the inside of its glass—he could not tell what. It opened and closed its mouth. It was memory. It shook its head. It put its hair's-breadth fingerbone to its nonexistent lips. Its tiny bones fell, its skull settled into nothing, it became a test tube and some specimen rubbish.

Billy sat on the steel where no great mollusc had been. He sat as if he were a specimen. He wondered what searing thing had not been overcome. He waited for whatever would happen, whoever would find him.

It was Baron and Collingswood who came, at last, into the room. They were not missing any colleague, Billy thought, carefully. They'd never had a third in their crew, though they stood often a little close together, a little close to a wall, as if they would be framed with another presence. They recalled enough, and they knew that something had happened, had finished.

Billy stood and waved with his handcuffed arms. The cops picked over the ruins of glass, spilt preservative, scattered specimen remains, scattered by no one.

"Billy," Baron said.

"It's okay now, I think," Billy said. They stared at each other a while. "Where's Simon?"

"He went," Collingswood said.

Baron and Collingswood muttered together. "Fuck this," Collingswood said. She undid Billy's locks.

"What's the crime?" Baron said to Billy. "You nearly came to work for me. What animal?" he said. "There's never been one here." He jerked his thumb at the door. "Piss off," he said, not unfriendly.

Billy smiled slowly. "I wouldn't have been—," he started to say. Collingswood interrupted.

"Please," she said. "Please just sod off. You were offered a job a while back and you said no."

"Whatever the circumstances," Baron said.

"We may be a man down," Collingswood said, "but we were always a man down." She sniffed. Looked at him thoughtfully. "Burns don't heal pretty," she said. "Always a little melty-looking scar. You can't fuss about that sort of shit, Billy."

Billy held out his hand. Baron raised an eyebrow and shook it. Billy turned and looked at Collingswood, standing at the edge of the room. She waved at him.

"Oh, Billy, Billy, Billy," she said. She smiled and winked at him. "You and me, eh? What didn't we do?" She blew him a quick kiss. "See you around," she said. "Till next apocalypse, eh. I know your bloody type, Billy. Be seeing *you*." She nodded farewell. He did not disobey.

BILLY WALKED THE CORRIDORS, ROUTES HE KNEW INTIMATELY, THAT he had not walked for weeks. He mooched. He left the Darwin Centre and reentered a night still frenetic with fights, thefts and heretic prophecies, but increasingly, epically *sheepish*, uncertain of its own anxieties, unsure as to why it felt like a final night, when clearly it was not and never had been.

In the tank room, Baron was scribbling in his notebook.

"Right," he said. "Honest to bloody blimey I've got no idea how we're going to write this up," he said. "Shall we, Collingswood?" He spoke briskly and did not meet her eye.

She paused before she answered him.

"I'm putting in for a transfer," she said. She met his shocked eyes. "Time there was another FSRC cell, 'boss. Boss.'" She air-quoted. "I'm going for promotion." Collingswood smiled.

PART SEVEN

HERO = BOTTLE

Chapter Eighty-Two

IN A QUIET PLACE, BY THE RAILWAY LINES IN A CUT IN THE CITY, discarded statues edged the stays. In a long-term moment of urban sentimentality, they were a line of retirement for no-longer revered nor desired mementos. In them Wati slept. Only his friends knew this.

He had crept over from Marge's crucifix after the end of the uncertain catastrophe that had not happened. He slept like one defeated. London was saved from whatever danger it was he had helped save it from, had there been such a thing, but his union had lost its fight, and the new contracts were punitive, feudal. Billy was glad for him that Wati could sleep through the worst of this, though he would excoriate himself for it when he woke, and would start the task of rebuilding the movement again.

"Are you sad?" Saira said. She sat opposite him. They were together in his flat. After all that night, after all the everything, he had found her. He had needed to be with someone who had seen whatever it was he had seen.

He had called Collingswood first. "Fuck off, Harrow," she had said, friendly enough. He had heard a squeal of static like the enthusiastic voice of a pig, and she had broken the connection. When he had tried to redial, his phone had become a toaster.

"Alright, alright," he had said. He had bought a new telephone and not called her again, but had tracked down Saira instead. It had not been hard. She retained the expertise she had learned, but she was not a Londonmancer anymore. Mostly she used her hungover knack to roll bits of London between her fingers until they were cigarettes, which she would smoke.

Neither of them were quite sure of details. They had seen the assault on the sea, though for what purpose they could not remember. "Are you?" she said. She spoke to Billy hesitantly. She was shy of this topic, despite all the time they had spent together recently.

"Not really," he said. "I never knew him."

The *him* was the man who had died: the earlier Billy, the first Billy, the Billy Harrow who had teleported out of the sea-house, in which they had all been for reasons they could all remember, though were not perfectly impressed with. He had been blown into bits smaller than atoms.

"He was brave," Billy said. "He did what he had to do." Saira nodded. He did not feel that he was praising himself, though he knew that he, this Billy, must be brave in exactly, precisely the same degree as his predecessor.

"Why did you . . . he . . . do it?" she said.

Billy shrugged. "I don't know. He had to. Like Dane said—you remember Dane?" Dane had died. That he was sure of. "Before the, before Grisamentum did him in." Grisamentum was gone too. "There are a lot of people who don't think twice about travelling like that. It's only a problem if you *know*." It all depended on how you looked at it whether you were troubled by the fact that it was always fatal.

"I keep trying to catch myself out," he said. "I keep trying to suddenly see if I remember things that only he could know. The first one. Secrets." He laughed. "I always do." Billy did not feel proprietorial about the memories he had inherited, when he had been born out of the molecules of the air, in the tank room, days before, at the dying end of a catastrophe.

I miss Dane, he thought. He was not sure of anything very concrete about Dane, not even in fact that he missed him, exactly; but whenever he thought of it, Billy was very sad that what had happened to Dane had. He deserved better.

• • •

When Marge and Paul rang his Bell, Billy invited them in, but they waited instead on the pavement. He came down. This was a valedictory organised in advance. Everyone trod carefully with each other just then.

Paul was in his old jacket. It was cleaned and patched. It would never look new, but it looked good. The scratches on his face were healing. Marge looked the same as she always had. They greeted each other with awkward heartfelt hugs.

"Where you going?" Billy said.

"Don't know yet," said Paul. "Maybe the country. Maybe another city."

"Really?" Billy said. "*Really?*"

Paul shrugged. Marge smiled. Every time Billy had spoken to her since he had saved history from whatever, she had been buoyed up, more the more she found out about where she lived now.

"It's all bollocks," said Paul. "You think this is the only place gods live?" He smiled. "There's no getting away from that now. Wherever you go, that'll be somewhere a god lives."

Once, Billy and Marge had sat down together, and over emotional hours he had told her what had happened to Leon—his murder at the hands of Goss and Subby, as part of the huge plot, the details of which were still pretty lacunaed. The wrong, the damaged edges of the details frustrated them both.

"You could ask Paul's back what really happened," Billy had said. "It was that bastard's plan. I think."

"How would we do that?" she said. "You think he'd even know, anyway?"

There were still those in the heresiopolitan wing of London who obeyed Paul as if he were the Tattoo, but not many. Most did not know details, but knew that he was not what he had been. Now Paul was a free operator, a roaming prison for a displaced kingpin. The Tattoo's troops were routed and scattered after the recent, most confusingly vague near-apocalypse.

"How would we do that?" Marge said again.

They were not watched, the streets contained no one paying attention. Paul untucked his shirt, turned and showed Billy his skin.

The Tattoo's eyes widened and narrowed frantically as he tried to speak. As if Billy would respect or listen to him. Across the lower part of Paul's back more ink had been added. He had had inked tattooed stitches, sewing up the erstwhile crime lord's mouth. Billy could hear an *mmm mmm mmm*.

"It wasn't easy," Paul said, "we had to find a savvy tattooist. And he kept trying to move, to purse his lips and that. Took a while."

"You weren't tempted to get him removed?" Billy said.

Paul put his shirt back on. He and Marge smiled. She raised her eyebrows. "If he gives me too much shit I might blind him," Paul said. Sadism? Really? Billy would have said not. Justice? Power.

"You're never going to tell us what did happen, are you?" Marge said suddenly.

"I don't *know*," Billy said. "Goss killed Leon. That's what started this. For no reason at all." They let that stand. "But then Paul killed Goss. You were there."

"I did," Paul said.

"I was," Marge said. "Okay." She even smiled. "Okay. And what else? What else happened?"

"I saved everything," Billy said. "And you did too."

"They're holding Byrne?" Saira said.

"I think they're getting her for the sea-house. Have to show the ocean that we're sorry."

"Whether or not she did it?"

"Whether or not."

"I heard the sea's started filling a new embassy."

"I heard the same."

Billy's flat was his again. He did not know what to make of it; he often wandered its little hallways in amazement. (Of course it was not his *again*. It had never been his—he had inherited it from his identical namesake. And he did not know why he had to do these prodding little thought-tests.) They looked over the street. It was nearly the end of the year.

"What year was it?" Saira said. "Year of the what? That just went?"

"I don't know," Billy said.

"Year of the bottle."

"It's *always* year of the bottle."

"Year of the bottle and of some animal."

"It's always that too."

So this was the universe, was it? Billy strained, and maybe it was nothing, maybe it was a quirk of his position—it looked through the window as if a fleeting bird stilled in the sky, for a snip of a second. Saira watched. Raised an eyebrow. Humans were still related to monkeys. All sorts of things might happen in that new old London.

Billy looked out at the city that was not as it had been the last time he had looked through the glass. Billy lived in Heresiopolis now, and would know when the next Armageddon came and failed. He drank now in different bars, and learnt different things.

He sipped his wine and poured more for himself and for Saira. It was the year of the bottle, Billy thought, the year of pickling time, flexing himself and feeling the clock hesitate as if he squeezed its throat. It was the year of the bottle once more.

He touched glasses with Saira. It was not the year of anything else. *So.*

It was coming up to the end of the world again, of course—it always was. But not so frantically as it had been, perhaps. Not with quite such agonies. Billy wasn't the angel of memory—he was far too human for that—but he could see memory-angelhood from where he stood. Put it that way. Did he have a history to protect? It seemed to him that the streets were no longer starving.

From outside the sky looked in at them. Billy was behind glass.

ABOUT THE AUTHOR

China Miéville is the author of numerous books, including *The City & The City, Embassytown, Railsea,* and *Perdido Street Station.* His works have won the World Fantasy Award, the Hugo Award, and the Arthur C. Clarke Award (three times). He lives and works in London.

chinamieville.net